THE MOUNTAIN
AND THE FEATHER

THE

BY JOHN ASHMEAD

MOUNTAIN
and the feather

HOUGHTON MIFFLIN COMPANY BOSTON
THE RIVERSIDE PRESS CAMBRIDGE
1 9 6 1

for Ann

Duty is heavier than a mountain, and so to be much regarded; Death lighter than a feather, and therefore to be despised.

Imperial Rescript issued to the Japanese Army and Navy at the beginning of the Russo-Japanese War

CONTENTS

Part One

CACTUS

February, 1943

The battle for Visaya Gulf was probably the last great naval battle ever to be fought on earth; during its course a few highly trained men on either side had it briefly in their power to change the history of the world.

It marked the climax — and the end of power at sea, for in the art of war, as in all affairs of men, at its conclusion again the pendulum of history resumed its silent swing.

BEGEL, The Battle for Visaya Gulf

❀

BORN violently long ago from volcanoes, the dim smudges on the horizon transfigured themselves anew into one green island. Chaplain Simon gripped his New Testament as a more primitive man might have gripped a fist hatchet. He stood beside you and asked you to join in the church services which would be held on the afterdeck. For Your Safe Arrival.

A pink hotel, gray ships, white houses on a silver sliver of beach, winked into view. The trade wind felt cool against your cheeks, and you braced your legs against the transport deck to counter the surging groundswell.

All day flying fish had leapt round the ship in bright arcs twenty feet high and a tenth of a mile long. In a sharp gust of wind, spray came aboard the well deck. You watched the bored enlisted men gather round a flying gurnard. Laughing, the men stretched out its pectoral fins to measure its wings, but the flying fish slithered through their hands. In the rush to catch it again, the sailors, not meaning to do so, trampled on it. A chief flung the dead fish overboard. It floated astern, white belly turned upward. The wind died down, and the school of flying fish vanished.

You meant to evade the Chaplain's invitation, but you would be polite about it. You liked Simon, Fisher of Men, with his bright shock of blond hair, his round, blue-eyed face reddened by the Pacific sun, his stout and sturdy figure with its suggestion of middle-aged plumpness in the rump.

And, in a way, you admired Simon. He was always hearty, always smiling, able to get along with the officers and with the men, with the WARDS who would replace the men in the air raid defenses of Hawaii, with the bored, slovenly ship's company. He played bridge, he sat and talked, he loaned cigarettes and Bibles, he spilled out toothbrushes, dental floss, New Testaments (Twentieth Century English Version) and Shorter Catechisms from a private cornucopia, he had a clean fresh smell of witch hazel about him. Constantly he hummed the Navy Hymn:

> Eternal Father! strong to save!
> Whose Arm doth bind the restless wave,
> Who bidd'st the mighty ocean deep
> Within its bounds appointed keep.

"No," you said. Your voice was abrupt, flat, in spite of yourself, almost rude. "No."

Simon did not seem to hear you. Mildly he said, as though that should make up your mind for you, "I've found the portable organ." He added wryly, "in a crate labeled GRAPEFRUIT JUICE."

It was typical of Simon to find the portable organ. From the moment he came on board he had steadily substituted order for chaos on the badly run transport. He had even cajoled the seasick mess stewards into doing their new tasks.

"You won't be sick if you work," he had said to the greenish-brown stewards, away from Louisiana for the first time in their lives.

It was not quite true, but it was pleasanter, the stewards agreed in their soft Cajun, to be seasick in the passenger officers' mess than in their cramped, foul bunkroom. And Chaplain Simon had moved kindly among them, his blond hair gleaming, his round face smiling, filling saltcellars, setting out napkins in the shape of swans, flicking at table crumbs.

"No work is too humble," he had said, looking sternly at the passenger officers. You and the other new ensigns had looked away. But the warrants, retreads, most of them, from the First World War, had laughed scornfully. He tried to explain about "dignity" — often, without realizing, he used the Spanish *dignidad* — but his embarrassed and puzzled audience slipped away from him.

Once Chaplain Simon had taken you with him, for Moral Support, to the hold occupied by hundreds of elderly Seabees, thickwaisted construction men, volunteers all. Ashore they put up hangars and Quonsets, laid roads and dug culverts, moved mountains of earth as though the world were their sandbox. But here, afloat, they lay groggily in their bunks and refused to clean up their vomit.

In his preaching voice, highpitched, and unimpressive, Chaplain Simon appealed to them: "Our enemies have a proverb," he said, "Duty is a mountain, death a feather." They groaned. Several called on Jesus in remarks without religious significance.

But there was always a will and a way. He threatened to take away their meals. A few hungry men found swabs, and order came slowly back to the Seabees' hold.

"I'm sorry," you said, perplexed at your surge of feeling.

"You're a —" he slurred over the word, "Catholic?"

You sensed that bluff, blond Chaplain Simon, Salesman of God, was shy about religion. For a moment, in a wave of liking for Simon, you wanted to explain.

You felt a gust of wind strike coolly against your cheek. All you said was "No, no," and you added, on the defensive, for it was no longer true, "I'm Episcopalian."

Had Chaplain Simon heard you? "A union," he said, a faraway look in his eyes. "Some day there'll be a union, Monty." Then, more briskly, in a tone that admitted denominations, after all, were of little account in a World Turned Foxhole, "I'm Jesus Coming, myself. Nondenominational branch."

The wind blew sharply between the boats and the ventilators and the two grimy stacks; there was the sweet cloying smell of baking bread. A dingy gull nickered hungrily at the ship and floated away again.

You thought of Stainer's *Crucifixion,* of flowers banked on the cathedral altars at Easter, of hot wax dribbled down your neck by the candleholding boy behind you. And the scrabble of earth flung against fir planks — ". . . of whom may we seek for succour but of thee, O Lord . . ."

You heard a crisp tread on the ladder to the boat deck. Then the sharp, even steps of Marine Major Begel, historian to all the armed forces, pacing out his constitutional. You eyed his short, rugged figure, and his squarish head, like a bulldog's, a little too heavy for his height. He carried a swagger stick under his arm, his short back was ramrod stiff.

With an effort you tried to remember Begel as Bradford Professor of History at Yale, with the right to pasture two cows on the campus. His researches in Spanish History had won him a red ribbon from King Alfonso and an enameled star from General Franco; his precise location of the eighteenth-century campus privies had enabled antiquaries to reconstruct the original Yale china pattern from sherds deposited — no one knew why — in the pedagogic privies after meals. A formal service for eight was now on sale in the University Bookstore.

You sniffed at a manly trace of English shaving lotion in the air.

Professor Begel had won flag rank in the American Historical Association; now he made no secret of his determination to win flag rank in the war. You were sure that senior officers of all three services approved his Great Man Theory of History; these correctly foresaw a series of books, each having as its initial photograph, not a ship, a division, a flight of planes, or even, most important of all, a simple heap of supplies — no, each volume would surely begin with a retouched portrait photo of a sternsmiling admiral or general.

Now Major Begel quartered the deck, back and forth, back and forth, saying softly to himself in a faintly British accent, *hup hoo hee haw, hup hoo hee haw.*

Chaplain Simon blushed slightly and stumbled over the hideous word: "An atheist?"

He looked shrewdly at you. No, Chaplain Simon was not to be deceived by your tanned figure, your dark coarse hair, your lean shoulders shaped by the summers spent working on the Connecticut roads. Surely, in your aquiline Mediterranean face, in your light gray-green eyes, he saw his real enemy, the intellectual.

O holy and most merciful Saviour, deliver us not into the bitter pains of eternal death.

Now he waited for you to tell him about evolution and the Heisenberg principle of uncertainty and the real age of the earth, he waited for you to fling at him your childish handful of pebbles, collected along the Eternal Shore — as if such mysteries mattered, before the Greatest Mystery of All.

And why not? Why not discuss the rights of the owner of the Gadarene swine? Would a just god make a pig psychotic?

Once, surprised and aware of yourself as you contemplated the purchase of a G.I. steel mirror, you had caught a glimpse in its bright, unbreakable surface of the dark, ironic face of our time — and point by point you had scanned that fragile face, in search of your own.

No, irony would be a cruelty to Chaplain Simon. Why not yield, abandon discussion, which Chaplain Simon could soon lead into rich green pastures of embarrassment, and go to the service.

But in spite of yourself, a memory of savage hurt, cicatrix beyond image or words, flashed through your mind.

"No," you blurted, "no, I'm not interested." It was your voice, and yet it was harsher than your voice. These were your words, and yet they were the harsh words, and the harsher miming, of the Ironical Man — the monkey on the back of the Ambiguity Addict — you were your own best Inside Dopester.

The wind died away, but you trembled. Chaplain Simon unconsciously swallowed and his ears wiggled ever so slightly. You sensed that Simon was pulled one way by his belief that he must be a Fisher of Men, and he was pulled in another way by an instinctive respect for your privacy. His superiors, no doubt, had sensed this defect when, before the war, they had assigned him to Foreign Missions — you could imagine the rather worldly spiritual director of his sect observing, sagely, "Some wines travel well."

Chaplain Simon sniffed and moved closer to you. "God," he said, shifting to his high, flat preaching voice. He waved at the pitching ship, the passenger Seabees, one of whom was having the dry heaves in the well deck, and he waved too at the expanse of sea and sky. The ship lurched, then banged down, hard.

"That's God," said Chaplain Simon, "the world." He tried to make himself clearer. "The world we never made." A look of joy flooded his face, and you sensed that Simon's Jehovah was Genesis.

No doubt Simon's conversion had come through conundrum, and what more riddling than that first great act of creation — when the world first hung pendant by its golden chain. Ah, if only your heart held words enough.

You saw the lips of Simon shape, but not sound, the words *Yonder! Yonder!*

Behind you on the boat deck the door to the radio shack swung open. You heard a series of meaningless dits and dahs. The door banged shut. The wind rose again, and you had to raise your voice, as though you and Chaplain Simon had suddenly grown deaf.

You could sense that Chaplain Simon was deeply moved. Perhaps at this moment he saw why he stood beside you and what he stood for, perhaps he knew — at this mystic moment — what Pythagorean proportion was being formed by ship, sea and sky.

On the way to San Francisco your tourist class Pullman had passed a long line of flatcars, loaded with tanks, moving sluggishly beside the worn green seat in which you sat. And from Japan were coming flatcars and shiploads of tanks and men, to clankclatter forward, crumple, flinch back, and grind and grind on again. You felt a spasm of uncontrollable emotion, something deep, atavistic, long waiting expression within you, like fear but beyond it, a savage, primitive joy.

Embarrassed, you realized that Chaplain Simon had taken your inattention for a grammar of assent and conversion. He was now telling you what God really was.

You were shocked. "Impudence," you nearly cried, "Impudence." And for a moment you disliked Simon. Why not convert Carl Napoleon Brandt, your bunkmate, or Major Begel. What expression had he seen on your face, forever invisible to you?

Major Begel, his constitutional finished, went by both of you to the ladder. He waited a moment for your salute, snapped it back, then said, "Good morning, padre," and was gone *hup hoo hee haw hup hoo hee* down the ladder.

You remembered how you had once taken Begel's course in History, *From the Fall of Rome to Modern Times.* Seated behind a post, one of six hundred students in the twenty-year-old Bradford Lecture Hall, you had watched Professor Begel push back and forth a chalky eraser attached to a long string.

"The pendulum of history," Professor Begel had said in his clear, slightly nasal voice, "I give you the pendulum of history, gentlemen."

Even behind your post, a mere freshman at Yale, you had liked the atmosphere Professor Begel tried to convey, that you were all — rich boys, poor boys — gentlemen scholars. Push went the eraser and puff — chalk dust fell to the platform.

Now Chaplain Simon kneaded your arm in farewell. With an effort you kept from flinching. But if you believed in anything, you believed in the community of men — why then this dislike of being touched?

Halfway down the ladder Chaplain Simon hesitated. No doubt he was thinking of the trimmers, forever buffeted by the winds at the gates of hell, beyond rebellion or belief. Shyly, delicately, Chaplain Simon looked back at you.

But his words were just the cheap religious cleverness of your times, the slick magazine god, of happiness and success — "You've got to take a stand on something," he said, "or you'll fall for nothing." And he meant to go on, for he had a dramatic weakness for exit lines: "No atheists in foxholes . . ." — but the wind rose, the organ bleated, the ship lurched, he stumbled and was gone.

From the afterdeck there came snatches of hymns and a sharp organ whine — "Never failing . . . And arm'd with cruel hate . . . let goods and kindred go, This MOR-tal LIFE al-so . . . forever." You were well within the Honolulu roads now, and the pitching motion of the ship changed to a glassy, level glide.

One of the Cajun mess stewards was singing the blues:

> If you should marry
> Tom, Dick or Harry,
> Life would be the bunk —
> I'd become a monk.

All yesterday and this morning there had been tantalizing patches of fragrance in the air; now came a rainbow burst of scent from hundreds of strange flowers; invisible they colored the tropic air. The sea had changed from dark to light green and the transport congealed in it, motionless. Slowly a coconut drifted past the transport, out to the sea. The destroyer escort stabbed like a gray dagger through the horizon and vanished. Chaplain Simon rushed his service to a decisive, sevenfold amen.

For you and for most of the transport passengers it was your first sea voyage, and now you turned your faces toward the Hawaiian harbor pilot, you became the intoxicated congregation of a jolly brown saint who smoked a cigar and wore his straw hat of freshly woven palm leaves like a yellow-green halo. Around his neck was a lei of pikake flowers, and the Navy captain of the transport, an elderly slack-jawed reserve officer, shook hands, then brooded at the opposite side of the bridge.

With much shouting and many waves of palm hat and cigar, the transport got under way again. Steadily the passengers came out on deck and silently lined the rails.

Your back stung from a painfully jovial slap. "Handsome Classen," cried Carl Napoleon Brandt. "How's Handsome Classen today?" Exuberant, he bellowed the first line of his version of the Army Air Corps song: "Here we go into the wild blue yonder — CUH RASH!"

"Bah," said Napoleon, shrugging his stocky shoulders in a gesture of amiable contempt for the other graduates of your training school. "Not one of you knows a deathblow."

It was true. Unlike Napoleon, who knew three — which he had promised his Japanese jujitsu teacher never to reveal, and never to use for purely personal advantage, you did not know a single deathblow. Nor could you, like Napoleon who had been a gym instructor in civilian life, enter the officers' mess by swinging along the overhead pipes, like an all too human jocko.

Napoleon drew a deep breath that seemed to double his barrel chest. Then he exhaled in a loud and lingering snort. "I'm ready," he said, in a tone free from self-dissatisfaction. He patted fondly his three-battery flashlight, his sheathknife — always ready to cut himself free from cordage should the transport be torpedoed, his watch officer's pistol — its holster lashed by a leather string to his leg so that he could draw quickly, frontier style, should any emergency demand rapid fire.

Napoleon indicated a WARD shaped like an overblown Venus. She was blond, gap-toothed, hardly pretty, but her breasts seemed about to burst through her nipple-tight bluesilk uniform. "She's hot for me," said Napoleon. He believed this to be the highest compliment a woman could receive.

Reflecting upon past strategies, Napoleon remarked, "When everything else fails, I always take a hot shower with the girl."

To you, this seemed a far more difficult feat than the simple act of seduction itself.

For the benefit of the WARD, Napoleon glanced sternly at the harbor. In a loud, carrying voice he said, "We'll beat the holy hell out of them." Then, with his fists, he made motions as of a fighter hammering his opponent in the kidneys and finally finishing off his invisible foe with a vicious rabbit punch in the neck.

Your transport was sailing past the great iron barrier nets, past the hospital, sailing as if on land, so thin was the blue slice of channel. Then the transport turned hard into the harbor, and you saw for the first time the sunken and gutted ships that still remained from December the seventh — the *Arizona* with a thousand men burned and forever trapped below, the *Oklahoma* — was that the *West Virginia?* — their names echoed through the transport in a great sighing sound. Gigantic strips of steel lay here and there, flung into limp red and blue tangles. *Remember Pearl Harbor.*

You stared across the harbor at Ford Island. A few men, black dots at that distance, clambered over the bottom of the capsized target battleship *Wyorada*. They were attaching cables to the keel. These led ashore to crates of machinery. The jehads of America — *Remember the Alamo — Remember the Maine — Remember Pearl Harbor — remember remember —*

Your first night on the Pacific, Major Begel had lectured to the assembled "casual" officers on the Pearl Harbor attack. Why, asked Begel dryly, had the Japanese not attacked the oil storage, or, more important still, the repair shops? Already *Pennsylvania, Maryland, California, Nevada,* were back in service. And that great line of dreadnaughts, Begel went on, neatly demolishing an inferior historian's research, did it matter so much any more? Carriers were the dreadnaughts of today. Point three (the crusher, you thought, used to Begel's technique), even with the battleships intact, you could have moved no more quickly toward the heart of Japan.

Last of all (you recognized the coming of the rhetorical climax), what had the Japanese really gained, aside from uniting a divided nation against them?

You and your fellows tried hard to think of Pearl Harbor as an

American victory. Bewildered applause, graciously acknowledged.

You looked at the water, once the bluest and clearest harbor water in the world, now murky with oil and rot and the dead, still in their steel chambers under the glassy cool translucent wave . . . *remember* . . .

Almost everyone was on the open decks of the transport now. On the main deck stood the elderly Seabees, the lean young enlisted men, the graying, potbellied chiefs. On the upper deck were the grizzled warrants, with faded ribbons from the First World War — some had seen Pearl Harbor last in 1917. Forward under the bridge deck stood the nervous, clear-cheeked young ensigns, their shoulder-boards glittering golden in the sun, among them the WARDS in their tight bluesilk uniforms.

On the main deck Napoleon had lined up his group of chiefs. On boarding the transport in San Francisco Napoleon had applied for shipboard duty, and the surprised and gratified ship's officer had put him in charge of a holdful of old Navy chiefs. These beer-bellied leatherlipped men had received their new commander-ensign with an amusement not always affectionate in character. Fortunately Napoleon was rarely aware of the reactions of others to himself. He immediately put his rotund charges through setting-up exercises and pushups, following these physical jerks with mental ones, consisting of classes in Japanese plane recognition, and the ship for the past week had rung to hoarse beery cries of Kate, Mavis and Jill, names given to Japanese planes for recognition purposes.

Napoleon paced up and down before his chiefs, complete with pistol, three-battery flashlight, and sheathknife. He was wasting no chance to practice plane recognition. "What's that plane?" he barked at them.

At mooring stations the special sea details of the crew lounged in dirty greaseblue dungarees, with a khaki sprinkling of ship's officers among them. High above them all, the jolly chocolate pilot with stubby cigar and green halo of palm nudged them to their berth, deep within the harbor.

Chaplain Simon saw to the hurried recrating of the portable organ in a box labeled only Juice. He stood at your side, and stared at the sunk and tortured craft of Pearl Harbor. His hands clutched white against the gray railing.

Simon struggled to tell you something. "Sometimes," he said, "sometimes . . ." His voice trailed off. His expression was remote and delicate, as if temporarily usurped by quite another person from the hearty, likable Drummer for the Deity. "Dignidad," he said shyly, and stopped.

He began again, "Once I saw an auto wreck —" he explained lamely, "a collision —" but the words would not come. Was he trying to say that no man believes all the time nor does any god expect him to . . . forgotten scraps and tags burned in your mind like stars . . . *suffer us not at our last hour . . . the earth and the sea shall give up their dead . . . for any pains of death, to fall from thee.*

A fly lit on Chaplain Simon's hand and he brushed it off. The moment was gone. Helplessly he kneaded your arm. As helplessly you kept yourself from flinching, and he moved away among the men, smiling, joking, saying goodbye, waving, shaking hands, patting shoulders.

Out snaked the heaving lines to the deck below, then the mooring lines, at bow and stern, at bow and quarter spring, at bow and quarter breast.

On the wharf you could see a cluster of senior officers, gold gleaming on the black bills of their caps. You turned and saw they were waving to Marine Major Begel who waved back with his swagger stick. An elderly woman among the group on the dock shook a lei of pink and white carnations at Major Begel.

Using Pearl Harbor as a gigantic blackboard, he was explaining to the group around him how the Japanese should have conducted their bomb attacks. "First wave — the repair shops." Waggle of swagger stick toward the Officers' Club.

"Second wave — oil tanks." Waggle of swagger stick toward Makalapa.

"Third wave —" indicating the capsized target battleship *Wyorada*, "battleships." Grand flourish of swagger stick. It was lucky for America that Major Begel had not flown with the Japanese air strike commander.

Napoleon barked again at his formation of chiefs, readying them for the landing. From far overhead zoomed the highpitched whine cf planes in descent. Down, diving down, they came in their squadrons, perhaps to welcome Major Begel, perhaps only wild in their diving joy. Fanged snakes of Emerson at play in their clearing, not to eat, not for love, only gliding.

Napoleon's voice shrilled through the ship. "Hit the deck, men, they're Kates," he screamed to his chiefs. He sprawled flat on the deck himself, with a clatter, thud, crash from sheathknife, revolver, and three-battery flashlight.

The planes swerved off, followed by their sound. Napoleon slowly picked himself up.

"Was that Kate or Jill?" asked one chief eagerly.

"I knew a girl in Panama named Jill," said a second chief. He thought for a moment. "She was a bitch."

"No," said the first chief, "her name was Kate."

"You jolthead," said the second chief, "you ever been in Panama?"

"No," said the first chief. "I never. How about you, Mr. Brandt, you ever been in Panama?"

"Carry on," said Napoleon, in a dignified tone. Usually he went down the ladders by swinging from the overhead handgrip, touching down at each deck with a yowl and a massy thump. But this time he retired within the ship slowly and silently.

The attention of the ship was immediately distracted from this incident, so gratifying to the enlisted men. A pretty Filipina drove up on a scooter, her newpenny face bright copper in the sun. At the gangway, now ready to be rolled into position, she left a message with a guard. Then with a flourish and saucy wriggle of her tightskirted little hips and deep pointed breasts, she was off. The enlisted men cheered her, and she waved back. The first chief began singing softly to himself:

> If you don't like my peaches
> Why do you shake my tree?

Steadily the slovenly crew in their dirty blue dungarees checked the lines, and only a few feet now separated the ship from the land.

You had secured a place at the railing, and the blond, gap-toothed WARD pressed against your back in the crowd. You could feel the curves of her hips and breasts, but she made no effort to hold away from you in the thronging group of ensigns and WARDS. You wanted to offer her your place at the rail, to ask her name, to look back at her.

You stood there, gazing in the distance at the sunken dread-naughts, imagining the curve of her breast from its soft pressure. The last delicate motion of the ship now stopped, the engines were silent, the mooring lines were doubled up, you were locked to the tropic land. You turned, but she was gone. You never saw her again.

CHAPTER TWO

March, 1943

The long days of inactivity, of waiting, of training, had at last borne their deadly fruit.
BEGEL, The Battle for Visaya Gulf

❋

ARMY CAPTAIN FEVERTON'S first order to Q was on Typing Posture. There had been "To much bad Typing Posture in Q," so you read on the bulletin board. Officers and men in Q would all, in the future, sit straight at your chairs and type with a relaxed wrist motion. Order #1 continued: "A typing error could loose the war." It was initialed "F, acting O in C, Capt., AUS, for General Waddleman."

Far in the distance you caught a glimpse of the capsized target battleship *Wyorada*. Men threaded cables into blocks and their tackle and attached cable ends between the bottom of the battleship and tiny motors ashore. Soon all this gear would pull the *Wyorada* upright, inch by half inch. Officially the Navy was determined to raise every ship sunk in the Pearl Harbor attack. The informed said, however, that the Navy would never succeed in raising the *Arizona*. There were hints that she would be preserved as an underwater monument, the first in American history.

Your Japanese dictionary, *Kenkyusha*, "The Researcher," dropped from your desk. For a moment you did not pick it up. Then you went to Feverton's desk and stood at attention. In so doing you showed your dutiful compliance with Order #3, "How to stand in presense of officer in charge."

Deliberately, he made you wait.

Captain Feverton, known as "Chuck" to his equals, and "Yes, cap'n" to junior officers and Negro mess stewards, had a large, chubby smiling face that seemed to have been pasted over his real features.

Perhaps this smile was the result of the long hot Missouri days spent before the war as the commercially jolly proprietor of a gas station (with three pumps, an ever changing mechanic, and a Negro boy). In the daytime Captain Feverton had wiped windshields, filled gas tanks, greased cars, and fixed flats; at night he took reserve officer courses in map reading, company organization, military law, and dreamed of Armageddon.

"All right, Classen," said Feverton sternly. "What's the meaning of this?"

You stared at Cartoon #1, from Junior Officer in Charge, for General Waddleman, ComGen Q and Related Bureaus. This was a crude diploma from the Erect Posture Typing School — as its coat of arms it had a reclining nude female with gigantism of the bosom. She was awarding a dwarfish, slobbering, but recognizable Captain Feverton a Master's Degree in Touch Technique. It was not an inspiring Work of Art, but underneath its crudity was a certain verve. You had to admit that.

While protesting your ignorance.

"Have you heard of Loyalty Up and Loyalty Down?" asked Feverton.

"No, sir."

Waving the cartoon, now rolled up like a marshal's baton. "I found this in the head."

On Feverton's desk you noticed your fitness report and qualification jacket.

"What kind of street would you say Loyalty is?"

You failed to answer.

"Loyalty is a two-way street, not a one-way street as some of you seem to suppose."

Feverton thumbed through your brown-covered qualification jacket.

"I see you were involved in some practical jokes while you were in college. You filled up the room of a tutor with crumpled newspapers. When the tutor dug through the newspapers he found a dead junkman's horse. The horse had to be butchered into quarters before he could be carried through the door."

"That is correct." One item had been omitted from the report. The tutor, your tutor, as it happened, was a fanatic admirer of Hitler.

Feverton indicated the ensigns of Q, hunched among green card files, map files, and letter files, green desks and tables, black type-writers, black mimeographing machines, green letter baskets and brown wastebaskets, green bookcases, black books, green books, brown books, blue books, great piles of maps printed in yellow and green and brown for land, and printed in blue for the sea, opened and apparently forgotten Japanese dictionaries, atlases and encyclopedias with black Japanese hieroglyphs trailing down the white pages. The long second-story room was perched on the lip of an extinct volcano that overlooked Pearl Harbor from the east.

"I see from your jackets," said Feverton, "that all of you have finished college."

"True, sir."

"And half of you have finished graduate school."

"Only Lieutenant Gordian Hannum has really finished, sir."

"I went to a two-year business college myself. I wonder if you gentlemen know what Life is about. Real Life. Life in the World Outside."

This was familiar dialogue. You had often heard it from your father.

"You know the World Inside," said Feverton, warming to one of his favorite topics. "I know the World Outside."

"Yes, sir."

"In the World Outside," said Feverton, clicking his pencil against his teeth, "Constructive Criticism is in demand. Very great demand. I have an insatiable hunger for Constructive Criticism myself.

"Destructive Criticism is not wanted. Destructive Criticism is negative."

"Are you suggesting, sir, that I drew the cartoon?"

Captain Feverton, reacting to something emotional, some tone of danger in your voice, dodged the issue. "Destructive Criticism," he said, staring at Pearl Harbor, "might even make us lose the war." Then, abrupt and harsh, "Carry on, Classen."

"But I understood, sir, that you wanted to see each of us about his current project."

Captain Feverton rubbed his hands briskly along his pink-chino-clad thighs.

You opened your file on the Kawaguchi Force. From the papers came a strange, sweet odor. You had prepared a summary of the career of the Kawaguchi Force — Force Rivermouth. It had taken part in the rape of Nanking, then it had swaggered and killed and raped and slapped its way through Burma, Borneo, Cebu, Mindanao, Palau and Truk before it went to its muddy, fungoid grave on Guadalcanal. There on CACTUS it left behind collapsible rubber boats, knee mortars, bottles of sake and beer, 150-mm guns, white rubber contraceptives, .25-caliber rifles, women's silk panties, corpses butchered for food, golden tins of dried kelp, a piece of rice paper with a seventeen-syllable poem: *Among flowers behold the cherry, among warriors the samurai.*

"That's historical junk," said Feverton, uninterested.

You opened your file on searches. You had made fragmentary records, from pilots' logs, from diaries, from captured orders, of search plane tracks out of Truk, Palau, Rarawa, Roi, Kwajalein.

"I'll take this one over," said Feverton. "RHIP," he explained, smiling his pasted on smile. "Rank has its privileges."

You opened your file, a brief one, on puzzling words. These were words containing the root *ketsu* — "decisive" — or *toku* — "special" — as one element in the whole word. As in *kessenbutai* — "decisive battle force" — or *tokubetsukōgeki* — "special attack." Did these refer to suicide forces or to suicide attacks? Did the Japanese have in reserve some ultimate human weapon?

Captain Feverton was not listening to you. For a moment, stout General Waddleman stuck his bland face inside Q, waved cheerily, and was gone. Q and its related bureaus were a Joint Command, Pacific Ocean Areas (called privately, by the irreverent ensigns of Q, "JOKEPOA"). Executive posts in this organization were staffed alternately by the Army and Navy. In gilt cap and army uniform of his own design, Brigadier General Waddleman, decorated for the longest retreat in American military history, from China to Burma to India, provided a remarkable capstone to a remarkable outfit.

Captain Feverton ordered you to forget the last file. He frowned and again clicked his pencil against his teeth. "Ideas can win the war, Classen." He held out a Japanese ethics text. "I want a translation of this chapter."

Obediently you checked it.

"All right, Classen, I'll be watching you from now on. It's your ball now, you run with it. Really run." Slowly, pointedly, he tore up Cartoon #1.

You watched a battered submarine sailing to her berth, a shell hole through the conning tower, black paint flaked off so that metal flesh gleamed jagged in the sun, a broom at the mast. The larger surface ships hooted a welcome. The crew of the submarine lined the saltrimed decks and yelled back.

(. . . and finally I urge all you newly commissioned ensigns to remember the glorious Anglo-American annals of the sea. Remember John Paul Jones on the sinking *Bonne Homme Richard*: "Surrender be damned, I have not yet begun to fight." Remember Lawrence, dying on the *Chesapeake*: "Fight her till she sinks and don't give up the ship." Remember Farragut at Mobile Bay: "Damn the torpedoes! . . . Go ahead!" Remember Dewey at Manila: "You may fire when you are ready, Gridley." Remember Beatty at Jutland, the greatest naval battle in history: "Chatfield, there seems to be something wrong with our bloody ships today, turn two points to port." Remember . . .)

You translated a few lines of Japanese on a scrap of diary paper taken from a Japanese soldier killed on CACTUS, on Guadalcanal: "Dec. 8 . . . today I lost my virginity to a Korean girl . . ." You stamped the scrap of paper SOUVENIR PASSED BY JOCPOA and put it to one side. The scrap of paper had a strange sweet odor. For a long time you had not realized that this odor, now part of the very wooden beams of Q, was the strange, sweet odor of the dead.

CHAPTER THREE

March, 1943

How few laymen realize what intricate preparations
must be made before a landing such as that on Visaya can
be successfully staged.

BEGEL, The Battle for Visaya Gulf

❋

"AH," said Arkansaw from his upper bunk. "We are favored with a
visit from the Admiral of the Typing Pool. No doubt, since he has
moved downtown, he retains a lingering but irrepressible fondness
for his still vacant upper bunk."

"Why does Feverton have to pick on the Typing Pool?" said
Napoleon, aggrieved. "It's my command."

"He seems to think its typing techniques need modernization," you
said. "Like using the touch system, for example."

"At least he has standards," said Gordian mildly.

Napoleon held up to the light Cartoon #5, a badly drawn venture
in the field of satirical pornography. "Look at that perspective," he
demanded.

"Why don't you just ask Feverton to take off his bars and fight?"

"And Prantz must go too," shouted Napoleon, kicking your lower
bunk.

"You were magnificent as temporary CO of today's coffee mess.
You even remembered one lump for Captain Feverton, two lumps
for Yeoman Prantz."

"Why don't you criticize Yeoman Prantz to that yeoman's ruddy
face?" suggested Arkansaw. "Like Ensign Brown." He offered
everyone a slice of Japanese canned octopus. Everyone refused.

"Prantz has a delicate touch. Not only did he cut the thirty copies of Brownie's orders to Guadalcanal himself. He tucked in with them a medical pamphlet on how to prevent the Guadalcanal crud from spreading all over your body."

"You're still in charge of the coffee mess tomorrow," said Arkansaw. "Just give Prantz a cupful of solid coffee grounds. No cream." He added reflectively, "They say you're too weak from the crud even to think about women on Guadalcanal."

"When did you find an apartment?" asked Gordian. "It's impossible to find an apartment in Honolulu."

"He ran an advertisement in the *Honolulu Bulletin* — 'Wanted, apartment, by young naval officer who likes to make noise.'"

"No one would answer an ad like that. Not in Honolulu," said Gordian.

"There was only one," said Arkansaw. "A Madam. She liked the spirits of the rash youth. She even gave him a housewarming party."

"A very gracious lady."

"Very," agreed Arkansaw. "At the end of the party she went around among the unconscious guests loosening their neckties, and — a very thoughtful touch — their belts."

"That was thoughtful."

"Don't be so goddamned ironical," said Napoleon.

"Better be nice to Prantz," said Arkansaw. "Remember your robin's-egg blue Packard convertible." He looked up from a copy of Lao-Tse's *The Way of Life* which he was reading in the Chinese. Instead of a T shirt or the regulation khaki shirt, he wore a striped Brooks Brothers shirt with a button-down collar, the kind of shirt he had always worn as a student at Columbia. He read from Lao-Tse: "A good knot is tied together without rope — it cannot be untied."

"And remember your passengers, Napoleon. We wouldn't like to lose our imaginary daily transport from Q to the fleshpots of Honolulu."

"Do you mean he's listed you all as passengers in his car to get a bigger gas ration?" asked Gordian.

"You're one of the passengers too, Gordian. Have you forgotten so soon your ride here this morning, the top down, the smell of the pineapple cannery the — "

"Napoleon," said Gordian sternly.

He pretended not to hear. His fist shot out in a left hook against an imaginary opponent, then came a right undercut seemingly aimed at his adversary's groin.

He grunted with satisfaction. Then, taking the part of Captain Feverton, he ran around the bunkroom, his hands on his crotch, bellowing like a man who has just been castrated.

"Perhaps we have at last been privileged to see one of the three secret deathblows."

"No," said Arkansaw, "that blow was surely a fate worse than death."

"Two wrongs do not make a rat," Gordian counseled.

"They help," said Napoleon. Grumpily he checked his watch. He began singing his favorite from the Dirty Hit Parade of the week:

> Monday I touched her on the ankle,
> Tuesday I touched her on the knee,
> Wednesday with success
> I lifted up her dress . . .

"I understand," interrupted Arkansaw, who spent much of his free time downtown or out at Green Point, though he had not yet moved out of the BOQ, "that if there's a girl in your apartment at the curfew hour, your Packard just spews out its gas and refuses to take the girl home. Some sort of secondary sexual characteristic. Might be worth a note in the *Automotive Times.*"

"Destructive Criticism," said Napoleon. "Do you want your stencils proofread or not?" The threat was a serious one. Napoleon had become an able, even expert proofreader, able to catch serious mistakes even though he had forgotten a great deal of his Japanese and habitually read *otō san,* the Japanese word for "father," as "Mr. Oto."

You and Arkansaw now speculated whether proofreading, like musical and mathematical ability, was an isolated talent, divorced from other mental qualities. Napoleon invited you to copulate, with each other or by yourselves, just as you chose.

"Another date?" you asked on seeing Napoleon smooth down his long black hair.

Napoleon reached for his favorite book of the moment from Arkansaw's small, choice library. This was Mary Shelley's *Frankenstein*. Napoleon was a great reader of books which had been made into movies, since he entertained the hope, often gratified, of finding sexy passages omitted in the screen version. He was beginning to give up hope about *Frankenstein,* even though you had pointed out to him that it was as badly written as a sex novel.

You grabbed the book from Napoleon and flung it to Gordian. He opened it, and read the monster's appeal to his creator: "I demand a creature of another sex, but as hideous as myself: the gratification is small, but it is all that I can receive, and it shall content me.'"

"Sounds like the one you were out with last night."

Gordian handed the book back to Napoleon.

"That's not my place," said Napoleon, injured. Gordian turned again to the ever continuing letter to his wife which occupied most of his leisure. This letter might just as well have been sent to his wife in one endless roll except for the postal and censoring regulations; to satisfy these, two or three times a day Gordian signed, sealed and mailed appropriate segments.

"He's the bride," snorted Napoleon. Though married he prided himself on his ability to prevent connubiality from degenerating into the vice of uxoriousness. Still he went, as did the rest, to Gordian for advice, and he did not become unforgivably insulting.

Every administration has its squirrel, and who else could match Lieutenant Gordian Hannum in informational nutmeats?

The Japanese Type 97 passenger flying boat could carry eighteen men for twenty hours at cruising speed. On Guadalcanal Japanese troops used the Model 2598 Ishikawajima Tankette. The Type 96 land attack plane Model 21 had a top speed of 203 knots, and the Type 1 land attack plane Model 22 had a top speed of 236 knots. The Ichiki Force on Guadalcanal was originally made up from the 2nd battalion, 28th infantry of the 7th division, 35th brigade (or Kawaguchi Force) of the 17th Army. The Type 91 improved airborne torpedo weighed 838 kilograms, had a speed of 42 knots, and in contrast to American torpedoes did not misfire. The cruiser *Nachi* had ten 8-inch guns and twelve 24-inch torpedo tubes; her top speed was 34½ knots. The 25th Air Flotilla lived at Rabaul.

The Yokosuka Fifth Special Naval Landing Force died on Guadalcanal. Our code name for Guadalcanal was CACTUS.

Whatever you wanted to know, Lieutenant Gordian Hannum always had the answer, or part of the answer.

You asked Gordian about the midget subs.

"*Tokushusenkōtei,*" said Gordian, in answer to your question. "The midget sub unit. There were four or five in the attack on Pearl Harbor. One was beached outside the entrance. We have its track chart."

"But the word means *special sub boat*. Why 'special'? And why were the boats called a special attack unit — *tokubetsukōgekitai?*"

Gordian hesitated.

"Does 'special' mean what we mean by suicide attack?"

Gordian answered fussily, "They don't call it a suicide attack, of course. That's what we call it."

"What do they call it, doc?" said Napoleon. As he often announced, he did not enjoy Gassing Around.

Gordian did not answer immediately. "Banzai attack," said Arkansaw, looking up from his reading in Buddhist *kōan,* problems intended to give the believer a feeling of *satori,* of enlightenment.

"Let's have the whiskey," said Napoleon impatiently.

Arkansaw proffered, but did not release, the bottle of bourbon, the last of your pooled liquor ration for the week.

"All things return to the one," said Arkansaw, "but what does the one return to?"

Together you shouted correctly, "Kwats."

Arkansaw handed over the bottle and returned to his text. He was only marking time until the lights were out and he could read the latest detective story in Braille.

His father, Professor Arthur Torrington, Sr., taught Semitic languages in a small Protestant college in Arkansas whose library made no serious provision for light reading. Arthur Torrington, Jr., learning that he could borrow books in Braille even in darkest Arkansas, had become a subscriber to the Braille lending library. Now he habitually read detective stories in Braille, but he preferred to read them in the dark, when, as he said, you could read Braille more quickly.

"True," said Gordian. "The Japanese call them banzai attacks."

"Do you think there'll be more 'special' units and 'special attacks'?" you asked. "Besides the midget sub attack at Pearl, and the banzai attacks on Guadalcanal?"

And was there, in fact, in this odd puzzling group of terms, in the doctrine of the Imperial Way, in the ambition for sure death with a sure hit, in the notion of having the eight corners of the world under one — Japanese — roof — was there a combining of forces and ideas, was there now forming some compound of patriotic ambition and suicidal despair which could flame out in some new weapon? In some new tactic?

Beyond the meaning of the words themselves you began to wonder if there might not hide some more important meaning, some future sense, waiting to be gathered — and used. Within yourself you felt some dark, unsuspected power of mind coiling and stretching toward — toward what? Toward events to come?

For a moment you wondered if you liked war. What would it feel like, not just to find out what your enemy had done, after he had acted, but to see in advance the action which he must surely — and fatally, because anticipated — carry out.

But you asked only about the word *gyokusai*.

"Death for the Emperor," explained Gordian.

"*Gyokusai*," said Arkansaw, not looking up from his Buddhist *kōan*. He described the Japanese kanji. "*Gyoku* — the king — a single line of power connecting the three lines of heaven, of man, of earth. And holding a dot, the orb. *Sai* — to kill, as with a rock. Death for the emperor — bring your own rock. *Gyokusai*."

Napoleon jumped to the floor from his old upper bunk with a thump which shook the whole room.

"Goodbye, *men*," he said. "Now for a date with a hag." He took out his appointment book, the product of thoroughgoing research by the amorous ensigns of Pearl, and looked her up on the list. You could never be too sure.

"Safe," he said, "the hag is at the age of consent."

"You mean you give them time to say yes?"

Napoleon leaped in the air and clicked his heels, ballet style. With both hands he traced the silhouette of a buxom female in the air.

What incident had made Napoleon, and the other Pearl Harbor

wolves, so tender on the subject of statutory rape, you never discovered. Perhaps they did not know themselves, but they had formed a defensive wolfpack whose main purpose was to get this vital statistic correct. They boasted of knowing the precise age of every nubile nymph in Hawaii.

Gordian looked shocked as Napoleon now tucked three or four aluminum-wrapped condoms in his shirt pocket, along with a tube of prophylactic jelly. For Gordian, though an anthropologist, only natives had sexual customs — Americans had morals.

And yet surely in the military-nautical ritual of intercourse there was much of anthropological interest — the unrolling of the ritual condom, the ritual wash with soap after intercourse, and the injection of the ritual jelly. Properly carried out, these rites made their sexual sectaries proof against venereal evil.

Gordian was all the more shocked because he had only just learned that Napoleon was married. Patiently at first, Napoleon tried to explain his marital ties. Gordian was still dismayed. In spite of his stay on Rarawa, or perhaps because of it, he took American marriage, if no other, seriously.

Gordian belonged to that small but optimistic band of teachers who marry their most sympathetic student. You remembered her from language school days as a thin, pretty girl with very wide, newlywed brown eyes. She was fond of red hibiscus in her hair, and bright-flowered, sarong-cut skirts. And always loose sweaters as if to try to conceal her large attractive breasts. Gordian's class had left for Pearl Harbor a half year before your own, and you remembered their farewell dance and how his wife liked to dance disturbingly close to her partner.

"What about Rarawa?" said Napoleon, who had read a few sections of Gordian's Ph.D. thesis with concentration. "You tell us the unmarried boys and girls are free to meet every night in the teenage hut and shape up for bush parties. After marriage, if the man of the hut goes away on a business trip peddling his coconuts —" Napoleon laughed significantly — "the wife can go to the recreation center for a little dirty boogie. And vice versa.

"I'm free to do what I want. And my wife's free to do what she wants. That's only common sense." And Napoleon punched an imaginary punching bag, first with his right, then with his left.

Napoleon had been amazed to learn from Gordian that some people in America (among them Gordian and his wife) did not believe in sleeping with a future spouse before the bridal night.

"How else could you be sure?" asked Napoleon. "I mean, really sure?" This time it was Napoleon who was shocked. "We were sure," he announced with pardonable pride.

An Annapolis ensign, his class ring gleaming on his finger, stuck his brown, closecropped head in their door, without the formality of knocking. "I'm O'Connor. Anybody here from the class of '42?"

Led by Arkansaw you all roared at him, "Kwats!"

He stuck his bright face further in the room. "What class is Kwats?" he asked suspiciously.

"There are four classes of Kwats," said Arkansaw. "The first is the holy sword of Vajaraja. The second is a golden lion seated on his rump. The third is a decoy. The fourth and best of all —" he paused for a reflective, nourishing pull at the bottle of bourbon, "is *not* Kwats."

Well coached, you added, "They should all be summoned in a loud clear tone, especially the last."

"Oh," said the Annapolis ensign, "reserve officers." He might have said something more, but he saw that Gordian was a lieutenant, and two ranks above him.

"Yes," said Arkansaw. "College men all. And you, Mr. O'Connor, are from the trade school?"

The door slammed shut. Down the hall they could hear the question repeated at door after door: "Anyone here from the class of '42?"

Napoleon tipped his cap at a suitably rakish angle. In imitation of army air force pilots he had taken the grommet out of his cap, and its rim drooped stylishly over his ears, suggesting constant use of earphones in aerial combat. On his chest he had pinned the Pacific Campaign Ribbon with one combat star, awarded by himself to himself for distinguished service on the transport which had brought him to Pearl.

"What will it be this evening," you asked. "Dolphins or wings?"

Depending on his estimate of the evening's target, Napoleon transferred himself at night into either submarines or aviation. "It puts them at ease," Napoleon explained, "and costs only a few pennies for the insignia."

Now he pinned on himself a parachuter's badge.

"The Navy doesn't have paratroopers," said Gordian.

"We're still in training," said Napoleon, "for a secret mission. So long, you dogs. Tomorrow it's Captain Feverton's turn." He drew his hand across his throat and made a gurgling sound, as of blood gushing out. Slowly he sank to the floor as the imaginary vital fluid drained from his veins. Then, cap between his teeth, he walked out the doorway on his hands. You could hear him pinwheeling down the corridor, a favored mode of exit.

From the hallway came a crash. You looked down the corridor. Napoleon had attempted a backward somersault to regain his feet. In so doing he had planted his large shoes on the chest of young Annapolis-trained O'Connor. Both had gone to the ground.

You reported to Arkansaw and Gordian.

"They're back on their feet now. Napoleon is moving in a jerky, mechanical way. What can the matter be? Ah — Napoleon is Frankenstein's monster again."

Frankenstein's monster was an act gradually perfected by Napoleon, to the delight of the Negro stewards of the BOQ, and the destruction, so far, of one chair and half of an upper bunk in the monster's implacable grip.

"He's advancing on Frankenstein, his creator, with slow, machine-like steps. The eminent young Frankenstein O'Connor, class of Annapolis '42, is retreating to the bulkhead. He tries to dodge. But the monster has punched the highspeed button in his own mechanical neck. He is too fast for young Frankenstein O'Connor.

"In his terror, Frankenstein seems to have forgotten how to turn his monster off.

"Oh, what a good monster it is. The monster squeezes Frankenstein with one arm, and points to his mechanical neck, to show O'Connor how to turn him off.

"But Frankenstein cannot seem to understand. Those years at Annapolis have taken their toll. The mind is no longer so keen as when he entered the Academy. Now the monster is squeezing Frankenstein with both arms. Frankenstein O'Connor is turning red. Now he's turning purple. Can nothing save Frankenstein for his Annapolis class reunion?

"Yes, there is something that may save Frankenstein! Monsters have a sex urge. Now the monster remembers. He has a date with another monster. He punches the button himself. The monster checks his appointment book again. Yes, the female is at the age of mechanical consent. He drools in an oily way, as only a mechanical monster can, and runs out of the BOQ.

"Young Frankenstein O'Connor gasps for breath. He is unable to call out. But the sight of his class ring revives him. He will live — live on for his class reunion. Faltering, then erect, he opens the next door — 'Is anyone here from the class of '42?' "

You closed the door of your bunkroom. "Continued in next week's Saturday performance. Free dishes to the ladies, if any."

CHAPTER FOUR

March, 1943

On October 20th, 1944, immediately after the landing of the first wave on the Visaya beaches, General Mac-Dazzle, Supreme Commander of the Allied Forces, signaled to Admiral Hornbull, "I want to thank you for returning me to the Philippines." Admiral Hornbull replied, "The officers and men of the United States Navy are proud to have had a part in returning the flag to the Philippines."

BEGEL, The Battle for Visaya Gulf

❀

ON YOUR day off you went to Honolulu. Inside the pink Royal Hawaiian Hotel, now taken over by the Navy as a rest hotel for submariners, you changed to swimming trunks in the Royal Suite, where once the Prince of Wales had changed his swimming trunks. In the corridors echoed the names of submarines — *Tambor, Grouper, Pollack, Tarpon, Growler, Dolphin, Plunger, Drum.* Scuttlebutt had it that several submarines had been lost in March, one off the coast of Japan.

Yesterday Napoleon had submitted his tenth request for transfer to PT boats. His yeomen admirers (several of whom he was tutoring in chest-expansion courses) had informed him that his request had been forwarded, as Navy Regulations required, but stamped DISAPPROVED.

You had done nothing to leave the dullness and uselessness of Q. And yet you knew now that, stifle it as you might, within you burned a desire, a fever, a flame — did you, like Napoleon, seek an enemy battle flag and an assault arrow on your combat ribbon? Did you wish, the Ironical Observer, merely to see a Modern Battle? Six days a week you sorted out trivia at Q, and on the seventh you rested.

On Waikiki beach at first you were painfully conscious of your dark blue issue trunks, which seemed to keep you in uniform still. You walked east toward Diamond Head, along the yellow-white crescent of beach. The water was bright bluegreen, darkening out beyond the reef. Everywhere on Oahu you felt islanded, besieged by water. How different from the landlocked, low rolling hills, the dull brown landscape of New England.

With envy you watched the light soaring flight of the surfriders, a dozen or so skimming in a ragged line along the foamycrested waves. You swam, powerfully though not very skillfully, in the surfheavy swells, and you noticed that most of the people around you swam easily and well, not like the summer swimmers of the Atlantic. There were no lifeguards, nor were they needed.

Stretched on the sand, propped on your elbows, you faced the beach. The barbed wire defenses, hastily erected after Pearl Harbor, had eroded or washed together in rusty clumps. But the war had long since moved away from Pearl and the barbed wire was tended only in the censoring regulations, which forbade you to photograph or discuss these now useless defenses.

You watched a stout brown Hawaiian father lower his two-year-old son for his first dip in the waves, and the chocolate infant clapped his pink palms on the water. A Hawaiian woman, about five feet eleven in height, weighing, you guessed, easily over two hundred and fifty pounds, was gathering seaweed. She wore a white holoku which clung wetly to her muscular trunk. With a quick, savage movement she caught a young octopus, carried it to her mouth, laughing at its flailing and sucking arms, and bit it in the eye. Then she held it, writhing and dead, high in the air for the beach to see before she dropped it back in her basket.

You lay near the beach house reserved for Army officers; now a girl came out and stood gazing out past Diamond Head, beyond the reef and the breaking surf. She wore a tight green bathing suit. She was taller than Japanese girls usually were, though not so tall as many Hawaiian Chinese. Her nose was slender, with a slight bridge, unlike the snub noses of the Hiroshima Japanese of Oahu. Her face was full and broad at the eyes, her hair was jet black, without the slightest trace of brown. Her figure was full and erect, almost rich in its lines, and still that of a young girl. Her arms, typically Asiatic, seemed slightly short, her knees turned in very slightly, but she carried herself gracefully, without seeming stiff and awkward, as she waited. It was a trick Oriental girls had to perfection, the art of standing still, the art of graceful patience.

Her coloring, fresh and young, seemed not "yellow," but through some gleam of the high Hawaiian sun, perhaps, it had a faint, mysterious violet tinge, so subtle as to be more fragrance than color.

You imagined her getting married in a year or two, and, somewhat heavier in figure no doubt, bringing her Hawaiian children to the beach. In the sand you traced some words:

> Against their Brydale day, which is not long:
> Sweete Themmes runne softly, till I end my song.

Waves came up on a rising tide and began to nibble at the archaic words. The girl, you realized, was watching what you had traced. But when you looked directly at her, she was smiling at the sky, at the horizon, at some mysterious and profound secret known only to women much admired by men.

There was an impatient, familiar voice from the Army officers' beach house. "Lani," it called. The greenclad statue came to life. She smiled again — this time you thought, perhaps you hoped — with a trace of amusement about the corners of her lips. And you sensed that she could see with her eyelids almost shut. She turned and ran into the water, diving in, and coming up some distance away from the point of her dive. She swam quickly and easily.

Captain Feverton loped out of the beach house. "Lani," he called again. You were surprised to see that he had a barrel chest but spindly long legs. He wore bright red tapa cloth bathing trunks. Angularly he floundered into the water, scraped bottom in a massive bellywhopper, got up, walked a few unsteady steps and fell forward with a great diving splash. Arms and legs thrashing, he churned his way out to her, with a great boiling of water, but not much perceptible forward movement. "Lani," he called again, his smiling face kept well above the waves, as if in fear that the pasted smile might wipe off.

Lani, you supposed, was for the common Hawaiian girl's name, Leilani, "Heavenly Wreath." Once a Hawaiian had explained the name to you as "Heavenly Reef." Perhaps that was an even better translation. You resolved, by an act of puritan will, not to be envious of Captain Feverton.

You stood up and walked along the beach, the water yawning at the dry sand under your feet. You stepped once into Lani's footprint, then ran along the beach on the hard wet sand at the water's edge, and plunged in. With hard vicious strokes you swam to calm water near the outermost reef, and there you rolled over on your back and floated, rocking, weightless, at the center of your china blue cup of sky. You let the tide drift you in to the beach again. Half asleep, against your will, you remembered

(THIS WAY TO THE PHILADELPHIA SESQUICENTENNIAL 1926, your mother and father drove you there in the new Model T Ford — any color you want so long as it's black. You had walked along the Avenue of Nations, fingering Japanese silks and Meissen china, sampling Polish ham and Wisconsin cheese. Above your head, from two pink pylons carved heralds proclaimed a new dawn, they reminded you of the nightly pageants on The Fall of Rome, The Creation of the World, The Birth of Man, The Evolution of the Dreadnaught, The Battle of Gettysburg.

Dewey's ancient flagship, *Olympia*, urged you to fire when you were ready Gridley. The new superdreadnaught *Wyorada* bade you carry a big stick and speak softly. Japanese troops tramped past, sightseeing in columns of fours. From a book exhibit window Ben Franklin sagely advised: "Rarely use venery but for health or offspring, never to dullness, weakness, or the injury of your own or another's peace or reputation."

You hated to leave, you remembered a last attempt to see again Washington's coat of arms, Paul Revere's forge, Jefferson's revolving desk.

A year later you had moved to Connecticut, to Palisades, to be near the Capital City office of your father's insurance company. Your father was proud of moving, he had beat out two others for the new job in the Capital City. "Competition," he liked to say, "made America what it is today" — happily he organized conferences, in Connecticut, in New Jersey, in Pennsylvania, to set standard insurance rates.

A year after the move, though the Model T was as good as new, you helped your father put it up on wooden blocks. It was the depression, there was no money to run it, everything extra went for your mother's illness. But your father kept the battery at a Palisades garage. For a long time your father kept the battery alive, but in the second year of your mother's illness he at last gave up and sold the car.

Once you saw the Model T, dented but still deep black and sturdy, in the dirt driveway of a small truck farm. You couldn't beat a good model T. In case of trouble, almost any pedal would stop it.

Under the sudorific Honolulu sun your breath slowed, came more evenly, and you sensed that part of you was falling toward sleep, you began to dream — clearly at first — of an army with coats of all colors, of rocks that blazed up and burned to ashes, of axes falling to the ground and changing to flowers, of a girl, nude to the waist, who walked out from the earth, you rushed past her toward a bluemouthed cavern, your dreams blurred and flowed by, ranging beyond reach

under your fingertips you felt the hot wet Hawaiian sand, you woke up).

Later that afternoon you wanted to do some shopping; you got off the downtown bus from Waikiki, but you had stayed on the bus too long, you had gone past the shopping district, down as far as River Street, in the area of the whorehouses.

Irregular columns of soldiers in khaki and sailors in whites inched forward in their "chow" lines. They trudged into wooden sheds, called, when they had names at all, the *Anchor*, the *Dreadnaught*, the *Golden Cock*, the *Catapult*. The men in line had a half-sleepy, flushed look. They did not talk much to each other, but patiently edged forward, alone in their long crowded lines, hundreds of men, perhaps a thousand or more, in an hour.

Each girl, you knew from Napoleon's professional landlady, had two little cubicles. While she serviced a man in one room, the next "date" got ready in the adjacent room; in that way no time was lost. A "date" cost $3, of which $2 went to the girl, and the rest to the Madam. She kept part for herself, and the rest went to interested members of the Honolulu police and legislature.

Near the entrance inside the door stood or sat the smiling, weary Madam. Each "date" had to strip his penis with his fingers, in so-called short-arm inspection, to show by absence of drip that he did not have gonorrhea. If he flunked this test, his service number was taken and telephoned to his military unit.

There was no test for syphilis, but once a week the girls were examined by military doctors for both syphilis and gonorrhea.

If an enlisted man caught either disease, he lost his pay until he recovered. Officers never caught these social diseases, but occasionally their medical jackets listed a disabling illness known as "undue exposure to actinic rays."

There was something primitively appealing about buying your sexual acts raw, naked, and sweaty, without any time wasted on courtship. Indeed, you were not supposed to kiss the whores. They permitted every other gross familiarity, with a surcharge for perversions such as Frenchy, but reserved that simple gesture of affection. In the heart of every vice lingered, like a worm in the bud, a virtue.

From the doorway of the *Dreadnaught,* Napoleon's landlady waved at you. Behind her shoulder you caught a glimpse of the full figure of a woman, in stepins and brassiere. Your loins ached sharply.

A jeep horn honked reproachfully at you. Chaplain Simon looked at you from the driver's seat.

"I mean, my bus . . ." you gave up, and climbed aboard the jeep.

"They bring in these girls," said Simon, "but not the men's wives."

You were silent during the brief ride back to the shopping district. "Dances," said Chaplain Simon, stopping to let you off, "at the university . . ." He shot off with a vigorous wave of his hand. "Dignity," he shouted back.

You walked by dingy, unhygienic tattoo shops, sleazy stores with windows full of purple silk pillows labeled "Honolulu" on one side and "Mother" on the other. There were bars that sold "Five Ulcers" rum, gin, and whiskey. Japanese and Chinese restaurants, open to the street, with low tables, and stools instead of chairs, offered bowls of rice, tomato beef, chicken hekka, chop suey, and Mandarin duck.

Many of the shops and banks and stores included the word "Comfrey" in their firm names; you halted at the Comfrey Jewelry Store. The pretty Chinese-Hawaiian salesgirl told you they were selling a lot of earrings now. Before every big move in the Pacific, she said innocently, the jewelry trade increased. You bought a pair of silver earrings made in the shape of tiny anthurium flowers. The girl asked if you wanted them mailed and you had her address them to A. W. Oman, Venusberg, Wyorada, USA. "Do you need a street number?" asked the pretty salesgirl. "It's a small town," you said.

The manager of the shop, a Chinese, came downstairs and asked you into the back of the shop. "Very fine beads," he said, in movie Chinese-English. "Mandarin beads. Real amber. You safe here." You sat down. Tea came, brought by the pretty salesgirl, and you sipped it. She sat down at her counter in the next room, letting the edge of the counter push under her full breasts. She smiled at you.

You detached one of the amber beads, held it over the ashtray and touched a match to it. The face of the Chinese store manager remained impassive. The bead burst into flame. They were very fine beads. Very fine plastic beads; if you never smoked you were perfectly safe. "Come upstairs," said the Chinese in his singsong Fu Manchu English. "I show you real goods. You safe here."

"Some other time," you said. As you left, you could hear "Fu Manchu" speaking perfect English to his pretty salesgirl. You looked back. She leaned against the front counter and smiled at you.

In the streets you felt oppressed by the aimless crowds of soldiers, of sailors, of starchshirted Marines. What had you to do with all this hurry of men? Gordian had his letters to his wife. Arkansaw would spend the evening with his new friends at Green Point. Feverton was probably dancing at La Hula Rhumba with his Lani. In a few hours Napoleon's blue Packard would be coughing to a lascivious halt.

You had your quiet backwater in which to spend the rest of the war. You had your list of words, your special units and decisive forces. You had a Boy's Manual of the Japanese Air Force. You had a primary school ethics text. You had a healthy longing for the pretty Chinese-Hawaiian salesgirl.

But you went back, aimlessly, to Waikiki. The crescent of shore darkened in the quick tropical sunset. Great arms of purple edged toward the red west, covered it, and turned the water a deep gloomy blue in their dark embrace. And at one corner of the horizon, just before it raced into the night, you saw the great convoy hurrying westward against Japan.

After dinner at the Moana Hotel you sat in the courtyard under a banyan tree. Red cigarette dots sparked in the night, ice tinkled in glasses, waves plashed, then sucked at the beach. Next door, at the Royal Hawaiian, a dance band played to the submariners.

Major Begel, wearing a white dress Marine uniform, in the center of a party of Navy captains and their wives, came through the Banyan court, glanced at you without recognizing you, and walked slowly on, his jaws clenched on a cigar.

You remembered an Edwards lecture of Professor Begel at Yale. Begel's audience, thanks to his lecture's title, "The Coming Struggle for Empire with Japan," had consisted of banner-carrying Veterans of Future Wars. Begel's vision had been, as always, large, even larger than his rhetoric. "When war comes," he had said to the future veterans, "you will fight, and in the long run, though not at first, you will fight well. But beyond this war," he added, for Begel had been as convinced of American victory as Tojo of Japanese triumph, "what will you put in the place of Japan's Greater East Asia? What power will you choose to exercise empire in China and Southeast Asia and in Japan? For all her greed, Japan has launched a powerful idea. You will not defeat that idea with the armies in which you will serve. And that idea is Greater East Asia." They had booed, and Professor Begel had acknowledged the boos as lesser men would have acknowledged applause. And then they had applauded, but he had walked out, pausing only long enough to snap: "No questions."

From Begel's table in the Banyan Court came fragments of his talk, above the noise of the submariners' band and the steady, slapping sound of the waves. "The real history of the CLEAN-SLATE operation — Banika Island — Pavuvu Island — no Japanese . . . all General Imamura's forces had been withdrawn . . . the Komandorski Islands . . . 26 March 1943 . . . *Salt Lake City* — chasing the salvoes . . . Japanese broke off the action first." Rich with expensive cigar smoke and the special fragrance of genuine Scotch whiskey, the party moved on.

That night you slept fitfully in your bunk room. A strange, snoring transient officer occupied Napoleon's old upper bunk. Overhead plane after plane from Hickham Field roared off in a practice alert, motors cold and still sputtering. A passage from Napoleon's *Frankenstein* came to mind. How that wretchedly written book lodged in one's memory: ". . . I was overcome by the sensation of helplessness, so often felt in frightful dreams, when you in vain endeavor to fly from an impending danger — and was rooted to the spot."

And rooted to your spot you lay there dreaming, at first of the beckoning Madam and the bareshouldered girl at her back, then of the Chinese-Hawaiian salesgirl at her counter — then you were alone, deeper in your dream, dreaming of deep blue flowers of gentian wavering in a blue cave — and beyond the cave, flickering and beckoning on, armed shadows, of a deeper, darker blue.

CHAPTER FIVE

March, 1943

> . . . *at the end of the war the temporary buildings on Makalapa which had housed the brain cells of the Pacific Fleet . . . were all torn down.*
>
> *Footnote 27,* BEGEL, The Battle for Visaya Gulf

*

GORDIAN's slender face and brown mustache nibbled at your idea, and rejected it, ever so kindly. And Gordian tried to divert your attack by saying, "Still, he wants to learn. After his last Man to Man talk with you he came to me to ask what 'ironical' meant."

You were both walking back to Makalapa and Q, from lunch at the Aiea Naval Hospital officers' mess. You were both full of thick noodle soup, rehydrated mashed potato, Swiss steak, ice cream and iced tea.

You went on with your argument, knowing that you often pushed an idea too far, and lost the full support of your audience. But you could not help yourself.

"It's a question not of whether he hates us — he does, surely, hate us just because we're intellectuals — but the real question is whether he's the type that wants to injure those he hates — 'I hate and I injure' —" You broke off at this parody of Catullus which gave you a personal satisfaction you immediately recognized as absurd. "And it won't do you any good to call it Destructive Criticism either."

You both walked slowly up the steep path to the edge of the shallow volcano on which Q's building sat. Coral dust stuck to your skin. There was no hurry. Ahead lay still another afternoon in the Document Assembly Center.

For all of America's Knowhow and Mechanical Genius, there was never, at Q or its related bureaus, any method of assembling a long mimeographed report except by having men walk around a table picking up single sheets from separate piles, one pile for each page.

Perhaps this was just as well, or the Army and Navy, in the Pacific at least, might have drowned in mimeographed documents. Each bureau chief in Q's building lay awake nights thinking up ways to keep Commander Wolfe from assigning that bureau chief's underlings for a morning, an afternoon, or sometimes in emergencies for three or four days, to the Document Assembly Room.

Not Captain Feverton, however. Anxious to keep his ship as taut as possible, he generously offered to Commander Wolfe, to General Waddleman, to The Admiral, or to anyone else at Pearl, all the ensigns in Q for any task at any time. And the Captain, before sending you to the basement, as he phrased it in Order #7, on this "Vitall Mision," lined you up, looked each of you in the eye, and said in an inspirational tone modeled on football movies about Knute Rockne, "It's your ball, men, you run with it. Really RUN."

Two or three times a week, you met in the Document Assembly Room and circled a long table piled high with fifty to a hundred stacks of mimeographed pages. Grimly you gathered the pages, one from each stack, and grimly you dropped the finished document off at the station of the Ensign Stapler at the end of the line. Softly you sang, whenever Captain Feverton appeared, in choruses led by Napoleon, "Ole Man River, he doan know *nuthin.*"

"I don't mind assembling the documents so much," said Gordian mildly. "Someone has to do it."

You both sat down in the shade and had a cigarette. You could see the harbor below and the steady procession of ships. A black submarine turned delicately into her berth. A cruiser edged out into the channel.

"Napoleon's request for transfer was rejected."

"I wouldn't refuse to go out," said Gordian, "but I couldn't volunteer."

"You heard that he took over the search files."

"Feverton? Have you done anything about them?"

" 'RHIP,' he said. He's got them all mucked up now." But your voice had a defensively ironic shading.

"Whatever unit you were in, whatever ship you were on," said Gordian, "there'd be a Captain Feverton." And, half a year wiser than you were in the ways of the Navy, he added, "He's better than the first two we had."

" 'Hardheels,' you mean."

"And the second one," said Gordian. "Don't forget 'Captain Fantasy.' "

Your first officer-in-charge, "Hardheels," had been under the impression, certainly correct, that you all needed whipping into shape. First, Hardheels had told you (this was in your old location, a corner of the sixth floor of a cement warehouse), that anywhere, afloat or ashore, you were always — in the Navy — aboard a ship.

Hands clasped behind his back, his massive, undershot jaw pushed forward, his class ring glinting in the sun, Hardheels crisply informed you of his horror on hearing the floor referred to as "the floor" rather than "the deck." "Walls," he went on, were "bulkheads," "windows" were "ports," and "stairs" were "ladders." "Two block that tie," he yelled at Napoleon. For a moment, the cement warehouse seemed to rock at anchor.

The helpful hints of Hardheels might have been more impressive had he been over five feet six — one grotesque rumor, assiduously spread by Napoleon, had it that he wore elevator shoes to get into Annapolis.

Hardheels was particularly cross about the morning dash for the warehouse elevator just before "oh eight hundred," and he now told you that the "elevator" was actually a "small boat" and you should conduct yourselves accordingly. Then he said "Carry on," in an ominous tone, and rolled away, his French heels clicking on the cement floor, or rather, "deck."

Gordian researched the rules for "small boats" in a handbook on naval courtesy. Junior officers, so it seemed, boarded such craft first, and debarked last. Next morning in the rush just before "oh eight hundred," you all respectfully pushed Hardheels aside and surged into the elevator ahead of him.

There was no room left for Hardheels himself, and the Filipina operator shut the door in his face. Hardheels reached his desk a few minutes late, and was chewed out by Commander Wolfe for setting a bad example to the new ensigns under his charge. That morning at "oh nine hundred" an unsigned memo informed you that the "elevator" had ceased to be a "small boat." Its nautical career had been of the briefest.

Later that week Hardheels, his metal heels clicking as he first stood on tiptoe, then rocked back, lined up the ensigns in Q and gave them what became known, after its third repetition, as his "You're here to die" pep talk.

This morbid monologue was based on participation in the fringes of the battle of Midway, three years of learning Japanese from a Mr. Naganuma in Japan, and a psychopathic desire to have war go on forever. Hardheels painted a gloomy canvas of a fifteen-year struggle, in the course of which death was certain, with the only consolation the possibility of a Soldier's Grave or Burial at Sea (rather than capture), though you could not believe so Powerful and Ruthless an Enemy as Hardheels described would stop to Honor the Fallen Dead. Indeed, the analysis of Hardheels, as he stood on tiptoe and rocked down "click" on his heels, held out only a dim prospect for Urn Burial by a Future Generation, and then not necessarily in One's Own Individual Pot.

After this speech the ensigns of Q adopted the phrase "You can't win" as a kind of password. The expression was used when the laundry got lost, when Hardheels assembled you for a talk, when rain fell during the outdoor movies.

Hardheels might still have been rocking his metal heels on Q's quarterdeck but for one tiny error. He made it his practice to criticize the work of the green ensigns of Q while turning in their manuscripts as his own.

Commander Wolfe, the real ruler of Q and its neighboring bureaus, did not object to this assumption of credit. By Navy reasoning, you were responsible, as officer-in-charge, for anything those under you did wrong, and so, logically, you were also to be given credit for anything they did right.

But Hardheels made a fatal mistake. For he wrote to Washington that the Japanese language training school of Q's new ensigns should be discontinued because their Japanese was so faulty.

A more orthodox officer than Wolfe might have objected to this outrageous by-passing of the chain of command. But Wolfe himself, an audacious manipulator of JOKEPOA, never went through the chain of command for anything important. No, it was the faulty logic of Hardheels which disturbed Wolfe.

For if the work of the new ensigns was good enough for Hardheels to submit as his own, then, reasoned Wolfe, the Japanese language school must have something to be said in its favor. Hardheels found himself with some thirty copies of new orders in his hands, transferring him to liaison with the hated General MacDazzle (no friend of Wolfe's) in Brisbane.

Once Hardheels understood that he was to leave Q forever, he mellowed in personality, even going so far as to reveal to the new ensigns that there were Japanese prisoners of war at Pearl. This fact he had previously concealed, even though one of their assigned tasks, theoretically, was the interrogation of POWS.

There were a few stolid infantrymen, a couple of excitable fishermen who spoke an odd dialect called Zu Zu Ben, a midget sub pilot — only survivor of the midget sub attack on Pearl, and a carrier torpedo plane pilot named Kawai — Pilot Officer "Riverwell."

There was a special bond between Hardheels and Riverwell, for Riverwell had gone to Etajima, the Japanese equivalent of Annapolis. Now, over three vanilla ice cream sodas, Kawai and Hardheels discussed hazing at their respective academies, while you took desultory notes.

Both agreed the hazing had been brutal. Etajima rated higher than Annapolis because at the Japanese Academy there had been several suicides, and one man had died of baseball-bat beatings by upperclassmen.

The hot Pearl Harbor afternoon wore on. According to his interrogation reports, Riverwell had flown in the attack on Pearl Harbor, and had subsequently been taken prisoner after a raid on Guadal while swimming "unconscious" in the water. The Japanese did not admit that their troops could be taken prisoner, and simply listed all missing men as dead. And Japanese prisoners usually rationalized their capture by stating that they had been taken while unconscious.

Riverwell's whole unit was called a *kessenbutai*, a decisive battle force. What was meant by this word? When he obeyed the wave-off of the landing officer's blue light on the morning of December 8 — the Japanese dating — he and his fellow carrier pilots had regarded the attack as suicidal, as one from which over half the flight might never return. But was that a banzai, a suicide attack?

Hardheels refused to let you ask Riverwell about these matters, and dutifully you noted down the information that Japanese aircraft carriers, unlike American ones, had no ice cream bars. The Marine chaser sat stiffly outside your barred waiting room, his short shotgun held across his knees. Through the partition you could hear a Marine guard saying to an American Marine prisoner: "Go ahead, you want to get out. Go over the wall. I'll shoot you. You'll get out. Go ahead. Go over the wall." The voice of the guard, quiet and deadly, hot as the afternoon itself, went on and on. You fetched a second round of vanilla sodas.

There was no criticism of your work from your second officer-in-charge, "Captain Fantasy." He was a tall, distinguished, Annapolis-bred commander, with gray-black hair and a gray mustache, waxed imperceptibly at the tips. There was no criticism for a simple reason — Captain Fantasy gave you almost no work at all.

Captain Fantasy was searching for the perfect phrase. He spent three days over the Japanese word *yūgeki*. He was trying to decide whether this vague method of attack referred to "ambush," "sneak," "delaying," or possibly even "judo" attack. Finally he settled on "diversion attack," took the afternoon off, and moved on to the next perfect phrase.

You had written in a report on Japanese blackout regulations the word "lighting." Captain Fantasy summoned you and asked, in a fatherly way, if you did not wish, on second thoughts, to change "lighting" to "the illumination of the electric lights."

"You can't win," said Arkansaw, and you agreed with him.

It was this incident, and others like it, which made Captain Fantasy assign to himself practically all the work of Q. No one else matched his high standards for felicity and accuracy of phrase. Sluggishly the work began to back up, first on his desk, then on an adjacent desk, which Captain Fantasy commandeered, then on an even longer table which he had made to order.

A great shipment then came from newly won CACTUS, from Guadalcanal. The boxes, and the papers they contained, were permeated with that strange rich odor which you later came to recognize as the odor of the dead. The worst documents were drycleaned, but the odor became part of Q.

Wolfe, after this shipment, took a strong interest in Captain Fantasy. His friends on Guadal had signaled to him that there was material of interest in this new shipment of documents. Several times a day he entered Q and glared fixedly at the tables on which the malodorous papers steadily accumulated, awaiting the delicate ministrations of Captain Fantasy. But Captain Fantasy, of the same rank as Wolfe, took no heed, except to refuse to wear a new plastic identity badge invented by Wolfe.

The strain of searching for the perfect word was relieved, for Captain Fantasy, by frequent trips to the Naval Officers' Pistol Range. There he selected a pistol from the brace on his specially carved Naval Officers' Pistol Board, aimed slowly at the target, and squeezed one hundred times. Captain Fantasy was horrified to discover that not even one ensign in Q had ever qualified on the pistol range. It was too late to recall their commissions but at least they could spend every afternoon at the range while they made up this gap in their military skills. Napoleon, overjoyed with this respite from supervising stencils, showed up at the pistol range with larger and larger weapons, until the chief at the pistol range pointed out to him that an officer who wished to qualify in the 105 howitzer should go to the *Army* range.

You had taken to Captain Fantasy your puzzling words, those with "decisive" as one element in the compound, or those with "special," as in "decisive battle force" and "special attack."

Captain Fantasy had smiled at you in a fatherly way and had put your jottings on one of his tables. You were assured that your problem would have a special heap all to itself. A wave of the hand told you there were more pressing matters. And further, Captain Fantasy suggested that you avoid using these words in any fixed translation until more information came as to what they really meant. In fact, it might be better not to translate such words at all. "Let the situation mature," said Captain Fantasy sagely. It was a phrase not lost on Captain Feverton, who then, as Army liaison officer, had the desk next to that of Captain Fantasy himself.

Doggedly searching for your word lists when Captain Fantasy

was at the pistol range, you had found in the mass of materials some curious documents without words, or without many words. These were Japanese search plane assignments. You persuaded Captain Fantasy to forward these to Wolfe. In a rage, for these were the documents referred to by his friends on Guadal, Wolfe came into Q, stood by the desk of Captain Fantasy and raised his heavy, dark eyebrows. It was a bodily gesture which had been known to make General Waddleman turn in his plump swivel chair like a Yo-Yo on a string. Captain Fantasy merely asked if Wolfe would like to meet him at the pistol range for a friendly round of fire.

Wolfe's solution was simple, though it would never have occurred to a reserve officer. Captain Fantasy was promoted from Commander to Captain. There was no position then at Q which really did full justice to his rank and talents (so Wolfe signaled Washington). No doubt, speculated Wolfe, there would be just such a position at the now expanding forward base of Noumea. Noumea in turn, Wolfe thought, might, after an indoctrination period, promote and forward Captain Fantasy to Brisbane where he could, perhaps, share an office with "Hardheels," to the endless confusion of the hated General MacDazzle, self-styled Supreme Commander, Pacific.

No doubt, you observed to Arkansaw, Captain Fantasy had been similarly promoted and forwarded from Washington. At the end of the war Captain Fantasy might well turn up Supreme Commander of the Allied Powers, a position he would have achieved by sheer lack of merit alone.

In a day, Captain Fantasy, his pistol board, his storage tables, almost all sign of his existence in Q had disappeared. Once you found a scrap of paper in his handwriting: "*toku* or *tokubetsu,* special, as in special attack, meaning suicide attack? *Hold.*"

You sat in the shade on the side of the extinct volcano and put out your cigarette. From the basement of Q came the strains of "Ole Man River, he doan know *nuthin,*" in the hoarse bellow of Napoleon.

"Time to return to the cotton-picking slavery of Q." You stood up. "It's his ideas I hate. Ideas that will Win the War."

But Gordian still sat, looking at the harbor. A look of disgust crossed his face. "You mean the censoring."

One of Captain Feverton's first ideas had been Preventing Spying by Censoring Officer Mail. How the ensigns of Q could be his Buddies on the Long Long Trail (a favored form of group salutation) and Potential Spies at the same time was hard to understand, except on a very taut ship indeed. Feverton's innovation here had hit Gordian especially hard.

Before Feverton's reform, the censoring of officer mail had been the merest of formalities. Each officer had written his own letter, sealed it, stamped it PASSED BY CENSOR, and initialed the censor's stamp with the initials of the censor, namely, himself.

But as Captain Feverton explained in Order #9: "One bad aple could win or loose the war." The next morning a rotten apple was left on his desk, with a cardboard placard: "Aple, Roten, one, government isue, Title I, for Spy Use Only."

The Captain frowned in the direction of Napoleon, corrected the spelling of "roten," then threw card and apple in the confidential trash basket. He went on reading the mail, his powerful shears at the ready, a strange tense smile on his face.

At first you thought this peculiar expression meant that the Captain had really found something objectionable in your letters. Then you watched the Captain more closely and saw that he was forming with his lips not only every word that he read, but every syllable in every word. Occasionally, on finishing a letter that he had particularly enjoyed, he would go over and congratulate its lucky author. Poor Gordian had been so honored several times.

The married men tried to deluge Captain Feverton by writing five and six letters a day to their wives (except for Gordian who had already reached this level of communication) but their wives at once suspected attempts to conceal unfaithfulness. The bachelors sent long letters to friends they had forgotten, and answered ads for kidney stones and gall bladder cures, describing their diuretic disabilities in hideous detail. Both groups wrote unkind things about the Army. They particularly called to the attention of their correspondents the Army's serious difficulties in finding men to do work worthy of the rank of captain.

Remarks about the Army were cut out by the powerful shears as military information. Remarks about Army captains were cut out as untruths. A third category — remarks which might be bad for home morale — usually took care of the rest of their letters.

On days when Captain Feverton was alert, a letter could end up with little more than a salutation and a complimentary close. Napoleon stormed into Q one day with a letter returned in some perplexity by his wife. She had written back that she wanted an epistle from him, not a paper doily. With a pair of shears Napoleon, to the delight of his yeomen, executed a number of combination fencing lunges and scissors cuts, aimed at all the extremities, but especially at the crotch of an imaginary captain. Then he had writhed on the floor in imitation of a basket case whose every limb, unto the last, had been removed.

"The Captain," Gordian had warned. Napoleon had stuffed the shredded letter in his mouth and eaten it, to scattered applause.

From Q on its volcano top came another melancholy chorus of "Ole Man River."

"We're late."

Gordian held a letter in his hands. The handwriting was not that of his wife.

"Brown," he said slowly. "You remember Brownie. Perhaps you could help me."

"Brownie?"

"I've got to write a letter to his mother."

"But there's no fighting on Guadalcanal."

"Suicide," said Gordian gently. "Someone ought to write to his family. No one seems to have known him very well, but I said I would. He used to talk to me once in a while." Hurriedly he said, on seeing some expression cross your face, "It's no use blaming Feverton or Prantz. No one knows about a suicide."

But you were not thinking of how Feverton, at the suggestion of Prantz, had ordered Ensign Brown to CACTUS. You were trying to remember Ensign Brown's face. No matter how you tried, you could not remember his face clearly.

Gordian stood up, beside you, and looked across the harbor. "They've started the winches," he said.

"Where?"

"On the *Wyorada*." Gordian rubbed his nose between his thumb and forefinger. "Don't get upset about Brownie," he said.

It was funny that you never felt like lying to Gordian. Not even polite lies. "I wasn't thinking about Brown. I was thinking about another use of 'special force' I found this morning. I wish to God I could think about him. But I can't really remember what he looked like. And yet I'd know him if he walked up the path here."

"But you'll help me with the letter?"

"I'll help you with the letter." And before entering Q you turned for another look at the *Wyorada*. Each of the motors ashore, you had heard, was less than one horsepower in strength, and yet, working very slowly, they would soon pull the capsized dreadnaught into an upright position. Some day soon you would go over to the island for a closer look.

"Let me write my own letter to Brown's mother."

Gordian said nothing more to you, he did not look at you as, single file, you entered the double fence of barbed wire, showed your plastic identity cards and your Navy ID cards, and returned the sentry's salute. But you knew, without the need for words, that Gordian was, now, your friend.

At another anguished bellow of "Ole Man River" you had to laugh.

"It's not so bad," said Gordian.

"No, it's not so bad. It's impossible."

CHAPTER SIX

April, 1943

The Yamato *was the equal, in tonnage, of five of our heavy cruisers; in three massy turrets she swung nine 18-inch guns, each of which weighed over 180 tons, and she outranged every American ship in her vicinity — why then did she falter with victory in her view?*

BEGEL, The Battle for Visaya Gulf

*

"No STAGS! No stags," warned the two Chinese girls who took tickets and sorted the money into wooden pigeonholes. Their voices chimed in silvery peals of laughter. You stood at the bottom of the University Gymnasium stairs and listened to the jazz band. Feet shuffled over the waxed floor overhead, and the band swung smoothly into "As Time Goes By":

A kiss is still a kiss, a sigh is just a sigh,
The fundamental things apply, as time goes by.

A few girls rustled past in long cotton Mother Hubbards, the missionary costume now authenticated as folkish dress by the Honolulu Chamber of Commerce. Then more girls, sprays of flowers, the heady scent of Chanel No. 5 cologne. And one beautiful girl in aqua and bluegreen, and a rhinestone tiara — she had brilliant eyes, and for a moment you thought she was Lani — Leilani — but she was not. She left behind her the scent of masses of white pikake flower leis, almost, it seemed, the odor of moonlight.

You stepped back to make room for a Hawaiian girl in a smart Fifth Avenue dress, a brown Aphrodite with her lovely chocolate arm linked in the white-uniformed arm of her sailor escort. The sailor, young, with good looks that smelled of money and of eastern prep schools, avoided your glance so as not to have to salute. Her picture, you recalled, had been printed in the *Honolulu Star Bulletin* as winner of a beauty contest. The two Chinese girls looked up from their tickets and wooden cashbox, and giggled in high silvery voices. "She's engaged," they said to each other, triumphantly, "engaged, engaged." They doubled their hands in their mouths, but still the giggles cascaded out between their fingers.

"Is that bad?"

"She was en*gaged* be*fore*" — more giggles, "and then *he* was *trans*ferred."

"Couldn't she wait?"

"But *he* was away so long" — more silvery giggles.

"How long?"

"Three months." Irresistible, chimesilvery peals, giggle after giggle, like the clear strike of hoof iron on stone.

"Pau, pau, pau," the two girls cried. You turned at the pinkwhite scent of carnations. Lani entered alone, in a long blue dress, a carnation lei flung carelessly on her bare golden shoulders. You tormented yourself by imagining profound thoughts behind her high, Madonnalike brow, and you prepared to go.

But her steady gaze made you glance at her sharply. She said to you softly, "Sailor." Her voice had a lilt of amusement, with an undertone that was faintly defensive, poised for flight. "You can come in with me."

She had the round olive face, you thought, of a virgin by Giotto, and, as so often in Giotto's faces, her golden skin held a faint rosy tinge. She wore no perfume, but now that she stood beside you, in her hair you sensed a dim fragrance, the sharp, faint trace of sandalwood. It was an odor that was always present in Honolulu's Buddhist temples. Her look seemed to double in intensity, then her eyes almost closed as she waited for your answer. In her patient waiting you caught a brief glimpse of something brooding and passive and alien that perturbed you deeply.

You bought your ticket from the two Chinese girls. One of them winked at you. They giggled again and went on calling to each other in their high chiming voices, "Away, away *so* long . . . pau, pau, pau."

A couple descended the stairs and you waited with Lani against the wall until they passed. Your overbold, overstrict New England mind, equally at the mercy of Sigmund Freud and Jonathan Edwards, saw Lani's figure through her tightly curved dress, and at the same time you thought that the expression in her eyes was one of goodness, of kindness, of naïveté. The band was now playing:

> And the thrill of the evening is when out Queenie skips,
> And the band plays the Polka while she strips . . .
> Take it off, take it off, soon it's all you can hear.

"What does 'pau' mean?"

She opened her eyes wide, their look charged with life and happiness, and said, almost closing her eyes again, with a gentle touch of mockery in her voice that made you think your own habitual irony naïve, "*Pau* means finish — the end."

At the top of the stairs, with a touch of her hand on yours that was tender — and mocking again, she left you and ran across the dance floor.

Helpless, spasmed with anguish, you found yourself propelled through a receiving line like a buck rabbit through a boa constrictor. At the mouth of the boa, cavernous, smiling jaws agape, stood the acting president of the university — "A wonderful mingling of the races we have here —" he called cheerfully to you, and skillfully shot you along to the next loop in the boa. This was a tall, thin-necked professor of Chinese with a yellow, greasy forehead, who swung you to one side and warned you against the Japanese monopoly of bean curd manufacture in the islands. The Japanese, it seemed, were deliberately withholding bean curd from the loyal Chinese citizens of the Territory. You swung round in the judo clutch of the professor of Japanese, who drew you a few steps further along, and warned you that the Army Island Commander was dangerously pro-Chinese and completely unaware of the menace of the Chinese Communists. Did you know that Sun Yat-sen had received his early training right here in Honolulu and did you know that his wife was a Communist? You did not.

The warm shoulder clutch and handshake of Professor Cobbett, Department of Sociology, twisted you along another loop in the line. Though you asked no questions you were told that yes, 40 per cent of the marriages last year had been interracial. The lovely oriental girls of the islands were attracted first of all to Caucasians or "whites," and second of all to Filipinos or "Flips." Last of all they were attracted to other orientals or "gooks." "Racial distance lends enchantment," said the professor waggishly. "Cobbett's Law."

A last dying spasm of the receptive boa, and a stoopshouldered Professor of English lamented that few of his students would ever go on to the Caucasian-dominated graduate schools of the mainland — never could he become scholastic Napoleon to a Grand Army of Graduate Disciples.

You were at last free to search for Lani, but she had reappeared in her assigned place on a stage at the end of the dance floor, among girls in similar blue dresses who formed the court for the Queen in the rhinestone crown. It was Lani's task to offer white pikake leis to those who were now formally presented to the Queen of Lei Day. This ceremony ended when the president was circled with a lei and kissed by the Queen. He showed signs of wishing to make a speech but the dancing, somewhat hurriedly, started again, in a rocky, jazzy rhythm. Lani disappeared.

Deep within you, checked, but not wholly subdued by excessive education, was an artless urge to enjoy yourself in the moment. Reckless, exhilarated, you cut in on the chocolate Aphrodite and her enlisted man.

Terrified, at first she danced at arm's length. Then, laughing at some rapid footwork of yours, steps in a wideswinging break which you had made up in sheer enjoyment of the music, she swung into a more natural position. Her warm cheek touched yours once, and suddenly, naturally, she let her rich figure unfold delicately within your arms. Quickly her sullen sailor cut back, his spoiled mouth shaped in a pout, and as she danced away she flung you a look at once long and curious, that almost made you blush. With great coolness you moralized to yourself that you were above all such flirtations.

But you found yourself standing next to a pretty Korean girl who stood stiffly still, her spirit and courage frozen. In silence she consented to dance with you, and in silence, when the music stopped, she stood by herself again.

Perplexed, you danced next with a tall Chinese girl who knew no Chinese and who advised you to buy your keepsakes at the Comfrey

Jewelry Store, the one which had sold you the inflammable amber. The store manager was her father. As you danced, you saw Lani swirl by in the tight shoulder clutch of the Sociology Professor. "Cobbett's Law . . ." you overheard, with an intense feeling of irritation that you immediately dismissed as childish.

When you were free again Lani had seemingly disappeared from the crowded dance floor, and you cut in on the stoopshouldered Professor of English. Your new partner was a Caucasian girl, or "haole" as she immediately styled herself. She could also be called a "wahini" or woman. And she was a "kamaaina" or oldtimer. "Pilikia" was the word for trouble, she said, gently frustrating your brief effort to hold her closer. And "malihini" was the word for newcomer.

"And you call rain 'liquid sunshine.' "

But nothing stopped her. If you went west you said you were going to Ewa. If you went east you said you were going to Waikiki. If you went south you said you were going makai, to the ocean. If you went north you said you were going mauka, to the mountains. Poi tasted better if it had been allowed to ferment for a few days. Menehunes were little folk who had warned of the Pearl Harbor attack but had not been believed by the unalert military officials.

You were amused and refreshed by her chatter, you danced together easily and correctly, almost impersonally, and you thought with a steady, ironical happiness, I shall never fall in love, love is impossible. And you asked: "What have the menehunes warned us of lately?" But your question, though not meant seriously, had the effect of making you see her for the first time — an odd piquant face which was somehow, quite suddenly, charming, and gold-washed hair — long, lovely legs.

"My name is Betty Comfrey," she said very simply. You looked at her again, and thought with relief that she was not, after all, so very pretty. She smiled and said quietly, "You like my dress, everyone does. There are lucky clothes, don't you think so?" Once more you were sure she was extraordinarily charming. You recalled the name Comfrey on shipping and trucks, on a private school fence, on the Comfrey Jewelry Store.

You could be born in a Comfrey Hospital, wet your Comfrey Diapers, be educated with Hawaiian princes and princesses in the

Comfrey Preparatory School, buy your wedding clothes in the Comfrey Department Store with a loan from the Comfrey Bank, you could slip a Comfrey diamond on your bride's ring finger and carry her over the threshold of a Comfrey-built house, whose lumber would have been freighted to Hawaii in Comfrey ships — and this lumber would have been sold back and forth among the cousinly members of the Comfrey clan, without the inconvenience and fuss of ever leaving the lumberyard, until you paid $77 a thousand board feet for lumber that had cost in the states $4.

And you could work off your frustrated feelings by hammering a Comfrey nail into that Comfrey lumber and then you could take a Comfrey aspirin when you hit your thumb and wanted to have a good cry in your Comfrey hanky.

And you were dancing with your arms encircling all that lumber, those ships and banks and jewelry stores and department stores and schools, and, cruelly reasonable, you saw her odd, piquant face as almost ugly, and you held her now, a little away from yourself. She smiled, as if interpreting your thoughts, your expression, as polite interest in herself, and then, irrationally, you thought her charming once more.

But when Betty Comfrey went on to inform you that the mainland soldiers had, alas, introduced race prejudice into the Paradise of the Pacific, you once again congratulated yourself on being immune to the sentiment of love.

And though she knew and waved to many dark-skinned lads on the dance floor, you began to see that she danced, by tacit agreement, white only, like the front half of a Southern bus. Only last week, continued Betty Comfrey, at a dance for colored soldiers from an ack-ack battalion, the oriental girls of the university had refused to attend, on learning that Caucasians like Betty Comfrey herself would not be there.

Before the war, said Betty firmly, tossing her goldwashed head, such acts of racial prejudice would have been impossible. And all these attitudes had been imported by mainlanders like yourself. It was the intermission, and Betty Comfrey frankly disinvolved herself from you with an ease of manner which made you homesick for the east.

When the music started again, regardless of her initial glance of humiliation and fear, you danced the stiffly proud Korean girl into a shadowy corner, hugged her tight, twirled her, pranced joyously round her like a lusty stallion during a South American number, and then hugged her again. Her inhibitions, her fear, her pride, all at last disappeared in the crude bongo-bongo of some Cuban dance, and she squealed with delight, hugged you back, pranced round you like a mare in heat, refused to tell you her name, her age, her telephone number, or even what subjects she studied at the university. But of her own accord she snuggled close. In the last furious dance she developed a new step of her own, a kind of South American jitterbug, which involved winding away from you at arm's length, and then suddenly recoiling with a final, sensuous collision. You abandoned yourself joyously to this maneuver until you came to your full collision stop in front of Lani and the English professor. "You dance very close," said Lani. These artless words excited you all the more.

The music stopped and you gazed after Lani's departing figure as if you could never tire of seeing her, and yet your right arm, absentmindedly, as if with an independent will of its own, held the Korean girl by the waist. Gently she disengaged herself to the tune of "Partings are sweet sorrow," and without a backward glance in your direction, as though you had never existed, she walked off with a Japanese boy, arms round each other's waists. Once the Japanese boy turned and stared at you in a viciously hostile way. You had not seen him on the dance floor, and you now understood that the Japanese boy did not know how to dance.

The acting president of the university waved to you and called again, "What a wonderful mingling of the races we have here." Professor Cobbett passed you, singing to the tune of the Christmas song, "Mingle bells, mingle bells, mingle all the way."

At the foot of the stairs the two Chinese girls counted the take, with a subtle and delicate expression of concentration on their ivory faces. You asked them what race Lani was. "Japanese-Korean," they said in their high chiming voices, surprised that you did not know. They turned to their piles of coins and bills and giggled again, and the sound of their chiming giggles clinked and blurred with the chime of silver against copper and nickel.

You stood under the projecting eave of the gym, watching a

sudden fall of liquid Hawaiian rain. The drops hissed without fury on the hot pavement. Soon would come wind and sun, clouds, another brief warm fall of rain, and sun again.

Lani walked at the edge of the tarred, rainswept road. Careless, without a raincoat, wearing a large yellow hibiscus as a rain hat, she let the water fall sparkling on the flower and herself. The rain dampened her brief cotton street dress against her full young figure. To better enjoy the rain she carried her shoes in her hand, and she ran and splashed in the puddles at the side of the road. She seemed to you happy and childish, and unaware, and with a sharp pang you thought, I shall always remember her like that.

Not wanting to avoid her, or follow her, for either might have spoiled your feeling of elation, you boarded the bus she selected — it was after all, also your bus — and with thoughts that were not clear to yourself, you found you were sitting beside her. She carried a book — through the silk of her furoshiki you could see it was on mineralogy. You would have preferred to have her not hold anything, and least of all that, and the feeling of elation was followed by boredom. You could think, in your mood, only of banality, and you said lamely, "You're wearing your shoes now."

You regretted this folly immediately, then you sensed that she was excited and aware that you had, in a way, followed her. She made no attempt to seem at ease. Her eyes opened wide, then closed almost shut in the maddening, now familiar way that she had.

"I can read —" she said, with a slow shake of her head — "and write too." Then, not unkindly, perhaps laughing at you, or at all men, sure of herself again, calmly, "Wrong angle, sailor."

You caught your breath and abandoned yourself to the delightful sensation of discovering what a new girl was like. Words came to your lips awkwardly, for you did not want to begin with her the Dialogue, that familiar preface to seduction that destroyed most of the possibility of talk between men and women in Honolulu. Your hesitation made you, as if in spite of yourself, sincere — at least you sounded sincere — and you said quietly, "I'll move to another seat, if you like."

She was disconcerted, even touched, and showed it by suddenly turning shy. The bus passed the Comfrey school and its studious princes and princesses. "Those are night-blooming cereus," she said, indicating a gray-green hedge. You felt that, could you have kissed her at that moment, she would have yielded. But the moment passed and the bus inconsiderately roared on.

"It flowers in the moonlight," she said. Her slow phrasing, her careful, correct manner of speech, these seemed to you perfection, after the rapid slovenly English of Honolulu, and you smiled with pleasure.

She said, reproving your smile, for this was the fear of the island girls always, "You're laughing at me." You protested. "No, you don't like Hawaii," she said. Her face was impassive again, with a slight trace of sadness, and again you thought of the grave young virgins of Giotto.

Clumsily you blurted, forced to the Dialogue by the fear that the bus would soon come to her stop, "Would you like to go out this evening —" then you changed the formula, really trapped in the Dialogue now, helpless, polite, seductive, repressing a leer, "We could go to dinner, dance perhaps, La Hula Rhumba —" Your voice faded away politely at the odd name, that of a night club where your bill was collected as you entered the door.

She frowned, the bus stopped, and you thought for a moment she was about to get off. But it was a stop for the busdriver who descended, bought and drank a bottle of pop, and climbed back aboard.

"Or the movies, at Waikiki," you suggested, willing to be with her on any terms. The movie at Waikiki had stars of light which drifted over its blue arched ceiling. It was the last word in palmfrond architecture.

"Or the Officers' Club at Pearl?" she said calmly. Or was her voice bitter?

You could take her there, of course, to a small square of dance floor, open to the sky, and with a view of the longnecked gantry cranes. It was called the Snake Pit, with seats at back for commanders and captains, seats on the front and one side for unattached, dateless junior officers who only sat and stared, and a few, a very few seats at the remaining side for the junior officers who brought practically all the girls, all the young ones, that is. And in the background would be the endless noises of men crowding up to the bar, of dropped and broken glasses, of the lines at the slot machines.

And if you refused Lani would surely think it was because she was half Japanese, because her skin was called yellow, though it was a mixture, in shading, of violet and rose.

She took a deep breath, almost a sigh, which revealed very clearly against her damp dress her heavy young figure, even to the tips of her breasts.

And full of the keenest pleasure that she sat next to you, suddenly you thought, I have been too eager, she will refuse.

And with a shock, you understood further that she was angry, but not showing it. "Let me guess," she said quietly, with a slow toss of her head. "You've just come into Pearl Harbor from a long dangerous battle at sea —" You began to laugh in protest, but she went on — "You're just about to go out on another dangerous mission. You've been giving your life for your country. And I should give — whatever I have to give, in return. And now you want to spend the evening talking and —" she looked at you with steady curious eyes — "and wrestling, sailor?"

You were charmed and stung by the slight trace of mocking insolence in her voice. Inflamed with sudden jealousy you wondered how Feverton had made out in the Dialogue. Not very well, you thought. And you were by that much comforted.

The busdriver stopped his diesel-electric engines again and went behind someone's lovely yelloworange hibiscus hedge to micturate. The passengers in the bus, caught up in the highpitched chatter of Honolulu, were unconcerned. With a whine the bus got under way again. At the next stop the busdriver's girl boarded the bus. Now she took tickets for the driver, and made change. Occasionally she caressed the back of the busdriver's neck or touched his hair. She was a tiny pretty girl with deep breasts and a loose redflowered Hawaiian shirt that was unbuttoned below the line of her brassière. She turned once, saw you and nodded. You remembered her driving up to your transport on her scooter. But had you met her since then?

"You're a wolf," said Lani, laughing, angry no longer, for reasons which you could not understand. She had followed closely your exchange of greetings with the Filipina girl, and had concluded that you were trying, even while you sat by Lani, to make time with the busdriver's girl.

The bus was approaching the center of Honolulu now, and it soon filled up with sailors. At the square before the library you and Lani struggled out of the bus. She still wore her pink carnation lei from the dance. Now, her eyes shining and brilliant, she put the lei over your head, waited a moment until the busdriver's girl was looking, then brushed her lips against your cheek with a soft velvet motion and walked away from you. Sailors on the bus applauded this scene. "Give it back to her, sir," they yelled. "Sock it in," they shouted. There was other encouragement, some of it not obscene.

Lani had to wait for the light to change, but she motioned you back. "Goodbye, sailor," she said firmly. "I have to go to the hospital now." She waved toward the end of the street. "The Comfrey Hospital. I'm in my last year of training as a nurse."

But you insisted on walking together with her across the street. At the curb she chose her words carefully. "We native girls think there must be something queer about a haole if he can't find a haole girl to go out with. Do you think we're wrong, sailor?" A gentle and endlessly subtle quality came into her voice. "And please don't call me," she said. But she took your hand and shook it firmly.

Had she mistaken your simplicity and power of feeling toward her for something else, for arrogance? No use to tell her that there were 270 men to one woman — of any race — in the islands. And 1000 men for every white woman. And perhaps there had been a streak of arrogance in your manner, however unwanted.

But that was only the surface of your conversation — beneath that surface was something delicate, mysterious, growing. You watched her walk toward the gates of the hospital. Across your face came the expression of a man intensely dissatisfied with himself. You waited, but she did not look back.

CHAPTER SEVEN

April, 1943

With the helpless enemy transports, over 500 of them,
almost in range of the mighty 18-inch guns of the Yamato,
Admiral Isoroku Yamamoto would never have permitted
the Japanese Fleet to turn back — but Admiral Yama-
moto was dead, ambushed by the U.S. Army Air Force
and by the intelligence offices of Makalapa.

BEGEL, The Battle for Visaya Gulf

✻

YOU PULLED another letter from the pile of enlisted mail. It began: "Honey, I was circumcised today. Ha! I'll be a good deal bigger now, the doc says. Ha! Honey, I'll bet you're glad, you little rascal. Ha!" Carefully you went through the letter with your censor's shears and cut out all the "Ha's."

Gordian, standing at your elbow, asked why.

"Partly to give them something to write to each other about. And partly because Feverton has volunteered us all for the censorship of enlisted men's mail in every office in Makalapa. And besides, this man's been writing about his circumcision every day for three weeks now."

"What about the man who writes five identical letters to five different sweethearts?" asked Arkansaw.

"You didn't put two of them into one envelope," said Gordian fussily.

"No," said Arkansaw. "I put all five into one envelope. But I have a feeling each girl will eventually see her copy."

Gravely you asked if the letter you held (which was marked on its unsealed flap SWAK — "sealed with a kiss") should be kissed after the censor, in accordance with the regulations, sealed it.

"A very fine point," said Arkansaw, "but the answer is no."

"Give me your letters," said Gordian. "Wolfe wants you to see him first, and then go out to the prisoner stockade to stand by when Kawai has his operation."

You had not talked to Wolfe before, except to call to his attention the search pattern documents. In his office you noted the plain desk with nothing on it, not even an ashtray. The desk was set at an angle across one corner of the room. On the wall was tacked a small newspaper picture of Admiral Yamamoto, planner of the Pearl Harbor attack. In Japanese Admiral Yamamoto's name meant "Foot of the Mountain."

Wolfe reminded you to be present during the whole of the operation. "Kawai will be grateful," said Wolfe, thinking you had not understood enough of his purpose to make sure that you carried out his orders intelligently.

And some day, you thought, we may want to use that gratitude.

Wolfe listened to a voice box by the side of his desk. It was the deep voice of The Admiral.

It was known that The Admiral kept on the walls of his office pictures of all the carriers the Japanese had used in the Pearl Harbor attack. As each was sunk, he personally drew a large black X through its picture.

The deep voice went silent. You saw Wolfe glowering at the newspaper picture of Admiral Mountainsfoot. For a moment you did not understand the expression on Wolfe's face. Then you recognized it for what it was — the dark look of revenge.

The Navy, you knew, was determined to get every carrier that had taken part in the Pearl Harbor attack. And it was determined to get Admiral Mountainsfoot, who had planned and ordered the attack. You drew in your breath at the thought that you were taking a part, however tenuous, in some scheme of Wolfe's.

On your way out of Q, you stopped at Feverton's desk, in a mood of some bravado, to leave off your completed translation of one section of the ethics text. It was not the section selected by Feverton.

"Classen," said Feverton, "you've dropped that ball for me. How can you run with a dropped ball?" And he smiled reasonably at Yeoman Prantz.

"Did you really want me to translate the section on the primary school child's view of Abraham Rinkan?" you asked, trying to keep your voice as polite and respectful as possible. "Or the section on Gafirudo and Herbert Fuba?"

Captain Feverton looked glumly at your translation from the ethics text of the life of Sakura Sōgorō, Mayor of Kōzu, in seventeenth century Japan.

For petitioning his ruler, the Shogun, for relief from the crushing taxes of the Shogun's vassal, Mayor "Cherry" and his wife were crucified, but first they were allowed to watch while their four young children were decapitated in front of them. "Though my body may die," said Mayor Cherry to the assembled townsfolk, "my spirit will live and guard your destinies."

The crucifixion had not been in vain, for the evil vassal was, very much later, banished, and the harsh taxes (on fields, ridge poles, abacuses, carrying poles, mats, newborn children, marriages, cows and horses, new houses, persons aged 15 to 60, all articles bought and sold, temples, silk clothes, bean paste, soy sauce, hoes, sickles and vinegar) were reduced to the more usual, bare subsistence level. A Buddhist temple was erected in honor of Mayor Cherry, for Buddha had tossed the head of one of the decapitated children outside the execution enclosure to the crowd of spectators.

After the story, the ethics text provided An Explanation, for those who needed to have their points belabored. Society, the explanation ran, was held together by the spirit of sacrifice — gisei seishin. Fruit from a fruit tree made itself attractive to animals in order to spread its seed and to increase the number of fruit trees in the world. Mothers gave their lives to save those of their children. Men lived by the sacrifices their ancestors had made. The spirit of sacrifice is the cause of the triumph of one nation of men over other nations of men. A candle, giving light to others, consumes itself. Among flowers, the cherry, among warriors — the samurai. Brief was bushidō, the way of the warrior, briefer still was gyokusai, death for the emperor. All men served an emperor, and in his service, duty was heavier than mountains, and so to be much regarded, but death was lighter than a feather, and so to be despised.

Feverton took some time over your translation. "I don't see any ideas here that will win the war," he objected.

You reminded him that Wolfe had wanted you to go to the stockade in time for Kawai's operation.

"Kawai," said Feverton reflectively. The gleam in his eyes you interpreted, correctly enough, as meaning that a new Idea that would Really Win the War was aborning.

At the stockade a Marine doctor performed the operation without any sort of anesthetic. Two chasers with shotguns, and a corpsman stood by as the doctor slowly extracted the bullet from the fleshy part of Kawai's thigh. It was a good operation. The Marine doctor knew what he was doing. Because he had been on Guadalcanal, on CACTUS as you had learned to call it, he omitted the anesthetic, that was all.

At the end of the operation Pilot Officer Riverwell began to talk, in Japanese too rapid and emotional for you to follow at first. It was some time before you realized that Riverwell wanted the extracted bullet to be placed in the bandage over the wound, so that the wound could heal faster. The Marine doctor became upset. "No," he yelled, "he might swallow it." He glared at Kawai.

The doctor packed up his kit and left. As he walked out, he called back bitterly, as though this remark explained everything, "I was on Guadalcanal."

Riverwell went on talking. He could not stop himself. He was in a state of shock from the operation.

"You were very brave." You did not think you would have behaved so well during the operation.

Riverwell, realizing the limits of your Japanese, said slowly and distinctly, "When a samurai's stomach is empty, it is a disgrace to feel hungry."

In his shock the day of his capture lived again for him. He had not told this story before, perhaps not even to himself. He had flown his torpedo plane down the slot to Guadal to attack American transports. He had come from Rabaul, and was expected to return to Buka, one of a large, hastily assembled *kessenbutai,* that familiar "decisive battle force."

But the landings at Guadal had taken the Japanese High Command by surprise. At that time, said Riverwell bitterly, the Army was busily shipping Japanese newspaper editors to the Philippines when they should have been sending supplies to the Solomons.

There was confusion at every level of the commands. By a mistake the planes of the decisive battle force were armed with bombs, rather than with the superb Japanese torpedo, such as he had used against the *Arizona* at Pearl. There was no time to change armament. As could have been predicted, his bombs missed their target. And his plane was badly damaged by machine gun and ack-ack fire; he himself was wounded.

Japanese aviation training was far more thorough than American, and even for this event he had been trained. Again and again he had been taught to dive at a simple ground target, the outline of a ship.

You did not at first understand. Astonished, as one might to a child, Riverwell explained. In case of serious injury to himself or to his plane he had been taught to crashdive the enemy. He was not to save himself. Almost every day of his training he had practiced this maneuver. That was the way of rectitude . . . *kōdōha,* the Imperial Way. That way, sure death meant a sure hit, *hisshi hitchū.* A man should strike when it was right to strike, and a man should die when it was right to die.

Riverwell stared at his hands, as if in disbelief, as if they belonged to some treacherous other self, which against his will had betrayed him. For those fine, those clever, those sensitive and discriminating hands had been unable to crash the target as his mind had directed. No, those hands, conscious, or unconscious, or half conscious of their ties, their obligations to their owner, had landed himself and his damaged plane in the water, in a last, unbelievable demonstration of their technical mastery.

"Dishonor," said Riverwell unbelievingly, still regarding those amazing hands. "Dishonor. A scar on a tree. Time makes it grow bigger."

He turned to you, and the two watching Marine chasers leaned vigilantly forward. You waved them back. As he might have asked for a cigarette, softly, without expression, Riverwell pleaded: "Give me something. Something to kill myself."

And you sensed that those incredible hands must have already refused to hang their owner, or to cut his throat with the razor blade he was given every morning. Perhaps now, Riverwell was thinking, these wonderfully trained hands would not refuse to convey a last tiny placebo to his lips.

From the Japanese ethics text you remembered an odd, completely Japanese proverb. To Riverwell you said: "To endure the unendurable, is really to endure." And you motioned to the Marine chasers to help Riverwell back to his cell.

Limping, but refusing assistance, Riverwell talked on, of *giri* — indebtedness or obligation. Riverwell did not want you to think of him as a man who was ignorant of *giri* — *giri shirazu*. He smiled, the wry hurt smile, the famous smile of Japan, that could substitute for tears, for deep emotions, for anything but laughter.

He was smiling at the new relation that had sprung up between Ensign Montgomery Classen and Pilot Officer Riverwell. You and he were caught up in a web of *giri*. And you were caught up in a similar, finer web of *on*. *On* also meant duty or obligation in a different sense, almost as a debt of gratitude. Kawai was not a man ignorant of *on* — *on shirazu*.

Riverwell tried to explain. If you fed a dog three days, he would remember you three years. That was *on* — obligation. On the other hand, duty, like the loincloth or cotton fundoshi which all male Japanese wore, could never be forgotten. That was *giri* — duty.

Duty then was the magic web thrown over a victim by the spider enchanter in a Kabuki play. A Japanese might not help someone who had fallen ill on a busy street because helper and helped would lay such burdens of *giri* on each other. Now you had helped Riverwell, and, as much as the person helped, you were caught in the web of duty. So the United States and Japan were entangling each other, regardless of the outcome of the war, though of course, Riverwell added, Japan would win. And now Riverwell almost forgot that you were present, his voice grew rich with the Japanese patriotic dream, as old as Japan itself or older — for it went back in time to the Emperor Jimmu and his phrase, *hakkō ichiū* — the inclusion of the eight corners of the world under one roof.

All the world was to be under the one, the divine family roof, that of the Emperor of Japan, that supreme authority to whom we are obedient because He is unselfish and because His Concern is the welfare and the peace of mankind. No president, no prime minister, could approach His Objective Love for all the people of the world.

Standing erect now in his cell, in spite of his wounded leg, Riverwell asserted that the Japanese, through their attack at Pearl Harbor, through the other battles of the Pacific war, were bringing real peace to the world.

And that was why a Japanese soldier had to give his life to his Emperor, to his country — and that was why he based his life on obedience to Emperor and country. And the Emperor's power lasted after death, for the Japanese took their places in the country of death according to the code of the warrior, *bushidō*. Heaven would show, in life and in death, the righteousness of the Japanese struggle.

Riverwell sank down on his cot, exhausted; the chasers prepared to lock the cell. You pressed his hand, slipping into his fingers the shapeless clump of lead that had been in his thigh.

Outside the cell you turned. Riverwell looked up at you with an expression of trust, of gratitude. Then he wedged the bullet between the layers of bandage, over the wound.

Only one thing was lacking now, a suitable occasion on which to betray that trust. You were your old ironical self again, ready to savor the exquisite inconsistency of the world and its wars. The barred entrance door clanged shut behind you. A file of American prisoners, followed by two Marine chasers with shotguns, stepped across the compound before you, in the blinding Hawaiian sunlight.

"Come on, you bastards," said one of the chasers, "sing." Raggedly they began:

> Lift your head up to the sky,
> Honey, Honey,
> Lift your head up to the sky,
> Baby, Baby —
> Lift your head and hold it high,
> Baker Company's passing by,
> Honey, Oh Baby mine.

Their shoulders snapped back, and the song forced them to catch the beat and march smartly. It was childish, and it worked.

That night in your bunkroom you handed back to Gordian his Ph.D. thesis on Rarawa in the Central Solomons. Heaped at the bottom of each page were little piles of footnotes, nutshells from which the kernel had been extracted. The text was heavy with ponderous observations about blood relationship groups, siblings, cross-cultural groupings, ritual care of seed yams, sacred fetishes, survival values, mating patterns (no one ever made love in anthropological Rarawa — they had mating patterns instead), and there was a chapter on love magic in which the sorcerer had to grasp and fondle and caress an object, preferably genital in origin or shape, associated with the beloved, and there was a chapter on hate magic, in which the sorcerer seized a ritual dagger of bone, leaped and twisted and turned, grimaced with hatred, thrust and pierced his imaginary victim — then, last but essential step in his dance, with a vicious jerk pulled out the dagger from its invisible magic wound.

Through the jargon and the intellection of the anthropologists, the dull verbal grips by which one academic mind acknowledged its brother, you had caught, in Gordian's Ph.D. thesis, glimpses of a cool Gauguin painting — violet shadows cast on rich chocolate breasts, the Southern Cross swinging in its palm tree fronds, dusky sensuous couplings in the dark. It was a side of Gordian you had not suspected. As you did, often enough, with the rest, you had fitted him into his type — young California intellectual and lecturer, and you ranged him beside your native Hawaiian girl, your Columbia intellectual, your small-town gas pump operator. And your own type, the Ironical Man Himself.

"You liked it there," you said as you handed back the thesis. And you had wondered, within every man, even within your own favored type, the Ironical Man, was there a dusky knowledge, an indestructible — because passionate — truth? An anger? — or a love?

"I'd like to go back," said Gordian simply.

And you had an odd image of the young bachelor anthropologist crawling studiously in the dark toward the frondwoven, offlimits girls' hut for a night of observation. But then, you guessed, a warm brown arm, and even warmer bosom had surely pressed, however shyly (at least in Rarawan terms), against the young bachelor. Trembling, then passionate mouths had embraced. Paolo to his dark Francesca, Gordian had leafed the book of anthropology no more that night.

How else explain that his thesis advisers had praised his unusual understanding of the "feminine side," as they put it in their professional English, of Rarawan culture.

"But you see," Gordian had said, and his thin bony fingers pushed toward you a reconnaissance photo of Rarawa. Here was the Gauguin painting daubed with coconut log gun emplacements, with concrete tetrahedron snouts snuffing the surface of the water, with cement command posts, with wooden privies constructed over the water.

"Take the number of privies," said Gordian wryly, but with a certain pride, for he had invented the figure now known as 'Gordian's constant,' "multiply in my formula, and you have the number of Japanese occupying Rarawa."

"What about dysentery?"

"The formula allows for that too."

Engrossed in your conversation, you became aware that you were being watched. You looked up, at Arkansaw's upper bunk.

In that moment before the seer realizes he is seen, there is a moment of frankness. Now you saw flickering over Arkansaw's face a look of ruin, of absolute, complete degradation.

Before you could realize, could assimilate the look, it smoothed quickly away, became instead the familiar smile, the pleasant mocking laugh that you had so neatly labeled "Columbia intellectual." Arkansaw leaned over his bunk, addressing both you and Gordian.

"If you say Q is the Navy, you affirm. If you say Q is not the Navy, you deny. Beyond affirming and beyond denying, what do you say?"

In keeping with the joke, Gordian called out, "Kwats." But you were silent.

"Correct," said Arkansaw. Without transition he fell asleep. The empty bottle of bourbon rolled on the floor. Disapprovingly Gordian put it away.

Together you turned out the lights and opened the blackout curtains. The flowerladen tropic air came into the room like a tangible presence, carrying with it faint echoes of welded steel and of diesel boat exhaust from the Navy yard.

Overhead began a silent ack-ack practice. A plane zigged through the searchlight fingers, eluded the graywhite talons, was caught, zagged on to the next searchlight battery, eluded, was caught, and swerved careening on. Your room faced Japan, and you thought now of great ships and their trapped crewmen moldering in the Coral Sea, off Savo Island and in Ironbottom Sound, off Midway: the carriers *Wasp* and *Hornet* and *Yorktown* and *Red Castle* and *Increased Joy* and *Flying Dragon* and *Green Dragon;* the cruisers

Quincey, Vincennes, Canberra, Astoria, Atlanta, Juneau; the battle-ship *Hiei;* the destroyers *Floodtide, Cool Breeze, Morning Cloud, White Snow, Passing Shower, Peep of Day, Phosphorescent Foam, Valley Wind, Mist of Flowers, Sword's Swish.*

Marines on a night march were singing again:

> Lift your head up to the sky,
> Honey, Honey,
> Lift your head up to the sky,
> Baby, Baby —
> Lift your head and hold it high,
> Easy Company's passing by,
> Honey, Oh Baby mine.

And you felt, as you were supposed to feel, the leap of the heart, the call to be out there, in the war, in the fighting.

But you sensed the loneliness of Gordian standing next to you. How much worse than your own patriotic desire to join in the war, a desire in which was mixed a certain childish element.

Gestures of affection had not, for a long time, come easily to you. All love was only, in the end, as you knew, a loss. But you rested your hand lightly on Gordian's thin shoulder. You wanted to say something that would be of use to Gordian, but no words came. And then it turned out that he was thinking of his wife surely, but of another subject at the same time.

"The whole fleet," said Gordian slowly, as much to himself as to you. "Wolfe said today that before the end, the whole Japanese fleet would come out." He rubbed his nose between his thumb and forefinger. "You know, Wolfe warned that the Japanese fleet was up to something tricky the week before Pearl Harbor."

You put on your ironical coat of many colors. "We'll still be here, reading about the battle in *Time* Magazine." It was especially galling to be in the intelligence headquarters and never to know anything about the war but your own tiny corner of it. And what you read in the overseas edition of *Time.*

Gordian put airmail stamps on two letters to his wife. In the morning he would, you knew, write a third letter before breakfast.

"If I were only home," he said, "she needs me at home."

"Can't you get leave? You've been here the longest."

"At the end of two years."

The marching Marines sang on:

> Lift your head up to the sky,
> Honey, Honey . . .
> Honey, Oh Baby mine.

You had a quick sharp image of Gordian's wife with a red hibiscus flower in her hair.

"You belong with them," said Gordian, "with the Marines."

"You won't believe this, but I was in a pacifist movement once."

"You enjoy being ironical," said Gordian kindly. "I suppose there wasn't a girl in the pacifist cause, a really pretty girl."

"There was a girl." You laughed. "Good fellows being ironical together. That's what we have instead of God."

That night you had no dreams. Or, trained Freudian that you were, none that your superego would let your id bring to the surface. But you woke up once, convinced that Arkansaw had been watching you. And fell fitfully asleep again.

The next morning Arkansaw asked you, pleasantly enough, "Who's Leilani?" Then you knew what you had dreamed about.

CHAPTER EIGHT

April, 1943

> *There were two main routes by which the Japanese*
> *Fleet could attack our half-unloaded merchant ships:*
> *the first, through the straits to the north of Visaya Island,*
> *and the second, to the south, and through these straits*
> *the Japanese planned to extend their pincers . . .*
>
> BEGEL, The Battle for Visaya Gulf

＊

FOR SEVERAL days at a time Captain Feverton disappeared from
Q. Napoleon learned from his yeomen admirers that Feverton
was visiting the newly built prisoner stockades, far past the West
Loch in the direction of Ewa. In Feverton's absence the ensigns
of Q tried initialing their own letters and mailing them, a few at
first, then all of them. Captain Feverton did not notice, and they
realized he was busy with More Important Things.

"Here you are, Classen," he said. "It's your ball now, and I expect
you to run with it." In a loud, peppy voice: "Really run!"

Captain Feverton had concluded that Pilot Officer Kawai was
still withholding valuable information. To extract this information
Captain Feverton had invented a new technique, a new Idea that
could Win the War. He had threatened to broadcast to Japan, to
Kawai's relatives, the fact that he was a prisoner. Fear of this
disgrace was now, so Captain Feverton thought, making Kawai talk,
really talk, for the first time.

"Here," said Captain Feverton. He handed you a crude drawing
of a Japanese destroyer. Its guns were described, in the Captain's
handwriting, as "8-inch guns."

"Think of that," said the Captain, with his fixed, pasted-on smile. "Our destroyers have only 5-inch guns. No other country has 8-inch guns on a destroyer. That's probably the most amazing destroyer in the world. That destroyer could win or lose the war."

You stared at the sketch. It was, as the Captain said, a destroyer that could win or lose the war. But everything depended on which side tried to use the destroyer with 8-inch guns. Whichever side used the destroyer would lose, for the 8-inch guns and their turrets would be so heavy as to make the destroyer capsize, possibly at the moment of first launching.

Captain Feverton now handed over some sheets of copy paper in closely written Japanese. "When he began talking," said the Captain, "I gave him pencil and paper. Let him get it off his chest. Here it is, right off his chest."

The Captain looked stern. "Whose ball is it?"

"It's my ball."

"Right, now run with it. REALLY run!"

You took the sheets of copy paper back to your desk, thinking it might be just as well to bounce your ball a bit before you ran with it. You looked more closely at the pages of closely penciled Japanese. Then you began to smile, and you looked up, in your *Kenkyusha*, some very unusual words. You made a few tentative anatomical drawings and threw them in the confidential trash. Some of the positions were just barely possible, for a very athletic couple.

It was really too bad that Riverwell had not illustrated his text. The manuscript was about sexual life in some sort of Buddhist — or was it Taoist? — heaven. A great many extraordinary sexual possibilities were described in all their supernatural detail.

You put all the papers in a manila folder, called for transportation to the stockade, and got your cap.

"Commander Wolfe wants to see ya," said Yeoman Prantz. "Stop in his office on ya way out, will ya?" Prantz smiled hopefully. Since Wolfe never praised, such a summons meant usually a chewing out of a very exemplary kind.

Commander Wolfe sat behind his cattycornered desk. As always, there was nothing on the desk. Beside the desk, on its separate stand, stood the squawk box which was connected with The Admiral's office. On one wall was the familiar, yellowing picture of

Admiral Yamamoto. For the first time you noticed the clocks. They were set high above the doorway which connected the offices of Wolfe and General Waddleman. These clocks recorded the time in Washington, Tokyo, San Francisco, Delhi, London, and Pearl Harbor.

"You're going out to see Kawai," said Wolfe. He had thick dark eyebrows and light paleblue eyes. His shoulders were erect. He was said to have two other offices just like this one, in The Admiral's building, and at the Sub Base. You got the impression of a mind endlessly coiling about its prey, pressuring here, cracking there, finally crushing.

"Find out if Admiral Yamamoto is a punctual man," said Wolfe. "Don't let Kawai know what you're after. Take two or three hours. I want the answer this afternoon."

Near the Wahainu range you turned off the tarred highway onto a crushed coral road which ended at the prisoner stockade. From four wooden towers, searchlight lenses remorselessly contemplated a great square of barbed wire.

In one of the small cells used for interrogation you offered River-well a cigarette. He thanked you and put it in his shirt pocket to smoke later.

On the plain wood table you threw the sketch of the destroyer and the pages of pornography. Riverwell drew in his breath with a hiss, and took the cigarette out of his pocket again. You gave him a light with your Zippo lighter, and Riverwell admired your lighter.

You tried to look stern as you pointed to the 8-inch guns, but you had to laugh.

"Saa," said Riverwell. "I didn't know he was a friend of yours. He insisted, as you honorably know, that I tell him something." Riverwell was using language that was excessively polite, especially if you remembered that he was a rank above his interrogator, and you resolved, in the future, to award yourself, in the style of Napoleon, a rank above that of the prisoner you were talking to.

He stared at the distant green hills of the Wahainu range. Over these hills his flight of torpedo planes had flown on December 7.

Captain Feverton had been very clever, threatening to shame his relatives by news of his capture. But Kawai, helpless and a prisoner, had made a fool of the Captain.

In Japanese you never said that someone was mistaken, you always said it was different. Now Riverwell fingered the sketch of the destroyer and said, "It must have been different. Allow me to make a respectful apology." Again he was using excessively, and by Japanese standards, insultingly polite language.

"You used the Wahainu range as a check point?"

"We never meant to attack you here. For twenty years we planned an ambush attack, a yūgeki."

You suddenly recalled the fascination this word had had for Captain Fantasy.

Riverwell put out his cigarette. "But the ambush attack was to have been in the Marshall Islands. We were going to wait for you there."

"Did Admiral Yamamoto change that plan?"

"It was more a change in feeling. He felt the plans should change to kōgeki bōgyo, to Offensive Defense. And the ambush attack was shifted to take place in American waters."

"You were with Admiral Ichiba, then, on Admiral Yamamoto's staff?"

"I was not attached to Admiral Yamamoto's staff. I continued my flight training. But once in a while I made a respectful visit to Admiral Ichiba in his Tokyo house."

In Japan, you knew, a close relation often developed between two men, one older, the other younger. It was called *oyako* — parent-child relationship. Gordian, in his sociologese, had once referred to it as "surrogate parent-child relationship." Riverwell and Admiral Ichiba of the Japanese Planning Staff had had such a relationship. Ichiba meant, in Japanese, "marketplace."

After the successful Pearl Harbor attack, Riverwell had been entertained several times by Admiral Marketplace with others on the planning staff who wished to meet one of the "Eagles of the Air" who had carried out their brilliant plans. Admiral Marketplace and the others had spoken freely before the young aviator, who would one day, as Marketplace's protégé, undoubtedly join the planning staff. Riverwell was quick and curious, and with the shrewdness of his farmer-samurai ancestry had pieced together many details.

In the summer of 1940 Admiral Isoroku Yamamoto first thought of attacking Pearl Harbor by an ambush attack, by a *yūgeki* air raid.

Riverwell spoke slowly, making allowances for your stiff, still awkward, Japanese. Outside the prisoner stockade you could see a formation of Marines shaping up. They began counting off. They stood at attention, presenting their rifles to their lieutenant for inspection. The bolts snapped open and were rammed shut in a slow steady motion.

In January 1941, Admiral Yamamoto ordered the Chief of Staff of the 11th Air Fleet to make the plans for an attack to be delivered in eleven months. By April, eight months before the attack, with Yamamoto driving the planning staff hard, the plans were completed. In May, seven months before the ambush attack, a staff, consisting of a handful of Admirals (Marketplace among them) and one or two yeomen, had reviewed the plans. In July, six months before the attack, first training started. Everywhere in Japan, suddenly, appeared warnings against spies.

Once the thick volume of plans on the Pearl Harbor Attack, *Shinjuwan Kōgeki Keikaku,* had been left unguarded for a few hours in a public room in the Navy Department. Any foreigner who had walked in could have seen it.

And once, for a few days, rumors spread through Tokyo of a coming attack on Pearl Harbor. Ambassador Grew passed on these rumors to Washington. Fortunately he was not believed.

The torpedo pilots were ordered to train for torpedo attack against anchored ships in a shallow harbor. Some, like Riverwell, guessed the name of the harbor, but kept quiet.

The choice of attack route had not been easy. The Japanese fleet had to go far enough north to avoid flying boat search patrols from Pearl Harbor, and far enough south to avoid the patrols from Dutch Harbor and the Aleutians.

"We heard you had spies at Pearl Harbor and in the Aleutians."

Riverwell laughed. "We studied our submarine reports. And we took radio direction-finder fixes on your patrol planes. You are always careless with your radio." It was the professional speaking severely to the amateur. They had soon found the gap, a little above the 40⁰ line to a point two hundred miles due north of Honolulu.

"But Admiral Yamamoto was a very thorough man. That summer he sent a freighter along the attack route. It was seen by no one. That was about four months before the attack.

"In the attack itself we were following the principles of your own theorist, Admiral Mahan — especially his idea of — " here Riverwell used the English words in Japanese pronunciation, "konsentureshyun obu fuorsu."

The training had been brutal. At every stage, in the Air Academy, men who could not take the beatings with baseball bats, and even crueler punishments, had hanged themselves, and one man had bitten off his tongue and successfully bled to death. It was almost like being a cadet at Etajima all over again.

You got up to stretch, but Riverwell sat patiently still. The squad of Marines was now in the hands of its drill sergeant. He held a riding crop. Now he struck one Marine across the face with the riding crop. Japanese prisoners nearby who were painting the white edging stones of the pathways went stolidly on with their work. Sundazzle turned blinding yellow on the hot coral stone.

"But we knew if we were to win the war we had to be trained. Japan is a poor country."

Over four hundred carrier planes had trained at eight different fields in Japan. There were new armor-piercing bombs. There was a new, improved aerial torpedo.

"The main attack was to be the torpedo plane attack."

You knew from your *Boy's Manual of the Japanese Naval Air Force* that the usual method for torpedo attack was to release the torpedo at about 1000 or 1500 meters distance from the target. When dropped, the torpedo sank in the water to a depth of as much as 60 meters, then rose to its cruising depth of 4 meters or so. But Pearl Harbor was only 12 meters deep. The first plunge of the torpedo there would mean the loss of the torpedo as it nosedived into the bottom and exploded before it could rise to its cruising depth.

"Why did you stress torpedo attack?"

"We learned, through our diplomatic offices in Honolulu, that you had no anti-torpedo nets around your anchored battleships and carriers. You obviously thought such attacks were impossible. So Admiral Yamamoto ordered us to learn how to make such attacks."

Riverwell was small of stature, somewhat thickset around the waist, like a miniature sumo wrestler. His head was bald, and closecropped high up the sides. His face was severe, with two deep disciplined wrinkles at the sides of the mouth. The mongolian eyefold was not noticeable. Except for his coloring he could have passed for a South European. Perhaps somewhere far back, in the sixteenth century, or in the seventeenth, there had been inter-marriage with the Portuguese or the Dutch or the English in Japan at that time. In ten generations, Gordian had argued, you were potentially related to everyone on earth.

Perhaps Riverwell's torpedo had killed 200 or 300 of his distant relatives the moment it hit the *Arizona.*

You could imagine him at the controls of his plane. First he would say, as you knew from your *Boy's Manual, shireikan,* the command of readiness in general. Then he would say *totsugeki yōi,* the command to get ready for attack. Then *totsugeki seyo,* begin the attack. The plane would approach its target and there would be the command, *hassha yōi,* ready to fire! And then the last command, *utte, utte!* — Fire!

Riverwell and his fellow torpedo pilots had practiced in Kago-shima Bay because it contained a natural formation somewhat re-sembling Pearl Harbor. Again and again, day after day, they came in for their torpedo runs, making the last turn near the Kagoshima Department Store. Often the store had red and white balloons in the air, advertising special sales of soap, of toys, of charcoal-burning hibachis, of canned tangerines. The pilots sped by the bright bal-loons at a speed of 160 knots, trying to learn how to release their torpedoes only 500 meters away from the target, at heights so low their altimeters read zero. Gradually they learned.

But in a shallow harbor, even though launched at zero altitude, the torpedoes still hit bottom before they could return to running depth.

In October, two months before the attack date, Admiral Yama-moto came to Kagoshima to inspect their progress.

You stood up again, to hide your eagerness. Here was your chance to find out what Commander Wolfe wanted to know.

Before the stockade the Marines, their green shirts darkened with sweat, drilled rapidly in close order. You could not distinguish any longer which Marine had been cut by the sergeant's riding crop. They all looked alike to you.

"We don't like inspections. Sometimes the men have to stand for hours waiting for some General or Admiral."

"Yamamoto was not like that. He did not like people to be tardy."

You drew a deep breath. This was the information you wanted. You would wait long enough to check it, and then return to Q.

Riverwell continued. Admiral Yamamoto had been disappointed with his inspection. Training was scheduled to end soon, by November 15, about four weeks before the attack. All through October and into the first week of November there were experiments with special gear — new stabilizer fins, and different gyro settings.

Finally, the second week in November, three planes were chosen to make torpedo runs, their fliers picked as poor, average, and excellent in ability. Riverwell was the flier of excellent ability.

Two of the three modified torpedoes exploded on target. That meant, by Japanese reasoning, that in a flight of 40 planes there might be 27 hits on 8 ships. "Good enough," said Admiral Marketplace. Abruptly their training was canceled.

And to the highest officers of the fleet Admiral Yamamoto issued Fleet War Orders #1, dated November 5, which ordered "preparations for readiness for war."

All the pilot officers attended a last conference aboard the carrier *Akagi — Red Castle*. In the wardroom hung the Z flag of Admiral Togo.

You looked inquiringly at Kawai. Togo had flown the Z flag when he opened fire on the Russian warship *Osliabia* on 27 May 1904. Togo's annihilation of the Russian Fleet — twice he succeeded in the Naval Officer's Dream Maneuver of crossing the T — signaled the rise of Japan to the ranks of the world powers. The *Red Castle* would once more fly the Z flag during the Pearl Harbor attack, as Japan in this new battle rose to the rank of First World Power.

Once, with Admiral Marketplace, Riverwell had visited Togo's flagship, the *Mikasa*, which now floated permanently in concrete near the great Japanese naval base of Yokosuka. He had seen the small sea cabin of Admiral Togo, and he had sat, with Admiral Marketplace, in the sacred wardroom of the flagship.

Early in October Kawai had seen the *Red Castle* take aboard a large flat parcel from Naval Headquarters in Tokyo. It was four square yards in size. Ever since its arrival, fleet scuttlebutt said that the Japanese Chief of Operations spent some time each day alone, scrutinizing this mysterious object. Now it was revealed to the pilot officers. It was a large relief map of Pearl Harbor.

Studying it, they knew for sure, at last, the object of their training. There was a violent wind that evening, and the pilot officers stayed aboard the *Red Castle*. It did not matter, for they would not touch shore again until they returned from the attack.

Usually the Japanese Navy was very strict with its flyers. They could not drink the day before they flew. In some units they were not permitted to have sexual intercourse the day before they flew. If you broke any of the rules you went back in rank, and often you went to the stockade. You were lucky to get out of a Japanese stockade alive.

But on that evening, November 17, they had sake to drink. Everyone danced and sang. The commander of Riverwell's air group, of *kōkūtai* #23, did them the great honor of performing a dance. Finally he sang a dialect song from his native province. That was a remarkable party. But Riverwell, not used to drinking, had a hangover the next day.

"What did it mean when your torpedo plane unit was called a 'decisive' force?"

Riverwell did not understand the question. Sometimes you called a force or a unit "decisive" when it had a "special" mission. Sometimes you did not.

By November 23, all surface ships (the submarines sailed direct to Pearl Harbor on November 18) had sailed north to the desolate island of Etorofu in the Kuriles, north of Japan proper. None of the islanders were allowed off the island, even to fish, and the enlisted sailors were then told of the coming attack. They too sang and danced as their officers had done before them. But Riverwell observed that the highranking staff officers were not enthusiastic; perhaps, he thought, because of fatigue.

Ashore, radio stations continued to send radio traffic, pretending to be fleet vessels at anchor in southern Japan. Sailors were released on leave in Tokyo, in large numbers, to indicate that there were no special ship movements.

On November 26, thirteen days before X day, the striking force set sail, thirtyone ships, six of them carriers, with three subs far in the van. On the way a tiny patrol boat signaled: "We pray for your victory." The great carrier *Red Castle* replied politely, "Thank you — *arigatō*."

Every day Riverwell spent thirty minutes in his plane on the hangar deck of the carrier *Lucky Crane*. He moved the controls and practiced flying.

"The *Lucky Crane* was a good ship. She escaped at Midway."

"We were overwhelmed with material power," said Riverwell bitterly.

"At Midway you had the larger forces."

There was a smart rap on the door. A Marine orderly, unarmed as the stockade rules required, came to attention. "Commander Wolfe wants to know if you will be back at Pearl in half an hour."

"Yes."

Riverwell continued: "You are weak in spiritual power."

"Perhaps we need a commander like Admiral Yamamoto."

"He did not want war."

"He said he wanted to dictate peace in the White House."

"No," said Riverwell patiently, "he said we could not win the war unless we were strong enough to dictate peace in the White House."

"He must have been very efficient, to handle all that planning and training."

"He was very strict. Admiral Marketplace told me that you had to be right to the minute when you worked for him."

Riverwell handed you an article torn from one of the captured magazines which the prisoners were allowed to read. "Here," he said. "This article is about our spiritual power. It will enable us to win the war."

Then he said fatalistically, "I failed in spiritual power. Someday I shall kill myself." His face worked spasmodically. He looked down at those astonishing hands which, in spite of himself, had landed his plane safely on the waters.

You handed to Riverwell your cigarette lighter, as a gift. You might try to comfort an American soldier who said such a thing. But you had put Riverwell in a situation of indebtedness, of *on*, which temporarily overrode his duty, as he saw it, to kill himself, and forced him to thank you for the trifling gift. Obedient to the morality of the country which no longer regarded him as alive, he bowed to you.

The orderly knocked at the door again. Your car and driver were waiting.

Riverwell got to his feet and, without servility, bowed and saluted at the same time. You returned the salute. You picked up the sketch of the destroyer, and the pages of pornography.

"Those do not matter," said Riverwell. He scrutinized your face and saw some expression there of which you were unaware. Then he said, gravely, "I think you learned something of great value from me today."

Riverwell was taken back to his quarters by an unarmed Marine chaser. The orderly led you through the barbed wire gates. "If he had us as prisoners, instead of the other way round, I wouldn't give a fog for my testicles," said the orderly. The orderly had been on Guadalcanal. You glanced back at the stockade. The late afternoon sun glinted from the searchlight lenses and made your eyes ache.

The ugly command car jounced back to Pearl Harbor. The road wound between red fields studded with gray pineapples and green sugar cane. You picked up the article Riverwell had offered you. It was an essay comparing Japanese to American spiritual power. Its main point was the difference between Japanese and American underwear. American underwear caught you in the crotch. American underwear was harsh and binding and gave you no support. The Japanese loincloth or *fundoshi*, on the other hand, followed naturally the shape of your crotch, without harmful binding, or — alarming possibility to a Japanese — unnecessary and unwise looseness. The Japanese loincloth was, in a sense, the symbol of the Japanese state. The Japanese loincloth showed the greater spiritual power of the Japanese nation. This power was so strong as to find expression even in an apparently insignificant article such as the Japanese jockstrap.

At the entrance to Q you saw the busdriver's girl, the pert little Filipina messenger who had met your transport when it docked at Pearl. She noticed your stare and deliberately, saucily, stretched, revealing her high taut breasts under her thin Waikiki shirt. Mocking, but not unfriendly, she said to you, "You have pretty eyes." Laughing at your confusion before the highly interested gate sentry, she started her scooter. "Don't you want to know my name?" she said provocatively. The scooter roared off. "Maria," she called back. "Maria."

You reported to Commander Wolfe.

"All right," said Wolfe, impatient. "Is he punctual? Is he on time for inspections?"

"I think so, sir."

"Don't you know? I don't want your answer unless you know."

You thought over your conversation with Kawai.

"Admiral Yamamoto is punctual," you said, with more assurance than you felt. And yet you knew, by instinct, that you were right.

Wolfe looked at you, as if for the first time he really knew who you were. With a nod of his head, he dismissed you. "Close the door," he called.

Inside Wolfe's office you heard the squawk box to The Admiral come to life. "Yes," said Wolfe, ". . . punctual . . . April 18 . . . twenty minutes over the target . . ."

And as you walked away you heard one last phrase, ". . . risk . . . justified risk . . ."

The Ironical Man sat down at his desk and reviewed his brief history of Force Rivermouth, now in the stencil version. From Nanking it had gone to Burma . . .

CHAPTER NINE

April, 1943

Hear the noise of the engine — gō gō gō gō!
Lo, the Peregrine Falcon flies, his home the clouds!
The Rising Sun gleams on his wings —
We are fighter planes,
On our breast the mark of the red eagle!
Song of the 64th Imperial Air Regiment Quoted in
BEGEL, The Battle for Visaya Gulf

❁

YOU REPORTED to Captain Feverton that somehow Kawai had
made a mistake about the destroyer with the 8-inch guns. Perhaps
Kawai had been thinking of a cruiser.

"Destroyer is *kuchikukan*," said Captain Feverton firmly. "Cruiser
in *junyōkan*."

"Yes," you acknowledged. You added cheerfully, a shade too
respectfully, "Yes, sir." And you suggested helpfully, "Perhaps
Kawai confused inches and millimeters."

"Are you suggesting that his destroyer had 8-millimeter guns?"

"No," and you hurriedly added, "No, sir."

"Are you being —" he stumbled a little over the word, "ironical
again?"

You handed to Feverton the pages of the pornographic Paradise.
You had translated a few lines and given a summary of the rest.
Captain Feverton looked at the translation suspiciously. His face
turned red. He was smiling with that odd masklike smile that
seemed to cover his real face.

"I gave you the ball," said Captain Feverton, "and I told you to
run with it? Right?"

With an effort you kept yourself from answering, "Right!" Instead you said, with a little tug of anger, "The ship doesn't have 8-inch guns, and the document is just a piece of pornography."

"Never mind," said Captain Feverton, with the maddening air of One Who is Continually Frustrated by Stupid Subordinates.

Your anger began to grow, outside of, almost in spite of yourself. To your surprise, you found yourself saying heatedly, "It's crap, just crap."

"He's spoiled now," said Captain Feverton. "The ball has been permanently dropped."

"He's not spoiled. He's beginning to talk for the first time about the attack on Pearl Harbor. His file shows he's never given us the straight word on that before."

"Classen, I don't think you've got the feel for constructive criticism yet." With satisfaction he dusted off an oldie: "I can always tell a Yale man, but I can't tell him much. Ha ha." Prantz eagerly joined his laughter to that of Feverton. It was the third time that Feverton had advised you of his ability to tell Yale men.

"For your sake I'm going to overlook this dropped ball —" Feverton paused impressively — "we'll just let the situation mature. Now carry on."

Feverton was shuffling papers from one basket to another basket in a crisp, executive manner. There was just one thing wrong — he had forgotten the labels on the baskets, and was transferring papers from *Out* to *Pending* and from *Pending* to *In*.

You shrugged your shoulders and started to walk off.

"Just a minute, Classen," called Feverton. "When you leave my desk, I want a salute."

"Aye, aye, sir. But have I permission to get my cap first and put it on? In the Navy we are not allowed to salute indoors unless we are wearing a cap."

"I'm warning you, Classen," said Feverton, flushed and with a baffled look on his face. "You're fumbling that ball again."

You saluted without your cap.

The next morning you telephoned Leilani at the Nurses' Dormitory of the Comfrey Hospital.

"I want to leave a message for Miss Kim."

"She's assisting at an operation."

"What is the operation for?"

"The Comfrey Hospital doesn't give out such information."

"Can I leave a message?"

"If it's important."

"It's about canoes. Hawaiian canoes have a direct boom, Samoan canoes have an indirect boom, Raro Tona canoes have a branched boom, Tahitian canoes have an indirect convex aft boom, Cook Islands canoes use an indirect convex aft boom, with a Y-shaped connecting peg."

"We only take important messages."

"But those are war canoes. Doesn't the Comfrey Hospital Nurses' Dormitory know there's a war going on?"

"We know." Click.

You noticed that Captain Feverton was staring at you, his fixed grin on his face.

You had taken as little part as possible in the discussions of the Captain's character, or in the pranks against him. Now you began to feel yourself drawn into the emotional currents of Q, even though you had hoped to stay outside, working on your small collection of air force material, and your steadily growing heap of puzzling words.

Now you discovered that if you stared back at Captain Feverton, the Captain would look pointedly at your desk and laugh in a jolly manner. In spite of yourself, you became uneasy.

That evening you called Leilani Kim from the BOQ. She had left word for you. One word. No.

After two days of pointed looks from Feverton, Yeoman Prantz came over, cigar between his thick lips, a bright smile on his ruddy face.

"Captain wants to see ya," said Prantz, not taking the cigar out of his mouth.

You were usually indifferent about military courtesy from the lower ratings; now you waited, as though Prantz had not completed his sentence. It was a battle of wills, in which, without directly commanding Prantz to say the required "sir," you indicated by your savage silence that he had better say it.

Slowly, with great reluctance, Prantz added: "Sir." The smile on Prantz's face changed imperceptibly into a gloating expression.

"Remember, Mr. Classen," said Prantz, slurring over the "Mr." as much as he dared, "There's a right way, a wrong way — and, the Navy way." He added, "Ya don't mind if I mention it, do ya?" He smiled again and dropped his cigar ash in your ashtray. With relish now he said, "Sir."

Disturbed, you realized that Prantz, whom you hardly knew as a person, hated you. Hated you, no doubt, as oldtime Navy enlisted men hated the new wartime ensigns, commissioned as they never could be in the Navy's archaic caste structure. Hated you, too, as an outsider, as a reservist of the post–Pearl Harbor kind.

It made no difference that Prantz and the other old Navy men had been caught off guard at Pearl Harbor. It made no difference that the old Navy men could not possibly man their ships and win the war without the reserves.

And yet, you thought, so far as I can I have kept to myself, I have minded my own business.

And you began, just as Prantz desired, to react to his hostility. You stood at Captain Feverton's desk, full of contempt for the old Navy which was still issuing dud torpedoes to its submariners in spite of protest after protest made to its archaic Bureau of Ordnance. Navy officers, like those of the Army, you reflected, were trained in the only surviving eighteenth century military academies left in the world. No wonder these officers stressed the bayonet and close-order drill, or tried to raise all the battleships sunk at Pearl Harbor when everyone (meaning yourself especially) knew that the battleship had been replaced in the line by the carrier. And the third World War would find these same officers struggling to preserve the carrier over the new submarine, or the tank over the new rocket.

So you stood at Captain Feverton's desk, full of righteous, perhaps overrighteous contempt for the old Navy, for the old reserves (of whom Feverton was one), for the old Army. You and your friends would surely have done better in their places (but of course you had not chosen their places — at least, before the war).

Captain Feverton examined you closely, paying special attention to the polish on your shoes, to see if General Order #17 — "Shoes should be rubed with a dry cloth at termination of shine." — had been properly carried out.

Captain Feverton toyed with a ruler. Against it he clicked his censoring shears in a peculiar rhythm. At first you did not recognize the rhythm. The Captain smiled broadly. You noticed that the Captain's *In* basket was bulging. His *Pending* basket was bulging. His *Out* basket was empty.

The Captain coughed, delicately. "Perhaps you can guess why you're here." He laughed in a horribly jolly, man-to-man way.

You could not guess.

"Your desk," said the Captain, laughing impatiently. "It has a large metal band around the edge."

Startled, you stared at your desk. So it did. You had never noticed it before. Now it stood out in the row of dull green desks. It was, in fact, the one desk in Q with a metal band around the edge. The Captain now looked pointedly at his own, bandless desk.

"It's your ball," said Captain Feverton, "how do you propose to run with it?"

You struggled to get a grip on yourself, a hammerlock on your terrible-tempered id. You would not take Captain Feverton seriously as an opponent. You would remain serene, detached, outside the gossiping and backbiting of Q. Perhaps you would permit yourself a small, occasional gesture of irony. But that was all. You were to remain the actor as observer, the detached Ironical Man.

Let your work at Q stay as it was, for the most part incomprehensible, insignificant drudgery. That you accepted. But you wanted nothing to do with Captain Feverton.

The Captain smiled again, showing his large white teeth. All his fillings were gold, even in the front teeth.

"Do you not think it would be appropriate if your Officer-in-charge —" Captain Feverton laughed again — "had the desk with the metal band?" He tapped his censoring shears against the ruler. You recognized the rhythm. It was the V for Victory. Dit dit dit dah. Captain Feverton continued, "It might prevent confusion . . ." He smiled as at a joke which you both appreciated.

With a slow burning anger which you tried to check, you said, "I don't think anyone takes seriously the difference between the desks, sir."

"Prantz takes it seriously, don't you, Prantz?"

Prantz, in the desk in front of the Captain, now wriggled his plump shoulders in delight. He puffed furiously on his cigar. Prantz, you were sure, had suggested the switch.

Gordian looked across the room and caught your eye. His lips shaped soundlessly the sentence, "You can't win." You did not smile back, as Gordian wanted you to.

Captain Feverton went on tapping his ruler and smiling. "All the more reason for changing," said Feverton, "if you can't see the difference."

This reasonable argument was overheard by Napoleon, who made the mock motion of hitting an invisible opponent in the belly. Napoleon turned hastily to his stencils when Feverton glared at him.

"The other day a paper for me was left by mistake on your desk," said Feverton. "Right, Prantz?"

Prantz's plump shoulders quivered and trembled with meaning. "Right!" they shrieked soundlessly.

You were sure this was an outright lie. Perfectly still, composed except for the fact that your fingers were trembling, you said, "I don't think it's worth the bother of the change, sir."

"It's no bother, is it, Prantz? Prantz will help with the change, won't you?"

Prantz's shoulders wriggled in an ecstasy of unbotheredness, followed by a calmer mood of selfless helpfulness.

"Is that a request or an order, Captain?"

"A request and an order are very similar, Classen."

"Please state that as an order, Captain." But the moment you spoke you knew you had made yourself ridiculous.

Captain Feverton laughed. And you knew you were losing, not the desk with the metal band, for that did not matter, but you were losing control over yourself, as you had not done for years. And yet there was an odd relief in this uncontrollable anger.

And with a sense of shock you knew you knew you were being broken. Like a plebe or a rookie you were being made to pick up the cigarette butt carelessly dropped by someone else, and you were being made to eat it.

With an effort you kept yourself from trembling. So this was how you were broken. And mixed with your anger was a kind of ironical analysis, floating just under the surface of your emotions. You were broken by the nonsensical order from the moron, who stood for the whole moronic system. After you obeyed a number of these nonsensical orders you were combat-ready for the ultimate nonsensical order. For you had to obey first of all, not think. You had to act.

And you had to learn that you could not Quit and Go to Another Job. There was only one job. And perhaps you learned all this even better, because more bitterly, when you first obeyed the truly moronic order.

You and Captain Feverton were the chief actors in a military morality play, and Prantz was the fun-loving shepherd.

And it was just this point that the Annapolis men, the West Point men, the old reserves, could never understand. They would regard any complaint as the capricious lament, the whining, of the weakling reserve officer. But there was something more important in this ludicrous incident, there was your forced surrender of something independent inside yourself, some fragile element of yourself, that you could neither name nor part with. In the end, you might not even have to be given the moronic order, you yourself might well volunteer. Once force the wild horse to taste the sour steel spade of the bit, and even escaped, he could never feel so free again. Discipline and duty. At that moment you felt a deep loathing for the words. These were the words that worked the world's work and won the world's wars. To hell with the work and the wars of the world.

Your mother had lived by these words. And at this thought, unbidden and by chance — or was it by chance? — you remembered, and then quickly suppressed the memory of the sad, meaningless death of your mother.

In the desk before you Prantz took a deep, contented puff on his cigar, then typed away furiously with a high-pitched, steady clicking of the keys. You could see that he was typing over and over, "The quick brown fox jumped into the funhouse."

"You and Prantz move it over here," said the Captain impatiently. "Prantz wants to help you." Captain Feverton looked at his watch. "I'm due at Cincpac for a conference. Order of battle," he added importantly.

The Captain flexed his strong, large fingers. You noticed that he often held his fingers in a curved position, as if ready to have them pounce on his typewriter at an instant's notice.

"It's your ball again, Classen," said Captain Feverton. "Now bounce it." The familiar incongruous smile slid over his face.

Sick with suppressed rage, you and Prantz tugged and hauled the two desks into their new positions. It was your day at the coffee mess. Now you deliberately let Prantz get his own coffee. Prantz let a malicious gleam flicker briefly in his eyes.

"O.K., Mr. Classen," he said. "How do you feel about cold climates —" Again there was that soft insulting slur over the "sir."

"The last circle of Hell was the deep freeze. That was for traitors to their benefactors."

"I like that, Mr. Classen. I'll remember that, sir."

You put down your own coffee unfinished, and moved off.

"By the way, Mr. Classen, Captain Feverton thinks the junior officers in Q had better be careful about that native poon tang."

Arkansaw came over to your desk. "You must have some fatal fascination for Feverton," he said. "He's left orders you're to be put in charge of the atrocities file. What's the secret of your charm?"

You glanced at the top item, a diary. It read, "We cut open his side so that the liver was visible and then we made the prisoner walk. Today for the first time I have seen a living human organ."

You got up from your chair and walked unannounced into the office of Commander Wolfe.

He sat at his cattycornered desk. On the wall over the door, the six clocks noiselessly told of the silent flow of time around the world. The small newspaper picture of Admiral Yamamoto looked yellow and crumbly in the hot afternoon light. It was April 17. Whatever event was connected with Admiral Yamamoto would take place, if it happened at all, tomorrow, on April 18.

Commander Wolfe sat erect in his chair reading a single sheet of paper stamped BRITISH MOST SECRET. His black eyebrows were in sharp contrast to his graying hair. Outside the offices in which he worked he could often pass unnoticed. Sometimes enlisted men went by him without saluting. Those who knew the headquarters offices were aware that it was a rare JOCPOA idea that did not originate, pass through, or become emended and improved, in his hands.

Wolfe put down the paper stamped BRITISH MOST SECRET. "What do you want, Classen?" He spoke in a lowpitched rasping voice. He sounded tired. You were surprised to hear yourself referred to by name.

The squawk box stirred to life. There were rumblings and growlings at the other end.

Then you remembered. By Japan time, today was the 18th of April. A deep voice came through the speaker of the squawk box.

"Repeat that," said Wolfe. He added irreverently, "I can't hear you too well. Must be your big beer belly."

The deep voice gave some figures. They were map coordinates, in code. You did not recognize them.

The deep voice from the squawk box muttered and gurgled. "On time," it said. "He was right on time for inspection."

"We told you he was methodical," said Wolfe.

"A lucky thing," said the squawk box. "Our Lightnings could only wait there for him for twenty minutes. Over."

There was a rumble of static from the squawk box itself that sounded like an impersonal, demonic chuckle.

Wolfe turned the box off. He looked out the window, at the procession, never ending, of ships and supplies and submarines and tugs. He looked at the *Wyorada,* now about to be flipped over by the Lilliputian motors and their tiny packthreads. Then, unconscious of your presence, Wolfe took a thick copy pencil from his desk and drew a great black X through the crumbling newspaper picture of Admiral Yamamoto.

The heavy-set, bland features, mutilated by the thick black X, still stared impassively at Wolfe's office.

Somehow, through some headquarters agency of which you knew nothing, either here or at Noumea or at Brisbane or at Washington, Yamamoto had been trapped and killed. The Navy had now sunk all but one of the Japanese carriers which had taken part in the Pearl Harbor attack. It was determined to get the remaining carrier, and, best of all, the planner of that attack. A dozen, a hundred tiny pieces of information had fitted together, in Wolfe's mind, or in some other mind. And Yamamoto — Admiral Mountainsfoot — had died. *Remember Pearl Harbor.*

For this, Wolfe had had you win the gratitude of Kawai. And

then you and Kawai had fitted into the puzzle a fragment called "punctuality."

Wolfe glanced briefly, impatiently at you. There was the barest hint of a smile on his face. You had the feeling of a mind uncoiling, untensing. The rasping voice said, "All right, Classen, what do you want?"

"Nothing, sir."

The voice was disinterested. "Then get the hell out."

You left, only to be summoned back.

"The correct response to 'Get the hell out' is 'Aye, aye, sir.'" There was nothing joking about the voice, and yet, was a joke intended?

You replied correctly, even turning smartly. It was only when you left Wolfe's office that you realized it was the first time you had ever obeyed an order instinctively, without thinking it over, without question. Were you beginning to accept another kind of obedience, more destructive and insidious because more plausible, than that required by Feverton?

You sat down at your desk and looked at the harbor, at the men climbing over the *Wyorada.* You felt a ringing in your ears, as of the sudden snap of a metal band. The Ironical Man remained, but as a separate entity, a faceless, hunched figure within yourself.

For a second time that day, but in a more baffling and mysterious way, you had been broken.

That evening you insisted on talking to Lani herself on the phone, and she agreed to see you in the reception room of the Nurses' Dormitory. You believed — perhaps you only hoped — that she had been waiting for your call.

CHAPTER TEN

April, 1943

---

*On the Japanese destroyers men took moving pictures
of our crewmen floating in the water, but they made no
attempt to rescue them.*

BEGEL, The Battle for Visaya Gulf

❋

"WHAT IS your name in Korean?"

"First I was called Flatface. Because my nose is arched, like a
westerner's." She turned her pretty eyes impudently toward you.
"Then, when I was older, my mother called me Jade Princess, and
my mother took the name Jade Princess's Mother. But I named
myself Leilani when the war began." She looked at you with an
expression of audacity and innocence.

"Why did you join the Navy?"

"I wanted to see the world and meet girls who wore grass skirts."
She smiled sweetly. "I have a grass skirt. Shall I put it on for
you?" Quick and observant, chattering and lovely, she said, "I'm
your first, isn't that so?"

"First what?"

"First native girl." She tapped your arm warningly. "You'd
better remember that I'm part Japanese."

"And part Korean."

Her face took on a pretty and defenseless look. "Only the disloyal
part counts." She smoothed her starched uniform, and in an exaggerated, professional gesture took your pulse.

"Melanophilia," she said in her lively, innocent way. "Love of
dark women. The Honolulu serviceman's disease." She burst into

laughter at your heightened color. She was extremely pretty. "What do you prescribe?"

"Light golden women." With a wickedly charming smile, her honest and fresh brown eyes almost completely closed, "Betty Comfrey."

You sat bathed in orange electric light from flower-sewn shades, in a small room off the main reception hall of the Nurses' Dormitory. Through the open door, you could see the pretty oriental nurses walking up and down broad wooden stairs, past the duty matron. On the floor by the sofa was a paper bag, slightly crushed from your bus trip. It contained a carnation lei which you had originally meant to give to Leilani. But from a feeling of shyness you had not done so, and perhaps you might take it away with you and not give it to her at all.

In your lap was a photograph album whose pages you turned, wondering why she had brought it to you. And now, with a delicately mocking glance, she put *Don Giovanni* on the vic — the overture began, the wind instruments skipped from bar to bar in Mozartian sounds that shadowed the ugliness of Death, and then suddenly the light passionate allegro theme of Don Giovanni — the voice of life? of Mozart himself? — quick and bold as a sword.

Crescendos, a quaver, the clarinets and oboes in thirds, a pride of sustained trumpet and horn notes, wind instruments disguising themselves as violins, the shimmer of the seducer's passion. The overture ended, and Don Giovanni's servant, Leporello, began to lament his ignominious role as seducer's sentinel.

A group of student nurses, going up the broad waxed stairs, stopped chattering to stare boldly at Lani and you, and then burst into giggles. They had high round busts which their student uniforms, in starched blue and white stripes, seemed cleverly designed to accentuate.

You returned to the puzzling photograph album. "That's your father?"

"My Japanese father. *Aboji.*" Agreeably and innocently she let you hold her hand.

With an uncultivated air, she made you pronounce the soft and lilting Korean word for father after her: *aboji aboji.*

Her father had a gloomy, furious stare that seemed frozen into a permanent expression. He was in Korean costume, in a light cotton coat with sleeves to the elbows, the whole made of starched garments ironed together, and he wore trousers, white like the coat, the crotch as low as his knees. Over his coat he had flung a vest with three pockets; on his head was the blackrimmed, highcrowned horsehair hat of a Korean Yangpan. He puffed uneasily, with the air of a man in rented dress, on a three feet long pipe, and tried to advance one curled slipper nonchalantly in front of the other.

Three correct paces to the rear stood a woman in a flowered skirt and short jacket, wearing a necktie fixed to one side of her jacket. She also had curling slippers on her feet.

"Your mother?"

"Yes, *omoni*," said Leilani, quickly observing your glance.

"Once my mother didn't clean the white clothes to Father's taste. Each piece of clothing had to be beaten white, and then starched, and pasted and ironed together. So he dropped all the pieces in the cold mud, and she had to wash them again. I helped her." Her voice was not complaining — there was no trace of selfpity.

"It looks hot," you said of her mother's dress.

"In summer her midriff would be bare, and the skirt white." She turned the page to a picture of herself in just such a dress, and bursting into a little laugh, hastily turned the page again. But not before you had a chance to see that in this short jacketed costume, the tips of the woman's breasts were visible.

A close-up of her mother showed that her hair was done up in a bun transfixed by a pin of brass, and by small silver pins. You remembered Gordian's file of anthropological articles on Korea, and the information that these pins could be used by their possessor to clean one's ears, or to stick one's husband's testicles if he failed in the performance of his husbandly duties.

In another photograph, Lani's father, in Japanese cut, westernized clothes, stood beside their thatchcovered Korean house. At one end of the L-shaped structure which was the house proper, there was a kitchen and its stonewalled garden. The kitchen stove, Lani told you, had flues that ran, Korean fashion, under the floor of the bedroom next door. And in the kitchen stood three black iron pots set in stone, and a clay oven, kim ch'i jars for spicy hot cabbage, a slop jar for pigs' food, and straw rings to keep food jars off the clay floor in winter, and so prevent their freezing.

Se vuoi morir? — Do you wish to die? — Don Giovanni asked the

Commendatore, father of the girl he had just attempted to ravish. And then an orchestration of violins and basses swelled through the record player, like the flashing of swords and the ringing of steel on steel, as the injured father attempted to revenge Don Giovanni's effort to rape — or seduce — his daughter Donna Anna. Last of all, the musical hiss of musical steel into musical flesh. And a trio — the dying Commendatore, wounded to death in the duel of honor; Don Giovanni — the ironical, cynical observer of his opponent's death throes; and Leporello, the servant, afraid and trembling. And for the three last bars the orchestra became the final pulse beats of the Commendatore.

"Why did he marry her?"

Impudent and pretty, mockingly she said, "Don Giovanni's don't marry."

"I mean your father."

"She was a great beauty. And then the Japanese had threatened to take her family's farm." Her smile seemed monotonous, almost fixed. She fell silent, perfectly still, lost in the involutions of some thought of her own that she would never share with you. She had grown up in a country that changed very little, adjusting its national dress by a trifle every three hundred years or so.

Korea was a border country. It had survived, a weakling between giants, for over a thousand years. The cost of that survival was written on every Korean face, but most of all on the faces of the Korean women. You thought of the Korean and Belgian and Syrian women who, in the end, far more than the men, determine whether a border country will survive.

With a radiant smile she suddenly turned the pages of the album to another photograph of her father in Japanese yukata, a cotton, after-the-bath robe decorated with paper cranes as a pattern.

All her prettiness seemed for a moment to rest in her eyes. "In Korea we fall in love, as my mother did, after marriage." She clasped her hands demurely, but her glance took on a teasing quality.

You turned again to the photograph. Her father was seated in the maru, the wooden floor room. This room was used as a dining room and had a wooden, open court before it. Cut in the ridgepole here, Lani informed you, was the date 1783, and at one end of the ridgepole was the phrase "Dragon ascending into heaven," and at the opposite end of the ridgepole was the phrase "Tortoise sitting on the floor" — to link the house firmly between heaven and earth.

Hai sposo e padre — said Don Ottavio to his fiancée, bereaved of her father — You have found a father in me. But not content with that, she demanded vengeance as well, and the obliging Don Ottavio made a pact, not without comment on the sardonic harshness of the times, that demanded of its men and women such pacts.

The next page of the album showed views of the matang, the smooth hardened clay where you could lie in summer, or thresh grain in fall, or at New Year's, like the small girl in the foreground, jump in the New Year's game of teeter-totter.

Then you saw in the face of the young girl the face of Lani, placid, innocent, pretty even then — had any Korean child ever looked weak?

With a charming and agreeable firmness she said, "I'm not a baby, you know. I'm the eldest daughter. Each week I must do the religious duties of the family."

"And your father?"

The record changer had jammed. Again and again it said obstinately, *Hai sposo e padre, hai sposo e padre.*

"Our farm," she said. "Do you understand what it means to have a farm?"

The record player crankily stopped. Leilani indicated a picture of herself standing in a wet rice paddy. She wore the revealing short jacket of summer time, but she showed you the picture without embarrassment. The laughing prettiness left her eyes and was replaced by a look of strength, almost a look of crudity. This time her hand found yours and clung to it.

On the farm, she explained with eloquence, she had had to go down the rice rows in the flooded fields, killing all the frogs she found in the water, while the leeches stuck to her legs. To this day she loathed the sight, and the sound of frogs.

Fixing her charming glance on you, unconsciously and innocently holding your hand in both of hers, she tried to tell you of the childish farm toys, of dolls made of straw stalks with movable straw arms, of a pinwheel made of paper, of sorghum stalk and of bamboo, of how her brother could flick a paper bird in the air and make it seem to fly from the instep of his foot.

But always she came back to the steady, demanding ritual of the rice, of soaking the rice seeds in salt water, of the seedling plot, of seed-planting time, of irrigating, then drying the land, of distinguishing weeds and pulling them, of working for each other in the fields, while the drummer played his changu and the cymbalist clashed his brasses and the flutist blew his flute — though just before the war started the Japanese, so her father had written, had taken the village cymbals for their brass.

"He is still in Japan?"

"In Korea, watching over the farm." In winter and summer, in war and in peace, farms went on. No doubt, when summer came, as they always had done, he would strangle and eat the dog which had been raised during the winter for food — "Korean dogfood" — she said with innocent crudity. And in winter there was little to do except take care of the oxen and the goods in the storage huts which paralleled the L of the main house itself, while the women sewed and visited. And all through the year, on the farm, the seasons went on, and each man had his steady, assured place as he moved from unrecognizable babyhood (a very young baby could be legally killed since he did not, yet, really exist), to marriage, to fatherhood, to old age. And after death you survived as a name inscribed on the ancestral tablets which were kept in the principal bedroom next to the kitchen — from this warm vantage point your spirit would guard the farm after your body had died.

To lose the farm, to lose your land, was to lose your ancestry.

Even Lani's coming to America had been part of the inexorable demands of the farm, for she had had an American-Korean grandfather, and her mother had been able to come to Hawaii to bear her daughter, and somehow Leilani had secured from her American birth both American and Korean citizenship, and even more important, an American education. She could marry, now, a wealthier man, who would take her name and move to the farm, as without yet perhaps realizing its significance, her Japanese father had done.

An expression hovered briefly on her face that at first you thought monotonous and almost without intelligence, until you saw suddenly that it was an expression of strength. Her face was startlingly full across the cheekbones, and for all its aristocratic profile it was the instinctively wise face of the peasant girl, wise because instinctively she would always know what she wanted of life. And there was the further inner steeliness, under her innocent and light-hearted charm, of the borderland people.

Korea you knew as the cockpit of Asia. It had been invaded by the Chinese, by the Mongolians of Genghis Khan, and it had been invaded by the Japanese. Korea had been one kingdom under Tan-gun of immortal legend. It had been the three kingdoms of Silla and Koguryo and Paekche. It had been united again, and then it had become a province of Japan after the Japanese assassinated the last queen of Korea.

With a bleak gesture Lani told of men being hidden in their village and traveling north, by stages, at night, to Russian Siberia. And she told of the fierce, trained men who slipped back, hiding at night in the village — known to her mother and to Lani, but not to her Japanese father.

Korea was borderland.

The last picture in the album was of a Japanese college student in stiff black uniform and black, short-visored cap.

With a fatalistic and mocking smile, she explained, "I have never met him, but my father and mother arranged for us to be married when I am twenty. I am twenty now. Nineteen by your counting."

She smiled, charmingly amused at the lack of comprehension in your face. "You are not a person in Korea until you have children and show you can carry on the family. You see, you are — twenty-four?" she guessed accurately, "and still you are not a person."

This arranged marriage seemed to you to have an artless and tender joylessness about it, even though it spoke of a society secure, endlessly sure of itself, so sure that parents had only to speak, even to a daughter educated in America, and there would be no need to worry about love, for the steady course of life followed on, as one season followed the last.

You hit the side of the record changer, and freed the jammed records. With a grinding noise it started again, and Leilani closed the photograph album.

Zitto — mi pare sentir odor di femmina! — Don Giovanni told his servant to be quiet, he smelled a woman. But the girl was Donna Elvira whom he had already once betrayed, and he withdrew.

"He must always have a new girl," said Leilani, her fresh and brilliant glance fixed on you. And with a rapid, confiding and yet mocking gesture she put her arm in yours.

When Don Giovanni fled, Leporello, his servant, sang to Donna Elvira, in a sad, allegro aria, the Homeric catalogue of his master's score: 640 women in Italy, 230 in Germany, 100 in France, 91 in Turkey, but— *ma ma in Ispagna son gia mille e tre* — already, in Spain, 1003 — of every class, of every age.

And Don Giovanni had various tastes. In a slow andante waltz of sensual recollection, Leporello recalled his loves. First the orchestra mimicked a shimmering blonde, the quintessence of blond, sensuous delicacy. Next the orchestra was a brunette, praising herself for her faithfulness, and then the orchestra took on a plump and rounded feminine shape, for that was what Don Giovanni liked in winter. And for summer, a modulation to thinness and coolness. And among these women strolled others, in lightly descending chords, the pretty tiny women, and in large stately ascending chords, the pompous fullblown ones. Next angular, unpitying music, the music of the spinsters — a Don Giovanni would ravish any woman so long as she was new and could provide another brief entry in his book.

But the Don's real interest was always the Young Beginner — you can imagine, Leporello assured Donna Elvira — *voi sapete quel que fa! voi sapete* — and laughing the flutes imagined, the basses imagined sotto voce, the strings imagined, the oboes and bassoons imagined — lust is charming, said the shimmering sounds, and how much more charming with the young beginner! *sua passion predominante è la giovin principiante.*

The needle wibbled crazily across the record, and a lizard, his rough coat golden in the orange electric light, his tongue flickering angrily, scurried from the turntable to the floor. Leilani turned the player off.

In a somewhat uncultivated voice, her pretty eyes turning curiously toward you, "Do you prefer the young beginner too?"

Suddenly she disengaged her arm from yours.

A haole nursing supervisor, with a pursy look on her middle-aged face that said quite clearly what hanky-panky she thought you and Lani had been up to, came to summon her back to duty.

Troubled, you shook hands. Lani's smile took on a placid and monotonous quality, she seemed tired, far younger than her nine-teen years, and her broad face lost briefly its look of endurance and strength.

After she left the room, you remembered the crushed brown paper bag, and you took out the carnation lei. Ignoring the pro-testing receptionist you ran halfway up the waxed wooden stairs and gave Leilani the carnations.

With a charming soft cry she held the woven fragrant rope of pink and white flowers to her cheek. Standing on the halfway land-ing in her stiffly innocent uniform, she seemed suddenly beyond your reach. Smiling brilliantly, she said in her lilting Korean, "Annyong-hi kasipsio."

She started up the stairs, still holding the carnations to her cheek. As you went to the door you did a little hop and a skip. You turned, not knowing why, to see that Leilani was laughing at you. She ran prettily down the stairs, slipped her hand agreeably in yours, and led you in a tender and perplexing manner to the door. There she innocently linked her arm in yours and leaned against you briefly.

You said goodbye again, her face was sweet and bright, with just a trace of superficiality.

You started to shake hands, but in a completely natural manner she caught your hand quickly to her breast, lowered her soft cheek to brush your fingers, and ran away.

Back at the BOQ you found your suitcase lying open on your bunk. Beside it lay a jumble of your clothes, ready to be packed. Arkansaw had packed his, and so had Gordian. On the deck stood another bag, tagged with Napoleon's name and rank. On top of the bag was an empty box stamped *One (1) Government Issue Killer Stiletto.* The box fell clattering to the deck.

On your bunk was a folder containing your orders from the Ad-miral JOCPOA to Ensign Classen, Subject Temporary Additional Duty with the forces of the Commander, North Pacific, wherever he may be. A small penciled notation, in the familiar handwriting of Prantz, read, "Good luck from a buddy."

Down the hall you heard singing, not sober, not drunk:

> There were four flies once on a time
> Who made up their minds to change their clime;

So they flew away with a buzz and a hum
And showed their mother a well-cleaned bum.

One was red and one was blue
And one had spots on his to rah loo . . .

Defiant of the blackout regulations, you opened the curtains and looked at the velvety midnight sky. You caught your breath, in a sharp, quick feeling of dizziness. You had a vision of yourself, a monster without a goal, plunging and falling from space to space. The singers approached your door, and you went to it, to welcome them.

Part Two

LANDGRAB

CHAPTER ELEVEN

June, 1943

Just as the symphony buff recognizes the first and second violins, the French horns, the trumpets, the bass drums, so the experienced amphibforce veteran can, in a landing, recognize the LCI rockets, the LCI mortars, the 5-inch destroyer guns, the aerial bombs, the battleship main batteries.

BEGEL, The Battle for Visaya Gulf

❉

WAR CORRESPONDENT BULFLASH put down the glossy picture of a Japanese movie star. He had kept it as a souvenir of Attu and had just showed it to everyone as a picture of a genuine geisha. "Wouldn't that make you jack off a quart?" he said, leering. He wolfed down his second drink.

"Can't seem to stop," he said nervously. "It's this damn light."

The light did have an unnerving quality. At 9 P.M. it still had not darkened enough to be called twilight, and for all but a few hours of the night, you had learned, it would stay just as light.

"Do you think pilot Job will take off tomorrow?"

"In our three weeks on Kodiak," said Napoleon Brandt, in a tone that defied challenge, "I have learned that there are two whores here. One of them may be free for fifteen delirious minutes, two years from today."

"I have enough money for two more meals," said Arkansaw. "The paymaster admits that Navy regs require him to pay us, but he still isn't going to do it."

"The Red Cross will lend us a little money tomorrow," said Gordian temperately.

Arkansaw flung his long frame on a short chrome-legged sofa, the main piece of furniture in the Kodiak Naval Officers' Bar. "Buy us another drink, Bulflash, and we'll tell you the secret history of Pearl Harbor."

Bulflash handed round drinks for everyone and a double for himself.

"Remind me to take out a life subscription to your scandal sheet," said Arkansaw.

"That pilot Job is a coward," said Napoleon, cradling his drink in both hands.

"I heard they send these pilots here for making mistakes somewhere else," said Bulflash, licking his lips. He was rapidly eating peanuts from a tin can, tossing them in the air and catching them in his mouth. His upper lip was thin and his lower lip was full. "A fine kind of punishment," he said, tossing two peanuts in the air and catching them both in his mouth. "Why, a pilot like that could put my life in danger."

"How much circulation would your paper lose if the rich man's Ernie Pyle never returned from the war?" asked Arkansaw.

"I've told you once," said Bulflash. "I'm the poor man's Ernie Pyle." He calculated. "200,000 readers." More peanuts flipped between his lips. "It's not a joking matter," he said.

"I'm on Job's side," said Gordian. He tasted his liquor and put it to one side unfinished. "If he thinks the weather is no good for flying, then I think the weather is no good for flying."

"We'll be here for years," said Napoleon. "We may even miss CLEANSWEEP," he said. "All because of that coward."

"There'll be delays," said Gordian. "You won't miss the operation. If you *really* want to be on it."

"What do you mean by that crack?" said Napoleon. "Do you want to bet who comes back with his own samurai sword and his own rising sun flag?"

"I hear the last plane from Kodiak to Adak is splashed all over the mountains a little north of here. Job may be smarter than he looks."

"A war correspondent's life is tough," said Bulflash. "I haven't been home for two months now. First it was Attu. Now this. Probably won't get home for another couple of months. Got a baby son I've seen only twice." More peanuts. His face took on a tragic but brave expression. "You know, some war correspondents have been killed in battle." He shuddered. "Attu," he said.

Bulflash had a considerable reputation in the North Pacific Area for having filed all his Attu front line dispatches from the security of Dutch Harbor. He had won a Reporter Prize for them, and indeed, they had given much of the feeling and immediacy of the fighting in a breathless kind of prose, interspersed with sentimental stories about enlisted men which were his stock in trade. Wherever possible he tried to indicate that the war was being won by the enlisted men in spite of their officers.

Still you had to like Bulflash. He was usually amiable, and he was never stingy. Even Gordian could not bear to part with an envelope or a sheet of note paper. Arkansaw begrudged the loan of a dictionary. Napoleon hoarded female telephone numbers. And you had to force yourself not to take down the names of book borrowers on a library card.

Arkansaw hit Bulflash for another drink. "Sure sounds like a tough life," he said. "One more round of drinks, and I promise to buy a copy of your book, *A Trench Rat at the Fighting Front.*"

"That's not the title of my book," said Bulflash. "I've told you a hundred times what the title of my book is."

"I remember now," said Arkansaw, sipping his refilled glass. "*A Trench Rat Goes to War.*"

"No, no. My book is *Let's Go, Joe Blow.*"

"I think I'll use that for the title of my new book," said Arkansaw. "The nice thing about a title is you can't copyright it. Yes, I like it," he said. "*Joe Blow, Trench Rat.*"

Bulflash munched moodily on his peanuts. "What's your line," he said abruptly to Arkansaw. "I don't figure you."

"Sutras," said Arkansaw. "Cloaks and sutras."

You and Gordian groaned.

"He means Buddhist sutras, especially Zen sect works."

"What the hell kind of work is that?"

"It's no work for an honest man," said Napoleon.

"But Arkansaw isn't an honest man."

The object of this discussion combed his hair and closed his eyes, seemingly asleep.

"What about you," said Bulflash, "what's your line?"

"Just bound for Adak like yourself." Then, feeling foolish at this unnecessary display of military secrecy, since Bulflash, however indiscreet, was hardly a spy. "On the headquarters staff."

Napoleon began doing pushups in a corner. There was nothing particularly remarkable in his easy up-and-down motion, except that he was supporting a full drink on the back of his neck.

"And him?" said Bulflash, hypnotized by this athletic spectacle.

"That's our coach. He keeps us physically fit. Mentally, we're on our own. Hey, coach."

"All right, men," said Napoleon. His eyes had a glassy, fixed quality. He swallowed his drink in one long gurgling glop. He put down the glass and smacked his lips. "At least we've got a good water boy on our team. Best damn water I ever tasted."

"Water!" protested Bulflash, indignant at the thought he might not have provided Napoleon with an honest drink.

"All right, line up," said Napoleon.

"It's best to humor him when he's like this. He's very powerful."

"Well, I'll be running along," said Bulflash nervously.

Napoleon's long arm shot out, whirled him around, and stood him at attention. Then he reached down and dragged Arkansaw into the line.

"Take my letter back," said Arkansaw sleepily. "I don't want to play on the football team any more. I've changed my sport to crocheting."

"Can't you stop him?" asked Bulflash. Napoleon took Bulflash by the jaw, then grabbed his neck like a chiropractor, expertly snapped it out of joint with a loud crack, and snapped it back in again.

"That'll teach you which goalpost is ours," said Napoleon. "Now let's forget the past and do better in the second half. I'm no man to hold a grudge."

He walked up and down the line while Bulflash, dazed, rubbed his neck. "All right, stomachs hard," said Napoleon. Quickly he ran along the line, tapping each man in the gut. Bulflash was unprepared, and had the breath forced out of him with a great whooshing noise.

"Been breaking training, eh?" said Napoleon severely. "Well, there's only one cure for that. The water cure."

"No, no." You and Arkansaw got down on your knees. "Spare him, coach, not that."

Gordian said judiciously, "He's going to kill somebody one of these days."

Bulflash paled. "What's he going to do?"

You and Arkansaw tried to hold Napoleon back. "Spare him, coach. He'll do better the second half. We promise."

Napoleon hesitated. They nudged Bulflash. "Tell him you'll do better. Give a pep talk."

"Look, coach," said Bulflash, alarmed. "I promise to carry the ball longer and harder than anybody."

"And in the right direction?"

"In the right direction."

"Where's that water boy," said Napoleon, looking accusingly at his empty glass.

"Here," said Bulflash. "Coming up." He handed Napoleon his own double whiskey. As Napoleon thirstily drank, Bulflash skipped out the door.

"That's the spirit," cried Napoleon after him. "Get in there and fight." He made as if to go after Bulflash, but Arkansaw waved in front of him his new copy of his beloved *Scientifiction Monthly*. On its cover a nude green thing, half woman (the upper half) and half plant (the lower half) was about to crush in her embrace — or was digest the proper word? — an advancing scientist in white jungle hat. Enraptured, Napoleon sank, still glassy eyed, back in a chair and fell asleep, holding *Scientifiction Monthly* in reading position.

The next morning, down at the hangar beside the plane, Napoleon sprinted back and forth to work off his hangover. Job and his co-pilot fussed about the plane, checking the load, the engines, the gas, the lubrication. The gear was quickly stowed aboard in its dirty white canvas seabags. Quietly you climbed the aluminum ladder and buckled yourself to a hard metal bucket seat. Forward of the double row of seats was a great disorderly heap of cargo, secured to the deck by thin wire cables.

The plane taxied slowly down the runway and the plane made a half turn into the wind. Job tested first the port engine, then the starboard engine, as the plane quivered against its brakes. Slowly the plane lumbered down the runway, then faster, the acceleration pressing you all backward. There was that uneasy, sluggish transition from the runway to the air, then the plane swooped upward in a long circle. But you were not allowed to release your seat belts, and the plane continued to circle the airfield. You all stared at each other. A dollop of sweat ran down the tip of Bulflash's sharp nose. Then another and another. Arkansaw began saying over and over *"Namiamidabutsu."* He kept on saying it long after it ceased to be funny.

In a long slow arc you entered the landing pattern and traced its circling geometry in the air. Below you could see a crash truck painted red and khaki, and whitely following it, an ambulance with a red cross on the roof. You made a sluggish approach, flaps down, and a surprisingly delicate, feathery landing. The crash truck and the ambulance raced beside you on the runway, waiting for something to happen. The plane stopped, and one motor after the other cut out, with brief, surly bangs.

Then you were allowed out of the plane. It looked big and fine standing there in one of the rare clear days of the Aleutians. A mechanic explained curtly that when aloft Job and his co-pilot had discovered that the wheels could not be retracted.

You were not allowed to leave the hangar area for three hours, while the mechanics worked on the wheels. None of you felt like talking. Napoleon sprinted some more. You walked by yourselves, or smoked, in a kind of self-enforced isolation, as though you had never met before.

It helped to think of Lani for a while, and then it did not help any more.

You were summoned to the plane again. At the end of the runway the plane's motors were warmed up for a long time. Just before Job was about to start, a jeep screeched up to the plane and the engines halted to idling speed again. A mechanic handed in two parachutes at the cockpit window, one for Job and one for his co-pilot.

Bulflash was not just sweating now. It was more like a man providing himself with his own personal shower. In a low, monotonous tone, Napoleon muttered over and over some suggestions for

Job's future. These would be invaluable, should Job ever desire to have intercourse with a duck.

Arkansaw drew out of his jacket a small, carefully wrapped object and untied it. Again you hurtled down the runway, while the acceleration flung you back along your bucket seats. Again you circled in the air, and once again, after an agonizing wait, you started on the interlaced circles of the landing pattern. Arkansaw spun round and round a tiny wheel. Bulflash looked up from his own private devotions, which consisted mainly of staring below at the crash truck and the ambulance.

"It's a prayer wheel," said Arkansaw. "Every time you turn it, it counts as one prayer. I'm just testing it."

"It's not turning fast enough," said Bulflash. "Let's plug it into the plane's electrical system."

With a hard bump you were down. The plane sagged to one side and your breath caught. From the crash truck the driver leaned out and shouted to Job as he raced alongside. The plane swung to a stop in a tight vicious circle.

Outside the plane Job said to you all curtly, "Flight's canceled for today." A sailor started to take the parachutes out of the cockpit. Job beckoned to him to leave them in, then he was gone in the jeep. You walked back to the BOQ, with the nauseous feeling that comes of returning suddenly to a place you think you have just left forever.

The next morning you took off and flew away without incident. In his relief Job buzzed some Kodiak bears, chasing them across the tundra in long, sickening swoops of the clumsy Dakota. First he buzzed the father bear, then the mama bear, and last the two frightened cubs. Napoleon turned green and advised you all that he was dying. Bulflash went to the back of the plane and coughed unhappily into the urine tube. Gordian calmly wrote to his wife, but your mouth went dry and your head felt giddy.

You started to land, apparently in the middle of the tundra, then you saw at the edge of a cleared metaled strip the usual quonsets and farther off the radio towers. Just as you set down, a sudden gust of wind, a williwaw, caught the plane and tipped the wingtip almost against the ground, and with a savage burst of speed, somehow Job got his heavy plane back in the air again, and you sped on.

At Dutch Harbor you landed and were fed at the Officers' Mess. At the entrance to the mess was a large printed sign: DUTCH HARBOR NAVAL PERSONNEL WILL NOT BE ALARMED AT THE APPEARANCE OF OFFICERS ARRIVING FROM ADAK.

On you flew through clouds and sunlit patches across the Aleutians to Adak. Fogs drifted in and cleared with bewildering rapidity. As soon as Job — or any pilot — had only one clear airfield on the route, he had orders to land immediately. The whole run was a great gamble with the weather, and with maddening compass gyrations.

For a long time ahead of you four volcanoes, arranged in a square, white with snow, beckoned you on. With an intense and mournful longing, you daydreamed of Leilani whom you hardly knew.

You were the first to see it, a dark splatter of khaki and aluminum against the middle of one of the blindingly white cones. The plane that had made the previous run. All of you watched until the dark splotch faded astern.

Still the Dakota droned on and the journey took on an endless character. In *Scientifiction Monthly* you read about the brilliant young biologist, Anderson. Fearful about the fate of Dr. Cristal, he slashed through the jungle with his native bearers. The native bearers fled. Very well, brilliant young Anderson would continue by himself. After all, if he really wanted to get ahead at Crumble University, he would marry Dr. Cristal's daughter. What better time to make a deal? The plants around him were enormous, some, on a gigantic scale, resembled Venus Flycatchers. Then he saw an antelope scurry into the path ahead. A plant reached out and swallowed the screaming beast, there was a leafy gurgle, and before his eyes the Venus Flycatcher took on antelope shape.

Young Anderson was filled with horror. Somewhere on this trail was there a plant that looked like Dr. Cristal — would indeed be like Dr. Cristal for the next hundred years or so? For suddenly Anderson remembered that these plants had two names in the native language — they were "kch" or "century" plants — or sometimes they were "kch kch" or "two century" plants.

Then he heard a highpitched call in the familiar, nagging voice of Dr. Cristal, followed by a rustle as a great green vine reached for him in a half friendly, half insinuating way. He stepped back nimbly, envisaging as he did so a new life, without Miss Cristal at his side. And Crumble University would surely need a new chairman of the biology department. This green horror could never effectively and sincerely (a favored word at Crumble University) direct biology majors.

Not daring to look, yet half knowing what he would find, brilliant young Anderson saw ahead of him in the murky jungle the green shape, still recognizable, of Dr. Cristal. There, slightly enlarged, but still visible, were the pot belly, the waddling legs — firmly rooted to the ground now, even the sun helmet and the pince-nez.

"I will not hurt you," said Dr. Cristal soothingly. Young Anderson stepped back, just in time to miss the long, looped vegetable fall of a rope that seemingly dropped from the skies.

"You're learning the ropes fast," called Anderson cheerily. He stepped to one side just as two leaves snapped shut, narrowly missing his hand. "That's taking a leaf out of the book," called Anderson.

"In the interests of science," said Dr. Cristal, "I command you to record my temperature." A green tentacle writhed toward Anderson. He sprinted for a clearing. "Too hot for me," he called back. "We must decide now on your last words to civilization. I was thinking of something like, 'Make my brilliant young assistant chairman and have him carry on my work.'"

From the ground near Anderson a vine burst out and sent forth a hundred twining creepers, one of which caught Anderson's foot and stung through his boot. But again he took successful evasive action. Dr. Cristal's aim was not yet good, but it was improving.

"Let's shake hands," said Dr. Cristal sadly, "a last farewell."

Quicker than you could say Jack Anderson, the young scientist fired his elephant gun into the ground at his feet. A huge root writhed in the hole, turned pale, and began to stink.

"You might at least say excuse me," said Dr. Cristal angrily. Vines now began to shoot up on all sides of brilliant young Anderson. He did not want to be hemmed in, nor did he want to kill Dr. Cristal unless forced to do so.

With a quick movement he picked up a large log, ran forward as the vines quivered at his legs in hungry ecstasy, and hurled it into a wavering fringed opening about at Dr. Cristal's pot belly — this, he judged, was the true mouth of the plant monster. Automatically the mouth closed over the log, and then began to assume its form. The shapes of Dr. Cristal and of the log battled for mastery in the voracious plant, but the brilliant young scientist had chosen a special, acidic log, even more acidic than Dr. Cristal. The plant hiccuped, woodenly. "That was hardly kind of you," said Dr. Cristal. "A tough wedge for a tough log," called brilliant young Anderson as he sped off to the nearest telegraph station.

When you landed in Adak it was evening, but still light. You waited on the metal-holed landing strip, waiting for a glimpse of Job, your pilot. His face was white with fatigue, the face of a man of fifty on a youth of twenty-two. He walked by without recognizing you as one of his passengers. In two days' time, he would, weather permitting, fly back to Kodiak. And in another two days he would return to Adak again.

In the jeep that waited to take you to the headquarters of ComNorPac, Napoleon had begun to sing:

> I don't want to be a soldier,
> I don't want to go to war . . .

And like madmen, relieved to be safe on this island which before the war had rented for $25 a year, you bellowed along with him, the driver joined in, even Gordian joined in:

> Monday I touched her on the ankle,
> Tuesday I touched her on the knee,
> Wednesday with success
> I lifted up her dress —

CHAPTER TWELVE

August, 1943

Before World War II military experts were unanimous in thinking a landing on an enemy coast against hostile troops was almost impossible because of the vulnerability of transports and open boats to air attack, but we had left certain crucial factors out of our reckoning.

BEGEL, The Battle for Visaya Gulf

❁

COLONEL MIST had a face like a hounddog and was six feet tall. It was widely believed in the regimental combat team that Colonel Mist had ordered a runner on Attu to bring him a roll of toilet paper under fire. It was also believed that he had arranged on Attu to have the officers of his staff provided with fresh white bread which they ate in a tightly shut tent so as not to arouse the envy of the enlisted men.

In the stand-up mess of the gently heaving transport, Colonel Mist reviewed, for the last time, the attack plans. Two battleships, two heavy cruisers, three light cruisers, and nine destroyers were to fire 2000 rounds. Then two heavy cruisers, some light cruisers, and five destroyers would fire another 1000 rounds. The air force would drop 1200 tons of bombs. There would be several tons of surrender leaflets for the survivors of this bombardment to read, some 100,000 leaflets in all. And then, at last, the landing of 34,000 troops against an estimated 10,000 Japanese on Zhutchka — or, as the Russian meant — Darling Beetle.

Next to you stood the Navy boat officer, worried because he had been provided with crews who had never landed through surf before, and who thought a diesel engine had spark plugs.

Colonel Mist droned on. His face serious, he wanted to tell you all about the most important thing he had learned in war. This was that a stitch in time saved nine.

Without a smile he took out of his pocket a small army sewing kit, complete with assorted needles and a hank of white, black, and khaki darning thread. If you sewed up those pesky holes while they were still little holes, those little holes could never turn into big holes. Dismissed.

You went back to your bunk and lay there as your stomach clutched at its condemned man's meal of French fries and steaks. In the bunk over your head the Red Cross man, originally weapon-less, fingered a long M–1 rifle and a heavy belt of ammunition which he had bought from Warrant Officer and Band Leader Sanky.

You had first met Sanky at the RCT staging base on Adak. There Sanky had been pulling from the mucky tundra a sign by a slit trench which read OFFICERS ONLY. You helped him uproot the sign from the gumbo and throw it in the odorous trench. "Think their shit doesn't stink," said Sanky aggrieved. Sanky now sat on the edge of his bunk, cleaning a .45. "There's nothing like a .45," he said, "for really close-in fighting." The Red Cross Man eyed the black automatic. "You see," Sanky explained, "you just hold the trigger down and she goes off." Sanky tossed the weapon up to the Red Cross man. "What did Martivet want?" he asked you.

Your transport was a Merchant Marine ship, but on the flag bridge Lieutenant Commander Martivet, formerly of your training school at the University of Wyorada, presided. He wore a sheepskin coat with collar to match, a black peaked cap, elbow-length fur gloves, and as accessory a three foot long spyglass in offgreen. Three signal-men stood alert on the flag bridge ready to send and receive messages.

"You should have reported to me at once," Martivet had said when you presented yourself to him. You explained that you were attached to the RCT.

"Suppose a message had come for you from Admiral Norcross?"

You did not think this a likely possibility.

Then jocosely, "How's that dwarf tree of yours?" Chagrined, you knew that your old drillmaster had confused you with Arkansaw. Martivet burst into song:

O Behring Sea, bleak Behring Sea,
So long we've hoped to sail o'er thee
For ne'er can sailor salty be,
Until he sails the Behring Sea,
And views Alaska's dreary shore,
And fills himself with Arctic lore.

He whipped the spyglass to his eye and trained it on the Aleutian fog. "Carry on," he had called, and your interview was over.

"Did the Japanese really shoot the stretcher bearers on Attu?" the Red Cross man asked Sanky.

"They sure did," said Sanky. "Between Chicago and Massacre. The stretcher bearers wore Red Cross armbands too."

The Red Cross man winced. Sanky went on: "They were yelling and screaming, 'Japanese boys kill American boys, Japanese drink blood.'"

"That was their last suicide attack, a *gyokusai* attack."

"I don't know what kind of attack you call it, but they ran right through the field hospital, pulled the blankets off the litter cases, made them stand up and cut them from head to foot with their swords. And all the time they were laughing.

"I was right in the middle of it, sound asleep when it started. I woke up fast when some Jap set up his machine gun right at the edge of my foxhole and fired across it."

"What did you do then?" asked the Red Cross man.

"Nothing," said Sanky scornfully. "When he moved his machine gun away, I went down the hill for more ammunition for the company. I walked through this group of characters in ponchos. My second trip, I figured they were Japs. Some were walking downhill, some up."

His rugged features wrinkled in concentration, Sanky held the barrel of the .45 up to the light.

"You shot them?" said the Red Cross man.

"I just walked through them carrying the boxes of ammunition, as polite as pie. I didn't bother them and they didn't bother me.

"You should have seen them the next day. There they lay where they'd blown their faces off with their handgrenades, brains scattered . . ."

Yorking noisily, the Red Cross man shot out into the passageway and ran down to the head.

"Now what made him throw egg in the fan?" asked Sanky, astonished. He threw his short torso back on his bunk and fell immediately asleep.

When the ship glided to a halt and began unloading the first wave, you stumbled topside, rubbing your eyes, but you quickly stumbled back to your bunk again where Sanky was still asleep. The bandsmen, your seven nisei interpreters and their guards (assigned to keep them from being shot by mistake by friendly forces), the Red Cross man, and you yourself, were all in the seventh wave of the attack. Your time was a long way off.

You woke briefly at the sound of a shot, and went back to sleep on hearing that still another man had blown his big toe off, to get out of combat duty.

When you awoke again it was because the air had turned acrid. Then smoke began coiling lazily down the passageway. A compartment door clanged shut and was dogged down. An alarm bell began to ring, stopped, started again, and stopped for good.

Should you go topside? Should you take your equipment? You had an M-1 rifle, ammunition, two orange grenades, you wore three pairs of socks under your shupacs, you wore light underwear, winter underwear, trousers, water-resistant trousers, a shirt, a water-resistant shirt, a parka, a hat, a parka hood. You carried an inner sleeping bag, an outer sleeping bag, a shelter half, a long knife, a long knife badge (for purposes of identification and publicity you were General Ferox's Long Knives), thirty pounds of dictionaries, a change of underwear, shirt and socks, messgear, two canteens, a gas mask, and a packboard. Rigged for action, you could not walk, only stumble.

You took your M-1, the ammunition, and the grenades and gas mask and went to the main deck. There you found three of your nisei interpreters and their guards. You had been told that if any of the nisei were shot by friendly forces, you would be court-martialed and shot in your turn. You ran back below to find a way forward, but the door was dogged down. You went topside again. There were a few sharp explosions, like handgrenades, and stuttering sounds, as of rifle ammunition. The ship was under way again.

On the bridge deck the Merchant Marine captain yelled and waved his arms. He was short and huckleberry faced, and he called now for slow, dead slow, and then stop.

Listlessly below him, some Merchant Marine sailors searched for water couplings but could not find them. They argued about pipe fittings. The rumor circulated among the crowds of soldiers on deck that the Merchant Marine cargo loaders had been smoking near the hold and had thrown their cigarettes down it, in defiance of the No Smoking rules. The Merchant Marine cargo loaders, some sixteen men in all, had no work to do aboard the transport, in fact, they could not have done the highly specialized unloading task, for which the Army provided its own trained crews. But the Union had forced the Army to take on the sixteen unwanted men in Seattle, and their job consisted of lounging around and informing all who cared to listen that they made $20 a day.

More Merchant Marine sailors shambled forward and connected two lengths of hose. There was a search for the nozzle which they had mislaid. This was found at last, and the hose was lowered into the forward hold. Valves turned. Out came clouds of live steam followed by a loud explosion from the hold.

Above the Merchant Marine captain, high on the flag bridge, you saw Lieutenant Commander Martivet. He waved his spyglass like a baton, and directed the sailors to another coupling. The captain pointed to still another one. Confused, the sailors connected two lengths of hose, from two different couplings, into each other. The hoses exploded. They tried again, dividing into two rival schools of hose coupling, and succeeded in directing two currents of live steam into the hold. There was a gratifying crunch when two bursts of steam hit the grenade ammunition boxes.

The transport broke out a flag with a blue St. Andrews cross on a yellow field, the breakdown flag. A destroyer came gracefully alongside.

"Do you think an officer should always go down with his ship?" you asked Sanky.

A new burst of ammunition made the deck tremble. The motionless transport sent a spasm of black smoke into the early morning sky.

From the flag bridge Lieutenant Commander Martivet was trying to persuade troops to jump over to the destroyer. The troops refused. Only yesterday a man had fallen off the stern of the transport. A destroyer had picked him up in twenty minutes, an excellent bit of rescue work. There had been just one difficulty. The man was dead from exposure to the cold Aleutian waters.

Sanky spat into the cold blue sea. "I'd say, when the water reaches the upper deck, it's time to follow the rats."

Martivet waggled his spyglass at you, and ordered you to lead the way to the destroyer. You got your gear together at the rail. In the Merchant Marine mess you noticed the sailors calmly eating breakfast.

"If we all have to jump," said Sanky to the Red Cross man, "I'm sure glad I've only got a fortyfive to carry."

You got ready to leap when the two ships kissed. As you jumped, the carbon dioxide of your belt life preserver inflated and you felt a paralyzing cramp in the stomach. One of the destroyer sailors had to free you from the lifebelt.

After three of your nisei and their guards followed you, other soldiers began jumping over to the destroyer. You found two more of your nisei. Two were still lost. You jumped back to get the rest of your gear including your gas mask. The gas mask was gone. "Where's the gas mask?" you asked a Merchant Marine sailor. He looked contemptuously at you, and went back to his breakfast. You jumped onto the destroyer again.

The destroyer deck began to slant under the weight of the soldiers and their gear. It was beginning to capsize. A net tender came alongside the destroyer and you all jumped over to that. The net tender began to capsize. Some men went over the side to landing craft, and others, like yourself, jumped back to the destroyer. Again the destroyer began to list. You were ordered to jump back to the transport. As you landed on its deck your life belt inflated again, and you sank to the deck, helpless in its carbon dioxide grip. The Merchant Marine sailors, still eating breakfast, looked stolidly at you. Sanky came to your rescue and freed you from the lifebelt. More ammunition exploded in the forward hold. You rounded up the two missing nisei and their guards, but you could only find one other Japanese-American interpreter from your group of seven. The rest you had started with were now lost.

With Sanky, the nisei, the bandsmen and their trumpets and tubas and slide trombones, and the Red Cross man, now armed with Sanky's .45, you clambered down landing nets into a waiting LCVP at the stern of the transport, thus constituting your own attack wave. As you left the transport Lieutenant Commander Martivet spotted you through his glass and bellowed at you through a megaphone. You waved at him and sailed on for the distant shores of Zhutchka.

One of the ideas of General Ferox for his Long Knives had been that in each sector the bandsmen should land first and play stirring martial airs while the combat troops followed and stormed the beaches. That the Japanese, who had shown no mercy to hospital orderlies, would, out of love for John Philip Sousa, spare the band, had seemed most unlikely to Sanky, and he had reported to Colonel Mist that he and his men would rather die first than carry out this order, since they would die first if they did obey it anyway.

But when you chugged up to your landing beach you found that the first LCT of the assault wave had broached. For two hours now there had been no way for the other vessels of the assault wave to get on shore. On went your tiny LCVP, down went the landing ramp, and you tumbled ashore, complete with tubas, cornets, slide trombones, thirty pounds of dictionaries, and a damnable heavy small wooden box that was Sanky's especial charge.

You waited to one side, sitting on your dictionaries, while the supplies and men of the assault wave were ferried ashore by your LCVP. The heavily laden men crunched past you along the volcanic sands. The sun disappeared and a dense brume settled just above your head, so that the men walking up the hillsides lost their heads, their shoulders, and their waists before they finally vanished from your level. The muskeg soon broke down under the tramping shupacs of the men, and turned to mud that sucked gluily at your ankles.

When Colonel Mist appeared the RCT headquarters could move forward at last, and you helped Sanky lash the heavy wooden box on his back, on his packboard.

"What's that damn box?"

"Medals," said Sanky in disgust. "To be awarded in the field, under fire."

Behind a double in the steeprising hill was a cave with a Japanese mountain gun, a .75. Its breech block was gone. The enlisted men assured you that a cup of hot coffee had been found beside it. You tried to tell them that Japanese usually drank tea, but they insisted that hot coffee was what had been found there. From the gun position yellow Japanese telephone wire ran up the hill and disappeared into the brume.

About four hundred feet above sea level, still on the western side of narrow-waisted Zhutchka, the RCT headquarters bedded down for the night. The main Japanese positions were across the volcanic central hills, on the eastern side of Zhutchka. No doubt, as on Attu, the Japanese would wait a while before disclosing their positions.

You dug your foxholes in a rough circle that included two hill spines, and a cave headquarters for Colonel Mist. To your left, over the next range of hills, was the RCT to which Arkansaw had been attached. Napoleon was with a southern landing force. And north, with the Canadian commandos, was quiet, temperate Gordian. The Canadian commandos had deliberately chosen the longest route to the main Japanese positions, because this route allowed them to sail across Zhutchka's one lake on their new Canadian commando rubber boats which they were very eager to use under fire.

You woke up sullenly, reluctant to quit a warm, sensuous dream in which you had just begun to caress Leilani's shoulder. Then you realized that what had awakened you was rifle fire. You sat upright, and your shelter half released several gallons of water into your foxhole. Five feet from your hole a new brook suddenly appeared, went right through the foxhole of the man nearest you, and dumped him, wet and cursing, a few yards farther down the slope. Sanky crawled from hole to hole. "All officers stay awake," he said softly. "No firing, all officers stay awake." For your benefit he explained that the bullets crackling overhead were from our own carbines, and not Japanese .25 rifles.

Through the night you crouched in your wet hole, listening to the whiplash crack of rifles and the reedy, whining sound of the bullets. Once you heard a steady burst of machine gun firing and again Sanky crawled from hole to hole whispering, "No firing, no firing."

In the drizzle of the next morning, down the long spur on your left, came the stretcher bearers — two, three, four — seven, eight — fourteen, fifteen — twentytwo, twentythree — thirtythree, thirty-four, thirtyfive, thirtysix, thirtyseven. And, after half an hour, thirtyeight and thirtynine. Two neighboring platoons, lost in the night and the fog, had fought it out all night, and their second lieutenants had been found dead in the morning — your enlisted men stated flatly that they had scooped each other's brains out with their .45's.

Colonel Mist was writing a report that would prove your landing beach an incredible mistake. Had there been any Japanese at all, the whole RCT could easily have been annihilated. He viewed with a profound suspicion your request to be allowed to go forward to battalion headquarters with the RCT runner.

You were not thinking of the practical excuse you gave, that of looking for Japanese documents at battalion headquarters. In an exaltedly selfconscious state you asked yourself, "Suppose I should kill a Japanese, a human being like myself?"

Colonel Mist let you go, with reluctance, and his dubious expression conveyed that you were an officer by virtue of your uniform rather than because of your common sense. Still, he let you go. Halfway up the hills, you stopped to catch your breath and you looked back. Thirty yards from the RCT headquarters mustard-yellow smoke puffed up. Colonel Mist ran out of his cave screaming and cursing. There was another burst, closer this time, and Colonel Mist ran back into his cave. "They's our own mortars," said the runner with professional interest. "Must be gettin the range." You both waited a moment to see if your heavy mortars would destroy their own headquarters, but there were no further bursts and you trudged on up to the top of the hill and the battalion CP. The battalion major thought the Japanese had all retreated to the highest ground in the north central section of Zhutchka. One of your missing nisei interpreters, confused about what he should do or not do, had let the battalion major take, as a souvenir, a diary which discussed Japanese plans for evacuation of Zhutchka by means of "counterradar." Near an abandoned Japanese machine gun position had been found another pot of hot coffee.

You sent the diary back to the RCT for immediate forwarding to

Ferox's headquarters. The battalion major did not like you for taking away his souvenir, even though you promised him a replacement. "Do you want to go to company headquarters?" he asked coolly. But he sent a squad of four men, and the nisei. To keep other patrols from shooting at the nisei, you arranged the squad in a diamond formation and put the nisei at the center of the diamond. You were walking downhill now, toward the eastern coast and the lower harbor, called Fishhook Bay, walking over muskeg, through streams, slipping at one point among hundreds of bright yellow oranges.

The captain of the company was eager to have your squad go forward, as you suggested, to Fishhook Bay. When the enlisted men refused to cross a small stream and enter the Japanese barracks at the Bay (their first patrol report said they had gone past the barracks) you knew that the company commander had sent you on to make sure that one of his patrols, at least, should reach the barracks area.

But you did not care about your squad, which you left by a small stream to wait your return. You went on to the barracks, thinking, Here I am, a separate human being, and near here, perhaps still hiding in the wreckage of the barracks, are other human beings who wish to kill me. And one part of your mind concentrated on this idea, while you observed that the wooden barracks had been blown up from outside by bombs, and from inside by Japanese hand-grenades. You saw sloping wooden platforms for bunks, library cards, a game of Japanese *go* with black and white stones, tins of dried food that had been pierced by bayonets to make them spoil, tubs of pickled *daikon*, sacks of rice, cans of tangerines and of lotus roots.

You had almost forgotten about the Japanese, about these separate human beings who wished to kill you, when you stumbled over a wire. You were deep in the wreckage, you could not get out in time, you waited. There was no hiss, no sputtering, nothing but the steady drizzle and a faint halloo from your faraway squad. The wire ran, you discovered, to a wet grenade that had not gone off.

When you jumped the small stream and rejoined the squad the foggy diffused light was turning to twilight. Somewhere, you kept thinking, another human being like yourself was wondering if his booby trap had worked. The route back into the hills led past one more Japanese hut and you entered it with your nisei. You kicked at a strange protuberance in the floor, and the nisei turned from yellow to lemongreen and rushed out of the hut. You had been kicking at an American destroyer shell, a dud, and now that you knew what they were you saw many more American dud shells pocked all over the landscape.

No longer were you sustained by the wild fervor with which you had advanced. You grew desperately tired in just a few minutes, and you could hardly climb back to the company headquarters. You were groggy, but alert enough to keep a man from drinking sulphuric acid under the impression that it was sake. And you assured the captain that a large block of black material with holes drilled through it was not gunpowder but pressed charcoal, *rentan*. From time to time someone tried to light one of the blocks of pressed charcoal, but nothing would make them burn. You spent the night at company headquarters in a Japanese cave, sitting on the trail of a Japanese mountain gun, you were cold and wet and happy. Outside the cave the men stationed on the company perimeter smoked cigarettes and laughed and talked.

The company captain told how he had killed two Japanese on Attu. He tried to be serious but he was obviously pleased and delighted at having killed, himself, two Japanese, and his men looked up to him for it. You thought that, had you met two Japanese among the huts and killed them, you might have talked and acted in just this way. And in the Japanese forces, somewhere perhaps at this very instant a Japanese captain told his men how he had killed a couple of Americans.

A few days later you were detached from your RCT headquarters, which had been marched from the west to the east coast just a little north of Fishhook Bay. (On that march, unable to carry your thirty pounds of dictionaries over the hills, you had simply thrown them away.)

Sanky joined you in your last hike, north to Gertrude Bay, on the upper eastern shore, and went with you when you left the road to examine Japanese positions. There were dummies cut from wood, like parka-clad sentries and there were dummies stuffed with tundra grass. There were trenches half dug, but looking real enough from the air, and there were real trenches leading up to concealed hill positions. And there were huge manmade caves.

From time to time along the main road roared great tractors drawing gigantic tractor trailers north to Gertrude Cove. Each tractor-trailer contained its colonel or major, his orderly, and a load of personal gear. Each colonel or major was going north to explain to General Ferox that he had known all along that Zhutchka was uninhabited. You and Sanky received a lift from one under the command of Marine Major Begel. There was nothing, Begel said curtly, to interest the historian in the landing on Zhutchka. Grim-browed, he was eager to hurry to the next scene of carnage and re-cord its history. With hardly a bump the mammoth tractor and its trailer crunched over a Japanese bicycle with a twowheeled bicycle trailer attached.

At Gertrude Cove American soldiers and sailors in the hundreds roamed through the wreckage looking for souvenirs. There was the steady popping of Japanese grenades, and screams of pain from men who had lost an arm or an eye or a few fingers in their efforts to disarm the grenades and make souvenirs of them. Here the Japanese buildings had been erected twenty feet below the ground level. By the side of a command building you could see a wounded Japanese dog squatting on a bundle of our surrender leaflets. The dog, snarling and wounded, refused to come out. "We dropped a hundred thousand surrender leaflets," said Sanky, "but I guess that dog just couldn't read."

Like ragpickers American officers and enlisted men slipped through the muddy area clutching their treasures — Japanese officers' opium pipes, Bat cigarettes, rice sacks, pornographic postcards, Japanese condoms, a calendar by which to make love, short skis, red dust for seal stamps, cans of salmon and tangerines (packed only two thirds full), dozens of records of that great Japanese-American favorite, "You are my sunshine, my only sunshine," bam-boo flutes, brown blankets with a blue star in one corner.

General Ferox and Admiral Norcross had established temporary headquarters in the Japanese headquarters building, and here your orders were stamped and endorsed over to a transport which waited in the harbor. The Japanese had been gone from Zhutchka for two weeks before you landed, and General Ferox was busily signing or-ders transferring all aviators who had, in that period, reported light to medium ack-ack fire. They were being sent to SoWesPac, so that they could see at first hand what ack-ack fire was really like. As you waited for your orders you could read the redpainted sign on the wall, "Americans you die like dogs we come back and kill you."

From Gordian you learned that Arkansaw had already returned to Pearl, and that he and his headquarters had got lost in the fog and had circled Zhutchka once before returning to Adak, without even landing. Napoleon had mysteriously developed a strained back just before leaving Adak, and he had never come to Zhutchka at all. Gordian was happily writing a report on the Japanese evacuation of Zhutchka; this was the kind of thing Gordian liked to do best and he had figured out pretty well what had happened.

The simultaneous Japanese occupation of Zhutchka and Attu had been part of the Japanese *jikyō hisshō* — Strenuous Efforts Certain Victory Policy, initiated with the Japanese disaster of Midway. But the Japanese failed to supply Attu and Zhutchka adequately, and though Japanese radio squads cleverly, as so often, analyzed careless American radio traffic and found out in advance about the Attu attack, the Japanese counterlanding plans came to nothing. On May 29 at 2130 Colonel Mountainpass sent his last radio message from Attu: "With deep gratitude for all your kindness, I pray for Your Excellency's victory." Then he killed his sick and wounded and led 150 men in a night suicide charge, in search of honorable death for the emperor. The death on Attu of 2576 Japanese soldiers had "depressed his Imperial Majesty a little" and the Japanese Army and Navy decided to make a real effort to rescue the 5000 troops still left on Zhutchka. They began evacuating men by submarine in June, but this took too long and cost them two submarines. After mid-July the Japanese fleet tried three times to get past the American blockade. They succeeded on July 29, reached the north harbor of Gertrude Cove at 1330, and in fifty minutes they took the 5000 men aboard two cruisers, eleven destroyers and five smaller ships. Behind them they left timed grenades to suggest activity, and they also left booby traps.

Gordian had never received your Japanese diary with its note about "counterradar." No doubt it had been restored to its original status of souvenir.

In one sense, said Gordian, the landing on Zhutchka had been unnecessary. With just the same effort the Americans could have taken and held undefended Paramushiro, almost at the heart of Japan. But that was now impossible. The Japanese had started powerful fortifications there.

Before you left Zhutchka you went with Sanky to see the two biggest caves, each of which could hold over a thousand men. The caves were heavily booby trapped. The passageways held a foot of water, and drifting lumber and strips of bandages caught at your ankles. The booby traps were of the simplest kind, not double or triple like the ingenious German ones.

And you went to see the Japanese airfield, half completed, with little dirt carts that men pushed by hand on metal rails. Already the American engineers had vetoed the Japanese airfield site as impractical because of cross winds. In fact the swearing American engineers thought the whole island of Zhutchka was impractical and they advocated abandoning it in favor of Adak. "They scramble like hell to get these islands," said Sanky, wise in the ways of Pacific war, "and soon as they get one, nobody wants it."

From a nearby cave you heard a familiar voice singing out loud and strong:

> We've reached the land of Arctic fame
> Where we are sure to win a name,
> We love the seals, the fog, the rain,
> And great renown shall surely gain.
> O Behring Sea, bleak Behring Sea . . .

There was a great boom, a puff of black smoke, and out from the cave, as if shot by guns, tumbled Lieutenant Commander Martivet. In fact he had, in a sense, been shot by guns.

In the cave was a Japanese .75 with the breech block left in, and the lanyard ready to pull. Lieutenant Commander Martivet, searching for souvenirs, had pulled it. The gun was aimed to fire its charge into a box of .75 ammunition. It was a stupid booby trap in one way, and yet, in another way, it was perfectly adapted to a certain kind of American mind. You helped Martivet pick himself up, and he limped off with his knapsack of souvenirs, still singing:

> For ne'er can sailor salty be,
> Until he sails the Behring Sea . . .

On the boat ride to your transport, you and Sanky persuaded the coxswain to stop off at a half-sunken Japanese freighter. Down in its wide open hull bobbed an unexploded 500-pound bomb. Two demolition officers were firing their pistols at the bomb.

You recollected that not once had you fired your M–1 rifle all the time you had been on Zhutchka. You raised it to your shoulder and aimed at the hold. But Sanky took the M–1 away from you and examined its muzzle closely. The gas port was clogged. No doubt the gas port had been clogged all during your stay on Zhutchka. Had you fired the M–1 at any time, it might well have blown your head off.

You were parched, your throat burned, you felt a strange taste in your mouth. Like the rash young officer you were, you had looked everywhere for death on Zhutchka, and death had been at your shoulder all the time, waiting on the tip of your rifle for you to fire at another human being.

Some deep affection made itself known between you and Sanky and you both began to laugh, while the demolition officers lazily fired at the 500-pound bomb.

You wanted to take a last look at Zhutchka when your transport pulled out of the harbor, but as so frequently, Zhutchka was covered with fog. You knew you would never see it again.

CHAPTER THIRTEEN

September, 1943

Of the battleships Maryland, West Virginia, Tennessee, California, Pennsylvania *and* Mississippi, *five had been salvaged at Pearl Harbor, and now they came back from the bottom of that harbor to wreak vengeance on the Japanese both afloat and ashore.*

BEGEL, The Battle for Visaya Gulf

❖

STILL WET from swimming at Waikiki beach, you walked down the hot sidewalk. Pupule Street was well shaded with poinciana trees which, in season, covered its tarry surface with bright red flowers. The sidewalks burned your bare feet and you walked quickly.

At the entrance to Pupule Court you halted.

You had been determinedly, doggedly rephrasing your speech — your lecture — in your mind, and yet you had been irritated at the tone of priggishness which its subject brought to the surface.

True, Arkansaw had already explained that the homosexuals were the only people one could talk to, about books, about New York, about plays, about music. By definition, homosexuals did not speak endlessly and monotonously of the drab arts of fuckery.

But you had heard rumors, insubstantial as yet, of an investigation.

Your lecture, vulnerable enough to the mockery of Arkansaw, was driven from your mind by the sight of the group sitting on the little porch, on the lanai, which you shared with Arkansaw. As you hesitated at the entrance, Pupule Court itself seemed to add its low persistent voice to their higher, happier ones.

Overhead the trade winds rustled in the palm fronds, and at night the rats rustled in the palm fronds too. From time to time, either rat-gnawed or ripened, the coconuts fell to the ground. Once in a great while they smashed someone's head, a type of incident never reported in Hawaiian tourist literature.

Pupule Court was the brain child (she had no physical children) of Mrs. Borogove. It consisted, in the beginning, of her two-story house, in which she lived with her husband, a minor factotum in the Comfrey system and a rabid golfer.

Once the Comfrey mortgaged house had been a pleasant enough structure, with a lawn at its sides and back. But Mrs. Borogove, a rentier from topknot to toe, had constructed a detached garage with a one-room apartment over it on the back lawn. In it she put a *pune* or couch-bed, a few rattan chairs, a shower and a toilet, but no cooking equipment or icebox, and like the other landlords of Waikiki she called this tourist slum a studio apartment.

Construction of the garage and the driveway leading to it had left a narrow strip of land beside the drive. On this Mrs. Borogove had erected two twin studio apartments, with room for four single occupants. Each apartment had three windows and its own poin-settia plant.

Next, by walling up a pantry in the main house and inserting an extra door, Mrs. Borogove had added still another studio apartment in back of the main house. Last of all, her keen rentier's eye had spied a small strip of unused land at the back of the garage. On this she had constructed, from cardboard and plywood and Scotch tape, a long and narrow studio leanto (it was hardly fair to call it an apartment), so narrow that guests had to sit in a row on the pune, with no room to stretch out their feet. In heavy rains, a section of the cardboard roof always collapsed.

Although every square inch of Pupule Court was now occupied by studio apartments, hardstand, garage, and house, Mrs. Borogove could not rest until she had rented the main house too, and then she moved herself and her husband to tiny, disagreeable quarters three blocks away, in another rentier's house.

Each apartment paid $45 a month, and the house paid $200 plus key money, so that Mrs. Borogove would have been comfort-ably off, except for her passion for lawsuits. At present she was suing the Hawaiians next door to her in her new apartment. Each night precisely at midnight they held their baby by the feet, upside down, outside her bedroom window, in order to make said infant cry and disturb sleep of said plaintiff (Borogove vs. Liliuokalani, 1942, 43).

Before the war Mrs. Borogove had rented mainly to tourists, to an occasional naval officer, and to the irremovable Prince Mokuaweoweo. When war began she was forced to admit defense workers. With their coming, each studio apartment, including the Prince's, acquired mysterious grease stains, even on the ceilings, as silent tribute to the agility and dirtiness of her new tenants. And then Betty Comfrey, in charge of the Red Cross rent files, had directed you to a vacancy at Pupule Court, and you in turn had found for Mrs. Borogove such notable tenants as Arkansaw, BIJ (Born in Japan) Standish, and Napoleon, who had been advised by the Ration Board to find real passengers for his robin's-egg blue Packard convertible, or else.

During the week Prince Mokuaweoweo got steadily drunker and drunker and turned up his radio louder and louder each night, for drunkenness had the effect of making him deaf. Then the police came to Pupule Court. The police were mostly Hawaiians, like the Prince himself, big and burly, darkly handsome men, and they tenderly lashed him into bed for the night, switched off his radio and took away his five-gallon can of gasoline.

On Sundays his divorced wife, Princess Mokuaweoweo, came to visit him with their dusky daughter, and every Sunday afternoon precisely at three-thirty (to the horrified fascination of Mrs. Borogove) the child was sent out of the garage apartment, the shades went down, and soft ululations purred through Pupule Court, until precisely 4 P.M.

Sundays had a sobering effect on Prince Mokuaweoweo, but by the middle of the week he would be back at his old tricks again, putting gasoline on cockroaches and lighting them as they scampered about his studio apartment floor, or sometimes launching them flaming from his second-story windows. Or he leaned out the window and spat gasoline from his mouth over a lighted match. Or he fell asleep in bed while smoking a cigar and using the top of the gasoline can as an ashtray.

From time to time these habits set his mattress, the curtains, or the apartment itself on fire. And the police would come, and, often enough, the fire department, and the fires would go out, the floors would mysteriously be repaired, the curtains would be replaced and new mattresses be found.

Mrs. Borogove's lawyer advised her strongly not to take this matter up in the courts, for all Hawaiians knew that Prince Mokuaweoweo still maintained close relations with one of the few remaining *kahunas* or witch doctors, and no one would act against him. And the Prince was not only superstitiously feared, he was loved by many Hawaiians, for as a young man he had been a great athlete whether in field, ocean, or bed. He had been on the Hawaiian track team, he had swum from island to island, and he had slept with most of the great American heiresses during their Hawaiian tours of duty.

Enjoined from this promising dusky lawsuit, Mrs. Borogove did what she could to uphold white purity against the dark encroaching tides. She was all the stricter with her new young ensigns. "There'll be none of That in the evening," she advised each in turn, patting her topknot. "That?" you had asked, honestly puzzled. And then, comprehending, you had laughed ironically, and for several evenings Mrs. Borogove had conducted night patrol outside Pupule Court.

All this then, was the voice, or rather the voices, of Pupule Court. And next to it on either side, and across the street as well, were similar courts, with girl secretaries, defense workers, officers and enlisted men, all jammed around the central hardstand or garage. And there were parties, every night great noisy parties, so loud and wild that only the evening before a girl had been raped in the court next to Pupule Court and no one had noticed her screams. And after curfew at 10 P.M. the voices, the music, the tinkle of glasses continued until midnight or so, when once more the rustle of palm fronds, and of the rats in the palm fronds, could be heard clearly again, in one of the hundreds of places where men stopped for a while during a war.

You stood at the entrance to your driveway, listening to the squeal of brakes, and a heavy, dull crash, followed by a tearing metallic crumpling sound. And then a short feminine scream.

Two cars had collided at the intersection just above Pupule Court and one had toppled on its side. From the window of the damaged car crawled a defense worker in aloha shirt and khaki pants. On his feet again, he remembered, crawled back in, found a bottle of whiskey and crawled out again. "Not safe," he said, pointing to the precious fifth. "Not safe in there." A police car appeared at the beach end of Pupule Street and drove slowly toward the accident.

Your beach towel still draped over your shoulders, you ran to the upset car. The door was jammed but you wrenched it open, cutting your thumb on the broken glass. You tried to help the girl out. She was not hurt, but she resisted your help because her blouse and brassière had been torn off. Then she recognized you and smiled. It was Maria, the Filipina messenger girl. Quickly you gave her your beach towel. She pulled it around her shoulders very slowly, letting you have a good look at her deep, perfect form.

Once out of the car, she noticed your cut. She wiped at the blood with a corner of the towel, then drew your forearm between her breasts and sucked the wound clean. The towel became disarrayed and she let you help her with it. Smiling and waving back at you, she and the defense worker went off in the police car. Another policeman stayed at the scene, taking notes.

"An old, and very dear friend?" said Betty Comfrey. She walked back with you to your tiny lanai. Prince Mokuaweoweo appeared at the garage apartment window and launched a flaming cockroach in the air. "Kala mai ia kapale," he said politely. "Hot."

"My God," said Betty Comfrey, bandaging your finger in approved Red Cross style. "Is it like this every afternoon here?"

This question, addressed to the air of Pupule Street, was answered from the air of Pupule Street by a loud, piercing blast of music from next door where the rape had taken place:

> Mairzy doats and dozy doats and liddle lamzy divey.
> A kiddley divey too, wouldn't you?

Arkansaw groaned and sprinted inside his studio apartment, one wall of which was shared with yours. He turned on his record player to full volume and held out the window Stravinsky's *Rites of Spring*. Sexual thumpings from the Rites battled the liddle lambzies. The music went off next door, and there was a piercing scream. You wondered whether to call the police.

Arkansaw reappeared holding a tray on which rested liqueur glasses, a bunch of bananas, a bottle of Benedictine and a note. The note was addressed to you from Mrs. Borogove and read simply, "Ants, ants, ants."

Betty Comfrey burst into tears.

"I wish I could be free like you," she cried.

"Honeychile," said Napoleon, exuberantly embracing her and belting her on the shoulder. His cure for all ailments was physical exertion. "Let's climb a mountain," he said, pushing a whole banana into his ample mouth. Betty Comfrey laughed, her eyes shining. In a simple white dress, which showed off her slender bare arms and shoulders, and with her long golden legs and goldwashed hair, she seemed the perfection of elegant breeding. She blushed slightly under your steady gaze and looked away. You had an odd feeling that the two of you had understood each other, though you had said nothing.

"We can't climb that one," said Betty Comfrey, rejecting the mountain to which Napoleon was pointing.

"How about that one," said Arkansaw, a quirky expression on his face.

"We can't climb that one either," said Betty. Then she explained very simply, "Daddy doesn't own it."

"Well, let's climb a mountain Daddy does own," said Napoleon impatiently, accustomed to Getting at the Heart of a Problem.

Sanky tried the tiny glass of Benedictine, put it down politely, only half consumed, and lifted up the kit bag he carried with him. From it came a bottle of sour mash bourbon.

After first offering it to the others, he took a long, easy swallow from the neck of the bottle. "They say if you wave a bottle like this a girl comes running down the corridor of your hotel, but no one came last night." In tune with the ever louder music from Prince Mokuaweoweo's apartment he hummed, "I'm not much to look at, nothin' to see." Betty stared at him, fascinated. You had a vision of the high school senior class visiting its first settlement house.

But Sanky remained natural, and amused.

"Your name's not Sanky, is it?" asked BIJ Standish.

"It's really Polymeropoulos," said Sanky. It was impossible to tell whether he was serious or not.

138

"You were on Attu?" said Betty Comfrey in her fine, educated voice.

Sanky sipped his whiskey from a glass unobtrusively brought out by Arkansaw. He was a solid, tough and sensual man, and yet he began to seem to you more subtle than you had supposed on Adak and Zhutchka.

"Attu was the worst," he said. "Of course then your friends from Q came up and helped us conquer three police dogs on Zhutchka. Operation Fubar."

"Fouled up beyond all recognition," BIJ Standish eagerly explained. "I was on Attu myself." BIJ, born in Japan of missionary parents, had retained his evangelicism, but without any powerful interest in religion. Instead, he had turned his missionary drive to the religion of democracy, as he understood democracy. As Arkansaw said, he could not crush a cockroach without first pointing out to the hapless insect that it might so easily, with a little more education, have been a *democratic* cockroach.

And BIJ collected democratic atrocity stories, an occupation parallel to that which Feverton had assigned you, in your collection of Japanese atrocity stories. Given the slightest chance, BIJ would go on for hours about how a Marine colonel on Adak had asked him to bring back from Zhutchka a necklace of Japanese ears for his child to play with. Or he told of how enlisted men had collected gold teeth and testicles for display in San Francisco bars. Or he told how a lieutenant colonel had lined up his seven Attu prisoners and accused them, to their very faces, of being apes.

A car backfired on Pupule Street and BIJ flattened himself on the ground, a stunt he often pulled to indicate nerves shattered from his two landings on Guadalcanal and Attu. Betty Comfrey's fine eyes widened in surprise and she wondered, no doubt, whether she was going to be called on a second time for a display of Red Cross expertise. But when no one else noticed him, BIJ sat up again and accepted a glass of Benedictine. He refused a banana chaser, however, to indicate that he was not appreciated as he should be.

An impatient honk from a Navy station wagon announced the arrival of Lieutenant Hobbes of the Supply Department, Betty Comfrey's most insistent suitor. He wore whites, and the Pacific

Campaign Ribbon, awarded, according to Napoleon (a stern critic of the ribbons of others), for successful delivery to the Hawaiian Sea Frontier of the one millionth can of pork and beans since the Pearl Harbor attack.

With a graceful swirl of her skirts, and a lovely glimpse of her knees, she settled by Lieutenant Hobbes.

"I love them all," said Sanky appreciatively. Napoleon, Arkansaw and BIJ Standish departed to a Mormon square dance, and you and Sanky sat alone on the little lanai.

"I'd like to play tiddly with her." He shrugged. "I suppose you think the water's shallowest where it bubbles."

On your door he saw the latest note addressed to you from Mrs. Borogove. It read: "You have been flushing your toilet too much lately."

"There's only one thing to do with a note like that," said Sanky. He went inside your apartment and did it. He came out on the lanai again, holding a stagy photograph of Leilani. She wore flowers round her neck and sat on the ground with a formal skirt carefully spread out before her.

"I suppose this is Miss Right? A little too dark for the home folks?"

Prince Mokuaweoweo appeared at the window of his apartment. He was holding a glass. "To Mrs. Borogove," he said, "okole maluna."

"What's that mean?"

"Bottoms up." Agreeably you all drank bottoms up, and Prince Mokuaweoweo retired. But you filled the water bucket and got out the number of the nearest fire department, just in case.

An expression on your face, a tone of voice over which you had no conscious control, must have conveyed something to Sanky. He examined the photograph more seriously. You had once again the uneasy feeling that you had been underrating Sanky.

"She's broken it off, hasn't she?"

"There was nothing to break off."

Sanky got up to go. "Crazy," he said. He was smiling. You shook hands. "You don't think much of Colonel Mist, do you?"

He paused, savoring his next remark. "Colonel Mist said you were one of the brightest junior officers he had ever seen. He also said you were a complete damn fool to go roaming all over Zhutchka like that, the second day you were ashore."

You winced. You usually thought of yourself as understanding and analyzing other people. Not the opposite. Was Sanky suggesting indirectly that Leilani Kim might know you better than you knew yourself?

"Crazy," Sanky said again. The word echoed in Pupule Court.

Prince Mokuaweoweo leaned amiably from his window. "In Hawaiian," he said, "the word for 'crazy' is 'pupule.'" He lit a match, and spurted a mouthful of gasoline over it, in a long falling flame. His curtains began to smolder.

"You take the water bucket up," you said. "I'll cross the street and phone the fire department."

"No, you take the water up," said Sanky reasonably, "and I'll phone."

"Prince," you called, running up the stairs. "Prince Mokuaweoweo. Put the cap back on the gas tank."

CHAPTER FOURTEEN

November, 1943

> *Step by step — Guadalcanal, Attu, Rarawa, New
> Guinea, Kwajalein, Peleliu — we had moved toward
> Visaya, the hard underbelly of the Japanese dragon.*
> BEGEL, The Battle for Visaya Gulf

✿

COMMANDER WOLFE's face flushed with rage. Captain Feverton
stood at his side, with the expression of a drowning man who
silently appeals for help.

Wolfe was comparing two charts. One, the attack chart recently
printed for Operation LANDGRAB, showed gun and trench positions on Rarawa, and reef and beach depths. On this map, the
island of Rarawa had an axis of 139°. The map, made up from
a study of Kodachrome air and submarine photo reconnaissance,
and from prisoner reports, had been assembled in Q.

The other chart, in Japanese, showed much the same trenches.
But it exposed many more reefs than the first map. It revealed
headquarters posts, and 8-inch gun positions marked Vickers-
Singapore. On it, Rarawa had an axis of 128°. A typed note attached
to the map read "Wake Island."

You were immediately sure whose typed note this was, and who
had mislabeled the captured Japanese map.

"This is your chance," said Gordian. You were astonished to
see his lips set in a vindictive, ferine line. This was a side of
Gordian's character you had not suspected. But Feverton's childishly wrinkled face made you ask yourself what Sanky would have
done. Napoleon tried to urge you on with a quick flicflac jump
and a V for Victory signal.

But when Wolfe dismissed Q, you still had said nothing.

Prantz went immediately to the desk of the shaken Feverton and began to talk rapidly, with many shrugs of his plump shoulders.

You returned to your final report on the Sendai Force. In the night attack against Port Arthur it had first won fame. In the Russo-Japanese War, the war which, like all wars, had whelped its autobiographical fiction — *Human Bullets* — *Nikudan*. And, so the myth, continuing irresistibly, grew, three Japanese soldiers had later made themselves into carriers of a bangalore torpedo, blowing up themselves along with a path through the Chinese barbed wire. No difference that the story was not true, for the Japanese believed it, and even made a monument of their myth.

But as yet you had heard no significant tales of Japanese human bullets in this war. Even though such an attack would surely surpass all standards of *gyokusai,* of death for the Emperor. You wrote out another card for your files. At its head was typed NIKUDAN.

"When the cart stops," said Arkansaw, "what should the driver do? Whip the cart or the horse? In other words, why this sudden tenderness about Feverton?"

"I wanted to tell Wolfe."

"I sense an attack of severe rockhappiness, Classen. You'd better come to the party tonight at Green Point."

A long level look, daring you. Then he said, "I regard prudery as the worst kind of avarice."

"Lao-Tse never said that."

He recognized your work folder. "The second Sendai Division. Giant snails for food, cultivation of papaya trees, first annihilate the enemy on the shore, then annihilate the enemy at the first line, and last, annihilate the enemy at the inner line."

Arkansaw fingered other papers in the folder. "Plans to occupy Midway. Drunken, drugged suicide charge on CACTUS, written up by Bulflash in famous dispatch from safety of adjacent island."

"There's more to it than that." You read from a newly found diary. Before the suicide charge, the hospitalized and sick patients had called out *gyokusai da, gyokusai da* — time for honorable death for the emperor. And then the healthy troops, among them the diarist, had killed them. And there had been the ceremony of *yōhai* — bowing in the direction of the emperor's palace and worshiping him. And a last entry of the diarist, that soldiers with malarial fever, too badly wounded even to know that this was the banzai attack, had called out in their final torments "*Kaasan Kaasan*" — "Mommy, Mommy."

There the diary ended.

Arkansaw flipped the diary back on your desk. "Gordian says that only Americans and Japanese call for their mommies when they die."

Prantz joined you. He had a sharp, knowledgeable smile on his thicklipped face. He took the cigar out of his mouth. "Wolfe wants to see ya," he said, insolently adding the "sir" just as you were about to remind him to do so.

Speculating what Wolfe had on his mind, you absentmindedly observed that the *Wyorada* was apparently flat on her side, held in this curious position by a hundred threads that tied the ancient dreadnaught to the shore.

The cramped flag plot of the battleship was crowded. On a plexiglas chart a yeoman crayoned ship positions, writing mirror style so that the officers on the other side of the transparent chart could read more easily. When a messenger entered, the lights automatically went off until the door was closed, so that no light could penetrate the blackout hangings, and the yeoman at the plexiglas cursed softly.

The battleship was the command ship both for the convoy of troops, of which it formed the center, and, in a general sense, for the carrier task force 150 miles away, awaiting an expected sortie of the Japanese fleet. Should the convoy be spotted by Japanese search planes before it reached the immediate vicinity of Rarawa, Operation LANDGRAB was to be canceled. Admiral Norcross could communicate with the other ships in the troop convoy by TBS — talk between ships — but there was radio silence between his ships and the carrier task force and Pearl Harbor — unless he had to order cancellation.

At long intervals, Admiral Norcross ordered a change in the zigzag pattern of the convoy. To make such a turn, and make it properly, to know in the dark just how each ship would answer her helm — given a following sea with waves of a certain height —

all that demanded a lifetime at sea and a knowledge of every ship in the Navy. All that, Admiral Norcross had.

In a corner lay the precious stack of corrected map overlays. But you had found there was no time to change the plan of attack, and no way, until radio silence ended, to inform the shore bombardment group of the new targets.

Through your thoughts there no longer raged the wild and primitive impressions that had overwhelmed you in Wolfe's office. True, Wolfe had never accused you of the mistake, but the triumphant grin of Prantz and the averted gaze of Feverton had made it clear why you were ordered to take the overlays to Admiral Norcross at sea.

You were becalmed now in an icy clarity of mind, far from the storming enthusiasm which had driven you across Zhutchka on that sophomoric second day. You seemed to observe yourself as if from a great height, and you were in a state in which no act of your own could have caused you a moment's surprise, for every act, from cowardice to heroism, seemed possible.

The door swung and the flag plot automatically blacked out. You blinked when the lights went on, and saw the softly swearing yeoman crayoning in a Japanese search plane on the plexiglas chart.

Every ten minutes a new position report moved the search plane an inch or so toward the convoy, in an irregular pattern. Admiral Norcross watched its position changes with an abstracted air.

In a corner stood General Ferox, his burly arms braced against the angle of the bulkheads as if to compel the armorplate to stretch and grow bigger. "There's no place on this ship where I'd like to die," said General Ferox. His blunt face was sallow green, not with seasickness, but with claustrophobia.

The battleship wallowed round clumsily, on a new zig ordered by Admiral Norcross to evade the search plane. They waited for the next position report. The plane, whether by accident or design, had conformed to their turn. Several men muttered to each other, and one man sighed.

From Combat Intelligence Center, deep within the bowels of the battleship, came the word that the plane, on this leg of its course, would be within range of the convoy's antiaircraft guns in three minutes.

Erratically, the plane seemed to turn back.

Perhaps it had not sighted them? The yeoman was about to erase the first part of its track when, in a whisper, you asked him to leave it on. You tried to recall the odd search patterns you had collected, before Feverton had taken them from you. Not all Japanese search patterns were simple and obvious affairs. A few had been mathematical nightmares.

And in a few minutes the plane turned again, now heading directly for the base course, though still at some distance because of Norcross's ingenious zig. But several ships had lost station, and Admiral Norcross did not intend to change the base course for a while, until they had recovered their rightful slots.

The orders recalling the convoy had been written up in Pearl. The Flag Secretary held them, waiting the pleasure of Admiral Norcross.

On a scratch pad you tried to fit the plane's path into one of several patterns. With a borrowed protractor you measured angles on the plexiglas. Admiral Norcross observed your activities without apparent interest. Nothing worked. Then you remembered the wind drift.

"Classen," said Admiral Norcross sharply.

The Japanese plane would shortly intersect the course of the convoy.

The lights went out, and an enlisted radio man entered. The Japanese plane, now nearing them, was sending a radio message. The radioman who could copy *kana* had written it out. The message blank read TORA TORA TORA.

Then you heard motors, unsynchronized, Japanese style. The plane was overhead.

Admiral Norcross's eyes seemed to dwindle in size. "Has he spotted us?"

You tried to visualize the search patterns. One was a combination of interlaced triangles. Another was a meander. A third was —

The plane turned again, as if leaving them. The phone rang softly. The plane was sending again. TORA TORA TORA.

"It means tiger," you said. "Tiger, tiger, tiger."

Admiral Norcross nodded. "Code," he grunted.

"It changes every day."

"The destroyers can still shoot him down."

Your nostrils widened, and you said, by some deeprooted hunter's instinct that you hardly knew existed within you, "He hasn't spotted us."

Admiral Norcross contemplated you with a glance that was almost hostile. "Could he be pretending not to have spotted us? Is this a trap?"

Yūgeki, you thought, the favored device of ambush attack. Then you remembered the simple booby traps of Zhutchka. Ambush attack would surely come, but not in this form.

"He's on the return leg of his search pattern."

Admiral Norcross did not seem either satisfied or dissatisfied with your answer. A few minutes later, when the Japanese plane had flown clear off the plexiglas chart, he sent his flag secretary to get your full name and serial number. Norcross had a reputation for never forgiving a mistake.

"Montgomery Classen, Ensign, USNR, 236781." When you curtly gave your name, it was as though you were talking about someone else, that odd chance acquaintance — yourself.

Waist-deep in water at the end of the pier, you got rid of your reversible snap-fastened coat and trousers, green inside and brown outside, designed so that like a chameleon you could change color with your surroundings. Except for two men with parts of a mountain howitzer strapped to their backs, you were alone. You had no recollection of how you had reached the sea end of the 1100 yard long pier, and you did not know what had happened to the rest of the desperate boatload commanded by General Ferox.

In the lagoon, a solitary rocket ship, with six racks holding seventy-two rockets each, paraded up and down the beach. From time to time it fired a rack. In a corner of the lagoon, a command ship hoisted Blue Peter and boats formed up around her. One of the Singapore guns shelled the transports, and they moved sluggishly seaward. You caught a glimpse of the red-hot fourteen-inch shells in an answering battleship salvo.

Only a few men of the 18,000-man invasion force had managed to make it to the shore. A few more men were scattered along one side of the long pier. Corpses and abandoned boats rocked in the dodging tide of the lagoon. One whole regiment had disappeared, and 75 out of 120 new amphtracs had been destroyed by shore batteries. The dodging tide kept out the regular landing boats, and by noon 1500 Americans were dead.

Every time the battleship fired, the radio tubes broke, but before all the spare tubes had gone, Ferox had learned that the 8th Army Air Force had bombed the wrong atoll by mistake.

At Pamama Atoll south of Rarawa, the landing was going easily, and the son of one of America's most important political persons had been given a Silver Star the moment he touched shore. Admiral Norcross had ordered these ships to return to Rarawa for badly needed gunfire support. They had signaled that the correspondents had to have a repetition of the Silver Star ceremony for the newsreel cameramen, and the ships could not return till evening.

Admiral Norcross initialed this signal with an evil expression on his face. Well aware of how Bulflash had covered the front at Guadalcanal and Attu, he ordered the poor man's Pyle into General Ferox's boat. You shoved off, a rubber raft full of wounded bumped against the battleship, and Admiral Norcross burst into tears.

Once in the boat, you had understood that Ferox, thinking the battle lost, intended to go where the battle was, and get himself killed losing it. Without once moving you rode the boat to the reef. You had then waded five hundred yards through water and coral and plunging fire — you must have done so, even though you could remember nothing. Now at the end of the long pier, you thought of your Zhutchka antics, of the heroic patroller who had charged over the hills in search of the departed enemy.

This time you checked the action of your .45. You had four clips for it, each tied in its own rubber condom. In your small combat pack you had three units of K rations, a set of underwear and a pair of socks, a shaving kit, toothbrush, spoon, and cup. And just two dictionaries this time. In your belt was a collapsible shovel.

You huddled waist-deep in the chilly blue water, and shivered. A Japanese machine gun spat at the pier. It was firing from one of the wooden latrines the Japanese had built out over the lagoon. Over one hundred Americans, well fanned out, started from the outer reef into the lagoon and toward the machine gun. Two or three managed to reach the latrine, they threw grenades, and the machine gun stopped. But the other men fell into the water or withdrew. Circles of vomit lapped against the pier. Soon another Japanese machine gunner was firing from the wooden shambles.

You thought of Gordian's constant, of a huge nude pasted on the curved ceiling of a submarine, of the clocks in the office of Commander Wolfe, of the touch of Lani's arm in yours as you said goodnight, of crow flight over piney woods.

Gone was the wild, primitive impulse to move forward, to reach the enemy. All that seemed, in your floating sensations of observing yourself, the actions of a stranger to yourself. But no fear took the place of impulse, instead you were in the grip of a mystical clarity that demanded your impartial admiration of the few surviving green coconut trees and of the red and purple hatchings on the water that heralded sunset.

A Japanese propaganda leaflet floated within reach of your hand: "For Reckless Yankee Doodle — Did you know about powerful Japanese Nautical Air had annihilated your Fleet and along with sending 1,289 and more airframes into sea waters had sunk 31 carriers 12 several battleships and a few cruisers."

A few more men joined your little group at the end of the pier, and in the twilight Reckless Yankee Doodle sloshed unobtrusively toward the beach. The Japanese machine gunners picked up your silhouettes immediately, they were low and accurate, very good you thought admiringly, oh jolly good shooting, and you scuttled crabwise over the beach and tumbled into a shallow foxhole near a coconut log revetment. A mortar shell landed squashily near you, and a man flung his cold wet arm over your shoulder. You complained softly, but machine gun fire swept the beach and he did not take his arm away. The beach was zeroed in, the machine gunners never stopped, and the arm began to tighten round your neck. A star shell turned the beach green, a burst of shells in succession blinded you, and you rolled the dead man out of your hole. Just over the embankment a Japanese spoke in English, "One two three, you can't catch me." You pushed the dead man farther away and four bullets softly plunked into him.

The star shells showed more and more Americans crawling onto the beach, behind the revetment, and you thought you heard the savage cursing voice of General Ferox bullying men on. Once you reached out to touch a passing American, but your hand closed on a large land crab.

You were pleased to find that you had no fear; still, at 2 A.M. you had an irresistible urge to defecate. You used your shovel as a receptacle and flung the matter out. There was a howl of rage nearby, quickly stifled when it drew Japanese fire. General Ferox, you thought. You lay on your back in your foxhole, laughing silently to yourself like a madman. Gordian's constant, you said.

Again came the idiotic Japanese taunt, "One two three, you can't catch me."

That morning General Ferox went along the embankment, ordering men forward. He wore his pearl-handled pistols in brass-studded holsters with leather drawstrings. "Go ahead," said Ferox grimly. You tried to explain that your job was to stay at headquarters. His hand tightened on his pistol. Suddenly you knew that Ferox was capable of shooting you if you disobeyed.

You tried not to look at the dead American you had pushed out of your foxhole. But you could not help seeing that his eyeballs were black. Since 0530, behind you the falling tide had revealed hundreds of American soldiers, their dead ears and mouths packed with sand.

Painfully flat, you wriggled over the embankment and crawled along the coral sand. You were in a throng of Japanese, all dead, all suicides, by their own rifles, by their tap grenades.

You had lived, then, through a suicide charge, without ever firing a shot in your own defense.

Ferox was over the embankment now and you wriggled slowly on, elbows and forearms bloody against the sharp coral sand. You knew that Ferox meant to kill the Japanese, or be killed himself.

Men recognized you were an officer from your .45. They crawled after you, quite aware that you did not know what you were doing, but they followed you anyway. Then you reached a line where everyone had stopped.

Ahead was a sunken command post, like the turret of a dreadnaught, with concrete walls six feet thick, scabbed by bombs and shells, but still intact. Ferox, near you, waited until he understood the Japanese lanes of fire. These had a narrow traverse and were deadly from the front. But you could, with luck, go between the lanes from the side. At either end of the American line, two flame-thrower men wabbled forward. You all fired to cover their lurching progress. With a last dancing movement they reached the top of the command post. But they did not ignite their flame throwers. To your intense surprise, they emptied their contents apparently into the roof, and then scrambled back, leaving the tank behind. On the return trip one was hit. Crabwise, he scurried into the sand. He was silent, and made no cry for a medic.

Now, at Ferox's harsh orders, the fire from your side redoubled, and a third man with a flame thrower edged through the traverse lines. He went slowly and steadily, one hundred feet, seventy-five feet, fifty feet — and then he fired for the roof in a long smoky blast that turned bright red, flickered up past the main port, and searched out the roof. There was a startling gush of flame, and fires came out of the vents. Then, from what had seemed merely more concrete, a thick door creaked open and dark cinders of men stumbled out, still with voices that could scream. The line of Americans started to fire, then stopped in horror. The men were burning. And you shot again, all of you shot furiously until there was no more writhing on the ground.

On the third day of the fighting the Japanese corpses began to blow up like frogs and burst. Everywhere there was the smell of flesh, and of roasted cindered flesh. And everywhere maggots ate into the dead flesh. On the third night one hundred Japanese with bamboo spears charged a machine gunner on your left. The American machine gunner got ninty-nine Japanese before the hundredth man with a spear transfixed him. Ferox, wounded in the arm, never rested, never waited for artillery to come up. On he drove the troops against the third of the island, in two isolated sectors, which was still held by the Japanese.

But you returned to the beach and strained over scorched and soggy documents. You knew that there had been 1497 men in the 7th Special Naval Landing Force, 1122 men in the 3rd Special Base Force, 1247 men in the 11th Pioneers, 970 men in the 4th Fleet Laborers' Battalion (half of these Koreans). And there were a few mysterious orders of no interest to Ferox which you saved for the files of Q, on future use of a *kessenbutai* — a decisive battle force.

And there were the first references you had seen to a *sō kessen* — a general decisive battle for which all Japanese commanders were to prepare. Idly you noted that many of the saved documents had been found at the air base headquarters of Rarawa. The Japanese air force, no doubt, like your own, had its own notions about security.

On the fifth day of the fighting, just twentyfive yards from you a soldier held up his helmet to show his buddy four holes in it, none of which had killed him. He laughed, and, dispassionately, you hit the ground by instinct, watching yourself take cover, and watching the mucky red burst of the mortar shell engulf and dissolve the soldier with four holes in his helmet. You picked yourself up, and went on with your translating.

Prisoner of war Wada, whose name meant Japanesefield, began his souvenir flag business on the seventh day. By that time, half the Americans on the island were souvenir hunters from the ships in the lagoon. Japanesefield painted Rising Sun flags on parachute silk and wrote signatures in different handwritings across the face of the flags. The soldiers shot these flags, ten flags at a time, to give them a realistic touch, and sold them to the souvenir hunters.

Japanesefield had been very amused by the American army bombers. Each time they had come over Rarawa they had deliberately dropped their bombs in the water, out of range of the Japanese ack-ack. All the men on the island used to come out and watch the American Army bombers. Japanesefield had a fine memory and he gave you all the dates of the air raids. When you returned to Q, you found that that part of your report had been cut out of the mimeographed version. Cut out by the Navy, to avoid a fight with the Army and General MacDazzle.

Japanesefield, a petty officer second class, in the Yokosuka Third Special Base Force, had been trained as a tank driver. He had taken part in battles at Shanghai, at Nanking, at Rabaul, and he had been on a transport during the battle of Midway.

But before all that, he had taken part in Japan's undeclared war with Russia, the battle of Nomanhan in Manchuria. He had been captured by the Russians, and even so he had escaped. Japanesefield was tough.

Tough enough to volunteer for Rarawa duty after a brief spell of home leave.

On the first day of the landing he had seen a tremendous fleet on the horizon. The very first destroyer salvo hit the main ammunition dump and caused a frightening explosion. The rest of the ammunition and stores had been destroyed by battleship, Navy plane and destroyer attacks. Then he saw boats approaching under covering fire — the boats sank, he saw American soldiers die, he watched American boats hung up on the coral from the safety of a hidden tank in the *kesshibutai* — the decisive battle force.

At night, and sometimes in the daytime, he and his fellows darted out and ran back and forth looking for food, and terrified the American soldiers. The second night he led a tank attack. In the middle of the attack he lost his nerve and returned to his hidden position, but the engine stopped and he was surrounded by American soldiers. Then the engine started again and he escaped.

When their tank fuel was gone, the tank had to become a gun platform, and the first command post was abandoned. Two of his friends were killed by a naval shell and he wept until he could not see. By the third night the Japanese had lost control of the coast and of the air. They sent a message to the Emperor that they would commit *gyokusai* — only *gyokusai* was left. They were in an air raid shelter waiting for night when an enemy plane discovered and bombed them. The trench turned to hell, and a flame thrower burned them.

Petty Officer Japanesefield lost consciousness for a whole day. When he at last woke up he was pinned down hand and foot and couldn't move. Only gradually did he realize that a burned corpse lay across his chest, and a burned thigh and leg across his foot. He could not believe he was alive, but he had only burns on his face. In the evening he came out. All was quiet, the Americans had even lit cooking fires. He had no weapons, no food, no water, no companions.

He was taken prisoner when he was searching for food.

"I knew my orders were to fight," said Petty Officer Japanesefield. "But I had no strength to fight, I had nothing to fight with, not a sword, not even a bamboo spear."

He stared at you, seeking some answer in your face. "It is regrettable that I lived," he said, "but I lived."

He went back to his flag painting. Every once in a while, instead of writing Japanese signatures, he wrote across the Rising Sun ball, "Death to the American Devils."

In the daytime you worked on Feverton's latest Idea that Would Win the War. This was the plan for painting Mount Fuji black. All night long, B 29's would drop cans of black paint on Mount Fuji. The next morning Japanese, as far away as Tokyo on a clear day, would wake up and see that Mount Fuji had turned black. Realizing the power of America, the Japanese would surrender. "Why not paint it red?" you asked ironically. "For greater visibility."

"Classen," said Feverton, pleased and smiling his detachable smile. "Rarawa's made a man of you. That's what I call constructive criticism." And you were made his assistant on the project.

In the evenings, when you could manage it, you went out to the hospital at the point of entrance to Pearl Harbor. First you had gone there to see Arkansaw, who was having a longish bout with mononucleosis. And one evening you had met Chaplain Simon, much thinner now, no longer rounded and chubby.

"Do you play checkers badly?" asked Simon. You allowed that you played checkers badly. You were needed, then, to play checkers with Gunner.

At first Gunner refused. "I don't want to bother people," said Gunner quietly. He stitched away at a leather wallet he was making. He lay in his bed in a highceilinged room. It was almost impossible to move him, because the bullet was at his spine. At any time, in a year, or two years, in five minutes, the bullet would move, and that would be the end of CPO Gunner. Perhaps the Navy would have insisted on flying Gunner back home, if he had not been an orphan.

Gunner had learned in the orphanage to be neat and clean and industrious and not to bother people and to keep his nose clean. "I always kept my nose clean," he said with satisfaction. He had no relatives, no girl friends — or none to whom he cared to write. "Tough titty," he said laconically. Then he added with a friendly grin, "For them and me."

Gunner went straight from the orphanage into the Navy. The Navy was his whole life. At the age of fifty or fifty-five he could retire, into an older men's Navy orphanage in Philadelphia. He liked checkers and he liked to play with you because he could easily beat you, and the doctors had forbidden him to play with the other enlisted men — their games were too exciting for him.

Gunner had been on the carrier that exploded the night before the Rarawa landing. There were still a lot of burned crewmen from the carrier at Hospital Point. Her deck had flown one hundred feet in the air. A machine gun bullet from an exploding, unmanned plane had hit Gunner in the spine. He refused to discuss it, saying only, "Tough titty."

Gunner liked to read Bulflash's columns, and admired very much the ones about Rarawa. Bulflash, said Gunner, had the enlisted man's point of view.

You had heard that Bulflash had been so shocked by actual combat he had been unable to write at all. But he had recovered quickly, and now titled his column, and his forthcoming book about Rarawa, "I Was There."

Chaplain Simon never explained his relation to Gunner. From time to time he looked in at the two of you playing checkers, his eyes serious and squinting painfully, as though he were looking down into a great depth of water.

Once you entered Gunner's high cool room and found Chaplain Simon on his knees beside the starchsheeted bed of Gunner. Gunner gazed at the ceiling. "I don't like to bother people," he said patiently, as if explaining something complex to a child, something he thought you all might understand when you were older. And he went on stitching at his leather wallet, with small, intricate stitches in a meander pattern.

One day you found all the room doors closed in Gunner's corridor, and out of Gunner's room a sheet-covered figure was wheeled down the hall. You stood against the wall, until the cart was gone.

The next day you went with Chaplain Simon to Haleiwa Naval Cemetery, a temporary cemetery — in war even the cemeteries had a dubious air of impermanence. Each day the Catholic and Protestant chaplains said their respective burial services, mostly for the skeletons from the waterfilled compartments of the *Wyorada* and the *Arizona*. Every third day or so the Jewish chaplain came, thus allowing for the Jewish percentage.

The *Wyorada* and *Arizona* corpses were a real problem, complained the CPO of the cemetery. The flesh got detached from the bones and floated to the ceilings of the waterfilled compartments.

The cemetery was very well run. There was a firing squad and taps were blown, and the flag was dipped in salute. There was a bulldozer permanently attached to the cemetery; each day it pushed a deep trench a little further along, and then went back and covered over the newly lowered boxes. When taps blew for CPO Gunner the bulldozer clanked forward, pushing the dirt in front of it.

That evening you called Leilani and tried to tell her not about yourself but about Gunner and how you behaved when taps blew for Gunner and how Chaplain Simon finally pulled you off the bulldozer before you could carry out your plan to end the war by destroying all the military cemeteries.

You were confused and perhaps you were a little drunk, but after a while you got it through your head that Leilani wanted to see you.

The wallet Gunner had been stitching disappeared. Perhaps one of the orderlies liked the meander pattern and took it. It was a funny thing about Gunner's carrier. More men died on the carrier than in storming ashore on Rarawa. Bulflash and several other correspondents wrote books about Rarawa, about Operation LAND-GRAB. But no one ever wrote a book about Gunner's carrier.

CHAPTER FIFTEEN

December, 1943

> *A pilot who had used up his bombs against the advancing Japanese battleships called back for instructions and was advised to strafe the battleships; when he had used his machinegun ammunition he called again and was advised to make dummy runs — and did so until he ran out of gas.*
>
> BEGEL, The Battle for Visaya Gulf

*

CONFUSED by smoke, by talk, by the raw odor of Five Ulcers Rum, you went out on the lanai, and listened to the tinkling blues from the termite-ridden piano:

> He pulled down the shade
> But he didn't make the grade
> In Naval Housing Area TWO.

Leilani, barefooted, and strikingly pretty came out and slipped her arm in yours. Then she motioned, smiling, to your shoes. You slipped them off, and she began, softly now so as not to attract the attention of the defense workers and their girls inside the house, to do a hula. She sang a rollicking song in a low, sweet, voice:

> I've had the blues bout my momma,
> Blues bout my papa, blues bout my sister Sue,
> I've had the blues bout my brother,
> Now I've got the blues about you.

The sound of air raid sirens made you both stop. Lani shivered. Far off, toward the harbor, searchlights snapped on, and tracer bullets floated up in the air. But there were always practice alerts, and from inside the house the blues tinkled on:

Beat me, Daddy, eight to the bar,
A plink, a plank, a plink plank plink plank plunkin on the keys,
A riff, a raff, a riff raff riff raff riffin out with ease,
Aw beat me Daddy eight to the bar.

The sirens throbbed to an end, and the party began to break up well before the curfew of ten o'clock. From the tiny house some thirty or so couples emerged, the men talking of how the Hawaiian government tried to keep defense workers from voting while collecting their taxes. They spoke sarcastically of the local graft known as dockage fees, and they discussed familiarly the prostitution ring and its grip on the local politicians.

For the girls there was the most recent story about how a sailor had followed a local girl off the bus and into the nearest hibiscus bush where he immediately attempted rape.

You picked up your cap inside the house. In the bathroom the overhead light was always left on, and the bathtub was kept full of water. Termites saw the reflection of the light in the bath water and flew into the water, drowning with a steady, quiet plop plop plop.

There were brass Korean chopsticks on a table, and you picked them up. Lani laughed. "No," she said, "if you hold the chopstocks near the end like that, you will have a bad wife."

Your host had married a Korean girl, and as you said goodnight, Lani showed you, in the garden, a small stone statue under a conical straw hat. "The spirit of the garden," she said. "There are spirits everywhere in a Korean house." Then, laughing at you, in a charming, tormenting manner, "Korean women are sorcerers, you know. They keep their spirits in the cooking pots, in the household kim ch'i jar."

Well briefed by Gordian in what he called animism you said, "Just ways of handing on the science of pickling."

Her voice highpitched on the last word, she said, "I don't know."

That she spoke Korean and Japanese fluently, if somewhat childishly, made her English all the more attractive to you. Its slow-spoken correctness was without the usual commonplaces of a girl of her age, and she said now, with perfect good grace, as you stole a quick look back at your hostess, a remarkably pretty girl, "You are too fond of moth-eyebrows — of wahinis." And after this pert remark, she walked slowly toward the bus stop in a quiet and dreamy mood.

You sensed in her all the strict conventionality of a well brought up Korean girl, and you felt too the lack of any real interest in the oriental husband and home which was intended for her. And this clash within her had made her both quick and dreamy at the same time, passive in countenance often, and highspirited in talk. She was not original or brilliant, but she was strange, exotic to you (for you lacked interest in "Oriental girls"), not because of her race, but because of her agreeable hesitation between her two worlds.

Waiting for the bus which would take you down the valley to the connecting bus for her house, you stood under a hedge of hibiscus, away from the small group of people at the curbing. You put your arm round her waist, on her silken dress. She stiffened and took your arm away, and yet, instinctively, you knew that she trusted her passions far more than you did. But her voice was irritated. "No," she said, vexed that you had misunderstood something important about her, "I don't want that."

Quietly, humbly, "It was kind . . . to take me to the party." The word hovered on the air, "Leilani . . ." And the keenest pleasure flooded within you like the tides.

Her pretty eyes restlessly searched your somber face, finding there something defensive, for all the surface toughness, something easily hurt. She replaced your arm round her waist, and with a swift, natural gesture, leaned her head against your shoulder, and, very briefly, touched your hand to her cheek. But she would not turn her honest, fresh eyes toward yours, and you tipped her head, so that you could find her lips, could let their pressure rest on yours.

Together empassioned, reckless, you flung yourselves into each other's arms, amazed at your strength, and you withdrew again, so that once more you stood side by side, touching, distant, touching again. But you remembered, you knew now, by touch, the shape of her strong hips and her firm full breasts. All your frustrated longing turned toward her, welled up in you, and yet a strange timidity dried in your mouth; she seemed all the more radiantly lovely.

Lost in your charmed silence, you did not take — nor did she urge you to take — the last bus that met a connecting bus for her home, and when the winding valley ended you both got off, with half a dozen hilly blocks to cross before you reached the area of cramped little houses where she lived. The streets turned greenwhite in the brightening moonlight, curfew had come. You walked arms round each others waists, concentrating on the differences between Leilani's pensive steps and your own.

A patrol car flashed its searchlight on a trash can, and an alley cat, muttering, carried a kitten to safer refuge. There was a crash of crumpling tin, and a shower of broken glass. In the distance a woman shouted. Then there was silence again.

"My sister lives near here," said Lani. Her voice burst into a little laugh. "We can go through the back yards to her place."

She pointed across the street. Impulsively, she began to run. Your feelings of tenderness turned, almost with relief, to a desire for action. "No," you said, Woodman, Pathfinder, Eternal Boy Scout, thinking that walking you might both attract less attention from the curfew patrol car than if you were running. You did not think your dubious pass, signed by Admiral John Paul Jones, would be of much help in this crisis. The patrol car whined into higher gear, and a long finger of light raced down the street, ran over your heads, flickered, doubled back, and then ran easily along with you.

From the other end of the street, farther down the valley, came a low, sniffing answering whine, a command car loaded with MP's.

Leilani indicated an alley, you darted down it, only to stop at a five foot high wire fence.

In a charming and provoking way, she waited to see what you would do. Behind the fence, on the back lanai, stood a dark, thickset man enjoying his evening pipe. He contemplated you both as though you were the hundredth couple to come that way, and stop at the fence.

"Don't just stand there," you called to the fat pipesmoker. "Catch her." Without waiting you pushed Lani up and over the fence, and the pipesmoker caught her as she tumbled home in a flurry of white petticoat on the other side. As he stood there holding her, an equally fat woman pipesmoker came out on the lanai and drank in this remarkable scene. You scrambled over the fence by yourself, scraped for a moment at the top, and landed in a half somersault, your feet stinging on the cement drive. At the entrance to the alley you could hear GI boondockers slapping briskly along the cement.

"Thanks," you said to the pipesmoker, trying to detach Lani from his grasp. Out of shock, placidity, or just from sheer manly pleasure, he still held Lani tightly, although she was now safely on the ground. Or would be when he lowered her another two inches. The pipe-smoking wife disappeared into the house and emerged holding a large aluminum frying pan. A car squealed to a stop at the entrance to the alley.

Pipe still in her mouth, the woman with the frying pan said to her husband: "Color-blind." He turned toward her in astonishment, dropping Lani. "Color-blind," she said again. From her vantage point on the lanai she clonked him on the head with the flat of the frying pan. He shook his head as though brushing off a fly, twisted the frying pan out of her hand, and threw it at her.

You and Lani ran along the side drive of the house, toward its front yard. At the entrance gate you turned just in time to see the pipesmoker give the back of his hand to his wife's jaw. She had fielded the frying pan and tried another blow which he neatly caught on his elbow. She raised the pan, taking aim again.

The Honolulu police climbed the fence, followed by MP's of the curfew patrol. The first of the MP's saw you, and started by the porch just in time to receive the blow of the frying pan on his helmet liner. Stunned, he dropped to the ground. The other police and MP's, confused, perhaps thinking that the two menacing pipe-smokers were the curfew violators, gathered at the lanai. Flashlights pricked through the night and whistles shrilled.

Lani beckoned you round the next corner. Again you were in a narrow alley which twisted between and in back of several houses like a wounded snake. You caromed against a trash barrel which boomed off a sidewall, toppled to the ground and sluggishly discharged a lifetime supply of empty rum bottles. As if suddenly manufactured from darkness, a Filipino stood before you in the posture of the statue of liberty. There was one slight difference between himself and the statue of liberty. He had substituted a machete for the torch of freedom. The machete was in excellent condition, a bright line of sharpness glittered along its edge.

The Filipino gave the machete a few test twirls and found it in working order. He informed the houses around him, in broken but all too clear English, that he had at last found the Peeping Tom who had been spying on his new bride. Now he was going to re-move from Peeping Tom those physical parts which had stimulated him to Peep. In just a moment there would be no further Peeps out of Tom.

Lani spoke rapidly, in a kind of pretty pigeon English that you could barely follow. But you gathered that she was suggesting that it was highly unlikely to find a Peeping Tom making his rounds with a Peeping Thomasina, and if the machete twirler would wait a moment, a squad of genuine Peeping Toms would soon come run-ning down this very alley. For the patrols, on the scent again, were drawing closer.

The machete twirler wavered, and you scrambled across his back yard to a wooden fence. Lani felt swiftly along the boards until one swung loose, and you both wriggled through. The board swung shut behind you, and the machete cracked it. You both scudded up a flight of cement steps, climbed a low iron fence, and crouched down in a bed of Bird of Paradise flowers. Ahead lay one more street to cross, and her sister's house. Behind you could be observed a dozen awakened householders full of helpful suggestions for the MP'S and the police.

The amuck machete wielder hacked away at the board fence and at the trash can. The householders, the police and the MP'S inquired into ancestral bastardy in their respective families, and found much of interest. Following the principle of fool me once, shame on you, fool me twice, shame on me, the Filipino charged the whole patrol. A shot was fired in the air to stop him. A second shot was fired at him, and ricocheted through your flower bed. Orange and blue flower birds fluttered to the ground. Whistles blew and a carload of police squealed round the corner.

"Now," you said. You both sprinted across the street and up the stairs to the lanai of her sister's house, where you stood behind bamboo blinds and caught your breath.

"I expect we brought a note of color into their drab lives. Thanks for saving my life."

"Your virility," Lani corrected, impudently.

Her sister, hearing your voices, came to the door in a light green dressing gown. She had the arched nose and slender face you had seen on paintings of old Japanese court beauties. She was beautiful, and when you compared Leilani to her, you saw the difference between beauty and charm.

Lani watched you with agreeable amusement. She knew very well how men looked at her sister.

"You were queen at the Lei Day celebration, at the University."

Lani's sister smiled, naïvely pleased that you had remembered, and led the way inside. The house was almost bare of furnishings, with a single sofa and no chairs in the living room, a half kitchen with an ugly chrome dinette set, a small bedroom for the baby and his crib, and a double bed which almost filled the remaining bedroom.

Her husband, a quiet reserved Chinese, smiled continually as if recalling some recent happiness. Your eyes turned naturally to the only picture in the living room. "It is a double mandala," he said. "The Great Illuminator looks down on men in the grip of the Five Lusts and is moved to Pity."

The Great Illuminator sat on a white lotus and wore a white halo round his head, while a circular pattern of figures around him showed the Nine Ideas that would, eventually, come true.

"Ensign Classen prefers the Dynamic Buddha," said Leilani. In the adjacent frame of the double mandala the Dynamic Buddha sat on a seed pod of red lotus flower, surrounded by lesser Buddhas, one to each petal of the lotus, and encircled by other deities who repressed folly and vice. On the double mandala was shown each hand and body movement of Buddhist ritual.

You slept on the sofa bed, just under Buddha the Great Illuminator. Half awake, you dreamed of Leilani, and her sister and husband, passing through endless kalpas of birth and death, while you watched unbelieving, forever outside the circles of rebirth and redeath. Still dreaming clearly, you remembered

(Three pine trees. And crows flying over the pines of Palisades, over fallreddened maples — two crows choked up, turned enough to confuse your single-shot .22, hurtled past, derisive, crying "caw caw caw."

You remembered rubberbooted workmen draining the ice pond — it was too deep for the children who lived in the tiny new homes of suburbia, at the corner where the spring bubbled up, it was over twenty feet deep, and you remembered the sound of the pump, draining the pond through a great rubber artery, while men shoveled gravel into the water, to make sure that it would never again be more than knee-deep.

Summer and winter you fished for the giant catfish, who had grown old and fat and scarred breaking boyish hooks and poles and snatching their bait — in winter while the icemen cut and sawed the blocks of ice, you could see the giant fish gliding under the ice, black against the deeper black below.

And you remembered your father calling you from your raft on the pond, you remembered the white clapboard house, with its tiny front porch, its two maple trees, its low barberry bushes, you remembered a dining room paper with blue flowers and curling red wreaths, your foot slipped again along the thick stair carpeting, you listened — there was no sound from your mother's room, you fumbled among the bottles of wintergreenflavored homogenized mineral oil, of aspirin chewing gum, of tincture of mercurochrome, of paregoric, and you found the ointment that was supposed to help your mother's skin where it was flamereddened by the too long continued X-rays. In the darkened room your mother smiled at you, I won't cry, she had said, trying to reassure you.

When you returned to the pond it was almost drained, even the deep pool had only a foot or so of water remaining. Workmen in their rubber boots, childlike, tramped in the muddy water, at first you did not realize they were kicking, flailing the water, trying to kill the old giant of a fish, but battered, still fighting, gasping into the sucking mud, the catfish whipped back and forth, the workmen threw rocks at him, you found a stone pushed in your hand, had you too flung it at the writhing soft velvet body?)

Slowly you forgot, you released yourself from sleep, you heard the baby stir, you heard Lani sing a lullaby in Japanese:

> Nennen korori yo, okorori yo
> Boya wa yoi ko da, nenneshi na.

The baby fell asleep. Half asleep yourself, you suddenly sat up, awake all at once, a trick you had learned on Rarawa.

Lani sat on the edge of the sofa bed, watching you with grave eyes. She smiled, and in a gently feminine way, "You like my sister," she said, "and Betty Comfrey and the bus driver's girl, you are a wolf." She was laughing now, in her tormenting way.

When you tried to kiss her she turned her head away and you wanted to pull her toward you, but she slipped easily away. She wore her slender sister's rather tight nightdress, and you were ruefully aware of its fit.

But she said, "I came to tell you a bedtime story — only if you behave." Her face wore a provoking smile.

"In Jivaka walked Subha, the bhikkuni — "

"What is bhikkuni?"

"Bhikkuni is nun."

You stirred uneasily. It was not a promising beginning.

"Now listen," she said sternly, in her soft, slowspoken English. "In Jivaka walked Subha, the bhikkuni. A gallant appeared and barred her way, and she said, 'Why do you block my path?' 'You are a beautiful woman,' said the gallant, 'the woodlands are flowering, you have eyes that seem lovely and languid. Take off your yellow robes, for I can give you precious stones and gold and pearls —' But Subha the bhikkuni asked, 'Why do you want my body? You call me beautiful but my body is filled with decay. You find my eyes lovely and languid, but they are carrion too.' 'Most of all I love your eyes,' replied the gallant, 'the eyes of a gazelle are a miracle, but your eyes are more miraculous than these.' 'You are blind,' she cried, 'my eye is merely a ball in the fork of a hollow and rotten tree, my eye is only a bubble made of film and tears.' 'But still I must take off your yellow robes and kiss your languid eyes.' And saying so he took hold of her yellow robes. Then Subha of Jivaka stepped back and tore out her eye. 'Here,' she said pitying him, 'here is what you wanted of me,' And the gallant's lust ended, and he prayed, too late, that Subha of Jivaka might recover her sight."

As quietly as she had come, Leilani left you. After a time the baby stirred and the singing began again:

> Boya no omori wa doko e itta
> Ano yama koete sato e itta.

You went to her room and softly asked her, in the words of the lullaby, "Where has the baby's nurse gone?"

"To the village," she replied, smiling agreeably, leaning over the crib, "she has crossed the mountains to the village." The baby fell asleep again. She got back in bed, still smiling, very sleepy.

Your hand, without your volition, slipped under the covers, under her thin nightdress, trembled on her full warm breasts, and hesitating, thinking she objected, you started to withdraw your hand, but she suddenly pressed your hand to her, and then you knew, both of you, breathless, knew that you had aroused some great and mindless force, some extraordinary indifferent joy which would lead its own life, regardless of your plans and your passions.

She sat up in bed, not minding the disarray of her thin nightdress, and you tried to discover in her pretty eyes what had happened between you, and found no answer. She caught your head and pulled it to her breasts, and her arms tightened in her charming and undefended way, she had no idea of concealing her radiant, sudden passion.

Almost irresponsibly, with a lazy arch of her back, she let your fingertips drift from her half-closed eyes to her swelling rigid breasts. But when you wished to go further, with audacity and innocence she said, using the crudest, most naïve words, that if you wished to take her you might, "but then I will never see you again." Exquisitely pretty, her face pale and grave, she waited for your answer.

Aching, half drunken with almost satisfied desire, and full of a wild, bitter pity for her helplessness, you could not meet her brilliant glance, you shrank from your profoundest feelings — and when she proudly turned her head away, you knew that whatever might come between you, there would always be this mark — you had hesitated too long.

The next morning Arkansaw called Gordian's attention to you. "You reek of pussy, Handsome Classen," said Arkansaw. "I can always tell." But Gordian, not joining the rag, said in an irritable, almost vindictive tone that seemed to be growing on him, "Your Green Point training, I suppose." Arkansaw flushed, then quickly recovered and became his usual mocking self.

"You have that rich, healthy, scrappy look of the morning-after tomcat," said Arkansaw. "Later we'll ask Napoleon for a professional opinion."

Worried about Gordian, thinking yourself a fool for your last night's behavior, irritated at Arkansaw, you turned to the work on your desk. There was a buck sheet, an action report for you to read, initial, and pass on to the next man. You stared at it in amazement.

"Yes," said Arkansaw, still probing away at your evening in a mood that seemed not so very far from jealousy, "we were scouted by a Japanese sub plane last night."

It had flown over Pearl when you and Lani had stood on the porch attempting to perform a hula dance. The tiny plane, hardly ten feet across, had panicked the powerful defenses of Pearl, and had completely paralyzed the Air Raid Defense Center. It had got away, and The Admiral wanted to know why. To make matters worse, General MacDazzle had requested a report and would surely make a good thing of the incident.

You dug into the pile of work before you. The Japanese diarist had carefully copied from the general orders of his fleet a phrase he very much admired: "The Decisive Battle Force will assemble for the Final Decisive Battle in the appropriate harbors and will consist of a Decoy Fleet and a Main Fleet divided into Ambush Attack Fleets." Then the diarist had continued in his less formal grasshand characters, "Before sailing I went to the Comfort Station and made pompom with one of the Comfort Women who had just arrived at Singapore. Afterwards we talked quietly and she said she would some day be free, or at least her child would be free, of The Three Poisons. Her school of flower arrangement is Ike-no-bo."

You called over to Gordian, "What are the 'Three Poisons'?"

Automatically he said, "Sensual Longing, Ignorance, Desire for a Separate Existence."

You wanted to go on, then you noticed that Gordian had not, as was his practice, completed his morning letter to his wife. Nor had he, this morning, paid any heed to mail call.

In the harbor you saw that the taget battleship *Wyorada* was now upright, though very low in the water, and supported by pontoons.

To your readers, ComNorPac, ComGenSoWesPac, ComBatDiv, ComCruDiv, ComDesDiv, ComDesRon, CincPacCincPoa, Jokepoa, you explained in a tidy footnote about the Three Poisons. And with your mind's voice this phrase said itself, "In Jivaka walked Subha, the bhikkuni." And in your tormented mind's eye, an admirably pretty face turned away from you.

CHAPTER SIXTEEN

December, 1943

Psychological surveys show that both veterans and non-veterans of combat are afraid of dying.
BEGEL, The Battle for Visaya Gulf

❋

"WILL YOU let Simon talk with you?"

"Tell it to the Chaplain, you mean?"

"He thinks whatever you decide about your wife, you ought to decide it face to face."

You walked at the rear of the Officers' Club in the Navy Yard, under the five-story high gantry cranes. A stubby Christmas tree stood forlornly at the back of the Officers' Club, discarded, but not yet taken away. The silvergray carrier had her red Baker flag twoblocked, and was taking on ammunition from a lighter. A yard oiler waited her turn to fuel the carrier. At the end of the wharf sat Chaplain Simon in his battered jeep, waiting for you to finish talking to Gordian.

Gordian listened to you calmly, far too calmly. Unwilling to meet his eyes directly, you glanced towards the sub base across the harbor. There the anchored subs often practiced firing their torpedoes by releasing slugs of water from the tubes.

You were the first to see the white torpedo streak approaching. One of the tubes, instead of a slug of water, must have contained a torpedo, and it was headed for the stern of the carrier. The alarm sounded on the carrier and you thought — almost forgetting the danger — they've got a damn good watch. But the alarm was useless.

You were knocked up in the air, and then set down hard on your rump. The torpedo explosion rang in your eardrums, then numbed them, and water showered over you. Dully, half in a state of shock, you managed to grasp the fact that the torpedo must have hit between the carrier and the yard oiler, without hurting either, or damaging anything except the wharf. Officers and enlisted men boiled out of the carrier and the Officers' Club. Signal lights blinked angrily between the carrier and the sub base. By some trick of the blast, the brownneedled Christmas tree now floated in the murky harbor water.

It was a moment before you knew, even though you must have said you were all right and waved goodbye, that Chaplain Simon had taken Gordian away with him. And an even longer moment before you knew that the contorted expression on Gordian's face was the expression that comes just before a shy, reserved man bursts into tears.

A very amused CPO politely explained that you were out of uniform, or more specifically, out of your uniform, since the seat of your pants had split. After repairs you returned to Q.

Feverton behaved with a delicacy of feeling you had not expected, gave you the rest of the day off to help Gordian pack, signed the necessary orders immediately, even provided Q's car and driver to take Gordian to the Army airport for the flight to San Francisco.

In the airport lounge a few women in gray poured pineapple juice, while a microphone voice monotonously intoned the litany of flight numbers.

"Dignity," said Gordian, "what does Chaplain Simon know about dignity?"

His face weary, "I know about every kind of human marriage," he said defiantly.

You sensed that in his distress Gordian half disliked your knowing about his wife's unfaithfulness and yet he was compelled to tell you more.

His lips hardened into a thin vindictive line. Alarmed at something you sensed in him, "Don't look for the man," you warned.

It was your habit, encouraged no doubt by excessive reading, to think only of yourself — always your best central character — as changing, while others stayed the same — stayed "flat." Now you saw Gordian's innerness eroding before your eyes, and — without his knowing it — so had his yearning passionate wife changed while he was away. He saw as faithless, as a betrayer, a woman who no longer existed, who had long ago changed to something other.

There was a delay at the gate. "I know you didn't like Q," said Gordian, "but I was happy there." And in this unsatisfactory way, he left you.

At Waikiki Beach you had found a spot far off along the reef, never visited by surf-boarders or other swimmers. You were by now a powerful, if slow swimmer, even in the heaviest surf. Alone, you tumbled and floated in the writhing greenwhite surges, you slipped off your trunks and hung them on a rusty barbed wire stake, you knew how to bodysurf, how to catch the waves just as they crested, how to fly on their foaming tips for a few precious yards before you tumbled over and over and down in the whitefall, deliberately mindless and buoyant as cork.

A small strong hand forced your head under, and you twisted down, caught a sturdy, well-shaped foot, which more powerful than you had imagined, easily kicked free from your grasp. Then you spanned your hands round a full, soft waist, which quickly wriggled free, and when your eyes cleared at last from the greening sea, you saw Leilani, ten yards away from you.

She had hung her suit on the barbed wire stake, on top of yours.

Her pretty eyes, her slightly monotonous and placid smile, showed no guilty awareness of anything strange.

"By being calm," she called, in a charming and teasing manner, "you may keep your head in the presence of a tiger."

She could still swim a little faster than you, no matter how calm you kept, but you continued powerfully and slowly after her.

Then in innocent wonder she asked, "Is there something to be ashamed of?" And deliberately she let you swim beside her. Together you dogpaddled, you crawled, you submarined, you butter-flied, you crested on the surf. The waves roughened and tumbled you together and you kissed her once as through shimmering green glass. Her pretty face turned pensive and dreamy, and as suddenly her eyes became agreeably mocking, she raced to the stake, slipped on her suit and headed for shore in a crawl that soon outdistanced your own slow strokes.

On the beach she stood gazing past you out to the sea, her fresh brown eyes staring at a convoy that trudged palely over the horizon, "That's where you really want to be. Not here on the beach."

"No, not now."

With an air of uncultivation she sat down almost like a man. "Korean girls are sorcerers — we know what you are thinking."

The hot sands were warm, and you pretended to doze, but against your will, the pretense quickly became a reality. When you woke again the beach had filled with strollers who eyed Lani hungrily, with lustful ballplayers who made a point of dropping the ball near you both and then running madly around you. Leilani ignored them, and in her innocent almost unassuming way, touched her fingers to the nape of your neck. In her tight green silk bathing suit she was wonderfully pretty.

"I'm sorry about Gordian. He should stay with his wife."

"Why so?"

"Because it's *her* fault." Her agreeable, almost placid expression was rippled by a troubled consciousness that she did not find it easy to express. "He should show pity to her."

"What would a girl do in Korea?"

She burst into a little laugh that was a tantalizing mixture of innocence and crudity. "Go to the Chinese doctor, and have an abortion."

She sat up, and her pretty and restless gaze wandered to the beach.

"Why don't you ever want me to meet you at your house?"

She shook her dark hair impatiently. "My mother doesn't like to have me go out with haoles. Does your father know about me?"

You sat beside her and your shoulder touched hers. "How did you know that my mother is dead? And how did you know about Gordian?"

"I guessed," she said, smiling brightly. And then, in her most tormenting manner, "Korean girls are born sorcerers." At once, from her almost audible vivacity she leaned back in a relaxed, even dreamlike fashion, and you found yourself being softly and persistently questioned, she was charmingly and yet insistently curious, and again and again she wanted to know about your mother and her last lingering days, and she wanted to know too, of the remote suicide of Ensign Brown, she wanted to know about Arkansaw's dwarf tree, you were perplexed and entranced by her lazy flow of questions.

Under the high, hypnotic sun, lulled by the sultry beach, you dreamed, alone — or was the dream shared with your enchanter? — of Satori, spiritual enlightenment, and you dreamed of Samadhi, the last step of the Noble Eightfold Path, and there was Nirvana to dream of, too, and beyond Nirvana there was Parinirvana, because there could be no limits set on the heavens of Buddhism, void followed endless void, infinity stacked its saddle curve on infinity, and life was a bridge without houses.

It was time for her to return to Comfrey Hospital. In the charming and irresponsible way she had at times, her bathing suit straps had been allowed to drop well below her shoulders. You stood facing each other and she said boldly, "You *are* ashamed of me." You wished desperately to embrace her, or perhaps you wished simply to spank her, but the moment passed without your touching her, and she seemed almost disappointed as, with a quick, deft movement that was prettily, even indelicately feminine, she wriggled the straps over her shoulders.

Above you in the air two gallinules tumbled about, redcrested birds whose heads had been marked with the fire they stole from the gods of Hawaii. Darting down they fell side by side, then flew off in separate directions. When you turned again, Leilani had vanished.

Back at Pupule Court you put on the record player a tiny disc cut by your father:

"I don't know what to say . . ." — long pause, sound of neighborly laughter, and cries of "Talk! Don't just stand there!" "Mr. Smith is right beside me, but he won't talk, must be shy or something . . ." — another long pause, more urging to talk and not waste the record. "Now I'm very glad to have my watch back that you wore in the Aleutians, even if you did get it scratched up a bit it has a sentimental value, and speaking of sentimental value, something you'll be interested in, Monty, at a bond rally I sat next to General Eisenhower, and I'll send you a picture you can keep for a souvenir, signed by both of us." — blank silence — "Now in your last letter you wrote about going out with a *chorine* and Aunt Ethel thought you meant chorus girl and not a Kore-an girl" — nervous laughter in the background — "We all appreciated your little joke about if, you say, I wouldn't let you bring home one *chorine* girl you'd bring home two and then how would I feel if I had to let you keep one, but joking aside . . ."

You snapped off the record player and put the disc in the bookcase. A letter fell to the floor. It was the letter, written but never sent, meant for the mother of Ensign Brown. You put the letter back, next to the record.

You knew your father had exaggerated ideas of your ability, and equally exaggerated hopes for your future. But you could never talk successfully with each other. Your habitual irony grated against his businesslike optimism — even though this optimism was a veneer over a view of life that was far more cynical than your own.

You dropped off to sleep as a child, back at your Grandma Brady's house for the summer, and she was telling you about Sam Brady, telling a story you knew by heart and which she never varied by a word, how they lay still for an hour, not daring to move. Then they crawled forward again, but Biggs who was to grasp the arms was delayed, and had not reached his post yet. A twig snapped, and a huge savage within reach of Gray's tomahawk sat up, then lay down. Fifteen minutes passed, before Biggs moved to his place. There was a low hiss which Brady passed on to Gray, who in turn signaled to Bevington. They worked rapidly, feeling for the heart, then stabbing. One Indian stabbed by Gray sprang to his feet to utter the warcry, just as Brady leaned over and tomahawked him. He fell dead across an Indian not yet reached. Brady knifed his heart and tomahawked him at the same time. They had slain all but one in just a few minutes when he started to run. Biggs from the stack of arms shot him with one of the Indian's rifles. The white women fled at the noise and at the sight of Brady and his spies dressed as Indians and painted red and green across their faces, but the women soon returned. Bevington killed three, Gray killed three, Sam Brady killed six and the thirteenth was killed by Biggs. The spring was known after that as Bloody Spring and as Brady's Run . . . you stirred and moved gently into a profound sleep, into a field of gentians blue gentians cool and blue . . .

CHAPTER SEVENTEEN

January, 1944

On the 23rd of October, early in the morning, the cruiser Firegod *and its sister ship* Buddha's Mother *were torpedoed and sunk. The younger Japanese sailors had not been taught to swim because of the rushed wartime training program and they drowned. But Admiral Chestnutfield and the older men swam to a rescue destroyer.*

Both the Firegod *and* Buddha's Mother *had triple hulls.*

BEGEL, The Battle for Visaya Gulf

❊

"BUT WHY can't I pick you up at your house?"

Leilani's pretty lips trembled, and she answered you again, "You know how my mother is about haoles." In a motion at once bold and submissive, she tried to draw your arm round her waist, with exquisite charm she confidingly touched her soft cheek to your shoulder.

You had not told her of your father's attitude, not so different, after all, from that of her mother. And in a dark and helpless mood you attacked her all the more, perhaps, because one wretched part of you agreed with your father.

Betty Comfrey, driving a warbuilt car whose rear end was not of metal, but of orange varnished wood, like a station wagon, or the rear end of a bee, slowed down and offered you a lift. As Lani walked within the Comfrey Hospital grounds she turned back once, and you saw that her eyes were brimming with tears. You immediately regretted having accepted the ride, but it was too late,

Betty Comfrey buzzed her way through jeeps, taxis, peeps, trucks, staff cars, Navy station wagons without once slowing down, or, even more miraculous, without once having to blow her horn. She was a brilliant driver, and knew you admired her for it.

Without stopping to let you off, she turned hard right away from the main street that led to Pearl Harbor, and she said, with her faint pink blush that went so well with her golden coloring, "I'm kidnaping you for a drink, I hope you don't mind." And then, with the fixed expression a woman often assumes when she is being perfectly fair about another woman, "She's very attractive, Leilani Kim."

But you said, "I've only just met her." And then you asked yourself what was it you were trying to conceal from her, why had you told this petty, unnecessary lie?

The beeshaped car wriggled quickly through the crowded center of Honolulu, between the great four-storied houses of the Chinese merchants, and the shacks of the Filipino poor and beyond the warehouses of prostitution till you reached Nuuanu Valley and the area of fine residences, small ones at first, hidden behind green fronds and red and yellow flowers. As the car climbed, the houses became larger, the trees and vines and branches crouched lower over the road until you seemed to be in a wet green tunnel that insinuated itself higher and higher in the air.

She turned at full speed into a narrow drive and the tires flung up handfuls of gravel in protest and you rode swiftly now between a double crescent of royal palms, steel-gray shafts that soared up and up, ending in tiny green tasseled crests.

Everywhere were red and yellow flowers, as though you had driven into a yellow and red and green conservatory made of wax by expert craftsmen.

She braked hard under an encolumned porte-cochere. Up one of the columns straggled the mud tunnel of a termite colony.

On the great lawn was a tiny swimming pool, ridiculously small in contrast to the rambling house and the stables that had been converted to garages. And near the pool stood a small brown shingled bungalow. "My studio house," she explained. In a natural gesture she swayed lightly against you, and still sitting in the car, pressed your arm. "I'm exhausted," she said.

A Filipino houseboy, smiling and handsome, drove the car off to the garage with an indifferent, deliberate grinding of the gears at which she winced.

"Today was Red Cross day for me," she explained, as if to make sure you understood that her fatigue came, like your own, from the war, and not from life in this idle luxurious house. "I must have received twenty indecent proposals in just an hour this morning. Coffee, doughnuts, dirty talk, that's my line." But the implied criticism of servicemen and their morals was robbed of its sting when she smiled at you as she had once smiled at Pupule Court, and in the following silence you experienced the odd sensation again that an understanding had been exchanged between you. If it was a trick she had, it was a charming trick.

But then she spoiled the effect by adding, "And then this afternoon the university girls refused to go to the dance tomorrow because it's for the Negro ack-ack battalion."

"Didn't they refuse because the Caucasian girls weren't going?"

Betty Comfrey was wide-eyed. "But we've never gone." And with sudden hostility, "Your friend Leilani Kim started that."

"I always thought it was us servicemen who brought racial prejudice to the island paradise."

"That too," she said shortly, leading the way into the hall, past sugarcane flowers in dusty Chinese vases. On one wall of the hallway hung a painting of a nude native girl with an anemone, or some bright red flower, in her hair. She had lavish, sensuous flesh, and, surprised that it seemed to invite the touch of the beholder, you saw that the painting had been done on velvet. A brass plaque on the frame read: "Enter Lavinia, ravished." The native girl seemed almost related to Betty Comfrey though more fully proportioned and less tall and slender.

"I'm sorry," said Betty, taking your hand warmly and guiding you into the living room. "I must be having the curse." By this frank womanly tone, you knew you were with a graduate of one of New York's finest finishing schools.

Over an unnecessary fireplace hung, in a gilt frame with baroque columns, an idealized portrait of Betty. At first you thought it was her first communion, but you immediately recovered and knew that it was in honor of her coming-out party. The painter had clearly been under orders to make a very charming girl seem beautiful and the whole effect was strained and off balance.

But you were not to stop in the living room. Its river of rattan furniture spilled over onto a huge lanai and there sat a wax image of President Harding. Without changing expression the image of Harding accepted a kiss from Betty Comfrey, and a whole new glass of some refreshing liquid from a Filipino butler.

The image of President Harding searched deep within that glass for an object, perhaps an ice cube of rare and unusual beauty. "Daddy," said Betty, trying to introduce you. She shrugged her shoulders, and sat down, crossing her long, lovely legs. She had a cruelly reasonable expression on her face.

The Filipino butler brought you a long and powerful planter's punch. In your nervousness you drank half of it quickly without realizing just how strong it was.

Mr. Comfrey had the economic assurance of a man who has inherited a great deal of money without either adding to it or diminishing it by his own efforts, and he now said, "All this used to be our farm." His remark, and his even more startling gesture, which took in the whole Pali, the Nuuanu Valley, even the island of Oahu itself, produced an impression on you, though not the one intended.

You had a touching recollection of your father trying to explain why, in a competitive capitalist society, it was necessary for the Hartford insurance companies to pay hundreds of thousands of dollars to the Missouri political machine to fix the fire insurance rates. Your mother had not cared about that, but you now remembered sharply how again and again she had asked your father why he had to leave St. Louis so suddenly that he had to abandon there his wedding anniversary suitcase in twotone calf.

"Then we began to educate them," said Mr. Comfrey. He indicated Betty's little shelf of University of Hawaii textbooks. "The university," he said, with a sour, baffled look.

Betty Comfrey's lips entertained a smile of sympathy for her father, but her pretty eyes suggested to you that there were subtler and more modern ways of discussing these topics. But these clear blue eyes were very far from approving the donating of the Comfrey estates to a charitable trust, as the last student editorial in the

University of Hawaii newspaper had brashly suggested. She crossed her silken knees, well aware of the effect of this gesture on you, and leaned back, stretching delicately like a Siamese cat. The automatic Don Juan within you wickedly observed that she wore no foundation garment.

"Worst thing we ever did was to found that university."

"Daddy, Daddy."

"And now they even want statehood." He summoned up twenty years of accumulated phlegm, shaped it into one word and spat that word on the air. "Pah."

Your powers of resentment were far quicker than you cared to admit to yourself, and now they awoke from their uneasy slumbers. You were becoming aware that Mr. Comfrey, like many uncommitted alcoholics of the wealthy variety, was far from being as drunk as he was pretending to be (just as later in the evening he would be equally far from being as sober as he would pretend). And you began to see that these remarks were intended mainly to irritate you, and that Mr. Comfrey instinctively disliked you. With possibly ignoble pleasure you began to think, I have failed to please this bastard. You could not help yourself, and some of this dislike extended subtly to his daughter.

Mr. Comfrey received another nourishing charge from the watching butler, and he shifted his sentences to a more telegraphic style, as though wishing to send his words the furthest distance at the cheapest rate.

"Grandfather Comfrey . . . no mistake . . . Hawaii one big farm . . . you Navy *People* . . ." (Betty was summoned to the phone) — "new ideas . . . unions . . . socialism bad . . . you be sorry."

With an effort you kept from saying at appropriate intervals, "Ugh, ugh." Mr. Comfrey settled comfortably in his rattan chair, sure that you wanted his daughter and would not, therefore, retaliate.

"Whites meant to run things," he said. "White man's country. Don't teach you that at Yale, do they?"

You had to concede that they had never taught you that at Yale.

Smiling with happiness, Betty returned. She had obviously talked to someone she liked very much, and you felt, for one who at times thought of himself as half engaged to Leilani Kim, an absurd pang of jealousy. "Arkansaw," she said, "he wants to speak to you for a moment."

Arkansaw's words were guarded and he used the tone of voice in which forthcoming operations were often discussed. "If you don't care about going," he said, half mockingly, "I'll see you don't have to." Arkansaw was pleased by your hesitation and took your silence as assent.

The phone was in the hallway, and before going back, you examined again the sensuous, dusky nude. She had been painted with extraordinary skill and the dark velvet lent a languorous glowing quality to the flesh of the model. It was the model herself who gave the picture its disturbing, pornographic quality, and her lovers, you imagined, had passed through fire.

On the lanai Betty and her father sat silent but Betty was not a girl who looked her best when quiet, and she brightened at your return. You knew now of your feelings of resentment, ill defined yet, but you thought you had them under control, and you began, innocently enough, "Your Grandfather Comfrey, he was a missionary, wasn't he?"

Her father answered curtly, "Yes."

You had a tendency to follow a new idea with excessive enthusiasm that you often later had cause to regret, and you did not notice the stiffening, frozen expression that crept over Betty's face.

"And then," you went on, recalling what was a very deficient knowledge of the history of Hawaii, "he went into business at the end of his life, didn't he?"

"After his retirement," said Betty, interrupting her father, the coloring high on her cheekbones.

More reminding yourself of a story than wishing to tell it to her, you remembered. The missionary Comfreys, following their founder's example, had bought land from their naked parishioners for their churches, and, very naturally, for their homes and garden plots, always able to congratulate themselves on the strict legality of their actions. Then they had wisely bought land in anticipation of their future needs, familial and public, and they had bought land to keep lay speculators from buying it. Last of all, they had openly bought land for Hawaii's future, rather than for the heavenly future the family founder had first had in mind. And now these few old landowners kept their land — for the commoners of Hawaii could own their houses, but not their land. And every few years, land rents were renegotiable.

All this you tried to sum up fairly (from your point of view) by saying, a little too judiciously, "Some Comfreys, I suppose, bought land while they were still active in the church —" Betty shook her head violently but you paid no attention — "but I suppose most were simply local residents who knew a good thing when they saw it."

You could not, if pressed, name a single church Comfrey who had bought land, but you had been well trained at Yale in this kind of mousetrap debate.

"They paid for everything they bought," said Betty.

When you saw her hurt and angry expression you wanted to stop, you felt your argument was shaky, however lucky your un-principled hit had been, but Mr. Comfrey leapt to life. "Give it to the pinko," he shouted. And he peered at you is if through an arrow slit.

He let his Filipino butler replace his own glass with a new one (glasses were never merely refilled in the Comfrey house), but he waved the butler away from you to indicate that Pinko had had one too many.

In the joy of argument, you knew, you tended to think more of your own logic than of others' feelings; still you did not want, for reasons which were not clear, to hurt Betty any more.

But you might have gone on anyway, had not Mrs. Comfrey entered. With her appearance the house, the hallway, the lanai, lost some of their hugeness and seemed more appropriate, in better proportion.

Mrs. Comfrey accepted without question your glance of admira-tion. She was one of the few older women you had ever known who deserved the title of beautiful. You had seen her face occasionally, minted on the finest of Grecian coins. She wore a Paris frock, she had the figure of a girl and yet she was in her forties, with beau-tifully dressed silvergray hair.

When you turned back to Betty she awaited this second inspec-tion, childishly biting her lower lip. People must often have looked first at her mother, then at her. And the portrait over the fireplace ensured that even when Betty was not there, guests could compare, at their leisure, daughter and mother.

As soft as demon snow in a Japanese play came Mrs. Comfrey's questions. Can one learn Korean more quickly if one knows Japanese? Were not the defense workers spoiling beautiful old Hawaii? Was it right to rank the European theater ahead of the American theater? Would not Mr. Classen enjoy seeing scenic spots of old Oahu, those not usually visited by the tourist?

Into the room strode Lieutenant Hobbes, to call for Betty. He had the soft, purry cat look of the Supply Branch. War in the Pacific was the Supply Force dream. Seven to ten times as much tonnage was needed for each soldier as in the European theater. In Lieutenant Hobbes's past was the heady aroma of Mory's, of Scroll and Key, of little black sheep that had ever so genteelly lost their way. And in his future was the law firm of Hobbes, Hobbes, Gamboge and Hobbes. It was a good solid future, very different from your own indefinite one, and with sympathy you saw why Betty might desperately want at times — only at times no doubt — to be free of it. And to climb mountains Daddy did not own.

Mrs. Comfrey's questions flowed relentlessly on. There were almost no pauses for Betty, and she was silent with the silence of long habit.

Cruel, cruel, cruel. Betty surely would have trouble extracting the bemused, enchanted Lieutenant Hobbes.

You excused yourself, asking Betty not to show you out, but she insisted on coming with you as far as the hallway.

Like most rather unargumentative girls, Betty thought arguments more serious than they ever, in your experience, actually were, and she said in delicate, indirect apology, "I'm sorry, I did kidnap you."

You liked her for this and for a slow smile which forgave anything you had done. Your resentment had dwindled to an innocent desire to tease her. "You're not allowed to go out with anyone until your parents have met them — that's why you brought me here."

A delicate goldenpink blush was your answer, and you were confused at having hit on the truth of the matter. Should you take her out, she did not want you to learn that you must first meet her parents.

"Did I pass?" Your voice was dry, ironical.

She met your eyes frankly, though she blushed more deeply. "No," she said, "the question now is 'did I pass?'"

You were shaking hands in goodbye; in a curious, catlike gesture she dug her fingernails into your palm, and was gone.

You were walking on the gravel drive under the royal palms when you jumped. In a corner of the grounds a loudspeaker suddenly blared at you in a raucous Negro voice, "bunk bunk BUNK —" then beat out, "I'd become a monk."

At the Comfrey Hospital you left garlands of flowers for Leilani — pikake, orchid, ginger, pink and white carnations. Back at Pupule Court Prince Mokuaweoweo invited you in for a select drinking and flame-throwing party, just for two. It was the Prince who first observed the tiny scratches in the palm of your hand and asked you hopefully, "Does she have a friend who bites?" But perhaps the deepest scratches had come when you wrestled the Prince for the gas tank cap, best two explosions out of three.

CHAPTER EIGHTEEN

January, 1944

A captured Japanese enlisted man termed the evasive maneuvering of the sacrificial Japanese decoy fleet the "Bon Odori" — the "Dance of the Dead" — still, it served its purpose, this morbid Dance, and its purpose was to lure, to decoy Admiral Hornbull to the north, away from the defenseless transports in the Gulf.

BEGEL, The Battle for Visaya Gulf

❀

NAPOLEON's blue Packard was sticky with its roof up. Cigarette ash dropped on your hand and you rubbed at a hot point of flame.

"Prantz is determined to send you on the Kwajalein operation," said Arkansaw.

"I'd just as soon go." But it was not true, not any more, and Arkansaw immediately recognized it for untruth. You had faced danger on Rarawa, no better and no worse than hundreds of others, but you had changed since Rarawa, you had a wild new joy in life. Never had it been so pleasant to live — sensations came at times like powerful blows.

"Duty is a feather, death a mountain," said Arkansaw in mockery.

From the shadowy, blacked out house on Green Point came sounds of laughter, of a piano, of singing and shouting. There was a burst of light from a suddenly opened door. You heard men's and women's voices singing:

> The monkey married the baboon's sister,
> Smacked his lips, and then he kissed her.

The door as suddenly slammed shut, and a fragrant drift of cigarette smoke reached the Packard. From the shore below the cliffs you were intently aware of the plashing and soughing of the waves.

"Let me fix it so that you stay here," pleaded Arkansaw gently.

Napoleon came to his car and wanted it. "Monty," he said in surprise. "I didn't know you went slumming. What you doing here man? What is it this week, light meat or dark meat? I hear you like a little of both."

He roared off in the darkness to a Navy nurses' party.

"Some bamboos grow straight, others crooked," said Arkansaw.

"Is that the latest signal from the Great Illuminator?"

Companionably you both walked toward the house but you were acutely aware that you had not firmly denied Arkansaw's offer to "fix it."

The house was in the shape of a U, with the lanai and the long living room forming the curve of the U. A kitchen, laundry and pantry sketched out one arm of the U, and three bedrooms in a row were the other arm. In the courtyard between the two arms was a small pool, in back of which grew violet flowers of deadly nightshade.

On one long wall of the living room were narrow bookshelves, containing not books but rare corals and shells, and the only light of the room came from panels of fluorescent light placed behind the largest shells, so that a pearl and pink light flowed through the room.

At a grand piano sat Arch Getty, the owner of the house, a handsome, stoutish man of about fifty. He was playing and singing, "Wie einst, Lili Marleen, wie einst Lili Marleen." He had a good, clean rhythmic touch on the piano, and in a pleasant way he stood up for applause. He wore a hibiscus flower over one ear, and as he stood up and bowed, his unfastened bathrobe opened enough to reveal that he wore nothing underneath it.

He sat down and began again, with a gentle flourish:

> For according to our mother you're our father,
> And that's good enough for us.

Easily he modulated into "Ich hätt' einen Kameraden," and winked at Arkansaw, and then "Heute gehört uns Deutschland, Morgen die ganze Welt." Clearly, it was to be an international evening. You felt an attack of shyness coming on, which two powerful drinks did not remove.

Arch Getty sat down beside you on a long, circular sofa, and leaned toward you. The bathrobe opened provocatively on soft, clean elderly flesh. He adjusted his hibiscus and you moved along the sofa half a foot. Inconspicuously he followed you.

"Do you find this a *gay* party?" he asked.

A shapely woman of about thirty played away at the piano. She played with great gusto "She lost it at the Astor."

"Quite gay," you said.

Arch Getty seemed encouraged by your inadvertent repetition of the adjective "gay."

Arkansaw always tells *me* about people he knows would get along with *us*. Why has he kept *you* a secret from *us?*"

You did not know why Arkansaw had kept *you* a secret from *them*.

"You like *books*, don't you? I can always tell." Your opinion of Getty went down somewhat. In your experience people who liked *books* rarely read *books*.

From an end table Arch brought out a first edition of Henry James's *American*, and the same volume in the New York edition. "Fascinating," he said, "the little *changes* between the first and the final editions." He moved closer and squeezed your upper arm. "Tell me," he said, "have you read the homo*sexual* letters of Henry James?" Strong squeeze of your arm.

You had not, and you moved a bit further along the circular sofa. "Some*times*," said Arch Getty, wagging his fingers in a "naughty boy" gesture, and wriggling his shoulders, "the New England *hippopotamus* stopped trying to pick up peas and picked up little *boys* instead." You discovered that his shoulder wriggle had propelled him next to you again. "Would you like to see the *dear* little letters? They're from Henry to an *Irish* actor. Terribly, *terribly* indiscreet."

In spite of yourself, you were curious. "You have the originals?"

"Oh no, dear boy, friends of the family bought them off the market *at once*, but I have a typescript. Before the war came I was planning to edit them in a small *private* edition to be published in Hong Kong. Why don't you drop in some time, in the *daytime*, and see them?"

By now there was very little that the shapely pianist had not made her heroine lose at the Astor and she had gone on to her own popular variant, "*I lost it at the Astor.*" Arch snatched a drink off a tray for you. The party was reaching the stage at which some highballs have almost all whiskey, and others have practically none. Yours was one of the 90 per cent whiskey variety.

A young Army aviator, a fresh downycheeked captain, was talking to Arkansaw. "We came in like this," he said, flying with his hands, "just twenty minutes of gas left in the Lightnings before we had to turn around, but I got one of the Bettys and watched her crash in flames. I thought at the time it must have been somebody important to send us all the way to Buka like that. Then a month later I read about the death of little ole Admiral Yamamoto."

Happy and smiling, delighted with the party, the Captain turned to you. "I hear you know something about Japan. What's it mean, a kind of building with a green cross on it? Every day we flew up the slot we'd stop and shoot up this building, just to run our guns off a little. What's it mean, that little ole green cross?"

"A hospital," you said.

"Gee, that's a shame," said the aviator seriously. "I wish I'd of known that. We could have just as easy run off our guns on some other building."

He began talking privately to Arkansaw again. He shook his head, refusing some request of Arkansaw's and once he flushed. Then he laughed again, and they disappeared in the courtyard.

"Your friend Arkansaw is very distinguished-looking," said Getty. But his compliment had a spiteful quality. You had moved by now to the end of the sofa.

Getty's hand lay briefly on your shoulder. "Behind you are the *poisonous* shells." You got up to look at the shells, forcing him to drop his hand. There were only a few, ranged between a Blood Ark and a Rock Venus, and you did not like them. When you returned you went to an armchair next to the sofa. But Getty brought a drink for you and one for himself, and sat comfortably on the arm of the sofa. You were irritated to notice that you were becoming coquettish in the face of this pursuit.

Major Begel, now promoted to Lieutenant Colonel, entered with a group of Marine officers and their wives. These elderly consorts had a hardbitten harddrinking look and though they wore no badges of rank, after a few minutes among them you could pretty well tell the military titles of their husbands. Colonel Begel went directly to the piano. There he kept time with a swizzle stick while the shapely pianist, at his request, informed the living room that the monkeys had no tails in Zamboanga.

The bosomy pianist had rushed to Captain Feverton on his arrival in the doorway. She embraced him with considerable strength. Someone turned the radio to dance music. Betty Comfrey, in a new limecolored dress, stood near the radio. She did not seem completely at ease. "Betty," you called. And when she looked pleased, you fled from Arch Getty and began dancing with her, in a small happy circle near the radio. Her warm smiling gaze confused you, and aroused vague longings, blurred memories of college football week-ends, of the dances afterward, of firegilt autumn leaves drifting among strolling couples in evening dress.

Arkansaw reappeared with ice, more whiskey, newly washed glasses. Assisting him was the Army captain who had shot up the building with a green cross on it, but who was very sorry about it.

"He looks like you," said Betty.

Stupidly, "Arkansaw?"

"That captain. The fly captain." And she examined him closely as if seeking the secret of his attractiveness — not to her, but to Arkansaw. In that moment the scales dropped from your eyes, though you willed them desperately to remain. And you thought of the parties which you had finally asked Arkansaw not to give at Pupule Court, even if he was not one of "them."

At the silent piano, using his swizzle stick instead of the black-board pointer, Begel explained to his captive audience how the Japanese, had lost at Attu, and had had to evacuate Zhutchka. His voice dominated, then silenced the room. The Japanese, said Colonel Begel, were like a barbarian trying to box. Hit him in one spot, his hands go there. Hit him in another spot, his hands go there.

Captain Feverton sat with the shapely pianist and listened approvingly. Holding her hand tightly, he explained in a loud voice that Zhutchka meant Charming Beetle in Russian.

Betty's eyes were like dark blue stones. Her voice was bitter and frustrated. "Oh, God, I'm tired of it," she said. "You can't know how tired." She was clutching your arm till it hurt. "I could fight another woman," she said. And looking at Arkansaw now through her eyes, what was suddenly suggested to you by his familiar mocking features was a woman. But when he waved at you both across the crowded room, the woman in him had vanished.

But the memory of the Investigator from the Adjutant's office kept nagging at you. The Investigator wore lieutenant j.g. bars, but you suspected, from his excessive satisfaction when he talked about Ensign Torrington's "case," that he was really an enlisted man. The Investigator had asked you bluntly if Arkansaw ever associated with queers, "fairies to you, sonny boy," and disliking him at once, you had lied automatically.

Arkansaw and the Captain were talking intently to each other as though the rest of the people in the crowded room did not exist — the scene between the two equally goodlooking men had its beauty, it was a kind of love which might be contemptible, but a tiny voice insisted within you that love — no matter what the kind — was never wholly contemptible. And the two of them were as helpless as you with your own more acceptable instincts — their passions were as powerful as your own, and were at times uniquely poignant because of the fear — an exquisite fear — of exposure, and disgrace.

Betty Comfrey had no such reasonings to sustain her; in her anguish she drew you into the courtyard behind the fountain and there flung herself into your arms, merely to forget her despair. You knew why she acted so, you meant only to comfort her, you would be loyal to Leilani, but as you stood in a tightening embrace, your bodies cared nothing for your schemes and your loyalties, her hand, half by accident, touched the side of your neck and then lingered there, and your own hands, timidly at first, began to rove and explore. She drew back, you thought with repugnance, but her eyes glistening, she look at your helplessly, in wonder. "I must sit down," she said, "we don't know what we're doing," and at that moment Arch Getty found you and she twisted from your arms, saying "I'll fix my face and be right back," but you knew she was not coming back.

"My cousin Betty," said Arch Getty reflectively. "*Actually* a cousin of my dear divorced wife." A spasm very like spite crossed his face. "She's *lesbo,* of course. Not *promiscuous* though. Too much *taste* for that." And he cocked his handsome head to one side, eager to see how you would take these outrageous remarks. He was disappointed when you refused to rise to the bait.

"Arkansaw's a *charming* fellow, don't you think. But not quite . . . *gay* enough." There was an odd accent on "gay," and a quick bold stare at you, and you began to be sure that gay was some sort of countersign among the brotherhood.

Smoothly he continued, "I'm glad I was able to help him out in his recent little *difficulties* —" his voice was mysterious — "Perhaps I can help *you* too."

"I'm all right," you said, and anger rose within you as you thought of the Investigator and his Torrington "case." You gripped Getty strongly, more strongly than you realized, and he winced. "Leave Arkansaw alone —" you said fiercely, "it's dangerous."

"For him?"

"For you." You dropped his arm roughly and reentered the house.

You might well have been all right, regardless of what Getty meant by his mysterious offer of help, if you had not accepted your fifth — or was it your sixth? — drink, handed to you, or rather ordered on you, by an expansively jovial Captain Feverton, whose arm was permanently attached to the waist of the shapely pianist. He grinned at you, patted Getty on the back, shouted "Boys will be boys." The feminine pianist found this remark hysterically funny. "Boys will be boys," she repeated, marveling at the wonderful rich humor of Captain Feverton. She wanted to know why he did not go on the stage. Thus encouraged, Captain Feverton winked at you and shouted again, "Boys will be boys."

After one sip of your drink, you knew you were stoned. There was only one thing for you to do, and you did it. You giggled.

But you were not too stoned to be able to extract your knee from piano-playing Arch Getty's strong fingers. Later — or was it much later? — Arch steered you by the arm into the courtyard again, to see the deadly nightshade.

"I don't want to see it," you said. "Besides it's related to the potato."

"Such a *clever* boy," said Arch Getty. "So strong and tall, and so *intelligent* and handsome." His piano-trained fingers propelled you toward a bedroom. But Arch Getty, mistakenly sensing victory, was a little too precipitate. "How about a feel?" he said softly.

Moronically you repeated his question, not understanding. When you did understand you could not at first break away. You heard your mother's voice, the echo of her voice, saying, Always thank your host and hostess. And Arch Getty was certainly your host. You giggled helplessly.

Host Getty was having some trouble with the bedroom door he wished to open. When he finally got the lock unjammed, you both discovered that someone had been sleeping in Getty's bed. That someone was Captain Feverton, who for reasons best known to himself rested better with his trousers around his ankles and one shoe off. He added that his rest would be more complete if you and Getty got the hell out. "Amen," said from the dark the shapely woman pianist.

You escaped to the lanai, built out over the steep cliffs and the cool sounding seas below. Arkansaw was standing alone at the railing, looking down at the tumbling waters. There was no moon, but the white surf was easily visible. He gripped your shoulder and bent you forward, so that you both leaned far over the rail. "The great modern temptation," he said, but his voice had lost its usual mocking note. "Men used to commit suicide when they lacked a woman, or food or wealth. Now you jump when you've had enough of your civilization, when you've seen all that you care to —" his hand tightened, "like Brownie —" he said savagely, but you were stronger than Arkansaw, and you twisted his hand from your shoulder abruptly.

Perhaps you might then have talked frankly to Arkansaw, but he chose to veil the woman in him from you, and you went back to an earlier lost stage of your relationship, and you and he stood there and Indian wrestled, almost like puppies, and you wrestled, shouting and laughing, best two hundred falls out of three hundred. The dark misty night and the wrestling cleared your head. You both stopped and you could hear Colonel Begel's voice in the living room.

He was telling of the battle of the radar pips. In this engagement the Navy fired, by radar, 500 14-inch shells, 450 8-inch shells, spotters made salvo corrections, ships dodged torpedo wakes, crews reported near misses from Japanese gunfire. The whole cost came to over $250,000 in ammunition, and a few days later the Navy learned there had been absolutely nothing there to fire at, the whole battle had been imaginary.

"We have too much history," said Arkansaw, listening to the

familiar voice. "History begins when civilization comes to an end."

"May I write that down?"

"Write this down too — when the historians appear, like Thucydides or Marcus Aurelius —"

"Or Begel —"

"Or Begel — that's the coming of the end. The Emperor Augustus never wrote history. Even General MacDazzle is writing a history. In three copies."

In the living room they were singing now:

> Mr. Finney had a turnip
> And it grew behind the barn,
> And it grew, and it grew,
> And the turnip did no harm.

You wanted to tell Arkansaw not to pretend any longer, with you at least, to be outside the homosexual group, not to pretend to join their parties because they could talk of the theater and of music and of the latest books. But you contented yourself with telling him about the Investigator — who had sworn you to secrecy but you did not care about that.

"Oh yes," said Arkansaw, amused. "They used two handsome Marine charmers as decoys, forgetting that the decoys might just possibly be on our side to begin with."

All this was said in a masculine, joking tone that indicated Arkansaw was not a member of "our side," though sympathetic to its claims to be more civilized than the "other side." But as though you were comparing a false note with a tuning fork, you heard the concealed, jarring vibration of the womanly attitude within him, which was not even now, not most of the time surely, known clearly to Arkansaw himself, so slowly and gradually had it developed.

"One more proposition and I may develop a very *gay* simper."

Arkansaw laughed. "You've learned the password. They're not so bad as the stage jokes make them out to be. Once Arch Getty finds out you're not really one of the gay ones, he lets you alone."

You observed you had not found this to be the case.

"We'll stay together and defend your virtue," he promised. But on your return to the living room, you were quickly separated, in a party which seemed to have more than caught its second wind.

Supply officer Hobbes announced that it took twenty times as much tonnage to support a man in the Pacific as it did in Europe. Reporter Bulflash described how he had landed with the first waves on Attu and had seen three hundred Japanese in the last suicide charge — even now it made him sick to remember how the Japanese had cut the heads off dead Americans along the trail between Massacre and Chichagof. Colonel Begel said that after General Ferox had been put in command the whole Attu operation had gone twice as rapidly. Reporter Bulflash asked if his newest Japanese photo of a geisha (actually a movie actress) didn't make you want to whistle and whoop and holler and cry Uncle, where's the nearest bedroom.

"Over there," said Arch Getty, "the nearest bedroom's over there." Somehow he had maneuvered you out in the courtyard again, and you could dimly recall pushing Getty ahead of you into the bedroom, then with half-drunken cunning, locking him inside his own bedroom. But a moment later Getty stood beside you again. "Ah," he said, smiling, "you forgot the master key — or should I say, the master's key." Colonel Begel said that on Rarawa two hundred laborers with spears rushed an American machine gunner — the gunner got one hundred and ninety-nine of them, and the two hundredth spear carrier got the gunner right through the heart with his bamboo spear. And this was a lesson to us about the hordes of Asia who were now awakening.

Host Getty sang that there was a boy moose for every girl moose and a boy goose for every girl goose and a girl moose for every goy moose and a girl goose for every goy goose.

Host Getty asked you if you had ever been to the fairy bars in San Francisco. You said you had. Host Getty asked you if you had ever been to the lesbo bars of New York. You said you had not. Host Getty asked you if you knew you were a queen — a great beauty to the homos — that was why they had enjoyed *so much* Arkansaw's parties at Pupule Court. You said you did not know you were a queen and you carried Host Getty over to his courtyard pool and dumped him into it.

Arch Getty, in new bathrobe and hibiscus, returned to the piano carrying a Navy .38 pistol and a box of cartridges. "Russian roulette," he called, "anyone can play," and he loaded one bullet in the pistol.

Arkansaw took the gun away from him, and Colonel Begel warned him he could be charged for firing a Navy bullet, even on sentry duty, to the extent of the actual cost of the bullet.

Brandishing the loaded pistol Arkansaw stood on the sofa and recited the fire sermon of Buddha while Arch Getty played "Hold that Tiger" obbligato, the ear was on fire and all cries received by the ear — all thuds oomphs cackles and shrieks — were on fire, the nose was on fire and all odors — all violet and rose and fruit odors, and all fried food and dung and animal odors — all all were on fire, all tastes were on fire — all bourbons and sour mashes and rice and blackeyed peas and ham and yams and honey — all men's tongues flamed with fire, and all eyes were on fire — all sights of country and town, of war and peace, of men and women — every image that entered the eye was on fire, and the mind was on fire, every nerve every ganglion was on fire every drop of nucleic acid in the nerves was on fire and everything that traveled through men's nerves was on fire all ideas all thoughts all impressions all sensations all hatreds and passions and griefs all selfishness all un- selfishness all despairings all all all were on fire, on fire with passion burning passion on fire with grief burning with grief all burning burning burning all all all. And Betty held Arkansaw's hand and tried to pull him down from the sofa and Lieutenant Hobbes tried to pull her away from Arkansaw and Arkansaw spun the chamber and spun the chamber while Arch Getty played "Hold that Tiger, Hold that Tiger" and Arkansaw aiming the gun at his own head pulled the trigger.

There was a click. Arch Getty played "Hold that Tiger" fortissimo. He seized the gun from Arkansaw and loaded it with two bullets, balanced at opposite sides.

"One bullet is the child's version," he said. "The weight of the bullet carries it down, away from the hammer. But *two* bullets —" And he threw the pistol back to Arkansaw.

You saw the stunned look of Betty and you heard Arkansaw spin the barrel and you waited, face turned. There was again the click of hammer on the empty chamber, and Betty burst into tears. With a whoop Arkansaw spun the barrel again and this time aimed the revolver at the piano. The bullet crashed through the strings and the sounding board with a weird echoing music.

"The Lost Chord," said Arch Getty happily. "I've found the Lost Chord." There was an acrid smell of powder in the room. Arkansaw said, "I played a chord into the air, it fell to earth I know not where, I've been losing a hell of a lot of chords lately."

Arkansaw wanted to fire another bullet into the piano and find the lost chord again, this time, perhaps, for keeps. But you and Lieutenant Hobbes pinned his arms to his sides and took the pistol away from him. There was the wailing horn of the shore patrol jeep in the distance. The neighbors had called the police, the guests hurried off into the Waikiki underground railway — the back routes that evaded the curfew patrols — and as so often at Green Point the party, officially at least, was over.

You slept fitfully, waking up every time a plane took off from Hickam field and flew low over Pupule Court, stuttering and coughing and biting its way into the cold clear upper air.

A long time ago you were a boy walking along High Street in Philadelphia in the year 1776 and you walked along the trails of your ancestor Sam Brady careful to step only on the rocky ground, on the high places and you followed that endlessly tracking and pursuing figure and you lay by the fire place with him doing verseabout, Sam Brady read you a verse and you replied with the next verse, "rejoice with the wife of thy youth," and you said the verse about "let her breasts satisfy thee at all times." And very much later, dazed, in a wave of sharp sudden drunkenness, you heard a soft strange and yet familiar voice tell of love, of his love for you. On and on the soft voice went, waited, rose, fell, withdrew, and once a hand touched but in sorrow withdrew when you shivered. And you fell asleep, not fully asleep but almost so ahead of you waited flowers of gentian in their blue caves and the waiting wavering arms of flame and of shadows and beyond these colors of deepest coldest blue a beckoning figure, obedient and voiceless for a time only.

But the gentian blue gentian faded you awoke full of happiness full of the keenest unreasoning desire for the coming day and for the evening when you would meet Leilani.

You had an afternoon watch and it was then that you learned Arkansaw had already boarded his Kwajalein transport — "in your place, Mr. Classen," said Prantz spitefully, "Mr. Classen, sir."

Distracted by this information you did not at first notice that the Inspector from the Adjutant's office had settled in the chair beside yours.

"How about Getty and Arthur Torrington, sonny boy?" he asked.

"Don't call me 'sonny boy' — anyway, Arkansaw — Torrington — has probably sailed by now."

"We can wait, sonny boy. We can wait." He lit a cigarette and let the match burn close to his fingers before he blew it out.

CHAPTER NINETEEN

February, 1944

> *Magellan had landed on the shores of Visaya Gulf in 1521, and by the 1560's the inhabitants (most of them) had been converted to Christianity; Visaya Gulf then was older, in terms of length of European settlement, than much of the Americas.*
>
> BEGEL, The Battle for Visaya Gulf

❋

I send you a last *Kōan:* A government official asked a great Zen master about a young goose kept in a beautiful glass bottle. What would happen to the goose? The goose grew larger and larger, yet the government official did not wish to break the bottle or injure the goose. How then should he remove the goose from the bottle? "Sir," said the great Zen master. "Yes," said the official. "There," said the master of Zen, "the goose is out."

You PUT the letter, which Sanky had brought you from Eniwetok, back in its crumpled envelope, set letter and envelope in an ashtray and touched them with a match.

Ever sensitive to flame, Prince Mokuaweoweo called down amiably to you, "Need some gas?" Politely you declined. "Some other time," said the Prince, disappointed.

Sanky sprawled on your tiny lanai and sipped appreciatively at his sour mash. He held the glass up to the light. "Just the juice of the pure natural grains."

"How did Arkansaw take it?"

"Pretty well. Do you know anybody who takes that sort of thing well, I mean very well?"

You did not.

"Besides, he already knows Braille." It had been impossible to convince Sanky that Arkansaw had not cleverly and deliberately learned Braille in anticipation of just this mortar shell which had wounded him.

"He went all through the landing on Kwajalein without a scratch, and then the moment he stepped ashore on Eniwetok —"

"But the other eye's all right?"

"Fine." Sanky was astonished at your naïveté in these matters. "It's not so bad." Blindness in one eye was a heavy price to pay for permanent retirement from the armed forces, but not an impossible price. And from Sanky's attitude toward you, you knew you were, in warfare, something of a spectator still, not the complete professional.

"When I first came here, you turned white as a sheet. What did you think I was going to tell you about him?"

"I'm not sure."

"Did you think I might tell you he'd committed suicide?"

Abruptly, "No."

"Why not? I've thought of it — haven't you? Everyone thinks of it sometime." Sanky was moody and irritable and you did not choose to explore further in these unsuspected depths. "He'll outlive us both," and Sanky shied a rock at a large rat that peeped out from your red poinsettias. It was very hard, you thought, to suffer the silver lining of a friend's cloud.

"Have you heard about the next landing?"

You had heard.

"After Kwajalein and Eniwetok I've got as much fight in me as a whipped potato."

"Don't be too upset. If you miss the next landing General Ferox will be sure to find you another one."

"And another and another. I'd like to screw him in an auger hole."

Sanky had had a bad time of it on Eniwetok. A sword-swinging Japanese officer, looking as if he could swallow Sanky whole without stopping to wait for vinegar and soy sauce, had charged him right at the beach line and had very nearly split him into two equal but noncommunicating parts.

Sanky went inside for his cap, and his spirits revived at the sight of Leilani's picture. Sanky was without sentimentality toward women. He found in them much to enjoy, and somewhat less to praise, but he admitted that Leilani charmed him the way a blacksnake charms a catbird. One day he had tracked her from the Comfrey Hospital to the university, and there he had looked her up, introducing himself as a friend of yours. And he had sat, taciturn and happy, on the little balcony that opened off the second floor of the library while Leilani did research for a nursing project. He even exempted her from his strictures on college girls — it was useless to explain she was in nurse's training, and not really a college girl — Sanky had fixed ideas rather than ideas in the usual sense.

He had once had a disastrous experience with a college girl and he stubbornly believed all college girls were like that one — teasers. Every embrace but the last, as he put it, horrified at the indecency of the Collegiate Approach to Sex.

You and Sanky said very little about Leilani and yet that little was surprisingly unfavorable to yourself. You had expected Sanky, with his often-repeated remark that he wanted marriage the way a cat wants trousers, not to apply higher standards to your pursuit of Leilani. But these higher standards were applied.

How she had won him to her side, you did not know. He had only a few adjectives like "stacked" and "built" that he ever applied to her, and a few odd comparisons, that she had "skin as soft as a mouse's belly," and that she was "all woman, enough to make a Quaker kick his grandmother."

Whenever he saw you, sooner or later he asked, always hopefully, "Did she give you the bag yet, boy?"

You did not tell him that two weeks ago she had hesitantly suggested that you and she see somewhat less of each other. "Why don't you go to hell and pump thunder at a nickel a clap?"

"Just remember one thing, boy — it's the longest pole gets the persimmon." He jiggled the ice in his sour mash.

"How often do you see her?" he asked.

"Two or three times a week."

"What do you do?"

"Swim, dance, listen to records, talk —"

"If it was raining mush, you'd be the only man without a spoon. You must be crazy as a bedbug."

You were hesitant. Leilani had no great supply of small talk, as did Betty Comfrey, nor any general interests. She did not mind silences, but these longer and more awkward pauses, these dried places in your shrinking river of talk, had begun to make you uneasy, and the river dwindled further still.

You had many theories of love, somewhat too strongly held — you knew, for example, that people in love talked together and that there was something a little ignoble about nontalking lovers. At first you and Leilani had fulfilled this prescription admirably. She was inexhaustibly, charmingly curious about you and your family, about your father's insurance business and your years at college (you did not tell her about Q or about your year of training for the Navy). And you learned still more about her Korean farm and her Korean mother whom you had never seen and who never wanted to see you.

To Sanky all this mention of "talk" and "listening to records" was frosting. He went right to the cake. "Do you sleep with her?"

Your face turned fire-red. Then joshing you, but with a maddening seriousness too, "Why don't you marry her?"

"As the old woman said when the hog ate the grindstone — nuts." But all this was very awkward talk and you wanted to turn aside from his biting gaze.

You could not explain to Sanky that you had taken your father's recorded warning more seriously than you cared to admit. Perhaps it was the shocking sound of his somewhat pontifical voice.

You knew very well that voice's real teachings — not its Official Moral Position, for that was a model, and not a wholly hypocritical one either, of propriety. But you knew almost by heart how the voice told (half jokingly) of its owner's escape from Missouri in the great insurance scandals, and you knew the voice's anecdotes about Negro women. (A southern plantation owner sent a beautiful young mulatto woman a great many gifts. She told him she had already given her heart to one of his field hands. "I never hoped to win your heart," he said politely.)

By such anecdotes, by such bits of humor, over the years the voice suggested very clearly to you the proper attitude to take toward the Official Moral Position.

But you and Leilani had not embraced again so passionately as you had done that one night at her sister's, nor had there been mention again between you of her offer (so you wrongly called it now) to sleep with you once and never see you again. And you drifted on through the mindless summer afternoons and nights of Hawaii, you had some weakness, some measure of vacillation in your character which was reinforced after the landing on Rarawa, after Arkansaw took what should really have been your place on Eniwetok.

Should you answer Sanky's question about marriage by saying that you often — and easily — imagined yourself sleeping with Leilani?

Craggy and wrinkle-eyed, Sanky asked you, "Have I put my hand in the tar barrel?"

"Up to your elbow."

"Good," and he was off, as he put it, like a jug handle.

It was, then, in no very easy spirit that you met Leilani at her Uncle Kim's luau that evening, and she scrutinized you with quiet and anxious eyes.

Uncle Kim was a stubby Korean gambler with gold front teeth and a head as round and brown and bald as a Spanish onion. He had won and lost his house three or four times now, and he was renting it for the evening from its new owner of one day. Should the nightly fan-tan game go well, he might win it back, and there were always his pinball machines, his kimch'i pickle plant, his tattooing shops and other less attractive enterprises about which you would never hear.

In Uncle Kim's back yard a pig had been cooking for twelve hours in a deep pit over hot stones. From time to time the cook dragged out one or two pound chunks of pig wrapped in ti leaves and served them to those who were hungry. On long trestle tables set up in the driveway were salt salmon mixed with onion, fresh pink poi paste and the darker fermented poi, orange pop at every place and whiskey at every adult place, along with little Japanese sake cups for drinking the whiskey, and beer bottles and tumblers for the necessary whiskey chaser, and scattered along the table were big bowls of mon doo — Korean dumplings stuffed with beef and bean sprouts and pine nuts and mushrooms, and platters of Chinese-Korean sweet and sour spare ribs. There were forty or more Chinese and Koreans, and some Hawaiians, and they sat down and ate for a while, and got up to make room for newcomers.

Wandering in this happy noisy throng you began to think, to realize for the first time, that Arkansaw had quit your life and you thought of all you had been through together — Napoleon's Frankenstein act, the parachutes for the pilots of the flight north to Adak, the comic horrors of Q. By disappearing, Arkansaw had taken all these people and events irrevocably into the past with him — you had only a small and fairly unscarred sense of past time as yet, and you were shocked still to think of people and events as being "over." And once your hand strayed unconsciously to your eye, as if searching for a wound, and your fingers tingled.

Lani had left your side at first, shy before her Korean friends and relatives (her mother, on learning you would be there, had refused to come). But she came to you again, and faced them, eyes downcast and half closed, but with bright stubborn glints in them.

This inconspicuous action took more courage than you realized at the time. Your ridiculous Korean was needed to put her at her ease and make her laugh. You had studied a little Korean with her, and the more Korean you had studied the more ground you had lost. There were hundreds of verb forms and dozens of levels of politeness and far too many alternate words for such a small country. When you were introduced to Uncle Kim you tried a few sentences on him and succeeded in using a child's level of politeness in your verbs.

Lani tried to teach you the different words for uncle — there was *bagbu,* uncle, your father's elder brother, and there was *sugbu,* uncle, your father's younger brother, and *samchon,* uncle, your father's brother in general, and *gomobu,* uncle, the husband of your father's sister, and *imobu,* uncle, the husband of your mother's sister, but you never did learn the right word for Uncle Kim, who was the stepbrother of Leilani's mother, but bafflingly enough, had the same surname as Leilani.

Mrs. Kim was Chinese, short, ugly (to your eyes), flatchested, and completely charming; she it was who had given Leilani the Chinese dress she had worn to the luau. The Chinese dress disturbed you, for its high neck, its sensuous side slits which exposed her thighs, its close fit at hips, breast and shoulders, its silky pale blue sheen and its pale gold pattern of flying cranes — all these combined to suggest an ancient culture which looked on your own as barbaric.

Quick and light stepping the dancers danced, in the darkening driveway under the frangipani fronds, in the dusky house they danced under waterfall sprays of gingerflowers, and the house and its grounds flowed with sounds, the soft, relaxed chattering of Korean, the highlow pitches of Cantonese and Hakka, nervous go-for-broke Hawaiian-American talk, and always songs:

> A kiss is still a kiss, a sigh is just a sigh,
> The fundamental things apply as time goes by.

In the echoing flowerfilled house your voices seemed to come from far distances, from other rooms; from more innocent and younger times.

You would say nothing of your scheme — worthy of Napoleon — to take Lani back to your room at Pupule Court. You were resolved, high minded, you barely touched her cheek to yours as a pledge to yourself, and then she stumbled, you caught her, and your hand brushed her cool thigh.

At once you asked her to go back with you and she said simply, "If you want me to." And she said, in a pretty and undefended manner, so softly that you almost could not hear her, "You will remember . . . that I am a young beginner."

At once you wished to take her home as usual, to the familiar scolding from her mother, you wished to match this generous surrender by your own. But retreat did not agree with one of your most powerful images — not the least desirable, but no less firmly held for that — of yourself as mastering any woman you were in love with.

At this crucial moment Mrs. Kim found you and led you both to a small balcony where she and her husband were sitting, watching the luau below. Far down the steep slope of Sierra Drive curved the winding road and its houses, gray green in the humpbacked moon's light. In high spirits, Mrs. Kim told how she had met young and handsome Mr. Kim in China at Shanghai. He had been sent there by his family to study Chinese; each day his teacher appeared and advised him to study, and each day he told his teacher of his great respect for teaching, and each week the teacher politely drew his salary for this Confucian exchange of amenities rather than learning.

Still, there in Shanghai he had met his future wife, whom he had won with his ability to play "Lovely Hula Hands" on the guitar, and he had taught her to play the ukelele. She was of a very wealthy Chinese family, from Peking, and she spoke pure Pekingese dialect, not Cantonese or Hakka like most of the Honolulu Chinese. After their engagement she visited his shabby student's rooms, and she ordered a cartload of furniture sent down from one of their three summer homes to his apartment. When they were married her family took over three floors of the biggest Shanghai hotel, and the short smiling groom had only three dollars to his name. And his guitar.

But Mrs. Kim had come back with her husband to Honolulu, in the fighting with the Japanese her family had been impoverished and scattered, and her mother and father were now dead, and her three summer homes, her houses in Peking and Shanghai, all the furniture and servants and land were gone. She knew how to cook now, and do the wash, and she could still play — with much laughter — "Lovely Hula Hands" on the ukelele. Mr. Kim, eager to demonstrate, brought out guitar and ukelele and Leilani danced, very stiffly in the tight Chinese dress. Down the hill slope Mr. Kim's mango trees gave off a heady, rotten smell — you had to put the mangoes in paper bags to keep fruit flies out, but that was the wrong kind of work for Mr. Kim.

Then Leilani asked Mrs. Kim to sing to her Chinese lute, the pi ba. With a shrewd glance at you, Mrs. Kim sang from the book of songs a tune that had been old when Pericles was scrounging funds for the Parthenon:

> The wilderness holds an antelope, dead,
> Wrapped in a white grass mat —
> To her breasts the young girl embraces the spring,
> And a courtier allures her on.
>
> The forest is oak and scrub,
> A wilderness, and in it the deer,

Wrapped in its matting tight —
And a girl, like a jewel.

"Don't toy with the clothes at my breasts,
Don't undress me — please —
The dog will bark — please —"

The song, in spite of its words, somehow suggested that to yield by
force or trick was better than never to yield at all; Mrs. Kim, you
thought, had a wicked sense of humor.

In a back room the fan-tan game began. It was time for Mr. Kim
to try to win back his house. To speed his guests on their way, he
sang now, the great patriotic song of exile from Korea:

Ariran, Ariran, Arari O!
Crossing the hills of Ariran —
There are twelve hills of Ariran,
And now I am crossing the last.

In the gardens, and in the house, the other Koreans joined in, and
Lani sang too in a low clear voice, and many of the Koreans had
tears in their eyes. The luau was over.

You rode an electric bus to Pupule Court. The rear end of the
bus was taken over by beach boys and their girls who stomped and
sang, and talking was impossible.

She had been to your apartment several times before; she had
always sat primly in the one armchair, and you had taken the bed-
pune, or the floor. She sat passively now on the pune, she did not
want the lights on. And you had an odd impression that only now
had she really sensed your intention, and you could dimly see that
intention growing and deepening as hurt in her dark brown eyes,
and nervously she began to talk of *menehunes,* the little people
who appeared about the time of Pearl Harbor and warned of the
attack but had not been believed, and you realized that she literally
believed in menehunes — she was not discussing them as "folk-
ways" as Betty Comfrey had done.

And you wanted this humble, superstitious tale to relieve you
from taking her seriously, you needed for your purpose a heart
stiffer than devil's horn, and you felt your sensations of conscience
go obediently limp within you, you drew on inherited memories —

movie and book memories — of white men and delightfully rounded native girls (you could love Tondelayo Technicolor in her land but you could live only in your own, and the ship drew away from the palmfringed shore, and grassskirted T.T. waved goodbye while sad and brooding you waved at her from the ship's stern).

Lani knelt appealingly on the floor, put her left arm round your knees and shyly touched your lips with her hand, she seemed marvelously pretty, and in response you as gently touched her cheeks, and again your purpose faltered, you were so inefficient a Don Juan that you had not imagined more of the seduction than enticing her into your room, and you were ludicrously worried at the thought of the unfamiliar machinery of the Chinese dress— you wondered almost in panic what both of you should do next.

But your hand fell naturally to her shoulder, and through the thin yielding silk of her Chinese dress you felt her breasts, they seemed to flutter dovelike under your hands, and then stilled again, stiffening at your touch, and she did not push your hands away, you stroked her breasts deliberately, and passion came, darker, more swift than nightfall in a tropic land, came as if to rescue you from a state that was very close to innocence, nor so very far from love either.

With Lani's help the dress came easily undone from her bare shoulders, her firm figure had needed nothing more beneath the dress, there was no more to undo, but she hugged the dress to her shoulders, she turned her broad strong face toward you. She could do nothing weakly, you thought, not even surrender.

The noises of Pupule Court sounded in your ears like thunder — Prince Mokuaweoweo's radio, BIJ taking a shower and singing "Old MacDonald Had a Farm," Napoleon's heavy running step — he rapped on your door — you and Lani were silent — he ran off to his Packard and zoomed down the street — a last gargling chorus, "with an oink oink here and an oink oink there."

She shook her head, freeing her hair from its silver pin and letting it fall down her bare back.

"Monty," she said — "Monty" — she used your name very rarely, and it came to you now with the insistence of a magic chant. Her eyes were eloquent.

"You mean, then, never to see me again? It's so much to you?"

she said in wonder. You strained her to you, and she suddenly let her tongue find yours. Her cheeks glistened with silent tears and she wanted your handkerchief. She fell passive in your hands as if a long-expected moment had come.

Bringing your palm to her still wet cheek she said, submissively, "What are you thinking?"

On Pupule Street a horn blatted and another answered it like a mechanical mating call. It was the last frantic, joyless hour before curfew, the drunks stumbled up and down the street, the Prince's radio advanced a perceptible notch in loudness, a party spilled out of the tiny lawn next door and as suddenly went back inside, the humpbacked moon rose higher in the sky.

"That you will last through anything."

"Are you ashamed of me?"

In your mind emerged a picture, like a print slowly developed in a dark room, of Palisades and the ice pond in early winter, after the scarlet leaves but before the snow. The picture turned brown and vanished.

Confused, too late, you said, "I love you."

"Love!" she said, and you were shocked to find you had made her angry; she did not know that, however little you might be able to mean, still you had said these words first to her. And the words, once said, took on a life of their own, their meaning grew upon you, branching and rebranching, coral-like, deep within your mind.

The three words grew on and on, and you had to touch Leilani, most of what you had was touch — your families would never agree, you shared no friends, and yet your hands, your bodies knew that touch was sacred, to touch was to begin to love.

She pushed you away, quick to strike at words unspoken but none the less said for that. "Don't pretend you might have married me — it would take too much courage to marry me," she cried. She struggled against you, the Chinese dress slipped from her shoulder and tore — very slightly — along a seam, and irritatingly enough, she burst into tears of regret for the dress. You tried to comfort her. She stood up, blindly intending to run away, there was a crash and the record made by your father fell from its case and rolled to the floor.

Automatically, she picked it up, then became childishly, even maddeningly curious about its tiny size; she insisted on hearing it. And you played it at last, you played all of it, even though it was cracked — "you wrote about going out with a *chorine* —" *duhcrack duhcrack* — "you'd bring home two and then how would I feel —" *duhcrack duhcrack.* The record shattered, it did not just break into pieces, it seemed to explode, and Lani, to your surprise, burst into laughter.

With the record, your image of yourself as Napoleonic seducer had shattered too.

"Do you understand now?" you said, bitter and chagrined, thinking falsely that she would be moved by the voice of your father as you always were, not realizing that to her it was merely an elderly voice in a somewhat strange tongue.

"Shall I take you home now . . . all the way home?" You were horrified as soon as you spoke, to hear the unintended note of ugliness that crept from your heart to your voice. Did human beings then talk so hatefully to one another?

Defenseless, she dressed herself, made ashamed and clumsy by something she saw in your eyes; too businesslike, you found a safety pin to tie together a torn lucky crane.

"It's not your father who keeps us apart," she said, far quicker in such matters than you were. "It's something to do with your mother, isn't it?"

Lately she had tried again and again to learn what your mother was like, as if she might find out more about you through this interrogation, and she was even completely convinced that your mother had passed on something of her character to you — just as Leilani intended to pass on something of herself to her own children.

But you knew that your mother, long since dead, was no longer the unique individual she had been in life, she was now not much more than a memory of yours, and in some sense, to speak the more honest truth, she had insensibly become — as the dead all slowly become in time — a mirror of your thoughts.

Lively and chattering, she did not notice how quietly you saw her to her home. Just before her house grew a large golden shower tree in the middle of the sidewalk. Half deliberately, you separated from her to pass it. Sensing at last something of your mood, she said quietly, "In Korea that means the two people will never meet again."

But a timid and pretty happiness shone in her eyes as she said, "You preferred, then, to see me again?"

With a shock you realized how humbly such an exquisite and lovely girl had valued herself in your eyes. But your sensual disappointment only grew in power, you coldly shook hands with her, while the happiness died stillborn in her radiant eyes.

On the way back you walked slowly, lost in a melancholy depression, you ached in mind and body with frustrated passion, you did not care whether the curfew patrol became unpleasant about your pass signed by Admiral John Paul Jones, and you thumbed rides of the early patrols themselves. They promised you they would be back for you in a few moments, and just before curfew a car screeched to a stop — it was Maria, in a very tousled and dirty blouse, her hair tangled. But she was bright-eyed and smiling, and she said, using not Filipino but Hawaiian, "Hele mai, come here." "Whose car is this?" "Hele mai, hele mai, does it matter?" It did not matter, and you lurched off in the ancient car which lacked completely its second gear. "It is the car of someone I do not like any more," she said.

You passed safely the last roadblock before your apartment, but she had to go on through the next and you both knew she would never make it; she made no objection to parking in the driveway of Pupule Court. Then she was in your little studio apartment, her hand nervously darting in and out of her purse in an odd trick she had, and she kept saying to your remarks, "Hoomalimali — flattery," and she laughed.

She insisted on taking a long, hot shower to wash off the memory of someone she did not like, and she finally came out, back curved, all wet, not dried at all, but wet and dripping and stark naked and clean, with drops of water glistening between her small deep breasts, and smelling of soap and very wet she flung herself in your lap, she was determined to rouse you, but she caught your wrists in her strong little hands and showed her teeth and said nonchalantly, "I like it short and hot — just the main bout, no preliminaries."

Half asleep, much later on, you thought you remembered asking if she knew of the nun Subha of Jivaka, and you thought you remembered her sleepy giggle and her hand going out, to feel in her purse.

Still very sleepy, you managed to struggle out to the drive, in time to see her car — the car of someone she disliked, scoot down Pupule Street — she had gone and your wallet had been emptied of all but its ID cards, though she had thoughtfully left you money for bus fare.

By the fading humpbacked moon, under the scarlet poincianas, a great circle of rats ran round and round, twenty or thirty rats, nose to tail. For a long time, fascinated, jingling the fifteen cents she had left, you watched them run and run and run.

CHAPTER TWENTY

March, 1944

At Visaya it was the Japanese, rather than ourselves who had in mind the philosophy set forth by John Paul Jones: "When an enemy thinks a design upon him improbable, he can always be surprised and attacked with advantage."

BEGEL, The Battle for Visaya Gulf

❖

WHEN FEVERTON arrived at the prisoner cages the prisoners were joyously uncrating a waist-high bottle of *shoyu* — soy sauce for eating with their rice. "Sauce," exclaimed Feverton. "What right have they got to have sauce?"

"Din tell me nothin bout no sauce," said the Marine chaser in charge of the uncrating.

Captain Feverton had just been made Major, and his new rank had brought with it new suspicions. Where was Standish getting so Japanese a product as soy sauce — "Made in Japan" soy sauce at that? Perhaps Feverton expected to hear that BIJ Standish had it unloaded offshore from Japanese submarines.

Patiently BIJ explained that he had got the sauce — "prewar soy sauce" — he said proudly, from a café in Honolulu on Nuuanu Street, at which many of Standish's interrogation section ate their evening meal.

At suppertime Major Feverton roared off to the little café on Nuuanu Street. He entered, smiling his pasted-on smile, and beaming at the Japanese music which the interrogation section of Q, the drunk Japanese proprietor and his shrewd wife were all singing at the top of their lungs. A jolly good fellow, Feverton joined in with the rest:

Kimi ga yo wa
Chiyo ni yachiyo ni.

"Has a good beat to it, maybe we should use it as a marching song," he said. "What's it mean?" The proprietor explained it was a wish, a wish that he might live for ten thousand years, till the pebbles turned to moss-covered rocks. "He?" asked Feverton. Overcome with emotion, the proprietor stood up and said, "The Emperor — banzai." It was the Japanese national anthem. Major Feverton grinned in anguish and left.

The next day, in JOKEPOA Order #69, all officers and men of Q were forbidden to eat at Japanese restaurants in Nuuanu Street, or even to enter such restaurants "for any purpose hereinafter whatsoever." BIJ Standish protested. Like others of the BIJ or Born-in-Japan clique, he was an expert on "prewar shoyu sauce." "Prewar shoyu sauce," said Standish hotly, "is not to be compared with wartime shoyu sauce." Prisoners, he went on, talked more freely if provided with prewar shoyu sauce. The Nuuanu café was the only reliable source of prewar sauce in Honolulu.

But Major Feverton, after the *Kimigayo* songfest, was rockhard. He opposed letting the prisoners have any kind of sauce, prewar, postwar, wartime, ketchup, A 1, Worcestershire, Diable or BarBQue.

Anyway, said Major Feverton, people who could not speak English, like the Japanese owners of the Nuuanu Café, were un-American and very probably disloyal.

You had occasionally eaten at the café, and you knew that, loyal or not, the Nuuanu Café owners, and many Japanese in that section of Honolulu, were convinced that America would win the war. Their reasoning was simple. They had never seen American officers, other than those from Q, and they had very naturally concluded that the farsighted American Admirals had raised all their naval officers in Japan.

After Order #69 BIJ no longer flung himself to the ground and called "Take cover, men!" when a car backfired on Pupule Street. The spirit had gone out of him. "Kataki uchi," he was heard to mutter, "kataki uchi" — in short, revenge! No one took Standish seriously, but revenge came anyway, in its own mindless time.

It began when General Waddleman, after a long interval, had his attention called to Q again. Napoleon, on night guard duty, mislaid the keys to General Waddleman's office and to his safe. In his circular English the General inquired of Napoleon, "My keys, you lost my keys, how dared you lose my keys, lost, my keys, have you lost my keys?" Napoleon's easy reply of "No sweat, General" was not well received. The next day, Waddleman's orders relieved every one in Q from serving in the delicate post of night watch officer.

And from time to time now, General Waddleman stuck his head in the door of Q, quickly retreating before the ever alert Major Feverton could make them all leap to their feet at attention.

Q was now almost double its original size — it had crept down the second-floor hallway, engulfing partitions in its progress, it had sent all of its yeomen (except Prantz) across the hall to a separate typing and steno room, and Standish's interrogation section had a whole large room to itself. By the sluggish upgrading of AlNavs, you and Napoleon had gone to lieutenant, junior grade, and Gordian, reserved and silent since his return from home, had become full lieutenant. BIJ Standish expected that a few more months would see him made Lieutenant Commander so that he could do full justice to his enlarged interrogation section.

Everywhere in Q now there were files and indexes, a dictionary of air terms you had written, a folder on methanol injection in Japanese engines, a report on tropical fish traps, your atrocity reports file, your indices to decoy fleets, *kesshibutai*, suicide attacks — but as yet no suicide units. And stored in the arsenals and hangars of Pearl you even had Japanese equipment awaiting transshipment to arsenals in the United States — machine guns and rifles and knee mortars and tanks and even airplanes — you had walked among rows of captured Japanese Zero planes. At the beginning of the war these had been the best fighters in the world, but no progress had been made, now they were only half the horsepower of the squat, heavy and powerful American fighters, and they were still made by handfitting methods, each cockpit was machined slightly differently from the next one. And back at Q were their maintenance manuals, for these and for all other Japanese planes, and you knew these pretty much by heart.

In his renewed interest in Q, General Waddleman discovered that several of its officers had been in Tokyo before the war, and a few, like Standish, had been born in Japan. He called all these into his office. A chubby figure in pink riding breeches, he tapped on his desk with his crop, the nearest thing he could find to a British officer's swagger stick. In his own brand of circular English he asked if they knew this geisha, Miss Perfect Trust, did they know her, Miss Perfect Trust, in the Yoshiwara district, when they had been in Japan, did they, Trust?

They had all known her (BIJ Standish, mindful of his missionary background, restated this proposition, "had known of her").

"Ichiban ii," said General Waddleman, translating for the benefit of the BIJ's, "Number one good, ichiban ii. Number One. Good." They stood there, respectful, puzzled. Surely he had not summoned them to practice pigeon Japanese? The General looked at the ceiling, put the tips of his fingers together, and said, "Now on the Chindwin . . ." They walked out, baffled.

General Waddleman went back to an argument he was carrying on with his opposite number on the staff of the hated General Mac-Dazzle in SoWesPac — General Kasmir. He and Kasmir were arguing over the best and most efficient way to address Army style postcards, and General Waddleman had a telling point to make to General Kasmir. Engrossed in this argument, and pleased with himself for keeping in mind the needs of Q, he assigned Lt. Cmdr. Seeberg, USN, ret., from the lieutenant commander officer pool to Q.

Not realizing what he had done to Army control of Q (for a retired officer would obviously be senior, in date of rank, to newly promoted Feverton), General Waddleman himself brought Seeberg in to Q, introduced him to Major Feverton, said "A desk you'll need, a desk, you'll need, a desk," and went back to his office to dictate a letter about the return address on the postcard, address, return on the postcard address. Major Feverton opened Seeberg's papers immediately to his date of rank, and slumped in his chair with hurt, crushed look.

Lieutenant Commander Seeberg, Annapolis '30, retired for physical disability (namely arthritis which had cocked his head to one side and sharpened his disposition), was a devoted reader of Homer Lea's *Valor of Ignorance*. On his forced retirement, he had lived in Japan for three years at his own expense, studying Japanese and the Yellow Peril of Homer Lea at the same time. He had been completely convinced that war with Japan would come, and that his knowledge of Japanese would make it possible for him to re-enter active service, and he had been right.

Lieutenant Commander Seeberg did not charge around Q in the Major's fashion. He held no mass meetings of Q, nor did he issue general orders, though he did not interfere with Major Feverton's enjoyment of these simple pleasures.

But Seeberg, his head tilted painfully to one side by his arthritis, believed that accuracy in facts was a very first duty of life, and he knew errors when he saw them, as the Major frequently did not. When still very young Commander Seeberg had taken for his model Xenophon's Temenus — when Temenus said something was there, it was there, and when Temenus said something was not there, it was not there. Those who fouled up Japanese map coordinates, locating a new Japanese airbase in Puget Sound, or those who read a negative Japanese order as a positive, soon faced the iceblue eyes of Commander Seeberg. And few were the members of Q who relished being questioned closely on their ability to distinguish between shoe polish and fecal matter.

Commander Seeberg's consolatory remarks — for he had a few of these — were largely papal in attributed origin. When the officers of Q had the job of translating material from long dead and thoroughly ripened Japanese he spurred them on by saying, "When rape is inevitable relax and enjoy it, as good Pope Adrian says." His usual response to complaints was, "We always file complaints carefully here — in the wastebasket, as good Pope Gregory advises."

To summon men, he was fond of hurling pencils about, like thunderbolts, to attract their attention. He had the chair by his desk sawed off, so rumor had it, and whoever sat there to talk to him kept sliding forward on his seat. And the same rumor had it that the venetian blinds at his desk were carefully adjusted so that dazzling shafts of sunlight shot into the victim's eyes. True, men slid forward in their chairs when talking to him, and often blinked their eyes.

After the first shock, it was not exactly clear to Major Feverton that Q had slipped from his grasp, especially since Seeberg did not take the desk with the metal band.

But when Commander Wolfe grumpily refused to consider Operation Newsreel until Seeberg, as "senior officer in Q," should have initialed it, the blow fell. Flushed and unhappy, Major Feverton brought the plans for Operation Newsreel to Commander Seeberg.

Operation Newsreel was the Major's scheme for making newsreels of American conquests to date, and then dropping the cans of film in the garden of the Imperial Palace. Emperor Hirohito would see these films on the Imperial Palace Film Projector, turn momentarily from yellow to white as he surrendered, and so America would Win the War.

Instead of signing his initials on the plans, Seeberg substituted a four-letter word which happened to begin with the same letter, then handed the plans back to the Major.

Feverton saw the word, smiled, lost control of his smile, flushed, turned orange color, started to speak, lost his tongue, and stamped away. He tore off the offending four-letter comment, and put it in the Confidential Trash. But he did not forward the plans, as he had a right to do, to General Waddleman. That day men fought to be Q's Confidential Trash Burner and Incinerator Officer. On the scrap of paper was a word as old as language itself. In fact, it probably, like so much of Lieutenant Commander Seeberg's vocabulary, preceded language.

The Major prepared a request for transfer. In approved business college style his thick fingers, curved just right, flew over the keys, and his back was straight, typing roller straight. Again he walked down the hall to Commander Wolfe's office. Again he walked back, informed that this too had to be initialed by Seeberg.

"Well, Major," said Seeberg pleasantly, "keep stirring the crap and you'll get splattered yourself, as good Pope Sebastian says. I can forward this — " his voice changed to a roar — "marked Disapproved." The Major flinched, amazed that so much noise should come from such a small hunched body.

For the first time Seeberg noticed on the Major's desk a large sign reading (perhaps it had been lettered by the Major himself): HAVE YOU KILLED YOUR JAP TODAY? Seeberg's eyes took on bright blue glints. His voice went to the decibel level needed for being heard in a destroyer during hurricane force winds. As all Q held its breath Lieutenant Commander Seeberg ripped up the sign and inquired, "Can't you tell shit from shoe polish?"

The Major fled. Commander Seeberg happily hummed:

> Dirty Gertie from Bizerte
> Hid a mousetrap 'neath her skirtie,
> Strapped it to her knee-cap purty,
> Made her boy friend's fingers hurtie.

Seeberg stopped humming when he saw an ensign carrying a cup of coffee to Yeoman Prantz. The ensign held out the sugar to Prantz.

"Prantz," said Seeberg in a voice with an icy rasp to it. Prantz half rose from his desk, as though suddenly kicked in the rear. Something in the tone, perhaps, reminded him of the old Navy in the days long before Q, when the *Wyorada* was still the greatest dreadnaught of the seas.

"Front and center, Prantz," said the Commander. Prantz ambled to the Commander's desk in his usual belly forward style.

"Regular Navy?" said Seeberg in disbelief. "Formerly of the *Wyorada?*"

Prantz rested his hand on Seeberg's desk and said, confused, amiable, superior, "Yes. Yes, sir."

"Take your hand off my desk," said Lieutenant Commander Seeberg in a voice that was nine parts dry ice and one part vocal chord. "And stand up," he roared. At the far end of Q several new ensigns stood up, then quickly sat down when they realized the command was, luckily, not for them.

Prantz looked appealingly at the Major but he was busy typing over and over on his typewriter, "Loyalty up and loyalty down."

"Make your own coffee," said Seeberg, "and drink it with the enlisted men." Q sighed, as with one breath. There was to be no false democracy in Q.

But Prantz was slow to perceive this new truth about human relations in Q. He gave it the old enlisted men's try. "I was only trying to carry out the Major's instructions —"

"Are you arguing with me, Prantz?" said Seeberg. His tone was one of detached scientific curiosity, of the kind that rises in the human breast when a rock is turned over and a new and delightfully squashable slug appears to view.

Prantz, his empire shattering, was desperate. "I don't think it's fair to change the regulations all of a sudden. I've got my rights too, damn it." He made the fatal mistake of shaking his fist in the air.

Lieutenant Commander Seeberg scribbled on a piece of paper and handed it to Prantz. "Cut these orders," he said, "and prepare the necessary copies for the Captain and the Paymaster." It was the order breaking Prantz back to Yeoman Third.

"But — "

"You'll have a chance to discuss it all at Captain's Mast tomorrow," said Seeberg. He roared again, "You'll find us all ears."

"But — "

"When did you last have sea duty, Prantz?"

"After I was trapped in the hull of the *Wyorada*," he said, with a touch of martyr's pride, "I was told I wouldn't need to have sea duty ever again."

"You look pretty fat and sassy to me," said Seeberg, "but maybe we shouldn't break a promise like that. Instead of sea duty, how about going in with the assault waves of the next big landing?"

"But — "

"As good Pope Vincent always says, don't throw stones until you've closed your own shutters. Carry on, Prantz."

The next day a finer, cleaner and more industrious Prantz sat at his desk in front of Major Feverton. His Yeoman First marks had been ripped off, but had not been replaced by third class markings. In fact, after a second argument at Captain's Mast, all hands had felt he should start again from the bottom as seaman. He had been assured that the officers of Q, and this was certainly true, would follow his progress with interest, with great interest, and that they had every confidence in his ability to rise through the ranks again however slowly.

Commander Seeberg stopped by Gordian's desk. "Whose mail is that you're censoring?" he asked. Major Feverton brightly volunteered, since he had just left it off, "That's our bit." Seeberg glared and Feverton hastily retired. "Is it from Q?" asked Seeberg. "No sir," said Gordian quietly. Seeberg grabbed up the letters and went from desk to desk, followed by Prantz holding a large sack.

When the sack was full, Seeberg told Feverton to deliver the sack to Wolfe. "Tell him to ram them up his ass," he said, laughing coarsely.

In a moment Wolfe was at the door. "Was that from you, Foul Mouth Harry?" he said to Seeberg.

"Hello, Tomato Guts. You look as if you need to get your ashes hauled."

Wolfe laughed sourly and retired.

"As good Pope Borgia always says, grab a commander where the hairs are short," said Seeberg, to the air of Q.

A pencil landed on your desk and you hurried to Seeberg. He held out a diary to you, with a beautifully typed translation in the fist of Feverton. The translation explained that "a drizzling rain entered Singapore." Seeberg pointed to the Japanese. In the crabbed hand of the dead Japanese diarist you read out loud: "The destroyer *Shigure* entered Singapore." "Shigure" meant drizzling rain, true enough, but it was also a destroyer name, and this was a Japanese naval rating's diary. Seeberg looked satisfied.

"What are you working on?" You showed him your atrocity collection. A diarist wrote of his American prisoners, "We strung them to a tree and bayoneted them. They took a long time to die." Vice-admiral Abe celebrated the Yasunkuni Shrine Festival in October 1942 by ordering nine American prisoners beheaded. A Japanese enlisted man who had been in the Philippines wrote: "I beheaded a man who had Japanese money — the Americans who fell of exhaustion were buried alive. I write down Tojo's words and felt refreshed: 'When opposing sides are exhausted, the side which has lost faith in victory will be defeated.'" A general order advised shooting down all parachuting American flyers. Seeberg snorted. "Crap," he said, "we started shooting down Japanese fliers first."

Seeberg flung at you a manual in bright red covers, titled *Japanese Combined Fleet Doctrine*. He opened it to a chapter headed "Decoy Fleets and Ambush Attacks." You saw that it was about the deployment of a Decoy Fleet and a Main Fleet (formed into Ambush Attack Fleets). You remembered that a diarist had quoted from this chapter. "I'll bet you ten chamber pots to your one that they use that scheme in their final fleet action," said Seeberg. "Work on it." He walked away and spun back. "I haven't got the time to check your work," he said bitterly.

It was several moments before you realized that he had paid you a compliment.

Prantz left a letter from Leilani at your desk. "It got mixed up in my mail for a couple of days, sir," he said. You knew he was lying, and you were pretty sure he had steamed it open.

"By the way," he said, "I hear some of that brown stuff is really hot. Do they all look white after a while? Do Oriental girls have their slits sideways?"

"What's bothering you, Prantz?"

"The need for poontang, sir. I got an irresistible craving for brown poontang. Got me a new shack job. Last name's Cam — Cam Shaft. Or is it Kim Cam Shaft?"

"If you've really got her you ought to be able to answer all your questions about their pussies."

"What officer on a ship is in charge of damage control, sir?"

"What are you getting at, Prantz?"

"It's simple, Mr. Classen. We kept the Navy together before the war. Even Feverton helped keep the Army going before the war. You come in after the war's started and in ninety days you're able to command somebody who's been in the Navy for ten years."

You had been trained for a year, not ninety days, but you didn't want to argue with Prantz.

"Let's get it straight," said Prantz, "I hate your guts — " He added slowly, "Sir."

The letter from Leilani wasn't much, just an announcement of her graduation from the nursing school two days ago. And a little note added by Leilani saying that she had signed on for the Army Nurse Corps. She was flying to the states for indoctrination courses, and would be sent to Europe because of her Japanese ancestry. It surprised you that you could remember how well Leilani walked, with the grace of perfect health. You got her house on the phone, her mother answered and you hung up. The Major called you over.

As was his wont in times of crisis, the Major was typing directly on the stencil so that his newest and hottest idea should hit the presses as quickly as possible.

He had classified it SECRET, then as you stood beside him he typed above the word SECRET the word TOP.

As a special favor he was now allowing you to see it before it went on to Commander Wolfe. It was a plan for painting the face of the Emperor of Japan on the decks of the American carriers. The Japanese dive bombers and torpedo bombers would be so overcome by reverence for the Emperor when they saw the Imperial Countenance that they woulld swerve away and probably crash harmlessly in the ocean. And that's how the War Would Be Won.

Commander Seeberg accepted this new plan dourly at first; some of the ensigns of Q claimed they had heard him say it was "as poor as piss in a pumpkin." But then he began to take an interest in it. He got on the intercom to CincPac and talked to an admiral there whom he called only "Beerbelly." There were several calls back and forth on the intercom that day. That evening, it was agreed that all those interested in this scheme would meet at the house of one of the admirals. Except for Feverton.

The next day Commander Seeberg asked the Major to let them know if he had any more ideas like that one up his sleeve, since it had been directly responsible for the biggest and best brawl on Makalapa in ten years. He was humming:

> She made a fine stew of the savage Zulu
> And she scrambled the Hottentot's brains;
> 'Twas a dainty menu when the cooking was through
> And she dined from her lovers' remains.

There was just one catch, said Seeberg, which might mean a slight delay in carrying out this brilliant scheme. There seemed to be a shortage of paint in the precise imperial yellow color of the Japanese imperial skin.

The admirals of Makalapa wanted to get that skin color just right. Some wanted deep yellow and some wanted orange yellow and some held out for yellow-belly yellow, but until the point was settled, they wouldn't paint the face on the decks of the American carriers. Goodnaturedly for once, Commander Seeberg roared at the Major, "Do the job right, or don't do the crapping job at all, as good Pope George the Eighteenth always says."

CHAPTER TWENTY-ONE

June, 1944

> *When the rescue nets were stretched between the de-*
> *stroyer and the burning carrier, the stronger men in the*
> *water climbed up over the heads of the weaker, who*
> *drowned.*
>
> BEGEL, The Battle for Visaya Gulf

❋

YOU AND PRANTZ had an arrangement. You were to provide him with liquor from your Officers' Hard Liquor Allowance. He was to arrange a jeep from the motor pool on occasional evenings. It was no part of the arrangement that Prantz should ask what color the poontang was this evening, but you put up with this question to get the jeep. Betty Comfrey had, very pleasantly, made it clear that she expected you to show up in your own transportation.

"Light poontang tonight?" said Prantz as he slipped you the keys to your jeep. "Very light," you said, "the only girl in an albino quintuplet."

You drove Betty to the Officers' Club in the Navy Yard. She was in tailored yellow seersucker; she was neat and trim and elegant, she danced with you effortlessly, she followed your rumba squares and butterfly breaks with amusement and you knew she liked to be held — not too firm, but held securely — in a sentimental slow-dipping foxtrot.

"Don't be frightened of me," she said coolly, "or I shall stop liking you."

Her voice had a finishing school edge to it and you wondered how much you really liked her. But her hand held yours more warmly than her words suggested, and she refused a Navy captain's invitation to dance, and smiled at you. She had refused a great many invitations since your arrival at the Club.

Out in the center of the Loch you could see a fine dark spiral of smoke that spun itself out from the ammunition ship *Achilles Victory*. Lighters clustered round her and invisible men strained furiously to unload her ammunition.

"Do you mind staying here? If she blows she'll take all Pearl Harbor with her."

"We're very much alike," she said. "We're both a little too fond of danger. In a civilized passive way. I think I might have made a very good campfollower."

"Campfollowers drink a lot." And you motioned to the waiter.

Her voice took on its cool defensive edge. "Don't try to make me drink too much," she said. But she dug her fingertips sharply into your palm, and then she released your hand entirely.

And she drank steadily on with you, drink for drink, always calm and golden and well bred, and together you watched the lighters unloading ammunition in the Loch, and you felt the tiny gnaw of danger, the more pronounced because the prettiness of Betty had something of the prettiness of a child.

A quietness fell on both of you that was very much like fatigue. Each day you left Q in desperate search of a means to put a world from your shoulders. You had all, at Q, been sorting freightcar loads of documents from Kwajalein and Eniwetok, and now it was beginning again from Saipan — diaries, tail wheel inventories, force general orders, new plane manuals, night torpedo tactics, shore defense lessons, papaya cultivation, snails as protein. You missed Gordian who had quietly left for Saipan and you did your work as if it were the work, the duty of a stranger who had borrowed your name and your tall hard body. The weather was strange and cloudy, unseasonal Kona weather, full of the threat, rarely fulfilled, of thunder and rain, and each day, as the work mounted, you sank for moments at a time into a state too listless and inattentive for dreams or daydreams; when you woke again it was often with a painful snap of the neck, and an unconscious movement of your foot to keep yourself from stumbling down, down, down.

Your own fatigue brought about a profound sympathy for Betty.

It was no easy matter to stand and wait at one side of the war, watching and nourishing and waiting; you suddenly became very much aware of her as a person.

She at once sensed your new interest, and deliberately, meaning to shock or to test you, she said, "Your friend Miss Kim is at Schofield in the Army Nurse Corps."

"She's in the States, in training."

"No, she's back. I saw her at the university yesterday." She examined you gravely, her small full upper lip almost in a pout, and she smiled prettily, pleased that you had not known of Leilani's return; she did not wish to regard Leilani as a rival to herself, no matter how light the flirtation between you.

You felt a mood of longing, intense as a physical injury, a melancholy feeling of life turning by you, like a globe revolving in its space — this evening, however trivial, was softly spinning itself away, never to return again, and it was your evening, no one else knew, or could know, its aimless, sweet quality.

In a rocking rhythm a combo from the orchestra played and sang:

Ah got de so'dier-man sadness, de so'dier-man blues,
Ah wanna do what ah want and wanna do it when ah choose.
Ah got de mean man, movin' van, yaller dog wid a can,
Holy hell, so'dier-man blues.

"I don't like people to play jazz like that," and Betty's pretty lips took on a childishly firm expression. It was time to go in to dinner.

The dinner party was hardly a success; neither of you hungered for food, and you both were on edge, you were both difficult, knowing that some sort of crisis would surely come in your relationship.

It was understood between you that affection was to be demonstrated in neatly regulated stages — after two or three dates (in this Collegiate Code) you could kiss the girl's hand, then you could kiss her lips; after one more ecstatic week (or sometimes two) you were allowed — respectfully — to fondle her breasts, and there you halted for a time, both of you murmuring passionately that you did not do these things with everyone, though of course you both did.

But this fixed "courtship pattern," as Gordian would have termed it, was tempered by acts of surprising tenderness that took you both unaware; one night she had held your head to her naked breast and had burst into tears at the evening's end, unwilling, almost unable, to release you. And another night you had stroked her hair for hours. And there were flaring moments of resentment, too, that you never expressed directly — "The missionaries came to Honolulu to do good, and they did well."

Wanting to be alone with each other, and yet half afraid that this night might settle everything between you, you took the American way out and went to the movie.

The picture began with a closeup of a Marine foxhole outpost, and a crude sign, "Tokyo 3380½ miles." In a brief, ugly second you realized that the unstirring young Marine in the foxhole was dead. Betty gasped and took your hand.

Next a helicopter view, taken from above like the scenes in the *Genji Monogatari* scrolls, of an All-American town with a midwest courthouse and square. The town you knew, from hundreds of movies, was Santa Rosa, California, which — the village virus as Proteus — could show the columns of the old South, the stucco of Florida, the brick of Oklahoma City, or, as now, American Edwardian. The helicoptered camera eye spiraled down to the Edwardian house and plunged through the ceiling to show Pop Attaboy clutching the blackbordered telegram that announced the death of his Dannylad. "I can't go on," said Pop Attaboy, looking up through the ceiling and right into the camera lens, where he saw not Jehovah, as you at first feared, but Ghostly Granpap.

The dead boy's dead grandfather wore a GAR hat and civil war uniform (in the versions for playing south of the Mason-Dixon line he wore Confederate uniform).

Ghostly Granpap, playing Virgil to Pop Attaboy's Dante, took Pop back through his memories of Dannylad.

First Dannylad played Indian and sold "limonad" for a scout ax, but gave his earnings instead to a beggar. Dannylad was befriended by a mongrel dog named Gassy, whose owner appeared on the stage long enough to sell Gassy to a millionaire dog fancier whose kennel men spent most of their long day beating Gassy to a pulp. But Gassy was a trick dog and knew how to pick kennel locks with his teeth; he escaped limping horribly on all four paws. By the next day Gassy had recovered and helped Dannylad trap a gang of robbers who were trying to carry away the millionaire's million from the storm cellar where he had always kept it ever since 1929. Dannylad refused a reward of $10,000 and took Gassy instead, with a lifetime supply of dogmeat.

It was time for Dannylad to grow up and go to college and say a sad farewell to aging Gassy. But Gassy followed Dannylad across the continent on just his four paws, arriving in time to stop the show (the first year at Dannylad's college was spent in rehearsing a wonderful number in which fifty coeds and fifty dancing cowboys did "We're in the Army now" on horseback at a coed rodeo — Dannylad and Lulukins rode the white horses and sang, while the rest rode Palomino horses and hummed).

A shot flickered across the screen — Pearl Harbor buzzed by Japanese planes, the flaming *Wyorada* turning turtle, the *Arizona* blowing up.

Dannylad immediately joined the Marines, while aged Gassy wagged his tail in approval (and the openair movie audience shouted "You'll be sorry.")

Hackie the taxidriver drove Dannylad to the Marine base, and signed up in the Marines himself — his taxi was very convenient for the dates with Lulukins which constituted part of Dannylad's basic training. At the Marine base Dannylad quickly made friends with an All-American football center who was Chappie the Chaplain, and he made friends — more slowly — with a brave boy who turned coward whenever a gun was fired and who was called Chicken, and he made friends last of all with the usual Hardboiled Sergeant who was called Egg. At the Marine base the boots and Lulukins and her friends had plenty of time for clever dance routines because that was the other part of their training, except for once when Dannylad, Hackie, Chappie, Chicken, and Egg all ran through the obstacle course.

Basic training successfully completed, the Marines went to sea, with many practical jokes on Sergeant Egg, and many serious moments with Chappie. And suddenly they landed on Guadalcanal and began a fight for their lives with Chinese movie extras.

Chicken kept on being a coward every time the guns fired (this was pretty much all the time now). He really disgraced himself on his first patrol, and Dannylad had to rescue his patrol, and then stand duty for Chicken at the outpost. When Dannylad was killed,

3380½ miles from Tokyo, Chicken at last learned his lesson and went on an All-American berserk, bayoneting, shooting, and finally braining a grand total of thirty Chinese movie extras.

Ghostly Granpap's equipment included a Ghostly Film Library, and he showed Pop Attaboy a bloodcurdling montage of scenes: American soldiers on retreat in Bataan, and Russian children being bled for blood plasma by German troops.

Chicken Warhero came to the States, on a bond-selling tour with Lulukins, his dancing partner. Sure enough, Ghostly Granpap led him right to Pop Attaboy. It wasn't easy for Chicken to stay with Pop Attaboy and Gassy, now the oldest dog in captivity with a lifetime supply of dogmeat. But Chicken stayed, and told about Dannylad and all he had learned from him about how to go berserk. Wonderdog Gassy was suspicious of Chicken Warhero at first (just as Lulukins had been until she got engaged to him on the first night of the bond-selling tour), but as he listened to Chicken's story he stopped growling, and finally licked Chicken's hand (in the very same spot where he had first bitten it), did a last trick, and died of duodenal ulcers.

Chicken and Lulukins and Pop Attaboy buried Gassy while a heavenly chorus played taps in thirds.

In the concluding shot Chicken danced with Lulukins, a patriotic soft-shoe routine at an aircraft workers' bond rally; emotionally overcome, Chicken and Lulukins promised the workers to name their first boy Dannylad.

A final sequence showed Pop Attaboy smiling his favorite smile — through his tears — while Ghostly Granpap and Ghostly Dannylad and hundreds of ghostly extras in all uniforms of all American wars sang mine eyes have seen the coming of their terrible swift sword mine ears have heard the trampling where the grapes of wrath are stored (in the versions for below the Mason-Dixon line the song of the soldier ghosts was changed to Dixie look away look away look away Dixieland).

You and Betty came out of the open air movie holding each others' hands tightly; your fingers tingled against hers and she didn't want to go anywhere else but to her home. At the entrance she had you turn to a part of the drive where you could silently coast downhill, out of the grounds, so as not to disturb her mother who was a light sleeper. You both had a drink in her small private house, and then another — ice and alcohol seemed to go with the muggy weather and its flashes of soundless lighting.

She leaned into your arms, looking curled up and golden and flushed, and you stopped for more ice in your drinks and then for more drinks in your drinks. When you kissed again some barrier, some resistance between both of you was gone, but your approaching triumph had a surprising ashen taste, you became suddenly like a man doing something expected of him, almost, the phrase leaped to mind, as though you were doing your duty.

She never wanted you to see her breasts and the lights had to be turned off. Then she fell asleep, as suddenly as a cat, only to wake up a quarter of an hour later and ask if you admired her legs. She had very beautiful legs, she said, and she let her skirt slip down to show you. Another round of drinks seemed like a very good idea but most certainly was not. It seemed a sensible idea to put the skirt away so that it would not become wrinkled, then you both became very wrinkle-conscious and took off lots more of your clothes so that they would not wrinkle. Betty found some blankets in a chest rather too conveniently located under the sofa, and spread them out, and a sheet on top, and you lay on these, on the floor, to keep the sofa from getting wrinkled.

But it was not to be one of the world's masterly scenes of seduction — at the very last moment it turned out that Betty Comfrey did not intend, this evening at least, to go through with It after all. She only did It with men she was in love with. How many men was that, you asked. She had only done It with three.

To the memory of doing It while in love she would always be faithful. You got up, very much the gentleman bounder, somewhat unsteady, but full of respect for people who did It while in love, in happy contrast to yourself who put passion above love, and above doing It too, if you wanted the honest to God truth, which so very few people did these days.

"Do you mind very much?" she asked. You made your best gentleman bounder bow and stumble in answer. But your exit lost something of its graciousness and Old World charm when you had to tiptoe back under the royal palm trees, knock on her door and ask to be allowed to come back inside and retrieve your trousers, which you unfortunately had left under her sofa cushions in a lunatic eagerness to keep them in press.

After knocking for some time, you entered, turned on the light, and found your trousers. Nude and golden in the cone of yellow light, Betty lay half curled up like a sleeping kitten; she stirred, her arms moved, she murmured your name. You knelt beside her and stroked her shoulder. You imagined yourself lying on top of her, forcing her legs apart — in a long sober moment you discovered that you — part of you — was capable, was even about to rape a drunken woman, and when you ran from her door you were running, too, from this newly discovered part of yourself in a race that could never end, that had always to be run again.

At your jeep you released the brake and pushed, and as it slowly gathered speed you looked back. On the lanai of the main house stood a shadowy white-robed figure — the beautiful figure of Betty's mother. She watched you and raised her arm — in farewell? to summon you back? The jeep accelerated and just in time you tumbled aboard.

At the bottom of the Nuuanu Valley road you were picked up by the shore patrol for being out after curfew without a pass. The shore patrol lieutenant informed you that your pass had been superseded by a pass stamped with the Cincpac seal, and signed, as he put it forcefully, "by a living Admiral," rather than by John Paul Jones. He also found much to criticize and little to praise in your jeep trip ticket which read "Jokepoa to Bob Hope and return." "Getting it regular, Mr. 236711?" asked the shore patrol lieutenant.

"Tomcats come from miles to take my postgraduate courses."

Back at Pupule Court you found two messages tacked to your door. One instructed you to report to Q immediately. The second asked you to call Lieutenant Kim at a Schofield number. It was a moment until you remembered that Lieutenant Kim was Leilani.

On your return trip through Honolulu the same shore patrol lieutenant arrested you again. "What kind of pills do you take, mister?" he asked. "I think we'd better put you under observation for a month to learn your secrets." Only a telephone call to Q enabled you to secure your release.

In Q all the lights were on, and Seeberg had piled on his desk a two foot high stack of charts indexed as *South Japan*.

The topmost chart was of the entrances to the Inland Sea. Pencil markings in Japanese showed new Japanese mine lanes at the eastern entrance. These corrected older markings.

Seeberg's phone rang and Wolfe answered it. "No," said Wolfe laconically into the phone. "No radio contact for two nights now."

The date received stamp showed that the chart had been in Q for at least two weeks. It had been sent on from Saipan by Gordian, and marked, in his hand, RUSH.

Somewhere, nosing against the mine defenses of the Inland Sea, was an American submarine, supplied with the correct information on the old mine lanes.

You thought of a submarine on which you had made a practice run. It had a life-size nude woman pasted on the curved ceiling of the officers' wardroom. You imagined the submarine disabled by a mine explosion, settling to the bottom, you saw men laboring to repair the damage, you smelled the slow exhaustion of air, you sweated in the growing heat, your lungs began to ache as chlorine gas drifted up from the batteries, and long after you all were dead the water would at last begin to enter, in tiny jets at high speed, flooding up and up toward the nude pasted on the curving ceiling of the wardroom.

"All right," said Seeberg viciously. "Who indexed these maps? And when?"

Wolfe answered Seeberg's phone again. You knew at once it was The Admiral. "Yes, sir," said Wolfe to The Admiral. You were startled to realize that Wolfe said "Sir" to anyone. "Overdue, presumed missing."

Seeberg's face had no trace of compassion or forgiveness. You had all had a hand in the sorting of these charts — Major Feverton, BIJ Standish, Napoleon — you had done some yourself. After Rarawa you and Gordian had discussed the need for better indexes to unused material, and you had invented a kind of system. It should have worked, but somehow it had not. And all of you worked steadily enough, but none of you worked at top speed anymore.

"We're all responsible, Commander," you said bluntly to Seeberg.

Wolfe was angry at both of you, and at himself as well. "Forget it," he shouted. He adjusted the venetian blinds behind Seeberg's desk to cut down the draft, with an air of studied self-preservation.

He sank wearily into Seeberg's chair, and you realized that in the time spent at Q you had gone from a youth to a young man, but Wolfe had slipped over that fine deadly line that separates age from old age. "Get these maps out of here," he said, more quietly.

Before you left Q you stopped at Seeberg's desk. "I haven't been out for some time, sir," you said.

Seeberg's eyes were frigid with contempt. "I know that."

"I want to go on the next landing."

"STALEMATE ONE suit you?"

"Yes."

"I'll think it over."

At 11 A.M. the next day, on the grounds of Q, within its double fence of barbed wire, you received the Bronze Star for your part in the landing on Rarawa, for saying to Admiral Norcross that the Japanese had not spotted the Rarawa invasion fleet. Seeberg watched you with eyes like ice. The ceremony had been arranged by Major Feverton; even so, it went off with that unconscious grace which the Navy could always summon from somewhere at such moments. You were assured your actions had been in accord with the highest and best traditions of the United States Navy.

General Waddleman, assuring you that your actions had been in the highest tradition of the Army, too, in the highest, they had been, of the Army, tradition, too — pinned the ribbon on your chest. Over his shoulder you caught a glimpse of the *Wyorada* before you stepped back, saluted, and were dismissed. She rode high and straight in the water, and men were at work dismantling her gun turrets and deck structure.

That evening at the Schofield Nurses' barracks you walked through verbena flowers, up the wooden porch steps, and left your name at the entrance hall. In the center of a round table a large block of ice slumped in a punch bowl big enough to sit in. As nurses came into the room, they chipped ice off the block, and from a side table they took two glasses, then they rushed off on their dates. Nurses, you thought, were trained to be efficient.

An admirably pretty girl entered the room. For a brief instant, almost unconsciously resentful of some subtle change in her appearance, you did not admit to yourself that she was, indeed, Leilani.

You drove long and silently, as if by instinct going back to Honolulu, to Waikiki, out past Green Point to an area of rich estates and deserted private streets. On one of these you parked Prantz's jeep. You were trying to forget his parting words: "Dark poontang tonight, Mr. Classen?"

She had brought ice, glasses, even whiskey, an unopened bottle. She seemed more experienced than the girl you had known before — lost in the illusion of separation you had thought of yourself as changing but you had imagined her as still the same.

At first you sat creakingly distant, voiceless as two clapperless bells. You found her unshrinking glance disconcerting.

Melting ice dripped on the floor of the jeep; the whiskey bottle stayed unopened. She laughed. "They don't work for us, do they?"

She suggested that you go to the Stepney estate whose Japanese gardener would let her in — the present owners of the estate, afraid of Japanese invasion after the attack on Pearl Harbor, had left the islands for the duration.

"They did not have the courage to live there," she said, not realizing how she took the tough realism of the borderer, of the Koreans, for granted.

You hesitated still. She took your hand, saying, "Houses belong to those who use them."

Within the grounds you sat beside a seawall covered with night-blooming cereus. Behind you, not far from the sea, was a mansion with room after room of whitesheeted furniture, and a Japanese banquet room — large beautifully written characters near the ceiling of one wall advised you to be like an arrow when things go well, and to be like an arrow when things go badly.

On the grounds were garages, orchid greenhouses, a gatehouse, an ornamental pool whose fountain was a laughing boy urinating into the water — the *mannequin pisse.*

"Betty Comfrey left the islands too, for a year at the beginning of the war," she said quietly. "Most of the white girls left."

She asked, simply enough, what you were thinking. You were thinking several things, almost simultaneously: that few women would be really pleased if they could know everything a man was thinking; that you had received a postcard from Betty asking you to see her again; and you were thinking of Seeberg — in a spasm of frenzy he had said, "I hope the men who worked on the charts will count to ninety each night. For the ninety men on the crew of that submarine." You would, none of you, count to ninety each night, and Seeberg would forget his rage. You told Lani of none of your thoughts. Instead, you traced together the Big Dipper, which she called, Korean fashion, by the name of the Bear, and you looked for Cetus, the Sea Monster, and Andromeda, so modest she hid her face with her hands while awaiting rescue by Perseus who killed the Sea Monster, and you looked for the Fishes: the Northern Fish, the Western Fish, the Southern Fish, and the Dolphin near Sagitta — Sagitta, the arrow flung from the bow.

You remembered a stanza from "Ariran":

> Many stars in the deep sky
> Many crimes in the life of man
> Ariran, Ariran, Arari O!
> Crossing the hills of Ariran.

Her face turned tawny in the rising full moon, it had an almost fantastic sweetness, and you thought again how strong she seemed, in the short column of her neck, in her full rounded legs, in her figure. Your arms touched, and you remembered that she had once said, jokingly, that when sleeves touched it was through the cause and effect, the En, of a previous existence. In a marriage, you thought, she would be the shaping partner, though seeming always herself to be shaped. Your passion wanted you to believe, too hopefully, that your inmost thoughts were in harmony, and hundreds of vague silvery fancies rocketed through your mind.

"In Korea," said Leilani, "the storyteller used to come on our street. He had colored paper pictures. I liked to have him tell the story of Frail Gotami."

Frail Gotami had been reborn in a poor house, and when she married, her poverty made her husband's family show contempt for her until she bore her husband a son. But the wheel of fate and illusion turned as it has always turned, and one day the son died.

Frail Gotami could not endure her son's death. She refused to accept it, and she went about the city carrying her dead son on her hip and asking for medicine. But those she asked for medicine only laughed at her and turned her away, until she reached the Tathagata, the Possessor of the Ten Forces, and she asked of him, "Give me medicine." He took pity on her, and in his pity he told her to fetch mustard seed from any house in the city where no one had ever died. And carrying her dead son on her hip she trudged from house to house, seeking that house in the city where no one had ever died. But after trying many houses she came to realize that all households, rich and poor, suffered grief and loss. None was exempt. There was no such mustard seed to be had, in this city, or in any other city where men lived.

And Frail Gotami carried her son to the burning ground.

So it was that Frail Gotami learned, as all must learn, that whatever is born dies, and she learned that the cure for grief is not to grieve for your own sorrow till numbness comes, but to grieve for the sorrow of others. For death comes to men, as floods to sleeping villages —

In you stirred restlessly your old, long-suffering acquaintance, the Ironical Man. "I was raised on the story of Tootles, the little locomotive who learned how to adjust to other locomotives and how never *never* to leave track. Tootles can't die because he has interchangeable parts."

"I told the story not for you but for myself," she said. Her face shone with a milky gentleness, she was beautiful in the flattering moonlight. "In Korea the elder sister carries her younger brother on her back. Younger brother was ill, and I carried him in the sunlight when he wanted it so, and at last he died. For a long time I refused to be comforted." Her face was pale. "But all such grief is not true grief — it is only wrath."

You thought and you spoke in broken fragments of sentences, in wild stirrings of desire — you forced your hand under her white silk slip to the secret smoothness beneath — fires ran through your flesh and your ears stunned.

She uttered a cry that seemed to be in a savage tongue, she fumbled open the buttons of her uniform, she took your hand and pressed it intimately to her. Undefended, helpless, in a crude stifled voice, "If you must sleep with someone then, take me."

She had fallen or collapsed to her knees by the stone seawall, her head struck against the ground. "We must have loved," she cried, "before we were born, in some former, unhappy birth."

The gnarled Japanese gardener, more pine than man, tapped on your shoulder, and called your attention to the artificial pond. He had turned on the fountain full blast, and the laughing boy statue urinated copiously in the water. Excited, the fish began tracing through air their voluptuous, mooncrazed arcs.

It was his way of telling you, politely, that he wished to lockup.

When you returned Leilani to her quarters, the block of ice had turned to warm water. Once you had visited a Honolulu temple with her, and she had showed you, among the objects of worship, a box containing the Lotus Sutra, and beside it a box holding a half-size replica of the Declaration of Independence. Before both boxes were equal piles of pink and white rice cakes, oranges, and pineapples.

You saw gathering behind her desperately pretty eyes the shadows of an intense and private grief. In a flurry of conflicting moods she swayed instinctively toward you. With a feeling of wretched urgency, holding out your hands, hoping to bridge a dizzily widening gap, you asked her to tell you what she was thinking at that moment, tell you honestly, and all.

Faintly, she murmured — No — then in helpless defiance, in a soft and lovely way, Never.

She was wonderfully, overwhelmingly pretty — you had lost her.

Alone in Pupule Court you opened the dusty drawer of a small rattan table, searching for forgotten cigarettes. There you found, in a half-illiterate hand, the telephone number of Maria. You tore it into pieces.

You dwindled to the center of a small flame, a whitehot dwarfish universe of sensuous passion — around you stretched forever an iceblue sky and the crackling music of spheres, a frozen infinite tinkling against which you could only burn the more fiercely.

But before you retrieved the torn bits of paper and went out to phone, you sat, your head pillowed on your arms, searching for a way to be faithful to some vague, never to be realized image of yourself, that you had lost far away, in Palisades, long ago, as a boy.

Part Three

STALEMATE

CHAPTER TWENTY-TWO

August, 1944

True enough, rescue organization work was not begun till the third day of the battle and some 400 ship-wrecked sailors died of drowning and exposure, but in any big land and sea battle there are bound to be mistakes.

BEGEL, The Battle for Visaya Gulf

❋

IN A SECOND curt talk about Operation STALEMATE Lieutenant Commander Seeberg did not commit himself about you, but he hinted that Major Feverton might soon be able to satisfy his suddenly insatiable appetite for combat.

Every free interval in the day — and Major Feverton now had two *Pending* baskets in recognition of the need for free intervals — the Major was to be found out on the pistol range. Needless to say, at twenty-five yards with a carbine he was devastatingly accurate.

On the Major's desk you spied an unusual form. It was an application for a campaign ribbon. It had never occurred to you to apply for a campaign ribbon, especially in advance of the campaign. You had in any event regarded ribbons, even your new decoration, as courting devices which you wore to impress the local girls if you lacked inner confidence. But the Major now informed you how important they were on your record, for your career.

"Career? What are you going to do after the war?" You remembered that the Major had gone to business college before the war, and had slowly worked his way up to owning his own gas station, with three pumps.

"I'm going to staff school, of course," said the Major. "It's a natural. I've already filled out the forms." He went back to work on his application for a campaign ribbon.

That afternoon, a relatively slack one, many members of Q busied themselves devising not only suitable ribbons, but even some highly unusual campaigns for the Major. *In* and *Out* baskets filled and emptied as these were carried back and forth by breathless yeomen. The Major noticed your industry and made a brief speech praising it. Commander Seeberg looked up for a moment, his head tipped to one side by his arthritis, his eyes blue and cold. Then he went back to reading the day's dispatches.

The Major might well have received one of his new decorations, with dire consequences for Q, when in came a group of new ensigns, wearing khaki coats, neckties, shoulderboards, and looking hot and uncomfortable in the sticky Pearl Harbor air.

The Major brightened. He was clearly hoping to be allowed by Commander Seeberg to tell them about loyalty up and loyalty down, and running with it when it was your ball, as it so often was for junior officers. But Commander Seeberg quickly dismissed them to let them arrange about their quarters. They were to report the next day.

Frustrated, the Major sent out the enlisted men, and called together the regulars of Q for a confidential talk on the combat rifle, the combat carbine, and the combat pistol, and how losing one's combat rifle, combat carbine or combat pistol, or forgetting the number of one's combat rifle, combat carbine, or combat pistol was like spitting on the flag. The Major patted his own carbine which went with him everywhere now, as an illustration of how the carbine should be part of one's own body. He had had its trigger filed to a hair trigger so as to be able to mow down multitudes of Japanese and he advised you all to do the same.

The enlisted men were allowed to resume their errands at the end of this confidential chat, and the Major began studying the fitness reports of the new draft of officers.

The Major happily sorted the fitness reports into little piles. Then he summoned you, after a brief suggestion from Prantz.

Your subsection of Q concentrated on airplanes for two reasons: (1) you had built model airplanes as a boy, (2) the Annapolis men on the staff of Q and many of its related bureaus, with a few exceptions, such as Wolfe, had no interest in airplanes. Battleships would win the war. Carriers and airplanes were a temporary phase.

In the next war, no doubt, the same men would concentrate on carriers and airplanes, while the winning weapon was regarded with aversion. Your airplane subsection in Q was hardly ever bothered by the Annapolis group and you were able to run it as you saw fit. Now the Major was discussing some proposed additions to your little group.

"You probably wouldn't want Grossman," said the Major kindly, looking over a folder. "He's one of the chosen race." He laughed appreciatively. Then he made a laborious Japanese joke. The Japanese word for nine was *kyū*, the word for one was *ichi*, and the word for ten was *jū*. The Major now said, laughing heartily, "He's *kyūichi*. Nine plus one equals *jū*. Get it?"

"I'll take him," you said coldly, suspecting that this was just what Prantz and the Major had really hoped for.

His first day Grossman smiled eagerly and perspired freely in the dusty, coral-laden air, but so did all the rest of you. He was really much more South European in ancestry than he was Jewish. In fact, he probably was not Jewish at all in any rational sense, since at some naval recruiting offices it was then the custom to list a man as Jewish if one grandparent still liked kosher frankfurters. No matter. As far as the Major was concerned, Grossman might just as well have walked into Q with a pushcart under one arm and a rabbi under the other. Prantz, now Yeoman Third, contented himself with asking if you had learned any Yiddish. "Just enough to say 'Put that yeoman in the gas chamber —'" you replied.

His second day Grossman decided that he liked it and was going to stay. He brought in a radio, earphones, a box of green pistachio candies and a green eyeshade. Then he took off his hair and smiled apologetically.

"Hot," he said to everyone who was interested — in other words, all of Q. "Isn't it just too obscene?"

He adjusted his eyeshade, his radio and his earphones, and popped a pistachio candy in his mouth. Then he began to work. He was writing an essay on hot jazz for *Downbeat*.

Grossman had three toupees, they soon learned, one for just after a haircut, one for a medium growth, and one for just before a haircut. You could set your lunar calendar by them. He arrived in medium growth, and by the time he reached full growth, the Major was boiling. By any standards, however relaxed, Grossman was hardly to be called military, and by the Major's standards he had come perilously close to spitting on the flag.

When word was passed to get ready for an inspection party of visiting brass, the Major decided on action.

First he tried glaring at Grossman. Grossman smiled sweetly back. The Major pointed to his earphones.

"Yes," said Grossman, "very fine program today."

The Major came over to Grossman's desk. Grossman offered the box of halfmelted pistachio candies, scrabbled around in it, and came up with an unusual treat, a green pistachio lollipop.

"Don't be shy," said Grossman when the Major drew back in horror, "take two or three."

"Stand at attention when your executive officer addresses you," the Major tried to roar in his best parade ground voice. It was not a good sentence for roaring, but Grossman took off his earphones.

"Static," he said, puzzled, and shook them. In a fury, the Major pulled Grossman to his feet. In so doing, he got the earphones and the cord tangled around his arm. Grossman dropped the box of pistachio candies. They rolled on the floor. He bent down to pick them up, and the radio cord got entangled around his feet and the Major's. The Major tried to back away, but he and Grossman were wrapped at the arms and legs in a tangle of wiring. The pistachio candies made the floor slippery, and the Major had trouble keeping his balance.

"Get me out of this," screamed the Major. The ground wire of the still connected radio had touched his pants with a vicious spark. In trying to lift the cord of the earphones over his and Grossman's head, he put his hand on Grossman's toupee. In the excitement it had come partly off, and now the gluey side stuck to the Major's fingers.

General Waddleman appeared at the door. With him was a grand inspection party, Admirals and Generals from the central and southwest Pacific, and from Stateside.

Fat and circular in figure and speech, "In here," said the General in his own peculiar oratory, "we have the brains of the Pacific in here, the real brains of the Pacific we have in here —" He stopped in astonishment at the sight of Grossman and the Major.

Grossman's hands were full of pistachio candies he was picking up from the floor. The Major was trying to disengage the toupee from his hand, and get clear of enough radio wire so that he could salute.

"Very secret stuff," said General Waddleman hurriedly, kicking a stray copy of *Downbeat* under a table. Smoothly he changed his pace from a forward to a backward motion. "I don't always understand it myself this secret stuff —" the ground wire of the radio made contact with a vicious shower of sparks and the Major leapt into the air — "it's hard to understand it myself this secret stuff it's hard to understand," continued General Waddleman, now herding his fascinated brass to the door.

Desperate, the Major broke free of wires and the gluey toupee, rushed by instinct to his desk, performed a brilliant rifle salute and grounded his carbine smartly. He had, unfortunately, forgotten there was still a bullet in it, left over from target practice, and he had forgotten about the hair trigger. With an impressive blast and a ripping noise, the bullet discharged through the ceiling. A few splinters drifted to the floor, and a voice, seemingly from the roof, shouted, "You frigging claybrain."

Smoothly General Waddleman herded his lingering Generals and Admirals out into the corridor. "Just remembered we need clearance for secret stuff hard to understand, special clearance, secret."

For the next few days Grossman with his new-haircut toupee, and his green eyeshade, but minus the radio, the pistachio candies, and the back issues of *Downbeat*, was shifted to BIJ Standish's interrogation section. But if anything, his oral Japanese was even weaker than his written. Nobody, it seemed, cared to know if a prisoner's father had two boy children and one girl child, and even fewer people cared if the morning-glories went *pika pika* along the fence when the sun came up, and that was pretty much Grossman's range in oral Japanese.

Back came Grossman to your section where he furtively ingested enormous amounts of pistachio candies. With great difficulty and considerable assistance he did a definitive study of the trigger mechanism on the old-style Japanese infantry rifle. This little success gave him new confidence and he began to improve.

But the Major was biding his time. "It's loyalty up and loyalty down," he told you, then added darkly, "or the opposite." You soon learned that the Major was deciding who should go out on the next operation. A few assignments were already settled. Commander Seeberg had been nearly run down by Napoleon in his blue Packard convertible, and in spite of an anguished squawk that he wanted to go, but not on Stalemate, the he-man of the Pacific was detached from Q. And Gordian, taciturn and solitary, had volunteered and had at once been accepted, even though he had only just returned from Saipan. And he too was gone from Q. But nothing had been said to you, and you pretended to look nervous and cowardly, and several times in the Major's hearing mentioned your anxiety about combat.

The Major, you knew, felt he had a sure eye for cowards and was fond of sending them to the front. A landing in the Pacific had usually a back and a front, and was sometimes a triangle or almost a circle, as at Rarawa, but the Major always talked of sending people to the front, especially cowards. If the Major had had his way, there would have been nobody in the front lines *but* cowards, and the whole war would undoubtedly have been very much different. Perhaps, you thought, by looking sufficiently nervous, you might be assigned to Operation STALEMATE at once.

The new operation grew in size; it was to be much more complex than anything previously attempted, and tension mounted in the inmates of Q. It became, of necessity, STALEMATE ONE and STALEMATE TWO, and was loudly whispered about in Honolulu bars. An unfortunate Army lieutenant was discharged for discussing it with his whore, and this incident spread the glad tidings even further. Some members of Q tried to appear inconspicuous and spent long hours in the head. They talked of heart trouble, previously ignored by unsympathetic doctors, and they publicly advertised their inability to keep secrets of any significance under torture. Others pleaded with Commander Seeberg and the Major, and asked desperately to be allowed to go.

The Major smiled grimly and resorted his piles of fitness reports. He changed his hair-trigger carbine for a hair-trigger burp gun — a kind of fat, sawed-off submachine gun. He patted this frequently now, talked of "hosing" instead of shooting Japanese, and the man who sat on the muzzle or hair-trigger side of the Major's desk offered a month's liquor ration for a new location, but found no takers. The Major made a particular point of toying with the hair trigger of the burp gun whenever Grossman looked his way. Grossman was hypnotized by the gun, and the huge quantity of bullets in its forearm-long magazine.

One afternoon Grossman stayed behind to talk to you after the day watch ended.

"It's about the new operation," he said. He was sweating. The drops of sweat rolled out from under his toupee and down his thick dark sideburns. There were dark patches of sweat under his arms, and sweat and salt stains on the back of his shirt. "I can't go out," said Grossman. "I've got a wife and two children." You stared at him.

"Obscene, isn't it?" said Grossman, "I'm only twenty-two." You were not thinking about his youth, but about the obvious fact that life did not seem to care how it reproduced itself, so long as it reproduced. It was an unworthy thought, and you tried to reject it without success.

Grossman continued: "I hear in your section the Commander lets you say who's to go out and who's to stay."

"Yes. Whoever does good work can either go or stay." You added, honestly, "Unless something special comes up. But I don't think this operation is that special."

"I'm scared," said Grossman. You wondered if he had listened to you at all.

"I've never been so scared. I can't sleep thinking about it. How obscene can you get?"

You did not know how obscene you could get. Grossman pulled out two pistachio candies, tried to decide between them, then compromised by popping them both into his mouth at once. He was revolting but he was strangely human and appealing. There could have been no war in a world made up of Grossmans, and the world might have been a very much finer, if stickier place. You patted him on the shoulder and your hand felt sugary. Then Grossman started to cry.

There was at the moment no one in Q except the evening duty officer at the far end of the room. Grossman cried softly, in great deep sobs. From time to time he reached for another piece of candy. You could not make him stop crying. At last you shook him violently. The duty officer did not look up. In fact the duty officer, as so often in Q in the evenings, was asleep.

Grossman shook your hand in gratitude. Chocolate bits and flecks of green pistachio candy stuck to your palm.

"I'll do what I can." You were reasonably sure that Grossman would not have to go.

But the next day Grossman could not wait. He appealed to the Major. You could tell what the subject was from the gleeful look on Major Feverton's face. Crushed, Grossman returned to his pitiful little section of a table, with its crumpled, halfhidden candy wrappers, its small stack of books and maps. In five minutes' work with a damp rag, all trace of his passage through Q could be erased.

The Major summoned you to his desk. "He's a coward," said Feverton. "There's only one thing to do. He's got to go on STALE-MATE ONE. I've already had Prantz put him on the list." The Major's face assumed a stern and leonine quality.

You had some vague notion of appealing to Commander Seeberg, but Seeberg as an Annapolis man would not overrule the Major except for some extraordinary reason, and certainly not for this.

Then Feverton said, "I wouldn't send a man anywhere I wouldn't go myself. I'm going too." He stared pointedly at you, and stroked his burp gun fondly.

Your heart leapt up. The Major was taking your bait. He said, not expecting you to answer yes, "You can go — if you *want* to. The Commander's approved it."

Major Feverton looked baffled when you agreed to go. You walked back to your desk. You were still unhappy about Grossman. There were several others who wanted to go out from your aviation section. It was hardly Grossman's turn.

Grossman tried to keep out of your way. Clearly he thought you had somehow helped to arrange for his departure.

"It may not be as bad as you think."

"You don't know how afraid I am." He ate some candy. "I love my wife," he said. Tears blinked in his eyes. Then he went back to his work table.

You knew you should not feel that way, but you began to be a little bored with Grossman's problem. Then too, you found it hard to take seriously someone who ate pistachio candy on such a scale. You tried to keep Grossman from your thoughts. And one day, after a last reproachful look, Grossman was gone on his part of the operation.

In a few days you would leave yourself. You made arrangements for one of the new ensigns of Q to take over your studio apartment at Pupule Court, and you boxed and stored your few possessions. In your footlocker you rearranged two blue uniforms, one of which you had never worn, a black wool Navy overcoat which you had never worn, six white uniforms of which you had only worn one, two pair of white gloves which you had never worn. On a shelf in a closet you found a small stone figure, almost shapeless, with a wide straw hat, a Korean guardian figure of the house and garden. Lani had told you firmly that she did not believe in such things, and she had left it here — to watch over you?

For months now you had resolutely felt the pain of her departure diminish, you even thought at times you had forgotten her. With the discovery of this humble figure your passion raged back as though she were in the room.

You phoned Schofield, Aunt Kim, Leilani's home, but the answer was everywhere the same — she had left the island. You packed the strawhatted figure in your footlocker along with the brand new, slightly moldy uniforms. Prince Mokuaweoweo watched you load the footlocker in your waiting jeep. "Aloha," he called.

Aloha meant hello and goodbye and homesickness and love and affection and a thousand things beside. You had observed Prince Mokuaweoweo stealing gas from your jeep. Pupule Court was in for a big evening and you would be sorry to miss it. Just warming up, the Prince shot a tongue of flame almost clear across Pupule Court. You pinched out a smoldering patch on the roof of your jeep. "Aloha," you called, "aloha."

CHAPTER TWENTY-THREE

September, 1944

Appendix II is reserved for items of less than primary historical importance, such as the "Song of the Suicide Corps":

> *If I fly by sea*
> > *I'll float back, a corpse,*
> *If I go by mountains*
> > *Let my corpse turn to grass,*
> *For my Emperor's sake*
> > *I shall not die in bed.*

BEGEL, The Battle for Visaya Gulf

*

YOU AND the Major went together to pick up your combat gear for Operation STALEMATE. At the Marine Base you were sent to a wrinkled over-age Marine Colonel for a forwarding endorsement on your orders. The Colonel's eyes had the genial quality of a pair of steel marbles.

Major Feverton, apparently unaware that one does not argue with a Marine Colonel of a certain facial cast, any more than one argues with a bull elephant of a certain facial cast, now said to the Marine Colonel: "I want to go on both STALEMATE ONE and STALEMATE TWO. My orders cover only STALEMATE ONE."

The Major made an imposing figure as he stood before the Colonel, four orange grenades strapped to his ammunition halter – he carried four grenades in case two should fail to go off. He wore a pistol in addition to his burp gun, in case either should jam. He had a collapsible pick and a collapsible shovel, in case either of these should get jammed. In his pack he had an air mattress, and on top of his pack he carried a blanket roll in case the air mattress should receive a puncture.

The Marine Colonel pointed to a small, curious looking tube with a handle. "What the —— hell is that?" asked the Colonel.

"A bicycle pump," said the Major, "for my air mattress."

"Where are you from?" asked the Marine Colonel.

"Q," said the Major.

"Q?" asked the Colonel. "As in Kewpie Doll?"

The Major nodded.

"What other operations have you been on?"

"None, Colonel."

"Mr. Classen," said the Colonel, "what operations have you been on?"

"Zhutchka. Rarawa. Sir."

"Rarawa, Beach Red, by any chance?"

"We were supposed to land on Beach Red, Colonel."

"Did you know a boy named Donohue? Corporal Donohue?"

"No, sir."

In that peculiarly icy tone which a member of the Marine corps saves for behavior that he regards as un-Marine: "Why do you want to go on both operations, Major?"

"Well, my orders read —" here the Major dropped his voice to an almost inaudible whisper, "that I am attached only to the first operation, and I want to join the second with Mr. Classen here."

"You may speak in a normal voice, Major Feverton," said the Colonel. "I am not a spy."

"After we take the two smaller islands of Angaur and Peleliu, I want to go on the Yap landing with Mr. Classen," said the Major stubbornly. He slapped you on the back.

You sidled away nervously. You too, were carrying a large pack. It was labeled TECHNICAL INTELLIGENCE INSTRUMENTS, HEAD-QUARTERS PERSONNEL ONLY and it had a tendency to clink and gurgle when moved rashly. You had no grenades and had accepted a pistol only under protest. Your gas-mask container was filled with an object which looked like a gas mask but terminated in a cork. You did not care to stand in front of the Marine Colonel any longer than was absolutely necessary.

The Major, eager to add two assault arrows to his campaign ribbon, now said in a tone which you found provoking, "We're buddies." Again he slapped you on the back. That did it. A carelessly packed jar fell out of your sack, hit the floor, and broke. It exuded an orange substance.

"What the hell is that?" roared the Colonel. For a rather small man he had powerful vocal chords, and believed in keeping them at a high state of training, too.

"Orange marmalade." You did not know whether you should get down on your hands and knees and clean it up, or possibly, under the circumstances, lick it up, but you did know that your pack was so heavy that if you knelt down you might not arise again.

"And what is the precise military function of orange marmalade?" asked the Colonel, breathing heavily.

You replied, looking straight ahead, "It makes a delicious old-fashioned, Colonel."

The Colonel seemed to find difficulty in controlling himself. He turned to the Major. He started to speak, choked, then got a grip on himself.

"I'm sure, Major Feverton, that if you want to go on both operations you will not find it difficult to arrange after the first landing has been completed. That's all."

He turned to you. "Now, Lieutenant Classen, do you want to go on both operations?"

With a straight face, you said, "I promised my mother never to volunteer."

With an equally straight face the Colonel said, "A boy's best friend is his mother. Always remember that."

"Aye, aye, sir. I thought of that when I promised her never to volunteer." You started to try to ease off your mountainous sack so that you could do something about the mess on the floor.

"No," said the Colonel, "I don't want to run the risk of damaging —" he peered sharply at the lettering on your pack — "any more of those technical intelligence instruments. They are probably desperately needed at the front."

"So I am informed, Colonel."

When you were both dismissed, the Major asked you what the

Marine Colonel had meant by his last remark. "We haven't got any technical instruments," said the Major. You shifted your pack so that the Major could not see the lettering, so vital if the lock of the pack was not to be broken by pilferers when you went, as all men must, occasionally, to the head. You shook hands and parted. As you waited for your transportation you scanned your orders which had been stamped and endorsed over to ComPhibPac by Colonel Donohue, USMC. You wondered what had happened to Corporal Donohue on Beach Red at Rarawa.

You were almost happy to board your transport in Honolulu Harbor. You had spent the last month studying Yap and you knew more about Yap, and cared less, than you knew (or cared) about any bit of real estate in the world. With Yap's Micronesian castaway police chief you had discussed the depth of every inch of water and every piece of coral offshore, you knew every Yap arrowheaded fishtrap, you knew Yap customs such as six feet wide stone dollars, you knew the diseases to be had by sleeping with the Yap girls, such as yaws, for a start. At least aboard your transport Colonel Mist, now Chief of Staff for General Ferox, could no longer make your life hell with still another demand for information about Yap.

But once aboard the transport, you stayed in the harbor for two days, with no one permitted ashore. On the second day you were informed that STALEMATE TWO had been canceled. There would be no landing on Yap. KING ONE, the landing scheduled for Mindanao, southernmost island of the Philippines, had also been canceled. Instead, your units would take part in KING TWO, the landing planned for Visaya in the central Philippines. It was a leap forward in the progress of the war that made you catch your breath; you heard that it was Admiral Hornbull's inspiration.

But now you had to waste time, acting as shiplocked reserve for the Angaur and Peleliu landings of STALEMATE ONE; after backstopping these you all would sail the long slow journey to Manus, New Guinea, where you would wait for MacDazzle's forces to join you.

At sea, the Army officers were reduced by the monotony of the journey to arguments about who had the right to hang out laundry first; finally they agreed to wash their jockstraps and skivvies in the order in which their commissions had been dated. But all were unhappy when the bitter fight was settled, for it had given them something to look forward to each day.

The trip went on and on; time slowed almost to a standstill. Your mind came back again and again, searching, recalling, to a time when you must have been five or six, and you at last remembered — half day dreaming —

(Each summer your mother liked to visit her mother for a month, at Coaltown Pa., where your Grandmother Brady lived alone — before the coal mines came it had been known as Brady's Run; once all of Coaltown had been given to Sam Brady for his services as a scout in the Revolution, and you remembered the alley behind the small Brady lot — forbidden ground, but you knew how to wriggle through the fence, and you were forbidden the slaughterhouse at the end of the alley, but nothing could keep you or other small boys from it on slaughtering days — how deftly the butcher danced up to the black bull; the wooden mallet was half a foot across, and you remembered the butcher and his helper laughing — for this was a joke they never tired of — they flung at you the bull's pizzle and testicles, and then they had to hold you off while you kicked and screamed and bit — "You've a temper, haven't you?" said the butcher, holding you off with one hand; they went back to their work).

A hand pulled sharply at your shoulder, and you sat up, to stare, blinkeyed, at another group of transports, like your own, twenty ships or more, with destroyers, and another and another, till your eye reached the horizon; across its tiny arc steamed destroyers, carriers, cruisers, all that morning long.

Major Feverton, you reflected wryly, would now get all the combat a human being could want. After his landing on Angaur, his units would be brought to Manus to join in the landing on Visaya, and that landing was almost certain to bring out the Japanese Navy and Air Force in full strength; it was thought the battle on land would last perhaps half a year.

The weather remained clear and calm as you sailed toward the equator. It was fortunate that no Japanese subs appeared, for very few crews had their minds on their assigned tasks.

Gangs of enlisted men roved the passageways of the transport, armed with fire hoses and socks filled with sand. The shellbacks who had crossed the equator battled the polliwogs who had not. The day of the crossing itself was a day, so you discovered, of revenge against the hated officer class. Neptune, Davy Jones and the rest were enlisted men, and it was a rare transport that did not soon have some luckless officer slung aloft in a bosun's chair, tied to a cargo mast, or a gallant crew of ensigns cleaning out the crew's heads.

The first victim of the formal initiation ceremonies was an MP captain. He was sent through the gauntlet twice, as a memorial salute from the ship's crew to all military police, and was then retired to Sick Bay with severe contusions of the buttocks; he was also literally suffering from shock, produced by 10,000 volt radio batteries.

Other officers were then herded before Neptune and his court, and sentenced to run the gauntlet. Any who protested were given a sympathy chit which entitled the bearer to one hundred words of sympathy from the nearest chaplain — and which also entitled its holder to the opportunity to start the gauntlet from the beginning again. Previous initiation counted for little, at least if you were an officer it counted for little. A submarine officer, a passenger on the transport, was sentenced to two trips through the gauntlet on the charge of trying to dodge under the equator.

Grimly you started by kissing the Royal Pork, the mustard-smeared belly of a fat, hairy sailor. Then you danced a Royal Jig on a damp platform which had been wired for 10,000 volts by the ship's electrician. Sailors poured buckets of salt water on your dancing feet to help conductivity, though you concluded after a few trial jigs that this was not really necessary.

Next you had a Royal Operation, on a table also wired for 10,000 volts. Kicking and squirming in agony, you were pinned down by rubbergloved assistants who swabbed your mouth with alum. The Royal Surgeon then stuffed your mouth with stale bread in his anxiety to provide you with the right postoperative care.

And then you were crammed in the Royal Coffin by the Royal Mortician. The Royal Coffin was a tinned box six and a half feet long, with an opening at either end for fire hoses, and a watertight lid. The lid was clamped shut, then both hoses were turned on. Gasping, close to drowning in the violent rush of water, you were released to the open air just at the moment when you thought you were going to lose consciousness forever.

At about this point you became convinced that the initiation was not really happening to you, for you were standing outside yourself, watching it go on, but not really taking part in it any more.

Ahead lay more Royal Hazards, leading up to a Royal Platform on which stood the Royal Barber, equipped with a mammoth electrified Royal Razor, Royal Shears, and Royal Hairtonic (waste oil); there he dealt out Royal Hairdos of a unique, electrifying kind. The Royal Barber's Chair was so arranged that it could be tipped over backwards plunging the polliwog into the Royal Pool for a Royal Rinse. There Royal Mermaids, their wigs made of floor mops, waited to club the polliwog every time his head emerged above water. There were a number of Royal Mermaids wearing mop wigs and you reflected, in your newfound detachment, that the large size of mop was stamped Harvard, while the small size was labeled Yale.

There was a brief, welcome interlude in the Royal Festivities when a destroyer came alongside the transport, slowed to the transport's speed and passed lines to deliver guardmail and take on icecream. Both Neptune and the Royal Barber were needed at the lines, and like the rest of the passengers, you went to the rail to watch the two ships maneuvering.

The destroyer was flying the Jolly Roger at the masthead. Its officers, smoking cigars, with their saltrimed caps askew, were on the bridge, watching the fun. A young lieutenant conned the ship, and the captain kept a nonchalant eye on the lines, occasionally flicking the ash from his cigar. Without apparent effort or audible orders, the destroyer kept station alongside, never gaining or losing, easing off and on with each slightest motion of the clumsy transport, so that the lines between them hardly needed to be tightened or loosened by the men who manned them.

Unlike the transport which had many polliwogs crossing the line for the first time, the destroyer had only a few, and these mostly enlisted men. But there were some Army officers, perhaps being transferred by the destroyer from a large passenger transport to a smaller faster attack transport in preparation for the Angaur landings.

Just below the open bridge of the destroyer King Neptune held his court and enlisted men ran about to do his bidding. Still the destroyer kept on easily beside the transport; for all the confusion and horseplay its lookouts steadily scanned the seas around them, the skull and crossbones fluttered black and white in the breeze.

With a shock you realized that two of the officers were Grossman and Feverton. Grossman waved a sheet of paper stamped with a ship's seal. He had already been initiated and had kept the proof; he was released and Neptune's court, a bit short of the needed manpower while the destroyer transferred guardmail and took on ice cream and messages, immediately drafted him as Royal Hoser; there he stood, bewildered, holding a firehose in his hands.

Major Feverton was less fortunate. He was obviously arguing with his captors, though the words did not carry well to the transport. The shellbacks on the transport urged on the shellbacks on the destroyer, though these hardly needed encouragement. Major Feverton appealed to the captain of the destroyer; the captain smiled, flicked the ash from his cigar, and pointed to the Jolly Roger at the mast.

Now for attempting to bypass the chain of Neptune's command, the Major was put, struggling valiantly, into a strait-jacket, his hands were tied at his back in the canvas sleeves; from his wrists hung an empty peanut tin and a large cardboard placard on his chest proclaimed him to all the world as "ashtray." At command he was supposed to serve as an ash receptacle; now Davy Jones broke out a cigar, lit it, and called the Major over to dispose of the match. The Major refused.

You shuddered at this folly. Neptune at once held up two fingers, the dread signal which meant that the Major would have to run the gauntlet twice. This invitation was refused by the Major. Then Neptune signaled to his newly appointed Royal Hoser.

At first Grossman hesitated. Behind him a Royal Mermaid put down his sandfilled sock and turned on the fire hose. The hose stiffened, and Grossman lurched forward, then got a grip on the nozzle. The first sputtering blast pinned the Major against a bulkhead quite by accident. But Grossman proved to be a quick study of the art of Royal Hosing.

"Grossman," screamed the Major, "that's an order, Grossman." But Grossman, a happy smile on his face as he began to realize the potentialities of Royal Hosing, had suddenly become one of Neptune's most loyal shellbacks. Quickly he mastered the subtleties of the Royal Hoser's art, as he delicately nudged the Major back and forth against the bulkheads, and learned to call for risings and fallings in the water pressure as these seemed desirable.

The lines between destroyer and transport were cast off, hauled aboard and faked down on the decks. The destroyer eased off, turning slightly away from the transport, and seeming at first to lose speed. Then she sailed on an opening course, skillfully and easily she gained speed, the foam creaming higher and higher at her bows, the captain still sitting in his chair on the bridge, drawing on his cigar, the young lieutenant still conning the ship, the Jolly Roger fluttering as the destroyer began her long, graceful heeling turn to the next ship in the formation.

With a sigh, you went back to your place in the gauntlet, recalled by a watchful Royal Mermaid whose wig mop was labeled Columbia. The wig seemed to be of medium size. Wearily you got down on your knees and began the required tour through the Royal Guts of the Universe, a long canvas tube lined with chicken guts, hog intestines, garbage, and other slop which they had lovingly accumulated, judging from the smell, ever since the ship had left Honolulu.

You went through the Guts of the Universe slowly at first, groping among the Royal Slime, but you soon picked up speed as the sandfilled socks searched for, and found your posterior through the canvas. You emerged from the Royal Guts, dripping with gunk, a finer, but not a cleaner man. Ahead, for you, lay the remaining hazards: the Royal Barber and the Royal Rinse and more Royal Mermaids with their sandfilled socks at the ready. You lurched forward. "Smile," said a Royal Mermaid, his hair covered with a mop stamped Harvard; the Mermaid touched you with an electrified Royal Wand. To use a favorite expression of Grossman's, How obscene could you get? You smiled.

CHAPTER TWENTY-FOUR

September, October, 1944

The unlucky cruiser Admiral Mahan, *named for the greatest American naval historian up to World War II, bent on the manila mooring lines and messenger, while the seagoing tug* Commodore Perry *hauled on board the heaving lines, mooring lines and messenger, dropping the lizard when the plow steel towing wire cut off the fire hydrant even though it had been secured by a pelican stopper on the towing padeye and puddened and keckled with copper; the wire was recovered in some confusion after it broke the bones of three men, and was led fair through the after chock while the lizard kept the wire free of the screws although there was some trouble with the thimble of the chain shackle bolt.*

BEGEL, The Battle for Visaya Gulf

❊

TWO NIGHTS later you saw on the transport's starboard quarter Angaur, lit up with star shells, tracers, and signal flares. Except for a faint rumble, like distant thunder, there was almost no sound. Ashore on that island were Grossman and the Major. For a long time men stood quietly at the rail, watching the red and yellow and white lights.

The following night the island was no longer visible and your convoy, its troops not needed as a reserve, had changed its course for Manus. Day after day now you plowed the calm sea, the ships keeping station in their intervals, wheeling to the flutter of signal flags by day and to the rheumatic voice of Talk Between Ships at night. Often you and the other casual officers slept on the boat deck, while the Army enlisted men covered every scrap of the main deck below.

You slept and dreamed fitfully because of the brief tropic rains, your dreams were sexual, ugly and powerful as life itself, made up in a confused vague way of the Ward who had pressed against you as your transport entered Pearl Harbor, of Maria, of a girl — a worker in a pacifist cause — whom you had known before the war and whose name you had forgotten, of Lani herself, of Betty Comfrey, of the whorehouses of River Street and the men moving steadily up the stairs to the whores, the dreams were as much a desire to survive as an act of sex or an instinct, and you woke from them unrefreshed, exhausted, you watched the Southern Cross and the strange tropical constellations swing in the dark space between the rocking cargo masts, you listened to hundreds of men in the dark around you — dreaming, waking, falling uneasily asleep again as you were doing.

From south and southwest, from the east and from the north, other transports and convoys were converging on Manus and Hollandia; the whole tempo of the war was quickening and changing — even on your isolated transport you could sense that much, and the first issue of the ship's mimeographed newspaper used most of its space, without editorial comment, to describe the latest coal strike.

At Manus you learned that Japanese resistance on Angaur had been fairly light; you expected Grossman and Feverton to put in an appearance there in the near future. Your transport was the assistant command ship for the landings in the southern sector of Visaya, and you thought they might also be attached, as you were, to the headquarters of the 23rd Corps, under the command of Ferox, recently promoted from Major to Lieutenant General.

After a week in Manus Harbor, half hoping, perhaps, to run into Grossman and Feverton, you spent a day ashore. The sketchy town was mainly Quonsets, Australian government offices, warehouses, with clumps of living quarters scattered through low, rolling hills. Not knowing where you were going, you accepted a lift on a low-slung truck, jumped aboard, and sat on a pile of wooden boxes in the open trunk.

The driver and his helper raced along a graded dirt road until they reached a large, seemingly endless grove of coconuts, with a sentry box at the side of the road. The sentry waved them on, saluting you in the sweeping Australian style. The driver turned to inform you that in this area no soldiers were permitted on foot. He slowed to a crawl, a grin on his face.

"There," he said, "there's the reason."

And there the reason was. Radiant brown women, magnificently formed, and nude from the waist up, except for an occasional armband, strolled or sat under the slender trees, near their palm-thatched, stilt-legged houses. Once in a while an arrogant brown buck strolled by, a strip of peroxided red hair in the middle of his topknot.

The driver looked ahead and back to guard against roving sentries. Then he stopped the truck. He and his helper were breast connoisseurs. Each day they deliberately drove through the village (though it was the longer of two available routes), stopped their truck in defiance of regulations, and discussed the bosoms which were displayed before them.

Now they eyed critically old women with long wrinkled dugs, young girls with virginal budding breasts, and every range of size and shape of breast between these two extremes.

A mere novice, you were content to listen, look, and learn.

"Myself," said the driver, turning to you for approval, "I like them young and firm, like two sassy little cupcakes." He pointed to a young and firm illustration of this principle, who walked timidly to within a few yards of the truck and gazed at them suspiciously, as if she could read their minds.

His helper disagreed. "I like them more mature and rounded, just before they start to fall. The kind that puts the cheater manufacturers out of business." The helper sighed. "Something you can get your hands into. Know what I mean?"

A perfect illustration of what the helper meant came alongside the truck, on the driver's side, and smiled at him. The three connoisseurs, for you were beginning to think of yourself with the other two, stared at part of her anatomy, trying, without much success, to do so judiciously. Flattered by your interest, she said, "Gum?"

"Oh you kid," said the driver, taking a deep breath and losing sight of his cupcake theory. His hands gripped the steering wheel. She wore in her jet-black hair a strange tropical flower with a heavy scent which drifted across the dusty truck.

"Look at that flower," said the helper.

"That's a passion flower," you said, trying to be helpful.

The driver groaned. In his excitement he straightened his shoulders and stretched back his arms. She laughed and imitated him. This action revealed the full glory of her figure. The driver seemed almost to whimper.

"You and your sassy little cupcakes," said the helper scornfully. The driver admitted he had been vanquished by the weight, size and shape of the evidence.

"Gum?" said the magnificent Hershey Bar Venus. She wriggled a bit in anticipation. The helper grabbed the driver just before he leaped out of the truck.

"Gum," said the driver, struggling weakly against the helper. "I'll give you your weight in chewing gum."

She leaned on the door of his truck.

"Stop it," said the driver, "I can't take any more."

His helper tugged his arm. "Engine," he said. Behind them on the road they could hear a car.

"Scram," said the driver weakly to his chocolate Venus. She stood there, perfect in figure and face.

"Gum?" she said. She was a woman of few ideas, but those she had she was determined not to lose.

The driver stepped on the gas and you all drove slowly on. The connoisseur's hour was over.

"They're putting barbed wire all around their village," said the driver morosely. "Now whaddye think of that?" No one thought very much of that.

On the return trip you asked what had been in the load of boxes.

"Dynamite," said the driver. "Costs us a truck every now and then, when we get some of that old stuff."

Somewhat shaken by this news, you decided to have alcohol and peanuts for supper at the Naval Officers' Club, a long bar near a small boat landing. You were checking to make sure about the last boat taxi that evening when you saw Grossman step ashore.

Grossman's toupees had been sent to the wrong operation and he was bald as an egg, but a tanned, yellowish egg that had been taking atabrine. In one hand he clutched a supply of bar chits sufficient for several lost weekends. On his arm was a slight scar which Grossman explained had been made by a sniper's bullet. Now he was, as he put it coarsely, a member in good standing of the Order of the Purple Fart. He had turned into that stock Pacific character, the Combat Veteran, who Had Had It, but Could Take Anything More They Could Give Him.

Grossman pulled out two of his many bar chits and ordered another round.

"No thanks."

"They were both for me anyway."

"What about the Major."

"As our Japanese cousins say, a hundred days' preaching amounts to one fart. He claims he has to return to Pearl to speed up Operation SHRINER."

Major Feverton had somewhere gotten the idea that all Japan went to its shrines once a week, on Shrinegoing Day, taking long railroad rides to do so. We were going to draw up a list of all Japanese shrines and on some suitable Shrinegoing Day American bombers would simultaneously destroy all the shrines. The Major had described in dramatic detail how the Japanese would react when they looked out of their train windows on Shrinegoing Day and saw that all their shrines were demolished. They would surrender practically by return of post.

"Don't drop that ball, now," he had shouted, intoxicated with the vision of having at last found the Idea that Would Win the War. "More shrines, more shrines!"

You had found the Major more shrines, especially more phallic shrines — with pictures.

"What's that?" he asked, of a piece of sculpture that looked like a mouse crawling up a log until you took a closer look, when it changed before your eyes into something rather naughty.

You explained. "Impossible," said the Major. He started to return the phallic shrine file, then, on second thought, kept it. "Might be an idea in this somewhere," he said. But you had never learned what the idea was.

Now in the Manus bar you protested to Grossman: "But he asked to go on the second operation."

"Not since it was shifted to Visaya. Come and see for yourself. He's over at the seaplane dock, waiting for transportation back to Pearl."

Grossman suddenly slipped off his chair. You helped him up and took away his bar chits.

"Where's your ship?"

"Military secret. Confidential trash."

You thought of one of Major Feverton's earliest schemes for improving efficiency in Q. All trash in Q was burned anyway, but the Major had decided that greater security could be maintained if the trash was divided into two piles, one labeled "Confidential Trash" and the other just "Trash," and burned separately.

You shook him. "Where's your ship?"

"Out there." He waved his hand, indicating about one hundred ships of all types in the harbor. He was babbling happily of combat. "Got to get back to ship, transfer to old buddies' ship. Take Major's place. Going to go out and shoot own Japanese. Capture Japanese flag. Frame it. Tell children. Two children. Tell wife. One wife."

With difficulty you led Grossman to the Officers' Club landing. Your transport's water taxi had come in on its last trip. You and Grossman were the only passengers.

Grossman waved wildly at one transport as you chugged through the water.

"What's the name of your ship?"

"Confidential," said Grossman, waggling a finger at his lips.

Patiently, "What's her name?"

"That's her name. Confidential. S.S. Confidential. Confidential Trash."

"Are you sure this is your ship?"

"Good old ship. S.S. Trashcan. Home away from home."

The coxswain swung the LCVP alongside and together you got Grossman started up the ship's ladder. Halfway up he slipped and fell back. He waved you off. "Never go up a ladder like that," he said. "You might hurt yourself. Now watch me and see how it's done."

Slowly and patiently he crawled up the ladder on his hands and knees. For a glorious moment at the top of the ladder he stood erect and saluted crisply the ship's ensign and the officer of the deck. Then he collapsed. This time he was out for good.

There was no Grossman listed on the transport. You gave up, and took him back to your own ship where you found him an empty bunk in your own cabin.

Too much alcohol, and the meeting with Grossman, had left you in a halfawake condition. You dreamed, or rather daydreamed since you knew you were still pretty much awake, that you were in a house with many rooms but only one door. Some five hundred children lived in the house even though it was old, with rotten beams for rooftrees. And the house was on fire but none of you wanted to leave — outside the house Leilani called to you all to leave but you refused and you played happily in the rotten flaming house. For each child then, Leilani brought his favorite toy to the one door and coaxed him from the house; you heard her call your name, when you suddenly awoke and sat bolt upright in your bunk, startled at the sound of a shot directly overhead. You heard feet running over the metal deck. The army stationed deck sentries at night, and you thought one of them might have discharged his rifle accidentally. Gradually you fell into an uneasy slumber again in which, knowing that you were dreaming, you dreamed of being in combat. It was evening, and your troops were securing the perimeter against the coming of darkness. A major who looked somewhat like Major Feverton kept saying that the Japanese always attacked at night, but soon it would be your ball and you would have to run with it. You forgot the rest of the dream.

The next morning it was your turn to go through the books of the KING TWO operation plans. There were four thick volumes describing the local air cover, the stationing of PT boats, the formations of old battleships, the escort carriers, the immense carrier force of Admiral Hornbull, the landing beaches for General Ferox in the eastern waist of Visaya, and the landing beaches for General MacDazzle on the northeast corner of Visaya. The Americans loved to make up such plans; what happened in actual practice was always very different. The plans that concerned General Ferox and his 23rd Corps had been made very economically by crossing out the word Yap wherever it occured, and substituting for it the word Visaya.

You leafed through the already thick folder of the day's signals. Among them was a signal assigning Grossman to your transport, so that was all right.

You went below and woke Grossman. Together you climbed topside to secure a boat to bring Grossman's gear aboard. You had to wait. There was a quiet throng by the accommodation ladder. A soldier was being taken off the ship in a litter. Slowly the word passed through the crowd that he had shot his foot the night before so that he would not have to take part in the Visaya landing. Impassively the troops watched him. More and more men tumbled out of the hatchways to see him off. Chaplain Simon stood by his litter. Once Chaplain Simon touched the wounded man's brow. He was murmuring to him only the word "dignity, dignity."

That afternoon you and Grossman went ashore to the seaplane dock to say goodbye to Major Feverton.

The Major's huge seaplane was about to take off. Its four engines were warming up, and conversation was not easy.

"You can still transfer, if you want to."

The Major, his contorted leonine face white-yellow in color, was not a well man. He was sitting on an inflated rubber tube.

"I'd like to," he said. He shifted his position uncomfortably. "Unfortunately my piles came back."

"Too bad, I didn't know you had piles."

"They come and they go," said the Major. He smiled bravely. "I concealed the fact that I had them so I could stay in the army."

It was a typically warm, muggy, Manus day. The Major wiped his face. If you went about like a native, practically nude, as you and the troops had soon discovered, it was not an uncomfortable climate. But in Western clothes it was always unpleasant. "They don't have any cokes here," said the Major. "Didn't have any during my operation either. Inefficiency, I call it."

Your voice was neutral. "Visaya looks big."

"Ought to have coke dispensers everywhere," said the Major. "I'm writing a memo on it."

He avoided looking directly at Grossman. Now he said, "You did a good job, Grossman. I'm going to tell them back at Q."

"You do that little thing," said Grossman. "And what's more you can take your frigging assault arrow and ram it up —" You kicked Grossman and he shut up. The Major turned red and pretended to overlook Grossman's remarks.

He dug into his pocket and held out a tattered clipping, almost as if he were begging for your approval. It was from his home-town newspaper. It had clearly been written up from a letter sent in by the Major. It told how the Major had gone ashore on Angaur with the first wave, had been under enemy machine gun and rifle fire, had been bombed and shelled. It ended as the Major told of seeing that our flag was still there in the morning. Perhaps it was true, but you thought it probably was not. There had been only sporadic resistance on Angaur.

"Shouldn't be here at all," said the Major fretfully, sensing that his clipping had not produced quite the effect he had hoped for. "I was to be evacuated on the first hospital plane, but they made me wait here instead. Inefficiency again. I was supposed to fly direct to Pearl. I've got to get Operation SHRINER off the ground."

You stooped to pick up a picture that had fallen from the Major's pocket. It was another pose of his wife and the two nondescript children. "Got to think of their interests," said the Major.

You remembered that once, in a twisted spasm of jealousy, you had insisted that Lani tell you why, once in a while, she went out on a calm, reserved date with Major Feverton. She had no precise answer; still she had said vaguely, for that was not all the answer, "He's very lonely." And then she said again, "Desperately lonely." And, her halfclosed teasing eyes widening in surprise, "Do you begrudge him that?"

The flying boat was nearly loaded now. "While I was in the hospital I thought up a new Idea," said the Major, more confident in tone.

You thought of Operation Shriner, and Operation Mount Fuji, and Operation Emperor's-Face-on-the-Carrier-Decks, and Operation Newsreel-in-the-Emperor's-Garden.

The Major put a curious sketch in your hands. It was a piece of typing paper neatly scissored in the form of a leaf. You did not recognize the shape of the leaf. On the other side of the leaf was a sketch of the usual combination surrender message and safe conduct pass which the propaganda offices had used on surrender leaflets without, so far, much success.

"It's a kiri leaf," said the Major proudly. Your face went blank.

"The kiri leaf stands for death," explained the Major. "All the leaflets will be cut in the form of the kiri leaf. They'll drop over the Japanese troops like leaves of death." He liked the phrase and repeated it. "Like leaves of death. Death on one side. Safe conduct on the other. I got the idea from 'leaf-let' — a little leaf. A propaganda leaf. Get it?"

"Yes," you said. Grossman, you noticed, was fumbling with the Major's luggage, seemingly tightening the straps is it lay in the boat which would take it to the after hatch of the flying boat.

"I'll have it all worked out when you get back. I've already sent Q a memo. When you return it will be your ball. You'll have first chance to run with it. Mustn't let the situation mature too long."

You felt strangely patient toward the Major. "All right," you said. "I'll run with it." The arguments, the hostility of Q, these seemed irrelevant in the humid, sticky air of Manus.

His back hunched as though his khaki uniform had turned to lead, Major Feverton boarded the flying boat. From the hatch he waved his kiri leaf and his rubber tube at you. Then he disappeared inside. The hatch door opened again for a small sack of mail. You saw the Major deflating his rubber tube.

Slowly and clumsily the flying boat taxied to the section of harbor reserved for its takeoff. At the end of its run the usual crash boat kept its bow pointed toward the flying boat. The crash boat was barely under way.

The flying boat surged heavily across the water, beginning to plane as it picked up speed. Inside the flying boat, you knew, the sound of the spray against the thin metal skin would seem like bullets piercing the hull. But you and Grossman, standing on the boat landing, heard only the low roar of the motors. The boat was skimming the waves now, and it began to make the transition from an ugly earthbound mechanism to something remote and graceful and airborne.

Then it shuddered to a stop, nosed over and plunged to the bottom like a stone.

There was no fire, no explosion. The sudden silence, after the roar of the motors, made you feel that you had, temporarily, gone deaf. The men in the crash boat, who had already started to leave their station, thinking the flying boat safely in the air, now went to the spot where it had sunk, and dropped a buoy marker. A few boats put out from a nearby transport, but there was nothing to be done.

As all of you watched, a great air bubble belched to the surface, a last gasp of air from the drowning lungs of a mechanical animal. Slowly gasoline slicks formed on the surface of the water, and turned the sunlight into patches of rainbow. One of the patches of gasoline flared up in a rush of flame, then went out. In the wake of the vainly circling boats the marker buoy nodded, back and forth, back and forth.

That evening on your transport you saw that Grossman had a burp gun among his gear.

"Where'd you get that?"

Grossman, his face yellowish with atabrine, and flushed with drinking, said proudly, "I liberated it from the Major today." He waved it wildly around the cabin. "I'll hose them," said Grossman. "I'll hose them down. Shoot my own Jap. Get myself his Rising Sun flag." He pointed the gun at you and went "Dededededede*duh*."

"You damn fool." You took the gun away, seized Grossman by the shoulders and shook him violently. Grossman crawled into his bunk and laughed himself asleep.

You started a letter to the Major's wife, then tore it up. You went out on deck. One of the Japanese-Americans on the headquarters staff was standing at the rail. You knew he was *kibei* and had been educated in Japan. You asked him what the kiri leaf really meant.

"Honorable death for the Emperor," said the *kibei*. You laughed shortly. That was a surrender leaflet to drop on troops making a last desperate stand!

It was dusk and you stood alone at the rail, watching the great armada of ships. Small boats chugged back and forth, trailing diesel exhaust. In the morning the armada was sailing.

Again you were in a dream of combat. You lay somewhere near the perimeter, neither awake nor asleep, in a deep, narrow foxhole, your carbine ready to your hand on a thin earthen shelf, your knife half eased out of its sheath. You heard a quiet, persistent rustle, and you knew you had to wake up; a Japanese soldier was crawling to the lip of the foxhole, would be at it in a moment, and in the next moment at your throat, but you lay there, helpless, paralyzed, unable to move, unable to wake up —

Shuddering, you found yourself in the hot sticky cabin. Around you were familiar noises, the steady whirr of the electric fan, the soft humming of the blowers, the husky breathing of sleeping men. You were saying softly over and over to yourself, without realizing it, *dignity, dignity, dignity.* You stopped.

You heard familiar, century-old calls — Now hear this — Set the special sea detail — Stand by your lines — Single up — Cast off the after lines — Secure the special sea detail and secure both anchors for sea — Set Condition Three — Ready to relieve you — I relieve you.

The ship trembled when the main engines came to life and the propellers bit into the water. A little later the ship seemed to float freely, no longer locked in the harbor. Then she purposefully developed her own rocking motion, and when she pitched and rolled in the old familiar way you knew you were underway for Visaya.

You had a singular feeling that part of your life, a kind of youth, had suddenly come to an end. You could not sentimentalize over the death of Major Feverton. You had not liked the Major, indeed, at times you had hated him. And yet Major Feverton was a man, and now, in a strange, bitter way, his death mattered to you.

Over the ship's loudspeaker system the bosun's pipe squealed, and the familiar phrases sounded: "Now hear this, now hear this . . . sweepers man your brooms . . . now hear this, now hear this . . . the smoking lamp is lit, on all weather decks . . . now hear this now hear this . . ."

That morning, you told yourself, you would write to Major Feverton's wife, and it would be a good letter and you would mean what you said.

But you felt strangely disinclined to leave your bunk. It was too early to get up, you tried to tell yourself. Then you admitted what the trouble really was. You were afraid to get up, to leave the safety of your bunk.

Shivering, you recalled your dream. Your fear of death had been a long time coming, much longer than for Grossman, or the Major, or for the soldier who had disabled himself. You had not really known fear at all on Zhutchka or Rarawa. But fear had, at last, and oh how surely, come.

Willing yourself to put on each piece of clothing, you slowly dressed. You felt close to Grossman, you even felt close to the late Major Feverton, AUS. For you no longer knew whether you could hold out, whether you could "do your duty." But you knew you were like many other men. It was not an uncomfortable feeling.

You thought with unbelievable longing of Q.

A letter had come from Arkansaw. He said nothing of his damaged sight. One sentence read: "Always remember, Huckleberry Finn plays it *straight* — he is the only character in the book who never laughs."

In your answer you would challenge him to a round of Book Sequels — mentally you listed *Dracula Goes to War, Snow White and the Seven Reds, Moby Dick, Jr.*

But first you went out on the boat deck. It was a clear, fine day. The ship's crew was getting ammunition ready for antiaircraft practice, and off in the sky you could see the target plane towing a silvery target cone. Far down the column of transports ships began to fire. Apparently nerveless, the target plane flew steadily down the column, its path marked by black and white puffs from bursting shells. Soon it would be over your transport.

Part Four

KING TWO

CHAPTER TWENTY-FIVE

October 23–27, 1944

The historical facts are these: at Jutland 172,000 tons of shipping was sunk (of some 1,600,000 tons of shipping engaged in battle) while at Visaya Gulf 342,000 tons was sunk (out of 2,000,000 tons engaged); at Jutland about 9600 German and British sailors were lost, while at Visaya over 16,000 Japanese and American sailors died, and these comparisons do not allow for 400 planes shot down at Visaya Gulf . . .

BEGEL, The Battle for Visaya Gulf

❂

THE JAPANESE and the American 20-mm. guns were both Swiss make, but the Japanese guns could fire for only 15 seconds at a time, while the American guns could fire for 250 seconds. Those additional 235 seconds spelled out one phrase, and that one phrase was "good old American knowhow." From such tiny matters the pendulum of history receives part of its push.

❂

230730 "Hell, with us the impossible takes a little longer, that's all," growled General Ferox. Hot and red-faced, he slapped his pearl-studded pistol holster and thrust forward the shoulder which bore his beloved Long Knife shoulder patch. But the gesture was somehow unconvincing.

"Manpower?" asked reporter Bulflash. He tugged judiciously at his belt and sweat ran down his sharp nose. He pretended to be taking notes on his folded copy paper, but he was actually drawing tiny pitchforks in rows.

"Fifty-one thousand men here in the 23rd Corps area, and 53,000 directly under General MacDazzle in the north."

"*Supreme* Commander MacDazzle?"

Ferox winced at the hated title. "A total of 202,500 men. Figures not for publication, of course."

"And the ships," said Bulflash, shifting to drawings of horned demons with tails wrapped round their waists.

You were surprised at the barely concealed sullenness of Admiral Norcross's reply, though you knew he had been trapped into this shoreline press conference. His eyes were inflamed and staring, and he rubbed them without satisfaction. "Five hundred and eleven ships," he said, "two hundred and eighteen of them Large Slow Targets."

Bulflash turned to Ferox again. "MacDazzle's press release for today was 'If God stays with me, I may get some remarkable results.' What's your opinion?"

"We've got the supplies, we've got the men —" unconsciously his hand patted his pearl-studded holster —" after that comes the Jesus Factor — the unpredictable."

Without much wanting to, you had admired Ferox, the combat general, fighting for a toehold on Rarawa. But now you saw him, like many generals in the too rapidly expanded American Army, promoted far beyond his ceiling of abilities. Rather than using clear verbal orders, he spent much of his staff's time in circulating foggy written directives. He constantly called staff meetings to get "ideas." He had no proper liaison with Army air or any plan for air control. In fact he had no precise notions of what to do on Visaya aside from clearing the landing beaches of Japanese, but these beaches had already been evacuated by the Japanese before the American landings.

In this unwise promotion to Corps Commander you read not defeat, but the unnecessary deaths of a regiment of men.

It was unpleasantly damp and hot inside the moist brown command tent. You were thinking of 250,000 tons of vehicles, of 200,000 tons of ammunition — ten tons for every Japanese on Visaya — and 200,000 tons of medical supplies, about one ton for each

American soldier. And you were thinking of the two ammo ships, *Hercules Victory* and *Achilles Victory* which had just arrived in Visaya Gulf, sent direct from San Francisco. Through a miscalculation, neither of these ships had been provided with Armor Piercing shells for Admiral Norcross's old fire-support battleships. Was that the Jesus Factor?

Bulflash bit into a sandwich. "Horsecock," he said of the sandwich bologna, spitting out a clove. "How about you, Admiral Norcross, what do you think of Admiral Hornbull's statement that we'll be home by Christmas?"

It was the same prediction Vice-admiral Hornbull had made last year. True, Vice-admiral Hornbull and the top members of his staff had gone home by that Christmas.

"Comment negative."

"Do you plan to ride the Emperor's white horse in Tokyo, like Admiral Hornbull?"

"Negative." The word gurgled in his throat.

Bulflash turned to the real business of the press conference. Rapidly he explained that a performance of *Swing Shift Sam and Swing Shift Susie* had been dedicated to all the officers and men of the Fourth Army and of the Second Fleet.

Ferox and Norcross both frowned. Immediately Bulflash improvised — "With the knowledge and approval of MacDazzle." Ferox and Norcross were to autograph this record after they had listened to it, and the autographed record would be flown back to the states and played in all the big factories of America as a souvenir of the liberation of the Philippine Islands.

A mechanical vic blared in the warm tent.

> Hip hip hip hooray
> We're on the front burner
> The flapjack turner
> Working on production for the U.S.A.

Admiral Norcross pushed out of the command tent. With a weak but angry look, Ferox signed the record. Without the slightest hesitation, Bulflash signed Norcross's name on the disc. He smiled, and said in an amiable, judicious manner, "Some day he'll thank me for this. Norcross's public image isn't half as good as Hornbull's."

He put the record on again, threw a peanut in the air and caught it in his mouth.

You turned the vic off, and the record snarled to a stop.

＊

The historian's task is a delicate and responsible one, never more so than when defining the beginning of a great event such as the battle for Visaya Gulf.

＊

230830   General Ferox walked back and forth while he talked. It was his practice, at crucial moments in a staff conference, to break the blackboard pointer across his hard little belly, and he now held it ready for this unnerving punctuation mark.

General Ferox wore two stars on his helmet liner (it was too hot to wear a helmet in the soggy Command Tent), on his collar, on his shoulder tabs. He wore two yellow grenades clipped to his ammo belt. At his waist, in addition to his pistol, he wore a sheath knife, the Long Knife of his blue and white shoulder patch.

You watched the conference with eyes bleared, as though you saw everything under water. This was Ferox's first morning ashore, but most of the 23rd Corps headquarters staff had been ashore ever since the 20th, and for three days and nights the miracle of sleep, this most simple and necessary of human pleasures, had been taken away from you. You wanted sleep, uninterrupted soundless sleep, and like a desert traveler in search of mirage you kept remembering the full boyish sleep of your almost forgotten life in Palisades.

"No," said Admiral Norcross, hardly even pretending to be polite. "No."

Norcross was dressed in plain khakis, without insignia of any kind. He was short of stature, and somewhat chubby, with the rounded white face that the Annapolis graduate so often assumes in late middle age.

General Ferox snapped the pointer in two across his hard little paunch. With a remote smile, Admiral Norcross beckoned to an aide, and Ferox was at once supplied with another pointer.

Ferox flung the new pointer on the ground. "I can't see any reason why we should take prisoners," he yelled.

"I can," said Admiral Norcross. He rubbed his inflamed eyes.

Outside the soggy tent, bulldozers whined and snuffled their way deeper into the ground, digging out Ferox's underground head-quarters. A stack of coconut logs, gathered for the six feet thick roof, tumbled with a roar to the ground from the back of a dusty truck.

The staff conference was over and you all went outside, blinking against the damp bright sunlight. The headquarters of the corps was within an immense coconut grove, but fairly close to the beach, and you could see the ships on the outer fringes of the Gulf begin-ning to make protective smoke.

From far off a Japanese plane crawled into the blue cup of sky overhead, followed hotly by an American navy fighter. The Japa-nese plane was trailing a dark thread of smoke when all the ship and shore ackack of the Americans opened up against it. But the Japanese plane flew on, tugging its dark thread behind it, and the American plane turned bright orange at the center, its wings seemed to spread away from a central ball of fire, then it blew to pieces. The sky cleared, you heard an explosion, and the Japanese plane vanished safely across the horizon, tugging its black thread of smoke behind it.

The plane had been a decoy, and Admiral Norcross was the first to point to the real attack. All this time a Japanese plane had flown in low, skimming the water, now it climbed suddenly — you waited for it to release its bomb as it nosed over and down. But the plane kept hurtling down, hugging a huge bomb under its fuselage, down and down, toward a cruiser at anchor in the center of the Gulf. A yellow flash of light with delicate purple edges, a whitehot sheet of thick flame; and then an invisible hand shook you back and forth, and the noises of far off explosions fumbled in your ear-drums.

"Jesus H. Christ," said Ferox.

Bits and pieces of forgotten conversations tumbled rapidly to-gether in your mind, fragments of long since read and forgotten Japanese documents — special attack — sure death sure hit — the way of the warrior, *gyokusai* — death for the Emperor. Dully you thought, each man serves an emperor, and in his service . . .

Other phrases raced in your mind, general decisive battle — decoy fleets — so long expected, the union you had just seen, of patriotic ambition, and suicidal despair!

"At once," said Norcross. "Report anything you learn at once." Ferox agreed, but you knew Norcross had meant his words for you. There was a new explosion from the flaming cruiser.

The lips of Admiral Norcross puckered thin and white with fury. "One of our own five-inch shells," he said. With his staff officers and aides he went to the beach, picking his way through hundreds of Negro service troops who were sprawled, sound asleep, among stacks of half unloaded supplies. The air raid continued, other planes came into and left the blue cup of sky, the cruiser explosions shook at the damp and sodden air; still the Negro service troops slept on, jaws agape, dark bodies beaded with silvery drops of sweat.

Ferox watched the lacecurtained Admiral's barge churn its way toward the command ship *Nasatch*. With satisfaction Ferox said, "There isn't a place on a ship where I'd like to die."

From a radio belonging to the G-2 unit there came a momentary blast of song, and then the familiar voice of Tokyo Rose. "My dear friends of the 23rd Corps," said an icy, musky voice. "Welcome ashore to your new headquarters. And welcome ashore to General Ferox too."

The General swung round as if stung in the rump.

"We'll send you something special tonight," the brassy feminine voice went on, "something that we wish we didn't have to send to the poor, helpless men who carry out your orders, General Ferox. And now a song, dedicated to all the generals who lead the peace-loving American soldiers to a war they don't really need to fight. And I dedicate this song to all their fun-loving wives, back in the United States with the fun-loving war workers":

> I'm goin' to buy a paper doll that I can call my own,
> A doll that other fellows cannot steal,
> And then the flirty flirty guys with their flirty flirty eyes
> Will have to flirt with dollies that are real.

"Turn that damn traitor off," shouted Ferox.

The air raid was over, but the smoke screen spread, it settled over the Gulf and the beach in a dark choking fog; a light rain began to fall.

＊

Or shall we trace its beginning to October 17th? By that date Admiral Richfield in Tokyo knew that there had been no "Taiwan Victory" greater than Tsushima, Jutland or Pearl Harbor, and he hurriedly called off pursuit of mythical stragglers by a Japanese heavy cruiser squadron. But trapped by his public relations office, he was too late to recall the nationwide victory ration of sake, or the main Japanese fleet, already steaming into position for VICTORY ONE OPERATION — the defense of the Philippines.

＊

231900   Gathered in a large circle round Sanky, you and the bandsmen and Sanky himself were having an after-K-ration liqueur, compounded of equal parts of your "technical intelligence instruments" and of a Philippine coconut milk brew known as *tuba*. The drummer, whose storage space within his drums made him the logical distillery officer (it was a happy accident that he came from a reliable moonshine district of Kentucky) had started up his apparatus but had not yet got into full production.

You were eager to see Sanky with his men. Warrant officer was a peculiar rank, somewhat rarer in the Army than in the Navy. But in both it stood for a man who, like the sergeant, was at home with enlisted men, but who, unlike the sergeant, was equally at home with officers. Perhaps warrant was what all officers or all noncommissioned officers, ideally, should be like, but the warrants alone moved easily between the two military worlds of rank and of work.

Sanky lit a cigar and began. "I was happy as a pig in Paradise," he said, "and I decided to go to church."

A flight of birds caught his eyes, but he went on quickly: "Not just any old church, mind you."

There was a snort of appreciation from the bandsmen. Sanky was famous for his knowledge of tactics. "I picked a little church in the suburbs of Diego, and I walked in, as meek as new milk."

"Come on, Sanky," said the piccolo, a thin pimply strip of a lad, new to the traditions of the 23rd Corps and of Sanky's bandsmen, and who liked his stories short and hot. "Get to the point, for Chrissakes." He threw candies into his mouth as he talked.

There were cries of protest from the glockenspiel and the trumpets, and the piccolo was variously advised to "let Sanky alone," "go shut up," "go take off your cock with a handsaw." On one point there was substantial agreement, and that was how the piccolo could best and most conveniently dispose of his excrement.

Sanky drank deep from the coconut which held his share of the fiery mixture.

"I began by making the acquaintance of one of the elders of the church — named Hardhack." He drew on his cigar. "Sort of fellow you itch to kick."

"The girls?" asked the piccolo coarsely. "When do we get to the girls for Chrissakes?" He threw more candies into his mouth.

There were vigorous suggestions, from tuba, flute and bass drum, as to how the piccolo could have intercourse with himself, or with his band instrument, just as he chose. Should either of these prospects fail to please, he was assured of a plentiful supply of volunteers eager to ram his piccolo up his rectum, as a kind of musical proctoscope.

Undisturbed, Sanky continued. "Then Elder Hardhack introduced me to a widow woman." The piccolo, about to leave the circle, spun round as though gripped by an invisible hand, and sat down. "As pretty as a peony," said Sanky. His expression indicated clearly that you could hardly call yourself a man until you had known a genuine widow woman.

"I'm just a natural born fool when it comes to such a woman," said Sanky. "I only found out by accident what a slummock she was."

He laughed at the memory. "But what lovely blond hair the cheeky slut had. Natural, too." There was a sigh. Sanky would know for sure if she had blond hair.

"Her shape?" asked the piccolo. "Jesus, man. What about her shape?" He opened a tin of K rations and began eating greedily.

The three trombones pulled the piccolo's gasproof jacket over his head, then punched him vigorously, appealing all the time to the Goddess Intercourse. The piccolo located his tin and ate again.

"Just hold still and let me knead this dough," said Sanky, "and then you can bake it as brown as you please."

It was getting darker now, and the tip of his cigar glowed red when he drew on it.

"She had white skin, just as soft and white —" he found his favorite phrase — "as a mouse's underbelly."

The circle laughed. This was a simile all could appreciate from firsthand experience, at least of the mouse.

"Broad shoulders, broad hips, and a narrow waist, one you could put your hands around. And her figure . . ." his glowing cigar traced two voluptuous circles in air, and that blond, whiteskinned, greatbreasted widow woman seemed almost to materialize out of the thick damp evening air.

"I went to school to her to learn woman tricks, and I do believe that in any properly run institution — I do not refer to the Army — I would have got my diploma.

"She had a neat little house — my how that woman loved chintz, she even had chintz on the bookshelves."

"She read books?" said the flutist.

"It was her husband's library, she said. Mostly detective stories — a few books on criminal trials. And one or two on toxicology, medical law, criminal psychology, that kind of thing."

The flutist had gone through high school, and now he said proudly, "Toxicology is the laws of toxics."

"What's toxics?" asked the piccolo scornfully.

The flutist subsided, crushed.

"The moment we entered the house she turned on the radio and began dancing by herself, as if she never wanted to stop — why she was just like a feather on her feet."

Bandsmen all, they nodded approval. It did not do for a bandsman to go out with an unrhythmical woman.

"At first she danced far away from me, and I felt just as limber as a dishrag. But soon she came closer, put her smooth white cheek next to mine, took it away again, as cunning as you please —" loud groans — "put it back again —" cheers — "and finally let her cheek sink against mine, you know the way they have, until she had me in the chompin stage of my passion."

"Yeeow," said the bass drum.

"And every once in a while she'd just sort of drift her whole figure up against me, and fling away again, until she had me grinning

just like a baked possum, and I had to stop dancing completely —"
he paused and winked — "course I stopped right in front of the
sofa."

The drummer cocked an ear toward a clump of nipa palm from
which issued an ominous rumbling. He ran between the fronds and
vanished from your view. There was a dull thud. Birds streaked
angrily across the sky. "Daggone it," said the drummer, coming
back, his face grimy. "Daggone it, she blew her top again. That
still might just as well be my old woman for all the good we're
getting out of her."

"Are you sure," said Sanky, "that you were raised in Kentucky,
and I quote, 'on a high hill where the maple logs grow'?"

Sanky tipped the last container from your collection of Technical
Intelligence Instruments into the tuba supply, and refilled his coconut. He proposed a toast: "To the backside of —"

There was agreement that it should be to the backside of the man
who had made this trip possible, namely, General Ferox.

"Well, soon enough," said Sanky, "the widow had me hot enough
to fry grease, but I'll spare you cornpone eaters the story of that
supper she cooked me of rare steak and French-fried tatoes and
strawberries and heavy whipped cream, and I'll go right to the
point where I gave a great deep belch that came from behind my
kidneys.

"She looked at me just the way a lady dog looks when it's puppy-
making time, and the rustle of her dress said 'I dare you,' and my
arm flew round her and said right back, 'I take that dare.'

"Then she went to her bedroom to change into something more
comfortable — oh, I tell you these widow women know just how
sugar is made."

There were weak cries of "More, more," but Sanky said, "Let the
dirt go before the broom, for a gentleman never tells, but I will
say one thing, that negligee she had changed to was every bit as hot
as horseradish."

Sanky drew on his cigar. "I've married once," he said thoughtfully. "You'd of thought I'd know the teeth and claws of the female
animal by now. Course it makes you preciate home cooking, whenever you eat out, as I used to say when my first wife got jealous."

"That was pretty much all the time, wasn't it?" said the piccolo.

"Some peaches get all the worms," said Sanky, "and the other peaches don't get a one."

"You calling me a worm, are you?" said the piccolo. But his friends pulled him down and saved him from a possible massacre.

"Well next thing I knew she'd just about fanned me to wedding heat," said Sanky. "But always remember, what you get over the devil's back is often lost under his belly.

"Now rest easy, men, for I'm coming to the point of this story.

"You remember that weekend we had a bad time with the desert training and got into Diego too late to go anywheres but the Red Lantern?"

The slide trombone groaned and covered his face with his hands. "Those girls were mercenary," said the slide trombone, more in sorrow than in anger.

"And who do you think I met there?" The stump of Sanky's cigar glowed red. "It was that same old church elder, Hardhack, grinning like a hyena. As sanctimonious as ever, just as if he'd swallowed a drowned mouse and was having trouble over the tail.

" 'You getting along fine with Mrs. Farnweather?' he asked.

" 'Old Farnweather must have been quite a reader.'

" 'Never read a book in his life.' Elder Hardhack smiled with a smile that I didn't like at all.

"I thought of all those books — detective stories, toxicology, criminal jurisprudence.

" 'How did he die?'

" 'From a steak that was too rare,' said Elder Hardhack, cackling like a goose that's just laid a genuine gilt egg. He laid a finger alongside his nose. 'But she got off.'

" 'Got off?'

" 'Fortunately, before the investigation, Mr. Farnweather had been burned to a crisp — all perfectly legal, of course, in the mortuary incinerator. And the ashes dropped from an airplane, all over San Diego. Who knows,' he said with a tremendously pious expression as he buckled his trousers, 'we might be walking on his ashes now.'

"The next morning, bright and early, I was at the public library."

"Looking up toxicology?" asked the piccolo.

Sanky's glance shriveled him. "In the suburban weekly paper I found the testimony at the trial — she had said the books were her husband's. She herself couldn't bear to read such things.

"A week later I went back for the last time, determined to have it out with the widow Farnweather, root hog or die.

" 'They're your books,' I said, but the moment I spoke I wanted to bite off my tongue and fling it out the window. She gave me a long cold look that sank to my belly like an icicle, and she took a long long time fixing our drinks.

" 'Sit down,' I said, 'and tell me why you said at the trial they were your husband's books?'

"She stroked my head, as smooth as a harlot at a christening, laughed, and went out to change into something more comfortable.

"While she was gone, I switched our drinks.

"She came back in a black lace negligee she knew I liked. 'Drink up,' she said. And eying each other in a funny way, we both drank sip for sip. I sat back, with a sigh of relief.

"Then suddenly, it hit me. I felt just exactly as if a firehose was coiled in my belly, lashing to get out. 'I'm dying,' I yelled, 'I'm dying.'

"And then that durned hose exploded inside my belly, and released a lifetime supply of soda gas for an elephant, and the soda began coming out of my mouth and my nose and my ears till I was breathing soda in, and coughin it out, and durned if I wasn't hearing soda too, why I never knew one human being could hold so much soda — I just slipped and slid and slithered out of that house and along the street, why for two city blocks I never had to move my legs at all, I just skied along on my own supply of soda.

"And all the time, somewheres in back of me, I could hear Elder Hardhack laughing and laughing."

Two doves flew side by side inland. It was dusk now, and Sanky stubbed out his cigar. He walked over to his double foxhole which he shared with no one.

"Did you ever see her again?" asked the tuba.

"Just before we landed on Attu," said Sanky, "I got a card from the elder Hardhack. Inviting me to the Hardhack-Farnweather nuptials."

His strong fingers gripped your arm and his blunt and craggy face wrinkled into an expression of melancholy that astonished you.

"You goddam fool," he said.

He settled down in his foxhole. But first he rose up on his elbow. "I always say, it's the longest pole gets the persimmon."

From beneath his shelter half came a soft gurgle and an arm flung out an empty coconut shell.

Far off, you could hear the unsynchronized beat of the motors of the Japanese bomber that would soon make its nightly run over your positions. And you could hear Sanky's teeth grating in his sleep.

✿

Or shall we say, more dramatically, that the psychological beginning came at Brunei Bay, North Borneo, on the 18th, when the crew of the Japanese battleship Warrior's Wealth (*with her sister ship* Classical Japan *the two greatest dreadnaughts in the world*) *began painting sections of the main deck black, to make the battleship seem smaller to American planes?*

This was to be the first sea battle for these gigantic ships; ominously enough, the crew of the Warrior's Wealth *called the fresh black paint the ship's death dress.*

Perhaps the problem of precisely when the Battle for Visaya Gulf began is insoluble.

✿

232000   You jumped as the Filipino ran jabbering and screaming past the Translation Tent. In his middle thirties, he had a rusty revolver which he triggersnapped at imaginary pursuers. He wore a flapping green bathrobe. Along with many things and people that had been liberated on purpose, the local insane asylum had been liberated by accident.

Grossman's uniform was a symphony in salt and sweat. "Twentynine," he said. "Since the beginning of the landing, twentynine of our planes have been shot down by our own guns."

The PA system turned on. "Take cover, take cover. There will be 50-caliber-machine gun bullets passing through this area. Take cover." The PA system abruptly turned off.

No one paid any attention. It was almost completely black now, time to find your holes and stay in them. But you all wanted to be together a moment longer. Even Sanky had waked up again.

"'Nude Tennis,'" said Sanky reflectively. "That article of yours called 'Nude Tennis.' What's that mean? What kind of game is that?"

"It's a symbolic game," said Grossman, impatient.

"Does it have a net?"

"In nude tennis, the net is always down."

"And *Penetration*. Why is the magazine that printed it called *Penetration*? Every time I read an article like that, it's in a magazine called *Echo* or *Accent* or *Furioso* or *Downbeat* or *Folio*. What's the matter with a good American name like *Saturday Evening Post* or *New Yorker* or *Newsweek*?"

"Those names are all used up."

"A name like *Saturday Evening Post* is never all used up."

At the latrine twenty yards away, fireflies hovered, darkly blue-gleaming, in a trembling pillar that grew waveringly higher. Far off, you could hear a Japanese plane, its unsynchronized motors warbling, flying straight down the eastern coast of Visaya. And you could hear the steadier-beating motors of the U.S. Army night fighters which had turned out to be unable to find Japanese planes in the dark.

Then, at last, the 50-caliber bullets came, hiss ouah — hiss ouah — hiss ouah. You dived for your holes like prairie dogs.

A nisei who could not say the l's that were part of all passwords tugged at your elbow. You and Grossman spent much of the night taking such nisei to the latrine.

"Now, listen," you whispered fiercely to the nisei who was clutching his trousers. "Say after me, 'Lollipop.'"

The tower of fireflies grew another half foot higher in galactic swirls of blue light.

"Roripop," he said.

"No, 'Lollipop.'"

"Roripop."

A faint whistle began, high in the sky, like a wire scratched across dark slate, it grew louder and more pointed in sound, it turned to a shriek — a blinding flash scraped hotly across your eyeballs, and, plunged into a blind world, you rocked inside thunders that bruised your shoulders.

A gray-green hemisphere of light rose in the trembling air and ascended fitfully till it flickered on the highest slopes of Sogod Hill.

"Six days firing for the Corps," shouted Sanky, pointing to the blazing ammunition dump. From its artificial volcanoes spewed tracer fire, M 1 bullets, mortar shells, chunks of cherry-red steel and lead.

With a soft, relentless sound, invisible giant scissors cut deep slashes — rip rip rip — through the Translation Tent.

You and Sanky lit cigarettes for each other, and your matches trembled out in your hands. The sweat lay all along your hands and arms and back. You were overcome by an exquisite sense of hopeless longing — you recalled Chaplain Simon — *man regains his dignity by doing penance for wicked pleasures* — another section of the ammunition dump caught, the ground trembled, and a crimson light mingled with the green, in the sky you heard the grinding drag of a gigantic chain.

It was no longer necessary to take the nisei to the latrine. The cloud of blue fireflies grew and trembled over the pits, grew again another half foot higher, in a long dancing spiral.

✿

Rear Admiral Westvillage, though senior in years, was junior in rank to Vice-admiral Island, with whose forces he was supposed to join. For a day and a night Rear Admiral Westvillage pushed on, driving his Second Ambush Attack Force — the old battleships Three Creators *and* Mountain Castle, *his heavy cruiser,* Superlative *and his four destroyers — by long detours, in order to elude both the searching American subs, and his pursuing junior, Vice-admiral Island, who would at once take command should these two Japanese forces join.*

In both aims Admiral Westvillage was successful. When at dawn he reached South Strait, at the bottom of Visaya Island, and ordered the Superlative *to fly her reconnaissance float plane over Visaya Gulf, neither the Americans nor Japanese Admiral Island knew where he was.*

So was revealed to the observant historian the fundamental weakness of a navy which relied mainly on seniority rather than merit.

✿

240650   A sickish yellow hand plucked at the dark blue sky. In the beach ammunition dump two huge areas smoldered, like red-glowing eyes, but half the dump was still usable.

At the height of the explosions a bulldozer operator had carved firelanes through the dump. Then he had driven off. No one knew who he was.

All through the Corps area men struggled to their feet with an air of lassitude. You found some hot water for shaving, a simple and innocent enough pleasure. Humming:

> Roses are red
> Violets are blue
> I like pecans
> Nuts to you —

you cut yourself on the chin.

A green plane with the red ball painted on its wings fishtailed across the Gulf. It was surprisingly fast for a float plane — the Japanese made the best float planes in the world — but it began to burn from the steady cannoning of a pursuing Grumman.

You could see this aerial battle, but you heard nothing.

"Why do the Japanese send a float plane over here?"

You shrugged.

The float plane disintegrated into small, gritty fragments, as if wiped from the blue sky by a dirty eraser. On the beach the hellish eyes of the ammunition fire turned bright red in a sudden breeze, then were hooded again. Men began to fling earth at them.

A dourfaced Colonel Mist gave orders to catch the madman who was cartwheeling round his tent. Lunatic lips howled and yelled, ate K ration crackers and spat the crumbs, fingernails tore the tattered green robe, scratched at scarred flesh, legs ran, tumbled, crawled and danced off into the coconut forest.

"How do you expect me to think?" shouted Colonel Mist.

You went back to your shaving, singing softly:

Roses are red
Violets are blue
I use Lifebuoy
Why don't you?

❁

*At 240810, just after the Japanese had mistakenly driven
off their own fighter plane escort sent down from Manila, Admiral Hornbull's search planes found the First
Ambush Attack Force of Admiral Chestnutfield and began to circle it.*

*In the meantime an American Army bomber reported
the sinking and destruction of a Japanese battleship at
the naval base of Yokosuka.*

*The Army pilot stayed at the scene long enough, he
said, to see the battleship capsize.*

True, in hitting the Mikasa, Togo's *old flagship of
1905, the bomber had delivered a blow which might
well have sunk her and made her capsize. Except that,
as a patriotic tourist attraction, Togo's flagship had long
ago been anchored solidly in a base of concrete.* (127)
NOTE 127: *The Army version differs from this account.*

❁

240830   A light rain spat against the crumbling roads. Startled,
you turned sharply, your hand on the carbine that tapped soggily
against your hip.

"Another madman," said Chaplain Simon gently.

Braying through clenched yellow teeth, the lunatic Filipino gy-
rated into the Corps area, kicking out at tents, at ammunition boxes,
at a field telephone.

When you looked up from your work again, Chaplain Simon had
moved quickly across the field to a newly arrived litter case. The
rain fell more strongly and Simon threw a dampening blanket over
the figure huddled on the litter, but a stonefaced man, friend to the
dead, protested, began arguing bitterly with Simon — "Not dead —"
he cried; rain and a driving wind blew toward you, blew bits and
pieces of Simon's words, phrases worn and rounded from ending

millions of lives — *Death is only a door* — *in the end all men die* — *he will not go to his family his family will come to him* — *of whom may we seek for succor* — *leave, forget, forgive* —

Back again ran the madman, biting, kicking, and a soldier who had not seen him the first time fired at him, and another soldier called wildly, "Fall back, retreat" — and another, confused in the hardsilver rain, fired at the first soldier, who hurled back a grenade and pulped a banana tree.

— *dignity* — went on Chaplain Simon, slowly, unaware.

Men began firing here and there across the field, at wavering bushes, at raindrops, at themselves, like scorpions stinging themselves, and everywhere men tumbled and slipped and crawled into the musty old Japanese trenches, you huddled at a trench angle, miserable, afraid, while Sanky ran by you shouting, "Piney woods tacky, you pinheaded wartheads, you momzers, hell, do you want your frigging rifles rammed up your dokuses?"

Dignity — you heard the voice of Simon, calm, assured — quiet fell again, and Sanky hoisted his helmet on his rifle.

Ping, and the helmet, badly dented, whirled off and over the trenchlip. Sanky shouted again, "You horses' caboose, you shadbellied aments, hell hell hell!" But the firing ravaged on, far worse than before. Gleaming gold, the cross of gold at his collar shining, Chaplain Simon stood erect, you remembered the chaplain's school where he had been trained in his duties —

Dignity, he said monotonously, calmly.

"Get down," shouted Sanky, "get down."

Digni —

There was a soft clunk, as of a stick jabbing into a melon, and Simon slumped softly to the ground, dead, while the raingusts lashed at your eyes, and the men fired against themselves.

❖

On the morning of the 24th Admiral Smallswamp flew off his few remaining pilots to lure Admiral Hornbull away from Visaya Gulf and North Strait, away from the First Ambush Attack Force, and up the eastern coast of Luzon.

Ablest of Japanese Admirals, Smallswamp was deter-

mined to make Hornbull conform to the moves of the weaker, Japanese fleet. He expected Hornbull, like a dog, as he phrased it, to go "sniff sniff sniff" at Smallswamp's Decoy Fleet of four useless carriers.

With his instinctive sailor's eye, Smallswamp had chosen well his sailing area, off Luzon, at Cape Deception.

And now the pendulum of history hung poised, balanced between the Japanese and the Americans.

✿

241000   "What was that word *dignidad* he was always using?" asked Sanky. "What did he mean by that?"

"Dignity. What you're worth. You gain or regain it by penance."

"Penance for what?"

"For wicked pleasures."

"That's too much for a hell-raiser like me."

You sat in your foxhole, too weary, after the tenth air raid of the day, to get out.

Tacked on a coconut tree, a poster of the confident jaw, the beetling brows, the piercing, double whammy eyes of Supreme Commander MacDazzle, glared at you. I HAVE RETURNED — said the legend. The expression on the face was the brooding look of a motheaten hawk.

Sanky went to the poster, as he always did, crossed out "I" and wrote in "WE." You drew the mustache, while Sanky, an expert in these matters, sketched in a bulging bosom and brassière.

Once Chaplain Simon had told you about the chaplain's school at William and Mary, where he had learned about "Bringing God to men and men to God — the Navy way," and where he had learned how to dive through burning oil into the swimming pool. Once, in training, he had been clumsy and burned himself.

Dignidad.

"When they make movies," said Sanky, "they always show a neat little hole where the bullet goes in. But they never show the scoop-shovel hole where it comes out."

"That's *dignidad* too."

"He was courteous," said Sanky.

Through green alerts, red alerts, and all clears, the green-robed madman had crouched by the Translation Tent, reciting.

"Does he know what he's saying?" asked Sanky.

"Probably not."

"How much does he remember of it?"

"He's at the sixth book now."

The idiot savant, in his rich Tagalog accent, droned on:

> Hinc exaudiri gemitus, et saeva sonare
> Verbera, tum stridor ferri tractaeque catenae.

Sanky motioned to you. "Let's go."

Your foxhole was safe, even comfortable, with a little earthen shelf for your shaving kit. You did not want to leave it.

"Wait a minute," you said, "he's just got Aeneas in hell."

❀

The Japanese had tripled the smaller AA batteries of the 72,000-ton Warrior's Wealth, *and this queen of battle-wagons could fire from her main batteries huge 18-inch shells that puffed out a tangle of silver balls and wire at attacking planes.*

At 1025 she took an aerial torpedo which made it impossible for her to steer except in a circle. At 1030 she was hit by three torpedoes, and at 1045 by five more; she lost control of her guns and her compass blew up. Fighting for her life, she somehow managed to resume speed and even keep up with the formations of the First Ambush Attack Force.

In unsailorlike fashion, the Japanese had defied the stern gods of the sea, by boasting that the Warrior's Wealth *was unsinkable.*

❀

241200   Sogod Hill. Through Gordian's binoculars you saw the broken Japanese bridge, clutching in splintered wooden fingers a trapped American tank. Across the coastal river, their tracks hanging in the air like broken elbows, two more American tanks, in the Japanese mine field at the foot of Sogod Hill.

The dog handlers had stopped on the first slopes of the hill, where it was deeply gouged by 155-mm shells from yesterday's unsuccessful attack. A messenger trotted down the dark slopes, and several men carrying cartons trudged up again. Dogfood. You offered Gordian the binoculars.

You remembered a pretty girl with a liking for sarong style skirts and red hibiscus flowers.

Bluntly, "What about your wife?"

"I've adopted the boy. That's the right thing to do, isn't it?"

"And your wife?"

"An anthropologist is a man who knows about every kind of human marriage but his own."

"That's a husband."

In a disinterested tone he read aloud from a sociological study of fear under combat.

Many soldiers (44 per cent) had a sinking feeling in the pit of the stomach, one third had "dry mouth" and a fifth had clammy hands. A lamentable 6 per cent urinated involuntarily, a shameful 5 per cent defecated, and a wretched 1 per cent vomited and fainted.

What were combat soldiers afraid of? Combat soldiers were most afraid of wounds in the abdomen. Next came wounds in the eyes, then wounds in the brain and genitals. Least of all the combat soldier feared wounds in the hands and legs.

Veterans feared being crippled, while green soldiers feared their own cowardice.

"What do combat dogs fear?"

"I've never studied the combat dog." Gordian focused his binoculars on the slopes of Sogod Hill. Round a bend in your trench Gordian's regimental headquarters was talking to the dog handlers by walkie-talkie radio.

Men, and a few women, were flushed out of holes on Sogod Hill.

"Those dogs are wonderful at finding refugees."

The rain began its daily drizzle. You huddled under your poncho, wishing you had not come to Sogod Hill to look for suicide attack documents.

"Remember Ensign Brown? The suicide on Guadalcanal."

A twig broke between your fingers. You tried to drop it, but the gummy ends stuck to your hand. Suddenly, Ensign Brown's face came to mind, and vanished again, lost to memory.

Gordian forgot what he was going to tell you in his concentration on the hill. He was cleanshaven now, not so much less mild and amiable as more resilient. He refused to let you borrow the binoculars.

A hundred yards further along the coastal river some American soldiers, wearing only their helmets, were bathing. Before them they pushed bits of soap on scraps of wood. A Japanese plane swung low and strafed the bathers. Their pale white bodies plunged to the eyebrows in the brown-red stream.

Under your poncho you translated your only find, Officer Deeplook's farewell note: "It is the period of sweating blood. We regret very much having caused the Emperor anxiety."

After Japanese Officer Deeplook had written this note, sometime late last night, he had tapped his grenade on his helmet to start the fuse, and then held the grenade to his chest.

You stamped the note SOUVENIR PASSED BY CINCPAC.

"They've opened fire," said Gordian. The dogs and the dog-handlers tumbled, yelling and yipping, back down the hill.

A concealed Japanese, his booming voice tunneling out to air through several cave mouths at once, called out, "Americans, you going dying. Americans, you going eat blood."

Halfway up the slope, one of the dogs ran back and forth in aimless circles, tripping over his intestines.

None of the men were hurt. Gordian rubbed his nose between thumb and forefinger reflectively, and turned his binoculars toward the Gulf. "Where's the command ship, the *Nasatch?*" he asked. He searched among the hundreds of ships but could not see her. "If the Japanese fleet is going to make a stand, this is about their last chance."

Near the broken Japanese bridge, engineers were fitting together the parts of a steel Bailey bridge. Behind them waited six 75-mm Mark 8 self-propelled howitzers and a mine detector team.

Dozens of souvenir hunters, soldiers and sailors from the shore working parties, scrambled like crabs over the lower ranges of the hill, looking for dead Japanese.

The wounded dog sat on his haunches and licked at his intestines. Then he began to eat them.

❋

On the 24th of October, in cooperation with VICTORY ONE operations, General Pasture, ComGen16thImpJap-DivKyoto, sent out a patrol of 150 men, led by a Filipino civilian, to attack American airfields in the American 23rd Corps area. Their orders, in typical Japanese military style, were to display the worth of the Imperial Army and annihilate American bandits.

From the objective historian's point of view, this was one more pathetic attempt to make land operations influence a battle at sea.

❋

241300   Miss Perfection Rapidslope was a very attractive girl, although her smooth complexion was somewhat heavily rice-powdered by American standards. Even in the baggy trousers of her wartime *mompe* her figure hinted strongly of rounded delights.

The question was what to do about Miss Perfection Rapidslope. Another and related question was what to do about her five girls who stood beside her, moving about in little hopping steps like so many birds, delicate and fluttering in gesture, but whose downcast eyes hinted at the delights of night. For Miss Rapidslope ran a "shop" in Manila, as she informed you in her delicious Kyoto drawl.

From your conversations with her, you had made up a unique brothel guide to Manila. These had been divided into "shops" for Navy officers, "shops" for Navy noncoms, and "shops" for Navy enlisted men.

The Japanese army boasted a similar but much larger establishment, beginning with an officers' "shop" elegantly entitled "Broadpines" and going on down to tens of anonymous houses for enlisted men.

And Miss Rapidslope had further information on "B" Comfort Unit in Penang (150 girls), and on K, S and A units, of 10, 25 and 20 girls respectively, in Macassar, Hong Kong and Singapore.

From the number of "shops" and their staff of comfort girls you could get a rough idea of the number of troops in Manila and elsewhere, and a very precise idea of the location of the top headquarters, since the officer "shops" were always a short walk from the main command posts. Given a little more time you might have worked out a "Classen's Constant" — comparable to Gordian's inspired formula for the Japanese privy.

With a charming flutter of her long dark eyelashes Miss Perfection Rapidslope explained that in September of this year the Japanese navy had sent all "special need personnel" and "comfort women" back to Japan. But Perfection, and five of her girls, touched by this consideration (the cruder Japanese army simply left its girls to fend for themselves), decided to remain.

She sighed, and her full breasts pressed against her thin blouse. It had been a long, strenuous war. Ever since its beginning, even elegant geisha had been reduced to walking the streets like the ordinary Japanese prostitutes called *gi*. And Perfection had been relieved when at last the opportunity came to use her services in 1943 — and to display Love Country Heart as well — by taking her "shop" first to Tainan.

In December 1943 she had made a second move, and with thirteen prostitutes and seventeen geisha she had sailed from Tainan to Manila, in a boat so small you could touch both railings simultaneously with your hands. Her delicate rice-powdered face trembled at the memory.

But then a lovely church had been found for her in Paco, a suburb of Manila, and her "shop," for the first time in its existence, had resounded to merry tunes on the pipe organ. Naval officers liked her redecorated church, and they came frequently to it to "play," as the Japanese idiom had it. How the naval officers adored her beds in the shape of boats, her mirrors on the ceiling and at odd angles on the walls, her phallic fountains and statues!

And how sensible of the Japanese high command, which by means of houses such as hers avoided female diseases such as yaws, and female spies like Mata Hari. And how considerate of the Navy, with its special orders for wages, its special housing and transportation — even the traditional New Year's gift of clothing for the geisha. And in Japan's rising tide, more and more geisha had come from the homeland, and prostitutes too, until Miss Rapidslope had reached a total of forty in her "shop."

And now — delicate eyelashes fluttered — that you had captured Perfection and her troupe, on their inter-island tour, what did you intend to do with them?

They were number one performers, they knew artistic erotic dances, not at all the usual brief and vulgar kind of thing.

Perhaps you would like to see the dance of Krishna and the cowgirls?

The cowgirls go in swimming, calling out their love for Krishna as they swim. Krishna steals quietly upon them, and makes their clothes into a bundle, then climbs into a tree. When the cowgirls come out of the water, hiding themselves with their hands as best they can, they are unable to find their clothes.

They see Krishna in the tree and run back to the water and hide. Krishna tells them to come out of the water, one by one, if they really want their clothes. They say they are in love with Krishna, but they cannot come out of the water naked.

Krishna says they cannot have their clothes back. They ask why Krishna treats them so badly when they are in love with Krishna.

At this point in her narrative Miss Perfection Rapidslope smiled a deviously enigmatic smile. Krishna says if they love him they must not be so bashful, and so they come out of the water, one by one, shielding themselves with their hands. Krishna tells them to lift up their hands — only then will he return their clothes.

All together they lift up their hands and run off the stage.

Do you not think that a very fine dance?

Suteki, you answered. Superlative.

❉

Before takeoff, standing together on the runway, the suicide pilot sang: "The Japanese heart is like the mountain cherry blossom of our farflung islands, blowing radiant in the rising morning sun."

Each phrase from this poem was used to designate a suicide unit, and according to Corporal Saltfield's charred diary, he had been assigned the phrase, "mountain cherry blossom". . . Nothing could be more remote from the American way of war than these suicide attacks.

And from the historian's perspective, in this battle at least, they counted for very little.

❉

241330   The medical area of the 23rd Corps was a quiet space under tattered coconut palms. There was a dentist, a line of waiting patients, and an assistant to the dentist who pumped a foot treadle for the whining drill. There was a doctor, often idle, since the worst cases went directly from regiment or division to the Station Hospital two miles north, on the coast road to Abuyog. And there were a few long green tents in which patients waited to be sent somewhere else.

The tent you wanted held seven Japanese, an old Filipino man, three Americans and a Filipino girl. But it did not hold pilot officer Victoryview, a suicide pilot, whom you had come to find.

The girl did not look pretty any more, but you could tell at once that she was a girl and that she had been very pretty once.

The dark green tent was hot, and you wiped the sweat off your face. The girl was receiving plasma in her arm and was moaning quietly. It was obviously some simple phrase like "Daddy help me" or "Mommy help me." Nobody knew what it was except that it was not in your little Tagalog phrase books. She had been raped over and over, just before the Japanese left, and she was bleeding to death quietly, deep inside her body.

The three Americans had been heavily doped with morphine. They were bandaged, and their plasma bottles were empty. They stared with glazed eyes at the roof of the tent as though they saw there some scene of incredible fascination. When you first saw that staring gaze you looked in spite of yourself at the damp green roof of the tent. Then you wiped the sweat off your face, but your gas-proofed green shirt held the wet, and your face stayed damp.

Even when the Japanese fighters came over on a strafing run, so close that you could see one goggled head in its green aluminum cockpit, the three Americans stared, entranced, at the green canvas roof. But you, and the medical orderly, fell flat on the soft damp floor of the tent, and the Japanese, none of whom had been given any morphine yet, for there was a shortage of morphine, rolled on top of their captors, their broken legs and burned faces and plaster casts getting all tangled together, and a Japanese with his leg in a cast fell on top of you.

The Japanese planes swung round and tried again but only a few bullets hit near the tent.

You moved the Japanese on top of you to the ground, as gently as you could, and side by side you and the prisoner laughed and smiled at each other when the planes missed for the last time and roared off.

The prisoner with the cast pointed to a spent bullet that had stuck in his cast at the hipbone. The Japanese prisoners sighed and drew in their breath with a hissing sound. The American soldiers smiled in their morphine dream, the girl cried over and over again a few simple words in her unintelligible liquid language, and you and the Japanese laughed and laughed with relief. The old Filipino man had a wide grin on his face, and, still laughing, you patted him on the shoulder. He was cold, and at once you knew he was dead and had been dead all through the strafing attack. The laughter on his face was the fixed sad laughter of the dead.

❖

At 241400 Admiral Smallswamp, worried that his planes had not yet lured Hornbull to the decoy fleet off Cape Deception, broke radio silence and sent a long message to Tokyo, hopefully expecting that Hornbull's fleet would intercept it. Smallswamp was less than 100 miles from Hornbull, but the Americans, with less skillful radio directionfinder crews than the Japanese, did not hear him.

There was a subtle lesson here, for the judicious naval historian.

❖

241400   On reaching the top of Sogod Hill, the battered American troops discovered that it was not one hill, as their maps indicated, but three. From the second of these hills the Japanese launched a successful counterattack, and the Americans were driven off the hill.

General MacDazzle interrupted his inspection trip of the 23rd Corps area just long enough to explain to General Ferox how unpleased he was with this turn of events.

Fortunately for Ferox, General MacDazzle had to take time out for a wire recorder interview, to be flown back to America and broadcast from there. In it he announced the end of organized resistance on Visaya.

A Marine standing near you said to another Marine of the Marine

Artillery Battalion "How many times was it that MacDazzle announced the end of resistance on Siak Island? Five times? Six times?"

"I'm pretty sure it was five times," said the second Marine. They linked arms and sang, softly at first, but louder as the men of the battalion stopped work and joined in:

> They called for the Army to come to Tulagi
> But Marvin MacDazzle said "No!"
> He said, "there's a reason, it isn't the season,
> Beside, there's no USO."
> Bless em all, bless em all,
> The long and the short and the tall!
> Bless all the pelicans and dogfaces too,
> Bless all the generals and above all bless you.

MacDazzle, hawk face expressionless, got into his command car for the trip back north to Abuyog, his headquarters. Before the cavalacade started, MacDazzle's press officer struck out from Bulflash's copy a complimentary reference to the Marine Artillery Battalion. "Public relationswise," said the press officer, "that battalion can consider itself annihilated." Turning too sharply, he tumbled up to his knees in an abandoned latrine slit. The two Marines helped him out courteously.

❀

Admiral Chestnutfield withdrew his battered First Ambush Attack Force and signaled Tokyo: "Expect no results against pursuing enemy, damage gradually increasing, unreasonable to advance, will retire out of air range one hour, intend advance 241700 in accordance with success of friendly planes."

Admiral Richfield answered: "Relying on heaven, the whole force will advance and attack."

The writing of great naval messages is an art, which the Japanese did not, on this occasion, show that they had mastered.

❀

241600   The pilot at the Station Hospital was not Victoryview, for whom you were still searching. His name was Highspirits. No one knew if he had been a suicide pilot or not. The skin of his face was all puffed up as though it had been fried in hot grease. He was burned in the throat too, inside his mouth, and you could not understand what he was trying to say. He shivered with cold.

There was a holder beside his litter for a plasma bottle. The holder was empty.

With his burned fingers Petty Officer Highspirits folded paper cranes. He had only a few sheets of paper, and after he had folded them all, painfully he flattened out the sheets and started all over again.

"Well — " said the medical officer.

"How much plasma do you have?"

He shrugged. The shrug was the universal gesture of the war. You wished there was a military law against it. "Very little," he said.

"So little that if you give him plasma some American soldier will die?"

The medical officer did not want to answer no, and he shrugged again. You tried to fight off a sharp little knife edge of dislike. You had a lot of business with the medical officer of the Station Hospital, and it was silly to get in an argument with him.

You tried again to talk to the pilot. But he made a few horrible sounds in his throat, and went on folding his paper cranes.

A Japanese with a broken leg raised himself on his elbow and repeated your question to Petty Officer Highspirits. But this helpful Japanese prisoner could not understand Highspirits much better than you could.

"Why is he making paper cranes?"

"When he has made a thousand paper cranes, he will get well."

"Do you believe that?"

"There's no help for it," said the prisoner with the broken leg. It was an expression that covered even more situations than the American shrug. It meant just about anything.

"Tell him to stop it," you said, "his fingers will never get well if he does that."

But Highspirits flattened out all his precious brown and yellow and white sheets of paper and began a new series of paper cranes.

"Here are his papers," said the medical officer. A glassine case, smelling of camphor and containing the day's flight code. Of no value, since the day was almost over. A picture of a wife and child, both holding Rising Sun flags. Taken on departure from the homeland, no doubt. And the usual small black diary.

You put the picture at Highspirit's hand. He went on folding his paper cranes.

The code you tucked in a pocket of your gasproof shirt.

"Will it save his life if you do give him plasma?"

"Who knows?" said the medical officer. He shrugged again.

You bastard, you thought, there's something in you that enjoys all this.

You opened the diary to the end, which, for a Japanese, was the beginning. In it was a poem.

"What does it say?" asked the medical officer.

"It's about the Japanese heart in the farflung islands, and how it's like mountain cherry blossoms in the sun." You noticed, but did not mention, the heavy line drawn beside the characters for "farflung islands."

"They'll never win the war," said the medical officer. "How did they dare attack us?"

You smiled. You had been told that your ironic smile was your best feature.

"They can always win the peace."

The medical officer's look promised you trouble at the Station Hospital from here on in. You resolved, not for the first time, to get a grip on yourself.

Across the road, near the bullet-pocked cathedral, you could see an American Army nurse. She walked along the dusty road, then crossed it, toward the administration tent of the Station Hospital. While she was still at some distance you thought, It's impossible to be any prettier than that.

The wind tugged at the nurse's dress and her hands smoothed her crisp brown uniform with a delicate feminine gesture. She seemed wonderfully clean and tanned, not the atabrine tan you had, but the tan of perfect health. She smiled at a sentry who saluted while she waved back prettily to make the sentry laugh — you saw now her fresh and honest brown eyes —

why had you not realized at once that she was Leilani?

Leilani looked along the row of tents to the one where you and the medical officer stood in the doorway —
why didn't she recognize you?

The stucco-yellow cathedral with its chipped plaster saints, the green tents with their huge red crosses, the ambulances crawling to either side of the road to disgorge litter after litter of bandaged mummies, the trucks, the bullock carts, the jeeps, the ducks, the alligators, all seemed transfixed by the golden dust they summoned from the alien Filipino land —

Leilani vanished, and a golden whirlpool of dust staggered down the road.

❖

So much for Phase One of the Battle for Visaya Gulf. Now with a dramatic thrill the historian records Phase Two.

The paratroop attack was to be coordinated with the advance of the Japanese Ambush Attack Forces; the Japanese paratroopers were supposed to reach the gulf by late afternoon, or by the evening of the 24th, but except for a few flights they were delayed, and finally all paratroop flights were recalled. One plane did not get the recall signal and it flew on, to crashland on Visaya beach. As the Japanese paratroopers unloaded demolition charges an American sergeant waded out and asked if they needed any help. "No," they said in English. "Everything O.K." The sergeant withdrew.

❖

241630　You stared down at Highspirits, lying in his litter and folding paper cranes.

You were thinking of the Japanese instructions to local commanders on how to dispose of Filipino civilians. "When shooting civilians assemble them in one place to save labor and ammunition, namely, in houses which will be burned down, or on the edge of a river. Use care in torturing prisoners, or they will make a fool of you. Kicking and beating are to be used only after all other methods have failed."

You closed the diary, first dog-earing the page which told how Highspirits, on Truk, had beheaded a captured American aviator.

The Truk garrison was notorious for its beheadings, and its American aviator liver feasts. You stopped reading in the diary at the point where Highspirits described the blood gushing from the neck of the dead American flyer.

Within the next tent an orderly knelt like a grimy angel, holding up a plasma bottle which dripped its fluid slowly into the veins of an unconscious American soldier. You thought of all the war monuments you had seen, tanks and guns and generals on horseback, and flagcarriers about to stick a flag into some brazen landscape.

"Well," said the medical officer, impatient. He shrugged in his irritating way.

At his shoulder appeared Lani. Her eyes widened at the sight of you, and her cheeks mantled in a delicate rosy flush. She was wonderfully fresh and pretty.

Deep within you, some gloriously untamed animal stretched lazily to its feet.

Leilani saw the diary; her hand flew to her mouth and at once dropped away in an almost invisible gesture. Her eyes darkened into a patient, waiting expression.

You felt that she would not criticize you for anything you did. But you knew she had read the diary.

The medical officer took your arm in his firm, unpleasant grip. He intended to have you take the responsibility for using the plasma — or refusing it.

Petty Officer Highspirits stopped folding his paper cranes and tried to speak to the Japanese with a broken leg. He was saying through his burned throat something that sounded, so deep and guttural it seemed, like "Buri, Buri, Buri."

Buri was an abandoned Japanese airfield, six miles west of Dulag airfield.

But the Japanese with the broken leg corrected you. Highspirits was saying again and again, "Giri, Giri, Giri — Duty, Duty, Duty."

"Let him have the plasma."

The medical officer dropped his fingers from your arm with an angry push. In the darkish tent, Lani's eyes grew wider still and shone brilliantly. The medical officer gave orders to a corpsman and left the tent.

With a quick, professional gesture, Lani traced a line along your cheek. You winced, and a flame of fire seemed to follow just above the light touch of her fingernail.

"Didn't you know you had been grazed by a bullet?" she said, wonderingly.

You turned and hunkered by the Japanese with the broken leg. "What was at Buri?"

He thought for a moment. "The 54th Airbase Company. The airfield was never finished. It was no good at all in the rainy season."

"How long did the Airbase Company work on it."

"I heard they were still there when your landings began."

Lani's fingers touched your head. "You must have something for it. Even a scratch is dangerous here." Her voice was cool, but her hand lingered.

Flushed from the plasma, Petty Officer Highspirits folded his paper cranes again. You put his notebook in your pocket and stood up. You did not know what you would do with the notebook.

Lani watched you gravely. You had not really thought of her as a nurse before. The late afternoon sun touched flecks of gold in her deep brown eyes. You tried to concentrate on her warm and radiant glance.

The sunlight dazzled, your eyes fell.

With a sighing sound the folded paper cranes, brown and yellow and white, sifted through the burned fingers of Highspirits, they nestled among his bandages, they fluttered to the dark, stained ground. His white, staring eyes looked at you. Unblinking.

"Now his spirit will go to the Yasukuni Shrine in Tokyo," said the Japanese prisoner with the broken leg.

With a gesture that was gentle and professional, and terrifyingly habitual, Lani covered the face of Highspirits.

"The Yasukuni Shrine doesn't exist. Our planes have burned it up."

Lani turned toward you, as if surprised by the harshness you could not keep from your voice.

"There's no help for it," said the prisoner submissively.

"How many paper cranes did he fold?"
"Not so many. Three hundred or so."

*

By 241900 only the second turret forward was out of water, but still the Warrior's Wealth *floated. Just as the sun went down the ship's machinery stopped. Captain Wildboarmouth ordered the crew to swim to the rescue destroyer* Beachwind.

The Warrior's Wealth *rolled over very slowly. Then her bow shot quickly into the air and fell back on the water with a grating, inhuman noise. She sank deep into the water; from the bottom of the sea a great orange-red ball of fire bubbled up high into the twilight air.*

So moved into the stirring pages of naval history the greatest dreadnaught ever built by man; with her died 1100 men, and Captain Wildboarmouth, world expert on naval gunnery.

*

241900   The dying sun gilded the scarpocks of the cathedral, it gleamed off the warm red crosses of the tents, rain fell to the road and flew back in the air again, in golden curls of wet spiral steam.

Twilight.

Three enlisted men, about to be discharged from the Station Hospital, watched you say goodbye. The khaki shirt stencil of one of them lettered itself in your mind. Pvt. Hyannis. His face was dark red under its tan. He took five pesos from a wallet with a horned animal head embossed on it, loaned the money to one of the enlisted men, and entered the transaction in a notebook.

You took Leilani's firm, pretty hand.

"They save it for officers," said one of the enlisted men, intending that you should hear him. You caught Hyannis staring innocently into the violet, darkening distance.

"I'm sorry about Feverton," said Leilani. You saw Feverton bowed under his leaden uniform, about to vanish forever behind a thin oval door.

"What did you see in him?"

She was attractively uneasy at being asked to define herself. Then, in her tormenting way, she found an answer: "Men are much more alike than you realize."

It was time for a fragile signal of goodbye. Even before you left, her pretty features seemed to blur and become indistinct, her smile took on a monotonous character.

Your driver spun the jeep around, and you saw Private Hyannis move quickly next to Leilani and say something to her. She flushed, then moved on, laughing at him in her mocking way. Swearing and sullen, he rejoined his two friends.

The bandage she had put on your cheek smelled clean and fresh. At a turn in the road you peeled it off and flung it to the ground.

❖

When ComBatDiv, Fifth Fleet signaled: "Advise that Japanese navigation lights have been turned on in North Visaya Strait" — Admiral Hornbull proudly replied: "We have that information. Advise that we have set a Classical Japan battleship afire, she is down at the bow. A second Classical Japan battleship has been sunk. Another battleship is badly damaged, and two remaining battleships are heavily hit. We have destroyed the North Visaya Force. The South Visaya Force has sustained thirteen crippling hits and is out of the action."

Alas, even the most prejudiced nautical historical buff must admit that the weakest of all naval arts is the art of naval reconnaissance, and Admiral Hornbull was sadly in error.

❖

250000 No one wanted the wounded three-year-old Filipino girl. She was not the responsibility of the 23rd Corps doctor. You hitched a ride to your old transport and learned that she was not the responsibility of its doctors; the civilian aid station refused her and the Filipino doctor explained that she was Japanese or half Japanese.

It was too dark to walk farther; halfway between beach and Corps area you bedded down in an old, damp foxhole; you bandaged her from your kit and guessed — what was a stateless child's dose of morphine? When she woke again it was midnight, too dark to guess at morphine again, you wanted to calm her, for Japanese reinforcements for Sogod Hill came through here, all noise was dangerous at night, but she started to scream and kick. You put your hand over her mouth and desperate she called out in Japanese *okaasan* — Mom*my* Mom*my*; Japanese rifle fire stuttered through bushes, trees, tattered at shrubbery, working its ragged way toward the cry. Mom*my* — Mom*my* — called the child in a highpitched wailing voice, and more firing came from the beach, you were being encircled, they thought you were torturing the three-year-old girl and you began to sing the lullaby you had learned once from Lani:

> Nennen korori yo, okorori yo
> Boya wa yoi ko da nen neshi na
> Boya no omori wa doko e itta
> Ano yama koete sato e itta.

In the fields around you the firing stopped; the child fell suddenly asleep, mouth open, a tiny drool of saliva on her cheek, wet lashes.

In the silence, for the first time you heard the noises of Visaya at night: crickets, land crabs, a falling leaf. And you yourself, not meaning to, fell asleep.

❉

Admiral Island had never approved of Victory One operations. He fired eight torpedoes at the two Hibuson Islands but failed to sink them. When he saw a flaming Japanese battleship split into two pieces, he reversed course, and his only further part in the action was, briefly, to collide with the disabled cruiser Superlative.

At the southern entrance to Visaya Gulf, at 250424, the guns of the six old American battleships fell silent. For a while the battleships sailed back and forth, still crossing the T, as it were, over 5000 dead Japanese and their commander, Admiral Westvillage.

Since the sixteenth century, when modern naval warfare began, it has been given to only a handful of men to witness the classic maneuver called "crossing the T."

When your naval historian returned to his sea cabin to write up his notes on this momentous encounter, his eyes

still blinded and his ears still deafened by the guns, for
a moment his pen refused to move.

❀

250630   Grossman slept on a cot which he insisted on perching
on top of the rampart of earth that guarded the Translation Tent
from Japanese bombs. You sang in his ear:

> Get up; for when all things are merry and glad,
> Good children should never be lazy and sad,
> For God gives day light, dear brother, that we
> May rejoice like the lark and may work like the bee.

Grossman sat up. He had three days' worth of sideburns on his
cheeks. Whoever had stolen his seabag was now the proud possessor of three transformations and a gross of pistachio lollipops.

"Look at that," he said, unable to take his eyes away from the
spectacle, "he doesn't even wink his eyes."

"Muerte muerte," replied the green-robed madman, his masklike
face fixed in a benign stupor.

"If only I could do that, I'd have my section eight in an hour.
I'm the one who needs a section eight."

In six days ashore, half the evacuated American casualties had
come under this merciful Clause Eight in Army regulations, which
permitted you to quit the irrationalities of combat if you were
insane.

"Tell it to *Penetration*."

"I'm telling them, don't you worry about *that*." In the best
tradition of modern writing, Grossman had already written one
autobiography (rejected) and had started on his second.

He scraped his fingers across his sideburns. "Have you heard
about the nude Japanese girl, the fighter pilot?"

"You mean the one whose hair blows back in the wind as she
dives to her death?"

"You saw her?"

"She's been seen diving down in five places now. Once on Mac-
Dazzle's headquarters."

"Is it true the landings on Visaya were located so as to protect
MacDazzle's coconut plantations?"

"Just for putting that in the form of a question they ought to take away your charter subscription to *Penetration*. Haven't you heard that the Japanese are planning to capture MacDazzle and hold him for ransom?"

"What's the ransom?"

"The Philippines."

Grossman stood before the madman, as if trying to memorize his actions.

"Muerte muerte," the madman obligingly croaked.

✿

> At 250658 the American Escort Carrier Fighter Director heard Japanese spoken on his interfighter net; then lookouts saw, on the horizon, first the towering mast of the battleship Classical Japan, and then the pagoda masts of the other Japanese battleships and cruisers. For a long time the masts climbed higher up the horizon, without ship bodies beneath them.
>
> Then green, yellow, red and blue gun splashes appeared in the water around the 16 American escort carriers.
>
> So began the stirring Third Phase, the climacteric, of the battle for the Gulf.

✿

250700   With the nisei translators you sorted out identification tags, Hachiman Temple wooden charms, toothbrushes, comfort bags, photographs, thousand stitch belts, letters from schoolgirls, letters from sweethearts, letters from wives and children, diaries, paybooks, field orders, general orders, supply orders for airplane tail wheels.

Much of it could be quickly stamped SOUVENIR PASSED BY CINCPAC. But you stopped short at the sight of a cloth tag clipped from a uniform: "68th Independent Mixed Brigade, 26th Division." A field order of the same, incomplete, no date. A paybook, 26th division. A scrap of an order headed TA OPERATION.

Reinforcements.

You could almost wipe the hot, heavy air of the Translation Tent from your face. You were reflecting that there were now 100,000

309

troops unloaded and ashore, and another 100,000 still on the transports, all of you seven thousand miles from your home bases, and still lacking usable airfields.

The shot of an army .45 crackled in the clearing. Troops began to yell at someone further in the coconut trees. There was a $50 fine now, since the death of Chaplain Simon, for every unnecessary shot fired.

Colonel Mist exploded from his tent. In a khaki handkerchief he held the hot slug which he had just dug out of his field desk. His face took on its deepest and most hounddog expression, for an instant you expected him to bay.

From the grove sauntered Grossman, scratching his sideburns with the butt of the .45. Grotesquely, with a manic motion, he saluted Colonel Mist.

"You could have killed me," said Colonel Mist. Tears seemed to shape themselves in the corners of his eyes at the thought.

Grossman stared at him, eyes unwinking, face frozen in a benign grin.

"Section eight," suggested a nearby soldier. Colonel Mist gave a little nod, as if beginning to reflect favorably on this analysis.

You held out to Colonel Mist the translated and tagged items. He forgot Grossman and immediately called out General Ferox, who came up, blinking, from his underground command post. "Hit the iron while it's hot," said Colonel Mist.

Grossman shot you a glance of purest hate.

"Goddamn it," said Ferox, "where the goddamn hell is that photo reconnaissance we ordered?"

"According to Washington, the China airforce hasn't answered."

"Goddamn it, can't they do anything but sit on their ass and eat chop suey?"

Ferox's face began to color a deep and nervous red. "Get Mac-Dazzle on the line," he shouted. "Get my jeep."

But it was impossible to get General Ferox's jeep, at least immediately. It had just been stolen by the Filipinos.

*

At 250732 the rain squall lifted and Admiral Chestnutfield's mighty First Ambush Attack Force opened fire again on the helpless escort carriers.

*But three U.S. destroyers and four destroyer escorts,
in a desperate effort to save the sixteen U.S. escort carriers, together attacked the Japanese battleships and
cruisers. By 250800 three U.S. destroyers from this puny,
if glorious defending force had been sunk.*

*Where was Admiral Hornbull? Except for the loss of
the* Warrior's Wealth, *the First Ambush Attack Force
had not even been damaged by Hornbull's aviators, and
yet Hornbull was well out of range and steaming blithely
toward Admiral Smallswamp's Decoy Fleet.*

*The sensitive naval annalist could discern the stirring
of history's mighty pendulum, seemingly toward the
Japanese.*

❈

250800   At Abuyog General MacDazzle approved distribution
among the Filipino civilians of several crates of posters and matchboxes. The posters were three feet high pictures of himself, with
the legend beneath, in Tagalog, in English, and Visayan, "I have
returned." The matchboxes had pasted on their covers a reduced
version of the poster.

"How do you see postwar relations between the United States
and the Philippines?" asked Bulflash.

"We shall all be brothers, with the United States the guiding
brother," said General MacDazzle.

"Why 'I have returned' — General, why not 'we'?"

"Because of Filipino psychology."

Bulflash struck a match on one of the matchboxes. The match-
head exploded and shot high in the air.

❈

*Dramatic historic moments came almost too fast to
record. A telephone talker on one of the escort carriers
reported: "18-inch shell passing through starboard side,
18-inch shell passing out port side —" These shells, the
mightiest Armor Piercing shells in the world, did not
meet enough resistance in the thin walls of the escort
carrier to make them explode.*

It was a salutary lesson for Naval Ordinance.

❀

250805   The engineering officer of Dulag airfield had never heard of *any* suicide pilot prisoner, let alone one named Victory-view. The engineer kicked at the soggy field.

"Half a foot of water whenever it rains," he said. He stamped on the ground, and water filled his boot print.

"It will never be used," said the engineer. "It's too shallow for flying boats."

"But the only reason for taking Visaya was to get airfields."

"We told Hornbull and MacDazzle about the water table and the rainy season. We told them to take Mindoro, not Visaya."

"We can't pull out of Visaya now."

"MacDazzle can't. I could. You could."

"Have you been to Buri airfield? Six miles west of here?"

"Now there's a real swimming pool, man. Makes this one look sick."

The engineer walked across his airfield, away from you, stamping hard in the soggy ground, and watching his footprints fill up with great satisfaction.

❀

At 250815 Admiral Norcross learned that Hornbull had not left even a picket ship guarding the entrance to Visaya Gulf. He ordered three of his old battleships to sail to a point between the Japanese First Ambush Attack Force and the 511 transports in the Gulf.

Your historian watched anxiously as Admiral Norcross read reports of the Armor Piercing shells available in his battleships, cruisers, and his two ammunition ships. There were not enough for a second naval battle.

❀

250820   A mile northeast of the Dulag airfield the road was jammed. An Army truck heavily laden with mortar ammunition for the front and an airfield base truck with a load of refrigerators for the airbase personnel had stopped nose to nose on the one-way muddy track. Neither truck was willing to leave the road and run the risk of getting permanently stuck in the swampy fields.

The mortar ammunition driver and two Army privates got out of

312

the cab. They carried Thompson submachine guns with the safety catches off. Out of the airbase truck came Private Hyannis and a flyboy lieutenant. Both held carbines.

You went over to Private Hyannis. "Empty out your pockets," you ordered him, holding out your hand. Startled, surly, he did so. You flung the goldfilled Japanese teeth into the mud. Turning, you waved your jeep driver off the road.

"I thought only hospitals were supposed to have refrigerators."

The flyboy lieutenant turned brick-red. "These are our own refrigerators," he said.

You motioned to a space near your jeep. "It's as muddy there as anywhere."

The flyboy lieutenant began to protest. The Army driver and the privates with the submachine guns lounged closer.

The lieutenant and Hyannis climbed into the truck. When it was backed into the mud, it settled lower and lower on one side, until it finally toppled over. A white refrigerator slid loose, halfway into the black slimy mire.

With its wire cable, the mortar truck pulled your jeep free of the mud, then it rumbled down the road.

Your driver racked the jeep along at a good clip.

"We didn't wave goodbye to Hyannis."

"He'd like to kill you, that Hyannis." The driver began to laugh. "Damned moneylender. We call him Tenpercent Hyannis."

"Ten per cent isn't so bad."

"Ten per cent a week is murder. Sir." It was the first time your driver had ever called you sir. But after a while he remembered a story he had been telling you earlier, about how the infantry shot unsatisfactory lieutenants in the back. You told how ensigns pushed unsatisfactory enlisted men over the side of your battleship at night, and soon things were on the same old comfortable footing between you.

✿

By 250825 Admiral Norcross knew for the first time that Hornbull and his badly wanted new battleships were at least 300 nautical miles from the crucial area, and steaming still further away. In plain language — not

the required code — he signalled Hornbull: "Request air
and battleship support. Norcross."

After he had sent this extraordinary plain-language
signal, he went to his sea cabin, propped open the door
so that all his excited staff could see, and calmly began
reading a detective story.

It was a moment for history.

❊

290845   In the Japanese *kempeitai* reports you read how the
Flip guerrillas Dulag and Miranda had fought each other. Dulag
had finally crushed Miranda, and late in 1943 the Japanese had
made a conciliation offer to the winner. The Japanese estimated
their own casualties as 7 officers and 208 enlisted men. The guerrillas on Visaya lost 2000 killed and 2300 prisoners.

From the Japanese files dropped a copy of the Philippine loyalty
oath:

I shall never allow myself nor any arm or ammunition
to be caught by the enemy. I shall never turn traitor to
my country nor the United States of America. I make this
loyalty oath without reservation, so help me God.

Handsome, West Point trained Lieutenant José Maria Garcia
smiled his engaging, aristocratic smile. "We had to be traitors," he
said, "we had to live."

Together, at Colonel Mist's order, you and Lieutenant Garcia
questioned the refugees, even though Garcia's theory was that most
of the Filipinos, his own people, were either traitors or had cooper-
ated with the Japanese.

On and on went the questioning. Are the Japanese reinforcing
their troops? Yes. Have you seen destroyers landing reinforcements? Yes. Did you see five destroyers? Yes. Were these destroyers American or Japanese? Yes. Did you see the Japanese evacuating their troops? Yes. Agreeable smiles, the fugitive, delicate
grimace of the small country caught between two large ones. Gifts
of cigarettes. Next please. Did you see the Japanese landing reinforcements? Yes.

The young girls, in bright dresses, had just come out of hiding and you looked at them with admiration and longing. You listened again to Lieutenant Garcia. A madman, face covered with acne, insisted on being questioned. "Why did you poison my food?" he asked. "Why did you take my brain out? Why did you put a snake in my stomach?" With a hideously cunning smile the madman exposed himself and ran off among the girls.

"Is that what you have to do to get a section eight?" said Grossman.

"It wouldn't hurt any."

On and on came the smiling refugees, and always the girls, like heavy headed flowers. Why should this lighthearted lightfingered people be bothered with your war?

When you discovered that the *kempeitai* reports of the Philippine civil war on Visaya had disappeared, you did not bother to report their loss.

❋

   History's pendulum would soon fulfill its curve; meanwhile conversations of nonchalant bravery filled the air:
     First Pilot: "*Hello, there's a Jappo on your tail.*"
     Second Pilot: "*Thanks loads, friend.*"

❋

250900   "What's divine wind, kamikaze?"

"The typhoon that blew away Kublai Khan."

Colonel Mist could not find Lieutenant Garcia and he brought the Filipino farmer over to you. The farmer munched on pieces of bread taken from a paper bag. "Hola amigo," said the farmer, his coarse features breaking into a smile. "Komusta kayo." After that, the conversation did not go very well, since the farmer spoke a kind of Tagalog-Visayan not in favor with the purist who wrote your official phrase book.

Gradually, through a combination of Spanish, Japanese, English and Visayan, you learned that the farmer was mainly bothered about his cows.

"Are we shooting the cows?" The stumpy farmer munched on his bread and laughed. "Skivvy, skivvy," he said. We weren't hurting the cows, but we were making them die of starvation.

At last you understood. You explained to Colonel Mist: "He

doesn't mind what your soldiers do to his cows as long as they untie them when they're through. But the soldiers must untie them when they're through. If the cows are left tied up all night they'll starve to death."

Colonel Mist blushed.

The farmer munched his bread and smiled agreeably.

"He offers you his cows. His cows are your cows."

An air raid began and you never heard Colonel Mist's answer. When the air raid was over the farmer had gone.

"When was kamikaze?"

"Off Hakozaki, 1281."

✿

A stern exchange of signals crackled through the skies: "Request air and battleship support. Norcross." "Have sent Admiral Abel Hornbull."

✿

250910   Deep in the underground shelter, Lieutenant Garcia saluted General Ferox and informed him that the Filipinos in the 23rd Corps area did not want powdered milk, a year's supply of toilet paper, or four thousand rat traps.

General Ferox saluted Lieutenant Garcia and informed him that his jeep had been stolen for the second time that day, from the MP post where it had been parked, locked in chains.

✿

There was a rich historical irony in the first success of Admiral Hornbull's attack on the Japanese Decoy Fleet, for it was scored against the cruiser Thousand Genera-tions Land. *Her Captain Castle had first suggested sui-cide attack tactics in June 1944, and the cruiser had taken part in the Pearl Harbor attack. She was hit at 250940.*

✿

250915   The Marine patted the Long Tom's barrel and ground his metal heel on a cigarette butt so that the black volcanic sand hid it completely. "I dunno," he said. "They never tell us nuttin."

All the guns of the Marine heavy artillery battery now faced out to sea, toward Visaya Gulf.

✿

Nautical annals show few finer examples of humor under fire than the telephone talker, Zhutchka Bay, who chanted over and over while his escort carrier was riddled with 18-inch shells: "Come one, come all, see the tassel-tossing ship with a shell hole in her bum, see her laugh, see her shake those double tassels, come one, come all."

✿

250920   "Floating in the water while unconscious?"

"Yes," said the nisei interpreter.

The interpreter was surly because the Japanese had refused to talk except to an officer. You listened to the PA system. "Green Alert," said a booming voice. "Green Alert."

Reluctant, the nisei handed over the diary. It was hard for the nisei interpreters. Only rarely did they become officers, and often enough their white officers knew less Japanese, certainly less spoken Japanese, than they did. But the nisei, even on the propaganda station KGEI, sometimes used feminine words or archaic words for war, or translated freedom from want by the Japanese word meaning freedom from sexual passion. The nisei interpreter wanted to write up the report on Victoryview because he was the first suicide pilot to be captured alive.

You scanned the diary. There was nothing much in the diary. Except for a small penciled note on the inside cover. Victoryview had written a bitter Japanese joke, Tennō Heika Baka Yarō, much as though the Emperor were to be styled in English, Imperial Son of a Bitch.

"Red Alert," boomed the PA system. "Red Alert."

"All right, bring him over."

✿

At 250920 Admiral Chestnutfield's ships were widely dispersed because he had ignored his chief of staff's ad-

vice for a controlled attack, and instead had ordered General Attack, which allowed his ships to attack at will.

He reread the radio unit interceptions of the plain language despatches between Norcross and Hornbull. Were these messages part of a trapping, decoying maneuver, as Japanese Fleet Doctrine required?

Undecided, at 0925 he gave the order to retire and reform, and he signaled Tokyo that he had sunk four large carriers and a cruiser. Before him, the way lay clear into the heart of Visaya Gulf.

One might read whole libraries for years without finding a greater opportunity presented to a naval commander. Sluggishly, the pendulum of history picked up speed as it plunged along its massy swing.

&

250945 Petty Officer Victoryview's face cracked in a gold-toothed smile. "General Blackfield?" he said. "The General relieved by General Mountainbottom in the Philippines? He played golf, he read, he took care of his personal life."

"And the chief of staff of General Mountainbottom?"

"When he was told of the American landings he said 'Very good, but where is Visaya Island?'"

Petty Officer Victoryview had already told you how, on September 21st, over two hundred ships and hundreds of planes had been caught and bombed at Manila; on that day the Japanese forces there had been rubbed away by the magic lamp of sake and women.

What you wanted to know most about was still unmentioned — his last suicidal attack, from which he had escaped without even a scratch. Because he was unwounded, there was no bond of *giri*, of indebtedness between you. But, to ask directly about his last battle, was, with a Japanese prisoner, to hazard all, he might turn silent for days. Perhaps you should send Victoryview up north to BIJ Standish's Abuyog Interrogation Center.

Standish's stockade was probably the most efficient, but certainly the most extraordinary one of its kind, since for all practical purposes it was being administered by a captured artillery officer, Major Milkwell, acting commander of the Sogod Hill defense system. The Japanese command had not taken Major Milkwell's advice on hedgehog defense, and in his spiny indignation Major Milkwell had taken the vows of prisonerhood with a fanatic dedication.

From soy sauce to regimental records, Major Milkwell knew just where the body was buried; he told Standish's officers who to talk to and what questions to ask, and he told them what to translate and what to ship to Pearl and to Brisbane. As frank in captivity as in freedom, he had given Standish blistering inefficiency reports on those American officers whose Japanese was not equal to the tasks he assigned them.

Petty Officer Victoryview was explaining how lack of oil in the homeland made it necessary for the battleships to train at Lingga anchorage, where they could gulp direct their draughts of natural bunker oil. Unfortunately the carriers had to train in Japan proper, where alone the Japanese could make aviation gas.

"Once," said Victoryview, "the naval officers made a plan for accepting American oil in return for joining in a war against Russia. But the plan was never presented to Imperial General Headquarters."

"Why did you use your old Pearl Harbor tactics at Saipan?"

"We had captured and copied your radar in the Philippines, but we could not keep up with your improvements, and our radar is still your old Philippines radar. When we were thirty or forty miles from your fleet, we found your fighters had been vectored toward us by your fighter director radar, and then came what you call 'the turkey shoot.'"

When Victoryview returned from that disaster to the carrier *Phoenix*, he found that the Japanese First Air Flotilla planes had forgotten their recognition signals and were being conscientiously shot down by the Combat Air Patrol of the *Phoenix*.

Always the Japanese deluded themselves, always their publicity tried to present a retreat such as Guadalcanal, a defeat such as Saipan, as a sublime and clever operation.

Victoryview smiled his chryselephantine smile, and struggled over the unfamiliar foreign word. "Autoreinji," he said.

The Japanese planes, so outstanding at the time of Pearl Harbor, had remained much the same, while the American planes improved even from week to week, and now the Japanese planes lacked the range of the American. And then there was the daring *tobi ishi*

sakusen — the American skipstone strategy, of bypassing the forti-
fied Japanese islands.

Slowly had come a change from *shukuhai,* the time of toasts, to
gyokusai, the time of honorable death for the Emperor. Japan was
a country of *sabi,* mellowed by age, not new and assertive, like
America. She was a country of *wabi,* of loneliness and isolation,
the antique bronze in a remote wing of history's museum.

"All clear," said the PA system, "All clear."

*

*One more scrap of historical dialogue has been pre-
served from the battered* Zhutchka Bay; *while the Japanese ships were reforming, her telephone talker shouted:
"Hell, they got away."*

*

251000   Always there was too much talk of duty, of spiritual
force, of flags. At Pearl the Japanese had flown the Tsushima flag,
the Z flag of Admiral Togo, and they had set the flagship *Mikasa*
in concrete, but the Japanese had not really won the Russo-Japanese
war, they had only told their people so, and in just one more
month of war with Russia, Japan would have collapsed. And the
Japanese had flown the Z flag again at Saipan and it had not
worked, and he had heard it was being flown aboard the carrier
Lucky Crane in this battle.

Now the Japanese spirit, like the divine wind, the *kamikaze,* that
had driven off the Mongol hordes of Kublai Khan, was supposed
to blow away the mechanized hordes of America.

After Saipan the word "special attack" took on its new meaning.
First in the submarines, in the Heaventurn unit, with its flag an "8"
in a circle, "what you call eightball." And on the 15th of September
Admiral Horseholder had made a suicide attack, stabbing his
plane, like the point of a sword, into an American carrier. Admiral
Horseholder had received, in honor, a two-grade promotion after
his death.

"Admiral Horseholder crashed in the water, only the wing of
his plane landed on the carrier."

These are turbulent operations, said Victoryview.

On the throne, bent forward, his face florid with anger, Ferox received his worried staff like the French Sun King. He was signing complicated orders for the renewed attack on Sogod Hill. "Red Alert," bellowed a confident voice through the PA system. Ferox insisted on taking the night's patrol reports from Colonel Mist, and studying them.

Victoryview had got on the subject of the so-called Japanese seaplane tenders. These kept in their secret holds not seaplanes, but dozens of Thundering Ocean Special Attack boats, ready to leap out from the mother pouch, and ambush a decoyed enemy America. Victoryview was talking more and more freely. His Japanese bubbled like quicksilver, a year ago you could hardly have followed such rapid talk, in the accent of the Edokko, the Child of Edo, the wise city boy.

Now you could easily listen to him, and at the same time watch the five whistling dots tumbling in the sky overhead. The dots enlarged themselves and straightened on course. You scrambled with a guard and Victoryview into a trench. After the thundering blasts you started to get out of the trench. As confidently as before the PA system boomed, "Red Alert, Red Alert."

❂

At last from Honolulu came the Admiral's thundering signal, as if from a nautical Zeus: "To Hornbull. All the world wants to know where your battleships and carriers are. The Admiral. Pearl."

❂

Plodding, at random, you asked, "What about Milky Way?"
"A new medium bomber. Some are at Manila. But not many."
"What bombs does it carry?"
"Cherry."
"Why 'Cherry'? Do you give your bombs names?"
But you got no clear answer to this apparently simple question, and with what seemed idiot persistence he went back to lamenting Japanese use of the outmoded Type 97 Carrier Attack and the Type 99 Carrier Bomber; neither maintenance men or pilots knew how to fly or repair the most recent planes; there were too many "muddy rope" pilots —

It was hopeless. You asked a nisei interpreter to get a jeep to take him to BIJ's stockade. But often enough a prisoner hated to have his interrogation end, he developed an irrational desire to please his interrogator, to provide him information, and Victoryview could not stop.

"The *Mercury* divebomber," he went on, "it's no good. It cannot be flown off a carrier when there are no winds."

There were fine new planes at Clark Field, Manila, in crates, and there were spare parts for disabled planes, but the maintenance men were unable to put the new planes together, let alone repair the older ones. At Saipan in June, and now at Manila, only 20 per cent of the Japanese planes were usable. The pilots were often sick, there were poor medical facilities. Training was at a low level; some maintenance men could not even read the plane manuals.

The driver told you he was ready.

In September Victoryview had gone to Davao. "We practiced skipbombing at Davao."

"That was the 201st Airgroup?"

"Yes."

"And its losses in September?"

"About half our planes."

"How good was your skipbombing?"

Victoryview's face took on a knowing, cityboy look. "It was close to being a suicide attack." More than anything else, Victoryview hated to be fooled.

But he was off again on the familiar story. Training had to be done in southern waters because of lack of oil, but aviation gas could be made only in Japan. Badly trained pilots were always getting lost, or cracking up their planes, around Saipan and Tinian and Halmahera and Palau and Biak.

"All right," you said to the driver.

But it was not all right. The jeep had been stolen.

*

By 251108 Admiral Hornbull's planes had partly crip-pled the Japanese Decoy Fleet, and his battleships were only forty miles away.

Admiral Hornbull had disregarded the plain-language

322

calls of Norcross. But he did not dare disregard the inquiry of the Admiral. At 251115 he ordered his fast battleships to reverse course. The historian notes suspiciously that he might perfectly well have let them steam ahead without their escort destroyers, but first he ordered them to top off their destroyers, and the new pursuit was suspended for a number of hours.

Unfortunately for the Japanese, who had succeeded beyond their hopes in luring Admiral Hornbull away from helpless Visaya Gulf, Admiral Smallswamp forgot to radio Admiral Chestnutfield of the bitter success of the Decoy Fleet.

Historywise, error was about to cancel error.

❀

"One thing we Japanese did well was wireless intercept." There was the engaging smile of the city boy who has pulled a fast one. "We knew when your two main bodies left Hollandia and Manus. But you are always careless with your radio."

You thought of the morning the armada had left Manus, and you thought of Japanese thousands of miles away knowing at once that you had left, and even guessing in a general way where you were going.

You sighed, this could go on forever. You told the nisei to find another driver and jeep.

In your pocket you still kept the diary of Highspirits. You turned it to the page containing the poem of Norinaga Motoori — Shikshima no yamato gokoro wo hito towaba asahi ni niori yamazakura bama — The Japanese of the farflung islands, in spirit were like mountain cherry blossoms radiant in the morning sun. Again you noticed the line drawn beside the phrase "farflung islands."

You showed the poem to Victoryview. The Japanese lacked stick-to-itiveness, he persisted mechanically. England had the John Bull spirit, but Japan was only capable now of "compromise peace."

His face seemed as if it were about to crumple and tear like a bit of soft Japanese paper. Then his countenance smoothed itself into the Japanese smile — all the difference between your two

countries was summoned into brief existence by that smile. His lips
hovered over a phrase, then he said with difficulty:
"My unit was called 'the Japanese heart.'"

＊

*In the waters near the re-forming Japanese floated about
1100 American survivors of the sunken destroyers.*

*Admiral Chestnutfield's navigator informed him at
1140 that he was within an hour and a half of the transports in Visaya Gulf. The Japanese Admiral still had intact four battleships, including the Classical Japan with
her 18-inch guns, and two heavy cruisers, two light
cruisers and ten destroyers. But weakly he talked to his
staff of going north and helping Admiral Smallswamp.*

*While waiting for his decision, the nonchalant Nips
took movies of the Americans struggling in the water,
but they offered no aid.*

*History's pendulum quickly gained speed, accelerat-
ing along its curve.*

＊

251215   You had now been over and over the same ground a
dozen times. You knew that he was one of a five-man suicide attack unit, with four or five additional planes assigned as escort —
and to report results. You knew that there had been five such five-
plane units, each named for a separate phrase in Motoori's poem
on the farflung islands. You knew that he had flown from Mabalacat and that Admirals Greatwestern and Luckystrike were in command of suicide attack, of the Divine Wind operations.

But you had found out very little about his methods of attack.
Perhaps there were no special tactics. But you had to be sure.

You remembered the chapter you had long ago translated on
decoy and ambush attack doctrine. All navies wrote volumes on
attack and defense doctrine — surely a program that must have
begun so far back as August would have something official, some
pamphlet on doctrine, by now.

"What did you do before takeoff?"

"Volunteers had to be reported to the Emperor, by radio, so they would feel calm and strong. The Emperor was to know the name of each of us while we were in flight. We wore a special brow-band with a red rising sun printed on it."

"Did you yourself volunteer?"

A smile wandered across his face and vanished. "On the 18th, a lieutenant commander flew to Mabalacat from Manila. He said he wanted to congratulate us on volunteering for suicide missions. From Motoori's poem, we were given the phrase 'Japanese heart' as the name of our unit. Then we were assigned old model Zeros with 250-kilogram bombs wired to them."

"Did anyone refuse?"

"Refuse?" His face was the allwise face of the Tokyo city boy.

"There was no provision for releasing the bombs?"

"None."

"Was there any other ceremony before you left?"

"The commander had brought white boxes containing the ashes — fingernails and hair — of the previous unit, the 'rising sun' unit. We wore these on our chests at the farewell dinner. The unit that came after us would wear our ashes at its farewell dinner."

"There was nothing else? No briefing session? No instructions?"

"There was some instruction." He was honestly, so far as you could tell, trying to remember.

"Did the commander give you your orders from memory?"

"I think he lectured us from a pamphlet."

"Did it have a title? Did he give his lecture a title?"

"Doctrine." After a painful silence he added, "Divine Wind Attack Doctrine." He corrected himself. "No, I don't really remember —"

"Did the Mabalacat airfield commander have written instructions?"

"Perhaps."

"Did you know the airfields on Visaya? Did you know Buri?"

"You could not land at Buri. It was never finished. But it was planned to complete it."

In a sudden burst of resentment, he added, "Opportunity in war comes and goes, like flashes of lightning. But this is ordering you to make an unreasonable advance with your eyes shut."

"What did you think of Divine Wind forces?"

"The night before I was to fly, I read a magazine article on increasing sword production in Japan. How could people at home write about increasing sword production when we Japanese were not even able to pay back one arrow against carriers and battleships — except by this terrible means? This special attack method —" he stopped, then went on again, "it was an attack beyond all military logic."

"What happened on your own suicide attack?"

His face lost animation, it seemed bloodless and he looked about restlessly.

"I started to dive down when I saw my target." He stopped again, and held his breath. "Then I heard machine gun bullets going *ba ri ba ri,* and the sound *ga-an* — the plane trembled — there was a great noise — *pa-TSU* — an explosion."

He was silent again. He began talking more rapidly: "Smoke puffed out — I was saying to myself, 'I'm done for' — I swung the plane over and down, all around me were flames, like red lotus."

He yawned, and said in a neutral voice, "Somehow I was saved."

There was nothing more to find out from Victoryview. You felt drained, you did not want to talk to him any more.

In your pocket was a detailed report of the capture of Victoryview. He had never made any suicide run at all; instead, he had landed his plane in the water, and he had swum eagerly to his rescuers.

You stood up, and he stood with you and saluted. You saluted back, as was required. "Life and death," he said, "are just the thinness of a sheet of paper apart."

Like a man who has once in his life opened the door to hell, every time he told the story he would tell it a little differently. You wished helplessly that you could have found a way to assure him that you believed all his versions.

*

Admiral Abel had launched, at extreme range, 46 fighters, 33 bombers, and 19 torpedo planes from the carriers Hancock, Hornet, *and* Wasp. *Their expected time of arrival over the threatened escort carriers was not till 1310, and they would not have enough range to protect the transport shipping at all.*

At 1236 Admiral Chestnutfield ordered the First Am-

*bush Attack Force to reverse course and sail north, away
from the helpless American shipping in the gulf. Slowly
the Classical Japan, mightiest fighting ship in the world,
heeled round.*

The pendulum of history at last had reached its prime.

❀

251300   A cold heavy rain fell to the ground and sent up a faintly
putrid smell. In the tightly shut staff tent you did not see at first
what the red-eyed staff officers were chewing on, but the fresh
smell soon informed you that they were wolfing down mouthfuls of
new bread, just obtained from an LST. A stray dog poked his
head under the tent flap and barked noisily. With a start, you
threw earth at him.

After you had eaten your piece of white bread you went outside.
The dark mud pulled at your shoe and sucked it half off, where
the laces had rotted.

❀

The Red Castle *and the* Green Dragon *had been lost at
Midway, the* Soaring Crane, *the* Increased Joy, *and the*
Flying Dragon *had been lost in the Philippines Sea. At
251440, still flying Admiral Togo's Z flag, the* Lucky
Crane, *last of the Pearl Harbor attack carriers, sank in the
center of the crippled Decoy Fleet.*

*It was an event to make the most experienced historian
pause and wonder.*

❀

251500   Perfection Rapidslope, with a graceful, birdlike bow
of her head, came to thank you. Yes, she was very comfortably
located in a nearby coastal town, under the protection of the
Marines.

You turned to see a Japanese enlisted man staggering through
the scattered men of the Corps headquarters, a dazed expression
on his face. On his back he carried a 50-kilo airplane bomb. He
was a one-man suicide charge, but he seemed to send through the
area a paralyzing aura of unbelievability. No one moved, and

Perfection Rapidslope went on pecking at her conversational tidbits, the weather, the clients, the chance of new dresses.

There was a sharp crack, a bullet went through his right buttock and out his bladder, he dropped on his knees screaming, the aircraft bomb rang out on a stone, but the fuse did not go off. The Japanese slumped over on his knees, closed his eyes as though a shadow had fallen across them, and pitched forward.

"There was just one thing." Miss Perfection Rapidslope fluttered her elbows in what, for her, was embarrassment.

"What was that?" Your voice was thick and dazed.

"The American radish."

"What about the American radish?"

"The American radish is too big for the Japanese girls."

"Is this serious?"

"Oh no, it is not serious. Day by day the Japanese container is getting bigger and bigger." Delicately she scratched herself. You noticed that under the thick layer of rice powder she suffered from scabies.

❋

On the afternoon of the 25th Admiral Norcross ordered a topspeed search for the survivors, but the rescue ships had been directed to the wrong position, and late in the afternoon the search was called off.

But that afternoon sharks began darting among the thousands or so American crewmen still floating in the water. Allowances must be made for the sluggishness of rescue operations; even so, here was a blemish on a magnificent battle of the sea.

❋

251600   In the ironcolor room Napoleon's face had lean and wolflike shadows. He was unable to sit still and moved restlessly about. An enlisted man came up with a samurai sword. Napoleon paid two cartons of cigarettes and added it to a box at his feet. In it were a dozen swords and half a hundred samurai flags. With a clucking voice he admired his collection and screwed it shut again.

You picked up a news magazine on Napoleon's desk. Around you stencils whirred. You could hear distant radio signals that seemed to come up the deck into your feet. You flipped open the magazine to a picture of a farm agency spokesman. He was looking at a pigpen and saying, "If we're a war industry, by God we've got to get our price."

On Napoleon's desk, ready for instant reference, was a copy of *Knifework* by Fairbairn and Sykes. A .22 pistol with silencer did duty as a page marker. And the usual copy of *Scientifiction Monthly* with a nude red creature, half gorgeously breasted female, half giraffe, about to kick to death a scientist in a brown jungle hat.

"For patrols," said Napoleon, twirling the pistol and snapfiring it.

"We run patrols all the time, if it's patrols you want. I'm thinking of taking a patrol to Buri, west of Dulag. Want to come?"

"Some day, Handsome Classen."

"Why not now?"

Another enlisted man came in and received half a carton of cigarettes for a samurai flag.

The loudspeaker of the *Nasatch* ordered you to lay up to the flag wardroom.

Napoleon, face averted, began singing:

> Nose nose nose nose,
> Who gave you your jolly red nose?
> Wine and whiskey, ginger and cloves,
> They gave me my jolly red nose.

He let the samurai flag sift through his fingers before he placed it neatly in the box.

✻

In the final assault up Sogod Hill, instead of seven pillboxes reported on the G 2 maps, the attacking troops found over 53 pillboxes, plus 17 caves, and hundreds of smaller holes.

But to the properly trained Naval and Marine historian, the items of greatest significance were a dozen coastal guns, still in crates, unassembled. Our assault on Visaya Gulf had come just in time.

251630 You always knew when you were in one of the rooms — tent, caravan, or flag plot, where high command was exercised. There were twenty or thirty of these in the world. Stalin had one. MacDazzle had one. Montgomery had one. Churchill had one. The Admiral had one at Pearl. And Norcross had one.

The power in these rooms had the crackling tang of ozone. Now, in The Admiral's country, aboard the command ship *Nasatch*, you were in such a room.

Admiral Norcross rubbed his inflamed eyes. He scanned your report of your interview with Japanese prisoner Victoryview. On the long green baize table, next to JOCPOA's translation of Japanese *Combined Fleet Doctrine* — open to your favorite chapter on "Decoy Fleets and Ambush Attacks" — were charts of South Strait, North Strait, and Cape Deception off Luzon.

A special list was now being kept on a chalkboard. Suicide attacks. One escort carrier sunk, this afternoon, by two suicide planes. Three more escort carriers badly damaged by three more planes in the same attack — a total of five Japanese planes had put four escort carriers out of action. And all the escort carriers would shortly have to be pulled out of action for repair and refit. When these were gone, the ground troops would have no air cover.

As if thinking out loud, not talking directly to you, Norcross said, "Approach run? Angle of attack? Diving angle? Favorite aiming points?"

He stared at your report, as if unable to believe it did not contain these vital bits of information.

Through an open port at your back you heard a sudden furious burst of typing, like a burst of machine gun fire.

"You hear that?" said a steward outside the port.

"You think I'm deaf?" said a second steward. "You go in there while he's writing his *story*, that Begel take your head off."

The typing showered on, rich, musical, copious.

"I read a little bit," said the first steward. "All about crossing some ole x or t or some such thing, like." He laughed. "Man, was he cross when I didn wake him up. Said I made him miss the greatest naval battle in his *story*." He laughed again. "Some crap, like."

"Why didn you call him?"

"I was busy man, real busy."

"Busy hiding in the head, I bet. But how come he slep through all that firing?"

"He's a powerful sleeper, that Begel. We crossed a dozen t's before he ever woke up."

"Carbon," shouted the voice of Begel. "Get me some more carbons."

The two stewards did not move. The second steward said softly, "Now there's this club, and she wears nothing but three bells, one on each tit and the third . . ."

A door clanged. "Carbon," shouted Begel. Effortlessly the two stewards disappeared.

The flag secretary said in a low voice to the navigator, "Hornbull will never admit he went north after a Decoy Fleet."

You could see from the tracks that Hornbull had sent ninety American warships after a decoy fleet of nineteen Japanese ships, and had left not even a picket ship behind. You could see that his battleships had steamed uselessly up the coast of Luzon after the Decoy Fleet. Now they were steaming uselessly back down, in pursuit of the First Ambush Attack Force.

And you could see that the Japanese Admiral had withdrawn from Visaya Gulf at the very moment when the wreath of victory needed only a slightly firmer grasp.

"Bigger than Jutland," said the flag secretary quietly. He tried to keep his voice neutral, but he was very pleased to have taken part in the battle. Already he spoke of it as though it were an event in a remote historic time.

"We'll send instructions to all commands to search suicide wreckage for a manual on doctrine," said Norcross. Carefully he initialed your interview with Victoryview. "Anything else?"

"I'll try Buri airfield. This afternoon if possible."

Norcross shook hands and turned immediately to the waiting clipboard of dispatches.

"The last big naval battle of the war," said the navigator softly.

"Of any war," said the flag secretary proudly. The navigator's hand unconsciously made the sign of the crossed T over South Strait.

On the main deck of the *Nasatch* you searched for Grossman.

He had come with you on the *Nasatch*, partly to see the latest copy of *Penetration*, and of *Downbeat*, and partly to try his arts on a Navy doctor. The Army doctor of the 23rd Corps had refused to take him seriously when he had tried interrogating the nisei translators as though they were Japanese prisoners. "A temperature of 105° or frothing at the mouth," the Army doctor had said. And Grossman had been unable to froth.

You watched a destroyer, a quarter of a mile from shore, hoisting the signal Blue Peter. Ashore, LST's had spread out their lips of swollen black sand, to disgorge generators, folding cots, boxes of ammo, plasma, alligators, amphtracs, cartons of K rations.

Enlisted men ran past you, and you heard leather scuffling across iron decks. Grossman was locked in the arms of the ship's chaplain. At first you had the unbelievable impression that they were dancing the Bunny Hug together. On an unusually brisk twirl, the two partners staggered to the rail and into the water. The Chaplain rescued himself, but Grossman got tangled in the rescue rope, and was hauled up, suspended by his heel. As he swung past you he rolled his eyeballs so the whites showed.

"Muerte, muerte," he croaked cheerfully.

❋

At 251630 Admiral Hornbull and his fast battleships and heavy cruisers steamed back toward the entrance to North Visaya Strait. En route, Admiral Hornbull began to write a special report on Admiral Norcross's cowardice in requesting aid.

A necessary, if at times acrimonious part of every sea battle is the post-combat argument of the Admirals and their historians. In this debate my own position is, quite simply . . .

❋

251645   The doctor clipped his words as precisely as though they had so many surgical bandages. "What did you think you were doing?"

"I always do what my eightball tells me," said Grossman, wriggling in his strait-jacket.

In a corner of the ship's sick bay, Napoleon was explaining to the corpsman how a movie actress had summoned him to her stateroom on the SuperChief train. "Bring that handsome man to my room," the movie actress had said to the porter.

With a patient and the corpsman, Napoleon began to sing a trio:

> Oh we are three jolly consumptives,
> Cough cough cough.
> We get a free ticket to Tokyo,
> Cough cough cough.

"All right," said Grossman, "the all clear has sounded. Take me out of this strait-jacket and we'll all have a rousing game of snap."

"You wrote this article?" said the doctor, holding a copy of *Penetration.*

"Yes, I wrote it," said Grossman, "but let's have the literary criticism after a costume change."

"I don't think you understand," said the doctor, gently enough. "You're sick." He tapped his head.

"Of course I'm sick. I've got to be sent back to the States and made well again."

"No," said the doctor. "You're *really* sick. We're collecting people like you for a special study project. On Saipan."

Grossman turned a horrified face toward you. "Why complain? You've got what you wanted." You patted him on the shoulder.

> We get a free ticket to Timbuktu,
> Cough cough cough —

sang the corpsman and the other patient. Weakly, then more strongly, Grossman joined them.

When you left the *Nasatch* in your amphtrac you could hear above the churning of its sluggish tracks that the trio was now singing lustily, "Oh violate me in violet time, in the vilest way that you know."

The Amphtrac left you off near the Marine Artillery. You noticed that its guns faced inland again. You patted the nearest gun barrel. Still hot, it stung your hand and left a tiny blister.

*

Fifty-one Japanese air transports carried elements of the 187th Glider Infantry, and of the 34th and 4th Airborne Raiding regiments. As they headed for Visaya Gulf each trooper was given a sip of Ruby Port. Twenty planes were assigned the Dulag airfield; of these, one third were shot down in the air. But history records that the rate of attrition in such attacks is always high.

*

252000   You felt in your pocket for some matches, and your fingers encountered the diary of Petty Officer Highspirits. You opened the diary and wrote (under your first entry, "C. Deception") "Lost, Oct. 25." You could keep a diary as well as any Japanese.

Wherever Buri airfield was, it was not where your map had said.

When you saw an abandoned Flip hut, standing drunkenly on its stilts, you decided to spend the night there, prepared to give its fleas a treat.

You heard sobbing, a woman crying helplessly. And, also from the hut, a voice like the voice of Hyannis, fuzzy and wrathful, somewhat thick with drink.

"First we're going to give you a swallow," said Hyannis's voice, "then we're going to touch you. And then we're going to give you another swallow. And then we're going to touch you.

"All right, who pays to go first?"

The woman screamed, highpitched, steady screaming like the ripping of silk. You had never heard Leilani scream and yet you knew it was her voice.

"What am I bid for the first date?" asked Hyannis.

*

Determining the conclusion of the battle for Visaya Gulf is not easy for the conscientious historian.

For on the ground, supposedly coordinated with the naval battle, but a day late, came the above-mentioned 150 Japanese infantry of the 16th division, guided toward Dulag airfield by a Filipino (the enlisted men were weak

*from a diet of coconuts and bananas — their officers
kept all the rations during their four-day march from
central Visaya).*

*Should we call this and other minor actions the Fourth
Phase of the battle for Visaya Gulf? Or shall we class
them more properly as belonging with the First Phase of
the battle for Luzon?*

❖

252010   The back of the jeep was full of supplies, for sale to
the Filipinos no doubt. You intended at first to remove the distributor of the jeep. Then you remembered what the *Combat
Sutra* said. The *Combat Sutra* said always leave the enemy a
path of retreat. You put the distributor cover back on, and ran
to the rear of the stiltlegged house.

Lani was sobbing, her breath came in deep soft heaves. Two
shadows held her wild hands and feet, and a third shadow prepared
to lower himself on her.

You swung your carbine to your shoulder. You and its barrel
flowed together into one living aiming creature.

❖

*For once, Tokyo Imperial General Headquarters under-
estimated its victory when it announced that the second
unit of the Divine Wind Special Attack Corps had sunk
one carrier, damaged one carrier, and sunk one heavy
cruiser.*

*But a few histories of this great battle — launched
perhaps a little too hastily after the conclusion of the
event — are surely wrong in terming these relatively
ineffectual suicide attacks the beginning of a new kind of
warfare.*

❖

252015   Rain fell on the roof of the hut, it poured through the
holes you had shot in the roof to frighten them off. In the darkness
of the squall you could hardly see Lani's face. "They'll be back
when they stop to think." You tried to hurry her.

From time to time she moved her head as though caught in air that stifled her. She began crying incoherently that they had told her you were hurt, not far from the Station Hospital, that she had fought them. You tried to help her with her torn neat uniform. She flung her arms once, wildly, as you forced her with you a little way into the iron tangles of the nipa palms, paralleling a thin track that led from the back of the hut, and you tried spreading your poncho as a shelter for her. She shivered at the sound of the jeep returning, and you heard them casting back and forth round the hut and then spanning in a wider circle. "I'm glad you did not kill them," she said, and you thought she was recovering, but when you touched her bruised forehead, she put out her hand to avert a blow, she flinched from you, did she even know who you were? and she plunged away from you along the nipa palms toward the west, you ran after her and behind you they heard and voices threatened, but it was dark now, the rain fell and drowned all sounds all tracks.

She eluded your touch, she could not stand touch, a bright red glow lit the horizon and faded into rumbling sounds, she scratched your hand and broke free, you had lost her in the irontangled palms.

❋

. . . the majority of American airfield service personnel around the field promptly deserted, leaving behind car-bines, rifles, grenades and even machine guns to be cap-tured by the Japanese. But the wise historian will sternly repress all speculations as to how these American troops would have fought, could they have benefited by Marine boot camp training.

❋

252200   Heavy thunder rolled and broke in your skull and forced you awake. Overhead a white green star shell floated in the cloudy sky. You stood on a hillside, on a sloping track.

Beside you stood a girl who pressed her cold hand in yours, and after a moment you remembered her name. Leilani.

Just in time you heard noises — teki da? mikata — sounds of a slap, Zuzu ben, Tokyo, Kyoto, Tagalog, and you saw the marching shadows, at their head a shadow carrying a bedraggled white flag, redballed in the center, a Filipino guide. They stumbled toward the dark plain, they fell out to pick at leeches on their legs, the ground trembled to their step, you caught Lani and forced her to the ground beside you, she caught her breath, not meaning to scream, but about to, and you pressed quickly expertly at the sides of her neck, she went limp, a Japanese straggler stepped off the path for a moment and the warm stream fell over your neck, orange lights glowed on the horizon and flickered down to dullish red, the lights vanished in a warm flooding rain.

Last of all followed the staring, grimacing madrunning man, washing his hands and his masklike face in the rain, he slowed to a stiff-legged walk, there were scars at his throat and, cavorting after the Japanese patrol, he twirled his Rising Sun banner.

*

Since the Japanese were using captured American weapons, General Terow thought his own American troops were firing at both sides of his large plywood house and puncturing his refrigerator, and he yelled out of the windows to the Japanese to stop firing or think of a reason why.

Your historian feels compelled to note that a Marine general does not usually take with him into combat a plywood house or a refrigerator.

*

260600   First you had stopped to pick up a bit of paper, dark in coloring, its Japanese words hard to understand. But it was the smell that saved you from walking, unannounced, into the very middle of the Japanese patrol's encampment.

You both blackened your faces with swamp mud and waited for the patrol to move from your path. Stubby Japanese soldiers ate cold rice balls, made tea, used the very center of the camp as their sewer.

The paper you had found ordered its holder (1) to destroy aircraft after jump-off — this phase to end when the moon rose, (2) at 2230 the bearer was to destroy materiel, ammunition and bridges,

(3) at 2330 to 0300 bearer was to destroy aircraft again, (4) from 0300 to 0600 bearer was to build defensive positions, (5) at 0600 bearer was to prepare for the future.

Machine gun bullets pattered softly from the sky, but you could see nothing there. About two miles behind you lay the airfield of Dulag, dotted with red, yellow and green parachutes. Rifle and mortar fire sparkled along the edges of the far away field.

Like a gigantic handclap, directly overhead, you heard the parachute open. The American pilot pulled at the end of his pendulum, a gust of wind scudded him before your position and he looked down at you and Lani before disappearing into a slight rise of the land.

"He's got away."

But you had spoken too soon. Men rushed about in the Japanese camp. Then you saw a Japanese corporal methodically hacking a log to the right length. A favorite Japanese sport was to put the log on top of the calf and under your thighs, then violently force you to kneel.

✿

The Colonel of the 3rd Airborne Raiding Regiment radioed the Emperor, via Manila Army headquarters, "For an exceedingly long time I have been in your debt. Now whatever I have learned will be carried out in my attack. Deign to be at ease — farewell." The Japanese colonel issued orders for the last attack, but he and his staff committed suicide by grenade.

From an American historian's point of view, it is not easy to understand the merits of these suicides.

✿

260615 In your carbine sights you found the kneeling American aviator, the trench he had dug, and last, the Japanese officer holding on high his twohanded sword. As your finger had been taught, it began to squeeze against the carbine trigger. Your hand whitened.

"Don't watch."

But you watched it all through the carbine sights. Nothing human was strange to you, not the beheading, not your own still and paralyzed hand.

❀

General Terow ordered that all Japanese in the neigh-borhood of Dulag airfield were to be killed by 260900. But history advises us that an order and its execution are two rather different events.

❀

260630   In a cave within the iron-green palms her eyes dark-ened, then opened suddenly; you thought of flowers at daylight. Her compassionate eyes forgave the Japanese, forgave herself, and with a quick and gentle motion she stretched her bare arm and shoulder to you — she tried to check herself, but her nature seemed to expand and illuminate the green cave of palms, deep reflections rose to the surface of her pretty, excited eyes. Her glance turned from you, hesitantly you touched her bare shoulder — she moved instinctively from your hand and again straightened, not quite lean-ing toward you. A pleasure beyond words tingled and burned in your arms, and hands, her voice seemed to come echoing from great distances, on your tongue was the taste of honey, and at just this moment, as her lips compassionately found yours, as you sensed her hesitation between womanhood and innocence, you tumbled over, head pillowed on her lap, her fingers stroking your hair, and you fell fast asleep.

In your dreaming you remembered the blue diamond eyes of the hummingbird, iron leaves held on their pillars an enormous blue room — through it passed gray ghosts with yellow and whitened faces, you watched the ghosts rest and comfort each other you watched them stumble and fall never to rise again, with wings you protected the palm-blue building from thunder and fire, and always you tasted honey, with blue-jeweled eyes you watched dragon's teeth, growing to giants, who fired tubes of steel, you let the giants run happily or in anguish through your blueceilinged palms, you tasted flower after orange-petaled flower, delicious, thrusting deep in the flower, armed with the taste of honey you suddenly dove against the intruders, *depart!* you warned *go!* you warned . . .

Violently awake, you sat up.

With a languorous infantine gesture of trust she turned her head inside your arm — "We must go" —

But you bent back upon her, ignoring her simple and timid protest, too late you read in her submissive eyes a latent but stirring defiance of your will, you at once knew that to take her now, to take fullest advantage of her compassion was to beggar yourself — of her — perhaps forever, and so knowing, and knowing too that her excitement could grow to match yours, you pressed her lips — her voice faded in your ears, her complexion seemed to pale in your sight, your heart beat violently against hers, you were unable to speak, to call out, your flesh tingled and swelled with fire, your eyes tightened and at last closed, your ears sang, and sweat drenched your back, and in a last violent trembling you had the feeling of moving close, to just this side, of death —

on a calm and greening sea, an orange lotus flowered, petal by petal —

With tears, wanly smiling — "We must go" —but still she waited.

Was it a bird, or an exquisite movement of the darting passionate air — *go*, said the trembling, mocking air, *go* —

Still the taste of honey lingered.

"We must go," she pleaded.

But lost in wonder, you smoothed her dress with your hand.

✿

By afternoon it was clear that there would be no further naval engagements; history's pendulum had completed its swing, and the greatest naval battle in the world was ended.

Officers and men visibly relaxed; aboard the Nasatch *I was presented with a small mongrel bitch. After she had devoured at one sitting three chapters of my manuscript, I christened her Clio, for the Muse of History.*

✿

261500   There was contempt in every wellproportioned inch of Perfection Rapidslope.

"Marines," she said in polite contempt. "We can take twentyfour

of these Marines a night. Twelve Marines a night is not enough
for my girls."

Delighted, General Ferox at once got on the phone to the Marine
Artillery.

"Take out the patrol," he said to you.

✿

Appendix VIII. Search and Rescue Operations.

*The searching ships failed to find the southward-drift-
ing American sailors, now reduced to 900 in number by
fatigue, exposure, sharks and other causes. Perhaps future historians will be able to amend my analysis,
but . . .*

✿

261600   You sat at the edge of a clearing, listening to Sanky
during the ten-minute break. He was telling about Rajah Panbet,
for whom he had once worked.

Rajah(in some towns he styled himself Doctor) Panbet, a miracle healer, had a Sinublastotherm, a large box lined with blue paper
which cured arthritis — a disease from which the Rajah suffered
very badly himself, in spite of morning, noon and evening dosages
of phlegm cutter. For wealthy sufferers he rented a cowloft where
you could inhale the air breathed out by cows, and practice chewing like a cow, for nature, as the Rajah liked to say, "will castigate
if you don't masticate."

The Sinublastotherm was lined with blue because blue was the
color of sexually excited frogs, and because blue was the color of
bions, the life-giving particles which mainly determined man's "orgasmic personality." A small brass cylinder containing blue paper
was available for home use, for those patients who lacked time or
money enough to be able to sit in the blue-lined box developing
their orgasmic personalities.

Rajah Panbet was a practitioner of iridiagnosis. There were forty
zones in the iris clockwise, and forty more counterclockwise, and
spots in these zones were a clue to sixty different kinds of mal-
function.

When these medical treatments failed, the Rajah prescribed

walking barefoot and eating alfalfa, preferably simultaneously. In the Rajah's book, it was disease that produced bacteria and not the reverse. Among his more striking remedies were those made from spiderwebs and from minced human cancers.

"One day," said Sanky, "a burlesque dancer came in for an iridiagnosis. Dr. Panbet was in the middle of his favorite prescription for attractive females, namely relaxing, under his soothing ministrations, all — and I do mean all — the openings of the body, when the burlesque dancer suddenly recollected that he had iridiagnosed her condition not from her good eye, but from her glass one.

"She was not at all upset by the Rajah's trickery, however, for she had become an admirer of his skill in the gentle art of relaxation, in fact she hired him on the spot as her booking agent."

And that was how Sanky lost his job as the Rajah's Assistant Health Engineer.

It began to drizzle lightly. Sanky was humming:

> The infantry, the infantry,
> With dirt behind their ears,
> They can whip their weight in wildcats,
> And drink their weight in beers . . .

There were no American planes in the sky, only Japanese, cavorting and tumbling through black ack-ack bursts.

"Seems to be something wrong with our bloody ships today, eh Classen?" called Sanky cheerfully. "All right, on your feet, you want to be sent out on a patrol?"

❖

Appendix X. Military Aftereffects of the Naval Triumph.

General Luckyblessing needed only one look at the demoralized division of General Pasture. He at once decided to evacuate his own headquarters to the neighboring island of Cebu. General Perch advised General Luckyblessing that he was violating the military code, and ordered him to stay, but General Luckyblessing replied that he appreciated the efforts of the 35th Army but he still thought it wisest to retreat to Cebu. General Mountainbottom, when appealed to in Manila, ordered the 35th Army to be self-sustaining and self-supporting, but refused General Perch any detailed information on how this desirable goal was to be achieved. General Perch then asked Imperial General Headquarters in Tokyo to court-martial General Luckyblessing, but received no answer whatsoever to his dispatch.

❀

261700   "I'll go first and draw the enemy's fire," said Sanky, with the air of a connoisseur of fine vinegar. He consulted the map which showed the approximate distance to Buri and its deserted Japanese airfield.

You and Sanky had quarreled bitterly when you learned it was not his turn for patrol. Now he turned you and the six enlisted men first left along the track, then to the right.

From far off you heard the firing of heavy guns.

"There's your thunder, where's my nickel?"

"I've got my money's worth. You don't need to pump any more for a while."

❀

Appendix X. After-effects of the Naval Triumph on Luzon.

In a hundred Manila streets Filipinos slipped out at night and tacked up posters: "Kill a Japanese — 5000 pesos for an officer's cap — 10,000 pesos for a flyer's jacket."

❀

261730   It was raining steadily, and you thought of poppies in May, scarlet and heavy under the rain.

"Is it the right place?" Sanky wanted to know.

Gingerly you took the paybook from the dead and swollen Japanese: 54th Airfield Co. Cmdr. Bearriver. The dead man's .25 rifle with its orange stock was no bigger than your boyhood .22.

Sanky's face went bloodless. Before the entrance to the command dugout were yellow wires leading to demolition blocks. Scattered among the blocks were American K 1 ration wrappings, of brown waxed paper. Steps covered with split bamboo led underground. Through the shimmering rain you could see, a hundred yards away, the half-completed, watery airfield.

You saw in Sanky's face that you would go into the boobytrapped dugout alone.

"Engineers are supposed to do this," you griped, trying to relieve your feelings of fear.

"There's been a Japanese patrol through here today. Don't take too long." He checked the map again. "The map says six miles west of Dulag, but we're closer to fourteen miles west."

You forced back a sudden feeling of dislike for Sanky, for anyone who could stand safely to one side while you did what you must do. With tender solicitude you lifted up, one by one, each of the five or six split bamboo sticks that covered the first earthen step, and you threw these to one side.

It took half an hour to go down the short flight of stairs. The bamboo flooring was springy, you began lifting it as you had done the steps, first slowly, then more quickly and carelessly. In a far corner you could see a pile of documents as high as the chamber. You recognized files of personnel, airforce orders, supply orders.

You tugged at another piece of flooring. Held by a string, it snapped off. Helpless, your breath sobbing faster and faster, you listened to the hiss of the fuse. You came to, realizing that you had been shouting to the men at the mouth of the dugout to get away.

In the damp, the fuse had sputtered out. "Hurry," called Sanky down the stairs. You tore through the stack of documents. You wanted only one thing. It must have come near the end, and it was not far from the top. *Suicide Tactics Manual, Recommended Attack Doctrine, Divine Wind Decisive Forces* . . . soon there will be pilots with only 100 hours of training. In September, using old methods of attack, we lost 1000 planes . . . in the *Combat Sutra* it says tactics are like sandals; the strong should wear them, but not cripples . . . we must have a *miteki hissatsu* — see the enemy must kill spirit . . . special attack or banzai penetration attack is in its origins a submarine idea and goes back to the first special sub attack on Pearl Harbor, it is based on the idea that we found our lives on obedience to Emperor and country . . . it is believed that we can gain 100 per cent efficiency if pilots are not worried about coming back . . . the *kiun* — the spirit of the times, leads inevitably to sure hit sure death thinking . . . the first point is absolute lookout, and the second point is spiritual power strong enough to drink up the enemy . . . the third point is vision that does not let a fly escape . . . fly at either 3000 meters or 6000 meters, but if picked up, fly at 80 to 90 meters . . . just before attack descend to 500 meters, when beginning attack go into a 45-degree dive and aim at . . .

"Come on," yelled Sanky. "You bucking for Admiral down there?"

❋

Appendix XI. Theories advanced in Previously Published Histories of the Battle for Visaya Gulf.

Although American Navy planes succeeded in their attack against Ormoc (the Japanese reinforcement harbor on the west coast of Visaya), and although they sank a Japanese destroyer, a light cruiser, and two out of three naval transports, the Japanese still managed to land half of their reinforcements and send them forward to take part in TA operations.

But this Pyrrhic victory of the Japanese, if it may be termed a victory at all, should hardly justify an experienced historian in arguing that the Battle for Visaya Gulf merely confirmed a foregone conclusion. Was it as nothing that the American Navy had sunk three Japanese battleships, one heavy carrier, three light carriers, six heavy cruisers, four light cruisers, nine destroyers — over 300,000 tons, almost half the Japanese naval tonnage?

❋

261745   Sanky stumbled first into the clearing. He held his carbine slackly in his hands and his eyes blinked from the misty glare of the late afternoon sun. A small Filipino house teetered on stilts at the far side of the clearing. On the house was a poster of MacDazzle, but the legend "I have returned" was scratched out — over it was written "Kilroy was here," and over that, in Japanese, "banzai."

To one side of the house was a cart, upside down. Before the house a girl wearing a dress made of flour sacks was pounding rice in a squat wooden bowl. You listened as if hypnotized to the soft rhythmic thud of the rice pole and the swishing sound of the rice in the bowl.

The girl picked up the bowl and tossed the rice high in the air, giving it a circular motion. Each time she skillfully let a little of the polished rice fall into a mat on the ground, while the chaff floated free. Once she laughed as she caught the rice high in the air.

When Sanky heard her laughter, as though it had been some kind of signal to him, he said to the patrol, "All right." From the nipa palms the rest of the patrol struggled into the clearing. The girl saw you all, and with a melancholy wriggle of her hips, she ran into the woods.

Sanky took an oil rag and ran it carefully over the breech mechanism of his carbine. You began to enjoy a rising tide of exhilaration about the pamphlet on suicide doctrine, a sense of optimism rocked its tiny craft higher and higher.

"I earned my pay today."

"You ought to write a book," said Sanky. "On the art of the patrol. You go out until you're shot, then you come back and report you were shot at. If you think it's important, then you're officer material. You look like officer material to me, Classen. I think I'll recommend you for promotion to ensign."

One of the enlisted men spoke up. "If you're in the airforce, after thirty-five missions you get a medal and a rest. What do you get in the army after thirty-five patrols?"

This was a litany of complaint. Sanky made the expected response. "A thirty-sixth patrol."

Happily you tried to explain to Sanky about Decoy Fleets and Ambush Attacks, about trying to make the enemy conform to your movements. "You study his doctrine, you trick him into going where you want him to be, then you attack." You had predicted where the document was, and you had found it. In your crystalline moment, you knew what it was to Command in Modern Battle.

The girl who had been pounding rice came back, looked at you timidly, and started her work again. Sanky watched her alertly.

"I don't like that," he said. He snapped to the patrol, "All right, on your feet." The men only groaned.

You and Sanky stood side by side, waiting for the men to get up. "Leilani," he said softly. "I'd marry her." Against the clear noonday light of his glance you measured your own darker, more ambiguous regard, and your eyes fell.

"I thought you didn't believe in marriage."

He shook you by the shoulders, and the men watched you curiously. As if baffled by your obtuseness, he could only repeat your words: "Didn't believe?"

"Can't you understand?" you cried, "she's refused."

"That." His eyes narrowed in contempt. "When you play with cats you expect to get clawed a bit."

The noise of the girl pounding rice suddenly stopped and she disappeared. A wheel of the upside down cart spun slowly in the air. You saw a mattock leaning against the cart. Sanky stiffened. He was in his thirties but he seemed to you well over forty, and his face, before your eyes, slipped on a mask of fatigue.

The man who was taking the point beat back and forth along the edge of the palms. He located a trail through a patch of swamp, and beckoned.

"All right," said Sanky to the men. "Ante up. No checkee, no shirtee, as our little yellow cousins say." They correctly understood this to mean follow the point. Rain drizzled again, then fell more insistently from the now copiously clouded sky.

You wanted to take the rear, but Sanky waved you ahead. "My turn to shave the lion," he said.

From the patch of swamp Sanky glanced back at the clearing. The tiny crack of a Japanese .25 rifle split through the air, and you thought of hunting crows in Palisades. Sanky stumbled. Instinctively you pitched your grenade over and behind the house, forgetting to count off before you threw it. You pulled the pin, counted, and threw a second grenade.

The men along the trail began to run. "Come on, Lieutenant," they called.

"Hit me, you bastards," Sanky pleaded. He slumped to the ground. "I'm going, I'm fading. Hit me."

You cradled his head, watching the world blacken before his eyes. Your grenades went off, there were Japanese cries, blind firing into the nipa palm, shouts in Japanese — mikata da mikata da, a girl's scream. Rain fell in a savage white burst. Sanky's open mouth began to fill with water. You tried to close his mouth but it slacked open again. The patrol shouted to you but your carbine felt cool and wet along your cheek, you argued that it made good military sense to wait in ambush, you would let three Japanese come round the house before you fired.

The last noise you heard as you fled down the path was the bellowing of a caribao, like the voice of a land in agony.

✽

Appendix XIV. Japanese Intelligence Operations.

General Pasture's intelligence branch was slow and inaccurate, but he solved this problem by listening in on the San Francisco broadcasts of the Office of War Information. These radioed the names and numbers of all American units opposed to him; the broadcasts were faster, and far more accurate, than the work of his own G-2, and very convenient since they were in Japanese.

But Americans find it next to impossible to master the art of military secrecy, as historian after historian knows.

✽

261800   The Japanese patrol, four times the size of your own, was smart, aggressive, eager for revenge. It followed along the trail at a good clip until your patrol taught it to follow on either side of the trail as well, and when it darkened in the patchy swamp — long before it was dark outside — the Japanese quit.

You missed your footing on the trail, you half swam, half walked, in a coiling green sea whose branches lashed your face, you dreamed you were crawling on your hands and knees, you dreamed you swayed across a one log bamboo bridge, everything you carried doubled and tripled in weight, the smallest burdens in your pockets burned your bodies like flames, you dreamed you squeezed through a row of upended palm logs lashed together in threes, you dreamed you saw a towering pillar of blue fireflies over a latrine.

In the G-2 dugout there was a new Repple Depple second lieutenant talking to an enlisted man. "Suppose you're standing under a building. Suppose a bomb goes off in the neighborhood. A tile drops from the roof and your shoulder is bruised. Do you get the purple heart?"

The coder prepared your message for the field radio: ". . . if the ship turns to port, counter with a 90-degree aileron roll . . ."

◆

Appendix XV. Japanese Redisposition of Forces after the Battle.

Admiral Greatwestern, ComFirstAirFleet, and Admiral Luckystrike, ComFirstAirFlotilla, ComFirstCombinedAir-Force, ComSecondAirFleet, urged all air groups and air bases to provide volunteers for suicide operations in order to display the Imperial Worth.

◆

270900   The Investigator sat down beside you. Automatically you went on sorting the flood of paybooks, diaries, insignia, charms, photographs, orders, unit files. "Well, sonny boy, ready to tell me now about your friend Arkansaw Torrington? We're closing out our case on him."

"If you're closing it, you don't need my help." The Investigator was wearing Major's leaves, but you did not call him Major. You were pretty sure he was still an enlisted man. "Don't you know he's been invalided out, with an honorable discharge?"

You were repairing your broken belt with a piece of cord. In your pocket was a letter from Arkansaw, suggesting that you transfer to Washington — "As always, I live outside of history," the letter ran. Less confusingly, it ended, "Everyday I spin my prayer wheel for you —"

"I'll be keeping in touch, sonny boy," said the Investigator. "We can always call Torrington back and give him a proper discharge."

He picked up a small wooden charm. "What's that say?" he asked.

"Namiamidabutsu."

He started to put it in his pocket.

"Just a minute," you said. And you stamped it SOUVENIR PASSED BY CINCPAC.

◆

Postscript A1.

In a cement and steel office at Pearl The Admiral detached from the bulkhead a picture of the Japanese carrier Lucky Crane. *In its place he put a chart whose thick, predictive line foretold the fate of 754,000 tons of Japanese oilers. Then he buckled on his pistol holster and went out for afternoon pistol practice.*

I am told he shot unusually well that afternoon.

✿

271100   "It will be simple to find a room in Abuyog," said Lieutenant Garcia. "It will be my pleasure."

The captured jeep thief strained against his bonds and the ropes round his wrists hissed like snakes. He made an obscene sign at you.

✿

Postscript A3.

General Perch radioed his farewell poem: "A soldier has not done his duty until he gives his life in war, and therefore a soldier is thankful to be at the front." General Mountainbottom radioed back to him, from Manila, "They say it is harder to live than to die."

Fortunately, American military communications do not permit the transmission of morbid poetry.

✿

271200   You sat in the long narrow wardroom of the LST, at one side of the hollow-gated warehouse that was its hull. Rich smells of cooking, of grilled steak and simmering peas, drifted into the wardroom. On a sidetable were piles of bologna sandwiches, bottles of coke, and gingerale, cheeses, even fresh bananas.

Commander Martivet looked fresh and clean. Under one arm he carried his spyglass. He went over to the porthole, and tapped at it, in some irritation, with his spyglass. A bird, perhaps a hummingbird, beat angrily at the porthole glass, rested, then drilled it again. Commander Martivet's LST was run like a battleship, the PA system was forever blasting some new command to be executed on the double, and Commander Martivet was unduly upset by the bird.

Together you checked off the list of Japanese prisoners and civilians who were being transferred in his LST to a collecting station at Abuyog. There was Major Milkwell whose regime had come to an abrupt end when, in the hearing of a visiting Marine Colonel, he advised BIJ Standish to get rid of all his Marine officer interpreters on the ground that their Japanese was hopelessly inadequate. And there was Perfection Rapidslope, who was also no longer wanted by the Corps.

The bird tapped furiously at the glass. The Commander tried flicking a napkin toward it, without success.

You meant to tell your old drillmaster that he had taken part in the greatest naval battle in the world. You meant to tell him that, however fumblingly, and with what near fatal mismanagement, one great naval power had smashed another. But instead of these strategic profundities, you blurted, indicating the name of Perfection Rapidslope, "Once she was forced to help her father sell her sister into prostitution."

"What the hell is that to me?" asked Martivet, toying with his spyglass. He had not asked you to stay for lunch, and you realized you were expected to leave.

"Nothing," you said. "Nothing." You were alive — a savage and terrible joy flooded and tingled along your veins.

From their respective sides of the glass, Martivet and the bird tapped furiously at each other.

✿

Postscript A5, Footnote 487.

The destroyer Beachwind *was not allowed to remain at the Manila docks; instead, the Japanese harbormaster sent her to the island of Corregidor. There she disembarked 1000 survivors of the lost* Warrior's Wealth. *But in spite of the slaps of the Japanese petty officers, and the orders for silence, the defeated crew managed to whisper to the garrison, "The superdreadnaught was sunk —" and the shocking news quickly spread to Manila.*

Naval history indicates that, far more than the loss of an army division, the loss of a great ship is a psychological as well as a material loss.

271800   Sanky's service was not so different from many others held on Visaya. True, you and his men had gone back ten miles, to bring him to the coast, where, as the tuba put it, he could watch the Philippine girls, and see the ships unloading things to eat, and more important, drink.

You all agreed that with him should go something you wanted more than anything else on Visaya. Once living persons — namely Philippine girls — were ruled out, there was substantial agreement. The brasses disappeared for a while, and came back, with a bottle of genuine Scotch. They announced that it had been liberated from "that LST over there," the one skippered by Martivet.

"You're sure he gave it to you of his own accord?"

"He couldn't help hisself," said the slide trombone.

So the Scotch was passed around, then, with a fair share left, corked and lowered in the ground. After the Chaplain finished, the bugler blew taps.

Sanky had picked his bandsmen well, and the bugler was the sweetest bugler you had ever heard. Every note rang true and clear. Once Sanky had told you that everyone had his own words for taps, even though taps had no words, and it was true, you had your words for taps too, and you said them now, to the bugler's call,

> Faraway, long ago
> Faraway, long ago, faraway,
> Long ago . . . faraway . . .
>
> Long ago.

*

It would be a dull historian indeed who failed to feel a thrill while watching the daring maneuver called "crossing the T." And within this grand tactical motion is contained one of those permanent strategic lessons which lie at the surface of naval history, waiting for the perceptive observer.

*

Part Five

OLYMPIC

CHAPTER TWENTY-SIX

February, 1945

Again and again I had to remind men that they owed not only the duty of combat for their country, they owed as well the duty of helping to record the history of the stirring scenes they had just witnessed.

At times I was greeted with indifference, laughter, or even objurgations, colorfully expressed. But I kept in mind a saying of the enemy, "to lack a nine foot hill for a basket of earth."

BEGEL, The Battle for Visaya Gulf,
Preface to the second revised edition

"WHEN did the Japanese start to make it" asked the Bomb Disposal Expert.

"In August, 1944. Just before our landings on Visaya. It takes six months of training to learn how to fly it."

The BDE brought out his stethoscope and listened to the metal nose of the crated suicide rocket. "Where did this one come from?"

"Iwojima. It's on its way to the U.S., to Aberdeen."

"I hear it's rough at Iwojima."

"I've been asked if I want to go there."

The BDE snorted. "There's only one answer to a question like that." With a jeweler's wrench the BDE tapped lightly at the nose fuse in order to loosen it. Your duty was a humble one. You merely told him which way to screw the fuse.

It was hot inside the parked transport plane, and the crated rocket plane took up most of the air space.

The BDE listened with his stethoscope again. "Now if this had been German — " He pointed to the sky.

You agreed. The Germans adored bombs within bombs, so arranged that when the bomb was disturbed, without even the pinball warning sign of TILT, the disturber went compulsively, in ridiculously small pieces, to his next existence.

The bomb expert pointed to some Japanese written on the half-unscrewed nose plug of the suicide rocket plane.

"Sakuradan," you said. "Cherry bomb."

"Why cherry?"

"The Japanese have a poem about it."

The BDE did not disappoint you, and the inevitable obscene remarks about losing your cherry followed.

With a clang the nose plug fell out, and you both caught at it. The BDE took a spoon from his shirt pocket, dipped through the nose plug into the 1800 kilos of explosive, and offered you a taste. You declined, and he had a second helping.

He replaced the plug, and started opening the three plugs at the rear of the TNT nose. While he worked away, you returned to the cockpit of "Cherry Bomb" to stare at the unfamiliar controls. A voice tube, that provided communications with the mother plane, hung down one side like a severed gray umbilical cord. On the cockpit a Japanese workman had scratched "Die in battle." Behind the cockpit, in a separate crate, was the tail section with five rocket motors, and short stubs of wings.

While you waited for the BDE to finish, you found yourself thinking of Coaltown, in western Pennsylvania. Each summer, your mother had taken you there for a month when you were still a boy, to visit Grandmother Brady. On the front porch of the old Brady house were two rocking chairs, and a long swing with ashtrays nailed on the arms. All the other houses had their front porches and swings and rockers, and in the evenings, after the dishes were washed, no chair or swing on the street was still; the chestnut trees dropped their early, still green burrs, and people strolled along the sidewalks, stopping to talk at this porch and at that, while miners returning from work, their mine lamps still turned on in their sooty caps, walked silently among the strollers.

Many of the strollers stopped to say hello to Grandmother Brady — once the Bradys had owned all of Coaltown — and you remembered Henry Grundweg, the jeweler, everyone bought his engagement ring, and wedding ring, and flatsilver from Henry Grundweg — once he had taken your hand in his and said, Do you know whose hand you are holding? — No, you had said, and Henry Grundweg tightened his nimble fingers on yours, and said, his voice rich with emotion, You are holding the hand that shook the hand of Thomas Edison.

Every night Henry Grundweg carried his slide trombone to the captain's walk on the roof of his house and played a few bars of a hymn. He played to the stars, he always said, not to the people below, but you could hear his trombone all over Coaltown. Just before curfew his slide trombone would tremble:

> Eternal Father! Strong to save!
> Whose Arm doth bind the restless wave,
> Who bidd'st the mighty ocean deep
> Within its bounds appointed keep.
> O hear us when we cry to thee
> For those in peril on the sea.

When the curfew horn blew, Henry Grundweg stopped; he never played after curfew. In your mind, Grundweg's thin face wrinkled and vanished.

The BDE screwed the rocket plugs back, and patted the TNT nose affectionately. He wiped his spoon clean and replaced it in his pocket. "All secure," he said.

Seeberg had wanted you to return to Q as soon as possible, but you admitted to yourself that you wished to postpone a final discussion of the Iwojima trip with Seeberg, and after you had left the Bomb Disposal Expert at his base, you went first to the POW stockade.

A big wired truck, like a cage on wheels, stood in the center of the barbed wire stockade. The searchlight lenses reflected the overhead sun from their four glassy orbs.

Pilot Officer Riverwell, small, thickset, now fat and glistening from the camp food, sat sunning himself on a bench outside the Japanese officers' quarters. He was very pleased to see you. Shyly he handed back your old, forgotten lighter. It was wrapped in tissue paper, in a small, beautifully made wooden box. On the lighter he had laboriously engraved three tiny fish hanging on a microscopic bamboo pole. The cloth fish, or carp ascending, swimming upstream, that were hung outside a Japanese house on boy's day, to show that a boy must, like the noble carp, fight his way upstream against the current of life.

Time moved at different rates outside and inside the prisoner stockade, and Riverwell, as though your last conversation had stopped only yesterday, began telling once more of December seventh.

You remembered on December seventh listening to the radio symphony concert in your room at Yale and reading Emerson — *If the red slayer think he slays or if the slain think he is slain they know not well the subtle ways I keep and pass and turn again* — Riverwell once more was telling you how the Z flag flew at the masthead of the *Red Castle*, the same Z flag that had flown at Tsushima back in 1905. And Riverwell was seeing again, as he talked, the *Lucky Crane*, and the lead plane with its wings painted red and yellow, he could see again the planes switching on their red and green navigation lights as a signal that their motors were warmed up, he could see again the glimmer of red and green lights dancing in the shimmer of the whirling propeller blades. And then had come from *Red Castle* the signal — Launch all planes! and the Captain of the *Red Castle* had signaled: I pray for your victory!

And they had all felt, that just as the United States took Guam and the Philippines in 1898, in fulfilment of manifest destiny, so now Japan was moving to fulfil her fate — carrying American aviation gas on her carriers, using American scrap steel to make her guns. And even the direction finding gear of the lead plane had been made in America — without error it had homed on the Honolulu radio and guided the Japanese planes to Pearl Harbor.

You tried to tell Riverwell that the *Lucky Crane* and the Z flag had both been sunk off Cape Deception, but he had no belief in your propaganda, probably he had not even heard you interrupt him, for he went proudly on, telling you just how his torpedo plane hit and sank the *Arizona* — Silently you listened until the guards summoned him into line for the truck. Obedient, he saluted, and left you.

You recalled a prisoner report that Admiral Koga, successor to Admiral Yamamoto, was fond of saying that Admiral Yamamoto had died at exactly the right time, in combat, and Koga envied him, for the Saga samurai of the clan of Koga believed that a fighter should select the time and place of his death, and the earlier in battle the better — "*Bushidō* — the way of the warrior, is to die" — Admiral Koga used to say.

And you recalled that Admiral Koga himself died in an airplane crash on a routine flight to Davao.

In the waiting line for the truck, a Japanese enlisted prisoner jostled against Riverwell. Without reflection, instinctively, Pilot Officer Riverwell slapped the enlisted man. A Marine guard came up, but the slapped prisoner bowed and saluted Riverwell.

Puzzled, the guard walked off. The line moved quietly aboard the huge, caged truck. Just before he climbed aboard, Riverwell stopped, indifferent to the urging guards. You thought he was going to turn and bow in your direction. But he bowed in the direction of Japan and the Imperial Palace, and never glanced back. And so Riverwell left Pearl Harbor for the second time.

Once a prisoner — perhaps it was Riverwell, but you could not remember now — had said — The life of man is a long distance and a heavy load.

There had been no point in telling Riverwell what he had really sunk at Pearl Harbor. From figuring and checking his course, you had long ago known that he had hit only the harmless target battleship *Wyorada*.

In your pocket your finger traced over and over the incised design on the lighter.

From Wolfe's old office a well-flung pencil hit you in the chest. On one bare wall hung a photograph of Wolfe, with his eyebrows now startlingly white. But Wolfe himself had moved on to the new advanced headquarters at Guam, leaving Seeberg in charge.

But Seeberg did not mention immediately Wolfe's proposal to send you into the thick of the fighting for Iwojima. Instead, he thrust the signal board at you, so hard that your hand stung. "It's a great day in fecal creek," he said grimly.

The upper dispatch, from Australia, was meaningless to you, announcing as it did merely the imminent arrival of Commodore Stellenbosch, to head a new Ideas, Communication, and Propaganda IntraService Section.

By officer messenger mail had come a stack of Stellenbosch

folders. By painting the Emperor's Face on the Decks of Carriers, Averting Dive Bombers, A Method of. Dropping Newsreels at the Bottom of the Emperor's Garden. Operation Shrineblast. Operation Fujiblack. And a new one, Proposal for colapsible ruber subarine.

"This Commodore," you said. "Is his hobby pistol shooting?"

Bluntly Seeberg specified how Stellenbosch might most satisfactorily self-inflict a wound with his brace of target pistols.

At last you remembered. It was Commander, now Commodore "Fantasy."

You put side by side the plans for a rubber submarine and the carrier deck portrait of the Emperor. "Combine projects," you suggested, "then let the situation mature."

"How?"

"Paint the Emperor's face on the deck of the rubber submarine. When it crash dives, it will break into a smile. That would frighten me off, if I were an aviator."

"For that remark I think I'll make you Stellenbosch's assistant." His face took on an evil grin.

"As our yellow cousins say, the wise man does not read the Sutras to cows."

Seeberg looked at you as if he were taking aim. He opened the *Suicide Attack File* and turned it toward you.

"Wolfe has sent a signal from Guam about you — but if you don't want to go —" You knew that, partly because he liked you, and partly because he thought you would do better in a dangerous task if you volunteered, Seeberg was rephrasing an order as a request. Apparently you were free to stay at Pearl, and yet you felt a change in Seeberg's character — he seemed to have crushed out of himself all the desires by which you were ridden.

His head twisted almost backwards by his arthritis, he watched you review the *File*.

At Mindoro, beginning with the landing on 13th December, 100 suicide attack aircraft had hit two LCI's, one escort carrier, two cruisers and one destroyer, as well as sixteen other ships. At Lingayen on Jan. 9, 1945, eighteen destroyers, one carrier, three escort carriers sunk or badly damaged, and lesser damage to eight other escort carriers. And in these attacks 200 Navy crewmen had been killed.

And now, since the landings had begun at Iwo on the 19th of February, already one carrier had been badly damaged, and an escort carrier had been sunk.

"It isn't that I don't want to go to Guam."

Unlike Wolfe, Seeberg always had material flowing over his desk. He picked up lovingly an orange-yellow volume titled *Combat Lessons of the Battle for Visaya Gulf.*

"You haven't signed the buck sheet," he said.

"I didn't learn any lessons from Visaya Gulf."

In the harbor below Q's hill, tugs maneuvered a battleship into drydock. Her bow — 2000 tons of the finest steel — had been sliced off in a collision with another battleship when a reserve lieutenant tried to maneuver the fleet while Admiral Hornbull took a nap.

"The Japanese aren't a naval power any more," said Seeberg harshly, "they're a suicide attack power."

In a moment, you thought, he would rephrase his request as the order it actually was. But he cocked his flinty head back at you, and said, "We expect to lose a quarter of a million America soldiers and sailors on the OLYMPIC landings. Most of them by suicide attacks."

It was forbidden to mention the word OLYMPIC, even if you knew it, except when talk was urgent. OLYMPIC, the last greatest military landing in history, the landing now being planned for Kyushu, for the southern mainland of Japan. All the energies of the Pacific forces, concentrated in a single bow, were slowly bending to launch a final flaming arrow.

From Seeberg's desk dropped a bit of scorched paper, scrawled in Japanese: "Pray for happiness in a future existence of the departed warrior." You returned it to its place in the *File.*

"The manual you found on Visaya was good. But Wolfe —" Seeberg corrected himself, "*we* want to know more. That piloted suicide rocket from Iwojima —"

"It's not very useful. The mother plane has to release it too near the target."

"What about the figures," said Seeberg, his blue eyes staring at yours. "One in four suicide attacks hits the target. One in thirty-three sinks a ship. The other day a Cherry Bomb split one of our destroyers in two."

It was all hopeless — what arguments could you plead against

going to Iwojima? If you counted high enough, say, to a quarter
of a million men, the single man no longer mattered. And part of
you was insanely pleased to think that extraordinary things happened to Classen, that Classen was being singled out for a special
expedition.

But you said, defiant still, "And if I don't want to go?"

From a locked drawer Seeberg produced a folder labelled *Top
Secret*. He was careful not to let you see it. "This is what we're
looking for.

"Rates of training and crew time. Details about the 3rd Air Fleet
at Kisarazu. The 601st Air Group. Captain Pinemountain. The
Chibaya Unit. The Divine Thunder Unit — supposedly equipped
with new model Cherry Bombs. The Kyushu suicide plane reserve
— is it still 2500 Army and 2500 Navy planes? New tactics — such
as suicide air-to-air ramming."

The folder sprang shut and he locked it in his drawer again.

"In the next war," you asked, "will whole nations circle each
other? Like suicide pilots looking for a chance to ram?"

His head twisted in reflection. "At the end of the First World
War, anybody who could tell sludge from shoe polish knew what
the Second World War was going to be like."

He pressed a buzzer on his desk. "You have a talent for war,
Classen."

"And if I prefer not to go to Iwo?"

"You don't always like to admit it, but you showed your talent at
Rarawa, at Visaya, and you'll show it again on Iwo — and after the
war."

High on the wall, time whirled round from clock to clock — 6 A.M.
at Tokyo, 11 A.M. the day before at Honolulu, 4 P.M. at New York,
9 P.M. at London —

His voice hard, sure of itself, he went on: "After the war, Wolfe
and I want you with those of us who are looking ahead to the Third
World War. To prevent it, or to win it if it comes. But we want you
only as a volunteer."

"Some of the Japanese suicide pilots have refused to go through
with their suicide attack. They've bailed out, or landed their planes
in the water. Suppose some of the pilots, a lot of the pilots, in the
next war, won't fly?"

"There won't be flying in the next war, the next *big* war." Impatiently he ground his thumb on his desk buzzer. "There'll be switches, rockets, men looking at clocks in a room very much like this one."

As if indifferent, he added, "In the end, obedience is simply an order you give to yourself." A yeoman appeared with your orders.

"Do I have to accept these orders?"

"You have a place reserved on the morning plane to Ulithi. The rest is up to you."

He observed you with a wry expression, as if he knew something he disliked, but had decided to accept, about you. Seeberg was very good. He had foreseen the coming of the war with Japan. No doubt he and Wolfe were already beginning to shift their energies, in part, to the next war. He was very good, but he was not good enough to make you pick up, of your own will, the orders on his desk.

Walking down the corridors of Q, away from Seeberg, you began to laugh. You had not been sustained by your powerful character, as Seeberg no doubt supposed. No, you wished to talk first with a girl, with Leilani.

But that afternoon you packed. And in the evening you went to the deserted estate of Mr. Stepney. The Japanese gardener led you past the greenhouses, past the mannequin pisse, to the banquet room, where the walls advised you in good times and in bad times to be like an arrow. You wondered who Mr. Stepney was, and what he would have thought of Leilani's instinctive adoption of his property.

Perhaps the world was shifting to an age in which only the tough borderland peoples, like the Koreans, would know how to survive. It was something for you and Mr. Stepney to think about.

The banquet room, lit by a yellow light, was in the Japanese style, with mats on the floor, sliding doors, and a veranda, narrow and wooden-floored, that faced the sea. Built-in cupboards held futon, and in the alcove was a simple flower arrangement of three lilies, standing for earth, man and sky. Beside the lilies reared a clay Tang horse — when you looked more closely you were pretty sure it was a very clever forgery.

On a scroll in the alcove, a quotation from the classics advised that a single bamboo dish holding rice, a single gourd with water, and a small hut on a narrow lane — all these were virtue. In the course of time, the scroll on virtue had become a very valuable and costly work, because of its calligraphy.

Lani entered with vivacity, wearing a light cotton dress that fluttered against her figure. She seemed strong, sturdy, in extraordinary health. You sat apart on the mats, like strangers; she was only a few days returned from Visaya, which you had left a month and a half ago.

She held to you the thin, familiar bouquet of gentle, insistent mockery: "You are trying to remember the Visaya Station Hospital?" And her passive and pretty eyes widened as if daring you to reply what you really were thinking of.

"I was trying to remember Abuyog," you began. But before you spoke you had suddenly recalled a tall high room with a balcony, closed and cooling shutters, bullet marks on the walls — and a girl who was painting on a strip of silk the poem, "More fleeting than the gleam of withered leaves, windblown, a thing called life —"

Seemingly indifferent, her eyes strayed here and there, to the Tang horse which she perversely called genuine, to the arrangement of lilies, and you were perplexed and charmed by her air of growing embarrassment.

She had let her dark hair grow unmilitarily long, and shook it now with a quick freeing gesture, as if struggling to release some inner feeling, but all she said was, "Mrs. Kim is being divorced by her husband."

"Did Kim gamble away her property as well as his own?"

"He has been very lucky lately, She will be well off. But she does not want a divorce." A hovering, fragile smile touched her lips. "Man's mind changes like the autumn sky," she said. And she added, tormentingly, "It takes very little to keep two people apart."

"Your promise, never to marry —"

"That —" she interrupted defiantly. "I am not a sentimentalist, like you."

In her eyes, as in a fortuneteller's crystal circle, you seemed to see the night, so many weeks ago, on which you had left Visaya, you had fallen asleep on the airport ground while waiting for your transport plane to take off, you had waked to the stitching traverse of airplane machine gun bullets across the field, everywhere you saw gasoline fires run their rivers across the airfield, lacing and interlacing in delicate patterns, an inch beyond the fires all was darkness — and you remembered in Abuyog a nude and lovely girl lying back against lace linen pillows, holding to herself her rounded arms, resisting, hiding, to be caught and seen and kissed the more.

Her hand, as if in spite of herself, in a pretty and timid gesture, touched yours, and as softly withdrew.

You had made out the check she asked for as a matter of course, and you handed it over to her.

She saw the amount and her eyes wondered if you had made a mistake. "I did not ask for so much."

Stubbornly you said, "You must take everything — or nothing."

"Nothing, then." And she pushed the check to one side.

Nervous tension drove through your fingers and made them clench. "You'll change your mind." And you really admired her peasantlike shrewdness — land was rarely for sale in Hawaii, but a little had come to the market after Pearl Harbor, sold by its frightened Caucasian owners, and now she had taken her chance to buy. It was like Leilani to find and use the vacant Stepney estate, and it was like her to know when the rare Hawaiian earth was for sale. Even in Abuyog, when she had let you spend nothing on her, she had been thinking of this, for she had said, with exaggerated impudence, that she would, in the end, demand her gift — "one never gets milk if one doesn't cry."

But now she would only say, almost in a whisper, "No."

You remembered an expression of Sanky's, which he had used only once with you, "Carrying gunpowder, why not jump in the fire?" And you blurted, "Sanky told me to marry you."

"Sanky," she said. As a child in Korea, Lani had learned to cry only rarely; now the tears just filled her eyes and were slowly blinked away.

"You cannot tell me why? It's not color?" She at once understood, correctly, that you were thinking of her prejudice, her possible objection, to *your* color. She hesitated for a long time, her pretty and expressive eyes half closed in a naïvely appealing glance. Then her face softened, settling into a deeper and deeper anguish.

"You said you would not ask me again —" You took her hand

as she spoke, and distracted, with her other hand she pushed a comb deeper into her long dark hair.

A voice that you knew was your own — and yet it seemed the voice of a stranger — now said her name, "Leilani."

You had learned that she drifted, rather than fought her craft of life through its decisions, and now she brought your hands to her cheeks, she charged all her prettiness to you in one lingering upward glance. But her eyes lowered again and she said in slow and gentle tones, her face suddenly meager, with an almost Korean lilt to her words, "You do think I was wrong —" she corrected herself, "that I *am* wrong."

She made fine, invisible, unnecessary adjustments to her dark hair. "It doesn't agree with your picture of your *kisaeng* that she should want land — you wish me to take life as it is, to show a love of loneliness and quiet things —"

Startingly she clapped her hands, and her old impudence returned. "Puppies don't fear tigers," she said. The gardener, who seemed to have been waiting behind the screens for his signal, burst into the room, struggling with two trays of Korean food. He disappeared, and she began to arrange dishes, tiny saucers, and bowls, and impatient, you touched her arm, but her gestures deftly expended themselves on brass and lacquer and porcelain, on kim ch'i and sauces.

You became insistent, you pushed the trays rudely to one side. She hid her defiant eyes in her hands. Your heart leaped, a pleasure beyond words tingled in your arms —

"Don't you understand how I could return?" she cried. "Didn't you know I was allowed to resign?"

Your breath ached in your lungs. You wanted to touch her drawn and anguished face, but she flung your hand from her. Abruptly she said, "I had an abortion — there is no child." And then, deliberately misunderstanding your silence, "You do not have to get your commander's permission to marry me." Her eyes searched yours, guessing for your answer before you could discover it yourself.

You took her hands by force in yours, you had the sensation of beginning to slide down an infinite precipice of glass and your hands tightened on hers.

"Why couldn't you tell me?"

In a somber and passionate tone, her face growing pale, she said, "Perhaps there are two kinds of people who must never marry."

"And the kinds?"

Naïvely, but with deep conviction, "Those of wrath — and those of grief."

In fierce and solitary possession of herself, she sat away from you, her breasts rigid and full, her back straight, her glance brilliantly pretty.

You held your hand to her face to offer touch — it was, perhaps, all you had ever had to offer, and she let you at last touch — you made out darkly, through your fingers, through your eyes, her high pale forehead, the hollow at her ears, her bridged nose, her delicate hair, and your hand fell to her shoulder, you became quickly aware of a faint fragrance of sandalwood that seemed to rise from her breasts. The world seemed, however briefly, rich in pleasure, full of climbing passions, and knowing that she was too proud to struggle, your heart leaped as you felt her lips part reluctantly against yours, she tried to break free but on her face lay a profound and enigmatic expression, the innocent cunning of generations of borderland women, deeper and shrewder and more ruthless than any mere man-made Machiavellism.

She did not wish the dinner she had prepared to go to waste, but you turned out the yellow light — her low dress fell easily from her shoulders, and below, her flesh was cold and marble to the touch. You flung open the sliding doors of the veranda, to let in the seacoast sound, while thoughts raced in your mind, that a woman should be seen at night, in a distance, or under a shadowy umbrella, that the able hawk hides his claws, that when day ended the way seemed long. You heard her lie back — all this, you said, will vanish in the morning and leave only charred wood in our hands — you stood faltering, a modern Joseph, stripped of your ironical coat of many colors —

At the noise of wood sliding on wood you spun round, but she was gone, the three lilies nodded in the stiffening seabreeze, you could see her purse on the floor, and the check beside it.

In despair you ran past a glassed-in jungle, past winged flowers, past a hedge that caught moonlight in white velvet cups, past a gnarled shrub that bowed and grinned, past a brazen urinating boy, past a tree that shrieked and sang in its torturing poles.

You caught up with her near a bed of freshly transplanted lilies, in her pretty superficial eyes *yes* and *no* struggled against each other, in the moonlight her white dress shone more and more brilliantly, her eyes deepened to points of light, and you began to sense, beyond their superficial and pretty gleam, the glow of a deeper passion that far outshone your own.

She laughed, all her charm and impudence flooded back. She bent to pick the lilies and you seized her arm while you cried "I adore —"

She interrupted, laughing, and tried to push you away. "Adore?" she teased gently, "We say even a sardine's head may become an object of faith. Perhaps you adore the flowers? the moonlight?"

"Yourself —"

"Ah, no one stays the same — tomorrow will come other winds, other selves, for both of us — you must prove to me —"

"Still?"

Her white dress fluttered at her back like the chrysalis wings of a medieval angel, she seemed transformed to an energy of air whom you might hardly hope to hold to earth. She barely hesitated, you strained to hear her delicate murmur, "Forever."

With her wonderfully fresh and pretty smile she held out to you her armful of lilies, you stood enraptured, and your two human illusions, lying by on a vacant, indifferent ocean, kissed, touched protected — a dream of life ahead grew between you, was glimpsed and vanished — you drew apart, silent, in wonder.

A Navy car stopped at the gate. Seeberg called from its rear window, then got out. The gate drifted open.

She shook her head wildly, and pulled at your hand.

"Your plane, Classen," said Seeberg impatiently.

"Sir?"

"Its departure time has been moved up." He said in a harsh voice, "I've brought your kit."

His words spun in your mind like juggernaut wheels, you searched for something other than yourself to fling before them, but you searched in vain. The lilies fell to the ground, and the tradewinds followed after them and nudged the flowers to the sidewalk, out into the road.

Leilani stifled a cry and ran inside the house.

"I found your gear packed," said Seeberg in triumph, thinking he had won.

"You knew? About Leilani and myself?"

"Surely you know that everyone at our headquarters is followed, is checked on."

But you had not known, and your affection, ironical, unemotional, moderate, but still affection, for the Navy suddenly died.

Misunderstanding, thinking you imagined a watching car now, at this moment, at the end of the road, he said, "Not all the time —"

"Just enough."

He ignored your remark. "You'll come with me," he said. It was not a request, not an order, a simple assertion. It was the final stage in your military education, that of being taken completely for granted.

"Even if she needs me, if we want —"

He broke in roughly.

"Pregnant women are usually in the best of health."

Your voice strangled in your mouth. "Then she lied?"

"Invented — she knows what she should do, even if you don't. She wished to save you from —"

But you did not stay for the rest of his sentence; overcome by instinct, you ran back to the empty room. Surely you would find Leilani there, waiting, to help you stand against Seeberg, against the men of wrath, against all that part of yourself — she would remain, to help you find some way from the men of wrath to the men of grief.

The gardener sat in a corner of the room, eating greedily from both trays at once, smiling at you, and blowing noisily into his tea. A brass rice bowl gleamed like gold in the yellow light.

With the stupidity of complete conviction he said, "She has left," and, more kindly, "Pau. Finish."

Her purse, your check — were both gone. There were a few pages of paper crumpled into a ball. You smoothed them out. They seemed to be a diary, of the briefest kind, that she had kept during your month together in Abuyog. The old man watched you closely.

You did not want the few pages, nor did you want him to read them either, and you put them hastily in your pocket. On the floor was a small, naïve mandala of Buddha on his lotus, perhaps spilled from her purse, and you rewrapped it on its wooden roll.

"He sees men sowing and plowing and fighting and thirsting with the Five Lusts," said the gardener, with satisfaction.

In Japanese you said, "These are myths for old men." You dropped the mandala on the floor. The gardener scolded you and picked it up.

"A fried pea doesn't break its pan by jumping up and down," he said. He went on eating noisily. "I am hungry," he said. He ate with the satisfaction of an old man who knows that he will see another dinner through.

In the garden the transplanted lilies wavered in the trade wind and stiffened again. From the cut stems drops of liquid spilled and sparkled in the moonlight. You sat in the Navy car, beside Seeberg.

The car ran swiftly along the darkened highway. Scurrying rat shadows fled before it, darted across the road, scattered under the palms. Halfway between Waikiki and the center of Honolulu, the car ground to a halt on one wheel rim, from which still hung festoons of synthetic rubber. The shadows came up to the car and hurried on. No one stopped, and you began to hope that you would fail to meet your plane.

But a swagger stick waggled out a car window at you, and Begel imperiously beckoned you aboard. So as not to waste a moment as he rode about, he had installed in his limousine a typewriter, with manuscript in it, a desk combined with a bar, and a dictaphone. Generously Begel served bourbon from his bar, to a speechless Seeberg and to yourself.

You assumed that the manuscript was on the battle for Visaya Gulf. But that was finished, Begel assured you; sternly he counseled you against spending too much time amassing your materials — the main thing was to write. And he was now writing on the B-29, and its new use in fire raids.

There had been some dark moments, Begel explained to Seeberg and yourself (at once placing you both in the role of Worshipful Student), when the B-29's, in their first raid on Truk, missed the island by a full mile, and it was realized that the great new planes could hit only areas, not targets. Should they write off the B-29's as a Washington mistake, or should they invent a new method of Pacific war, the fire raid? The answer was obvious. By ringing a great Japanese city with bombs, not only did the B-29's burn up Japanese homes — each home a miniature factory sweatshop — but the flames used up oxygen and the people went out like snuffed candles before the flames ever reached them.

The success of the B-29 fireraids had brought to the fore the Iwo campaign, for Iwojima was being assaulted at this moment mainly to provide an intermediate base for crippled Superforts. More artillery had been fired in the first day at Iwo than on D day in Europe, and this island, previously unknown to the world at large, was now finding its new role in the pages of history's unending volume.

Begel's large bulldog head sniffed the evening Honolulu air appreciatively. The grand strategy of the war was complete. The Japanese had dropped their guard, and all that was needed was the final haymaker — this, he asserted, would come through the B-29's.

Ill at ease in the completely unaccustomed part of Worshipful Student, Seeberg objected, but for once, he failed to quote a Pope or even to deliver his query about the difference between shoe polish and a less attractive substance. Crushingly, Begel dismissed the great operation, OLYMPIC. It would never be needed, he said, not allowing Seeberg to reply. The Japanese were desperate for oil. Their homes and factories were being burned. In the fall, their crops would be sprayed with kerosene and burned, by airplane. Begel's nostrils flared. It was time to return to Academe and begin writing the history of the war. OLYMPIC would never be needed.

"What's going to make the Japanese stop fighting?" you asked.

Begel stared at you, as if about to conclude he had known you somewhere before, but quickly he answered: "The logic of history. No nation can stand against the logic of history." His voice trembled with enthusiasm. What remarkable historic moments there had been in the war. Especially the Battle for Visaya Gulf. How his eyes shone as he talked about Visaya! He had been with the six old American battleships when at 250351 they capped the Japanese T and opened fire. At 250400 the Japanese battleship *Mountain*

Castle had split into two halves and had sunk, with only five survivors from 2000 men. At 250408 the battleship *Three Creators* was hit, and two minutes later, she also sank. Of the forces of Admiral Westvillage, only destroyer *Drizzle* had escaped. A holy radiance filled the eyes of Begel. "Only the historian who has taken part in events," he said sternly, "can move his readers." Very few officers, let alone historians, had ever taken part in this sublime maneuver, the crossing of the T.

"The historian," said Begel to a temporarily hypnotized Seeberg, "must be first, and last, a man of ACTION." He gaveled the deskbar with his swagger stick, and history seemed to surge through his rugged body like an electric current. As the car stopped at the airport, on each of you he pressed a first version of his article, "The Battle of Visaya Gulf, A Brief Preliminary Account." Hastily he took them from your hands to write his name and make them, as he said, "Presentation copies." His limousine drove off, its motor so silken smooth that you could hear the clacking of Begel's typewriter — he had leapt to work the moment the car door closed. In the distance his one star license plate winked, and you realized that Begel had overflown the rank of chicken colonel to his generality.

Seeberg walked by your side, still under Begel's spell. Inside the airport a line of new boots, fresh seabags at their sides, faced their new chief.

Tanned from hikes, and lolling on the beach, the chief surveyed them, smiling genially.

"All right," said the chief pleasantly. "This is the land of pineapples and grass skirts. Don't lift the pineapples."

"Aw, chief," said a fresh boot.

The chief's smile faded. "Jump up in the air, sailor," said the chief. "As high as you can. Jump up, sailor."

The boot jumped.

"Why did you disobey me?"

"But chief —"

"Who told told you to jump down?"

The line shaped up for your plane. Commander Seeberg, like a man coming out of anesthesia, began to sputter his thoughts of Brigadier General Begel and history. Aggrieved, he said, "When I took history at Annapolis we learned which Presidents were anti-

Navy Presidents. That's what I call *history*." Seeberg stared at his presentation copy of the *Battle for Visaya Gulf*, as if he were about to tear it to shreds. "What's this goddamn pendulum he's always gassing about?"

Your turn in line came, and there was no time for an answer. In a moment your plane flung you into the air over Honolulu. Below you there were dim lights on one side, but it was all dark on the other, and into that darkness over the westward ocean the plane steadily climbed. Your breath fogged the bullet window as you looked back at Honolulu; you traced a line with your finger on the glass. For a long while the line you had traced lingered on the window.

CHAPTER TWENTY-SEVEN

February, 1945

> We reject once and for all the defeatist theory of certain historians, that the happiest society is the one without a history.
>
> BEGEL, The Battle for Visaya Gulf, 3rd ed., Annex II,
> "Address on receiving the Mississippi Valley Historical
> Society Prize for Military History"

❋

THE BOW of the *Achilles Victory* towered high in the air and hung still. A coffee cup rolled out of its saucer, wabbled at the edge of the mess table, then smashed on the deck. The bow slid downward, and through a porthole you caught a brief glimpse of a toy destroyer on the horizon, surprisingly far off. Automatically you remembered her name — *Patra* — and forgot it again. Other names ran in your mind — *Wasp, Red Castle, Flying Dragon, Valley Wind, Mist of Flowers, Vincennes, Lucky Crane, Quincy, Arizona, Three Creators, Warrior's Wealth, Hornet* — as a child, at the Sesquicentennial, you recalled there had been a pageant, *The Evolution of the Dreadnaught.*

Thirstily you drank water, but your throat remained dry.

White foam drained across the porthole. "Our escort," said a lieutenant j.g. with bright new silver bars at his collar. He squinted out the port into the strange, graygreen air, cloud and mist streaked, lit from above the clouds by a flickering, invisible sun. "Her skipper's afraid *we* might blow *him* up."

Through your chair you felt the steady trembling of the ship, that stemmed from the winding propeller and shaft far below. One more day at sea. Bound for Iwojima. By fastest available surface transportation. Unloading by lighter at oh eight hundred tomorrow. Set special plane and submarine watches.

In your mind you saw Leilani observe you with grave and lovely eyes, you seemed to move towards her and she turned her head away. In your dreams, in your daydreams, in these five days aboard ship, she had taken on a disturbingly independent quality, she had come to seem not at all imagined, but almost real, as though she came into your thoughts at her wish, and not at yours. Again and again, you had to check an involuntary movement toward her image, as though you had started, in spite of yourself, to touch her hand.

"There's a right way, a wrong way, and the Navy way," said Engineer Rowan, in a tone that suggested he had settled this tremendous issue forever.

"Hot poo," said the lieutenant j.g. He was sorting out ship's mail for reforwarding at Iwojima. "Classen," he said in surprise. "Montgomery Classen." He tossed you a small package and some letters. On the package, addressed to A. W. Woman, Venusberg, Wyorada, was a blurry rubber stamp, ADDRESSEE MOVED. Crisscrossing this was another stamp, NO FORWARDING ADDRESS. A third rubber stamp urged you to MAIL EARLY BEAT THE CHRISTMAS RUSH. The canceled stamps recommended judicious investment in government bonds.

With the package was a letter from your father. Another letter, from Arkansaw. A postcard from Napoleon — he was having the patent files in Washington searched for any previous invention of a combination killer machete, can opener, whiskey flask and sword cane. So far, success. Competition, your father always said —

The lieutenant j.g. fingered his new silver bars and fiddled with the radio. The ship's bow foozled its way high into the air again. The Korean words for uncle burbled through your mind: *bagbu sugbu samchon gomobu imobu* — and words from a forgotten song — *There are twelve hills of Ariran and now I am crossing the last.* Leilani, her face the lovely olive color of a Giotto maiden, bent over a table in a room in Abuyog, Visaya, writing on a scroll — *windblown, a thing called life.* She seemed as though she were in the room, and yet you knew, painfully, that she was not. You clenched your hands together. She vanished.

The lieutenant j.g. turned up the volume of the wardroom radio.

Oh, Shenandoah, I long to hear you, Away, you rolling river. The
music dissolved into the familiar lilting voice of Tokyo Rose.

"Hot poo," said the lieutenant j.g. The bow of the ship staggered
down and started crazily upward again. "To all you homesick
sailors," said Tokyo Rose, "on your way to Iwojima —" The lieutenant j.g. wriggled in his chair. Tokyo Rose began listing ships,
captains, executive officers, crew members, junior officers.

"That's me," said the lieutenant j.g., jumping in his seat. "She
said my name! Hot poo!"

Engineer Rowan raised his burly eyebrows. Moving quickly and
easily, as though his joints were daily and generously lubricated,
he helped himself from a pot of coffee that had just arrived
after a fifteen-minute wait. You wanted more water but it was all
gone.

Calmly he said, "There must be ten thousand seagoing school-
boys in the Navy named Higgins."

"Hot poo," said Lieutenant j.g. Higgins, uncomforted by this
analysis. "They *know* I'm coming."

The ship corkscrewed its nose high into the air and then buried
it in the sea again. Rowan held his coffee level in both hands, as
though suspending it in gimbals.

From Tokyo the old sea shanty started again: *Oh, Shenandoah,
I long to hear you, Away, we're bound away, Cross the wide
Missouri —*

Lieutenant j.g. Higgins dialed another station. Distorted by
shortwave, the music sounded hollow, it rose and fell round half a
world from Italy. Faintly you heard, *Sua passion predominante è
la giovin principante.* Higgins snapped the radio off. He rolled back
the breakfast tablecloth at his place, and began to toss dice on the
cleared patch of green baize.

"Just promise me one thing, Higgins. Next time we're in Honolulu, be sure to get your oil changed."

"O.K., Mr. Rowan, O.K. But what made the *Hercules Victory*
blow up in the middle of Naples Bay? Santa Claus? Wham bam."

"Thank you ma'am," answered Engineer Rowan. A dirty machinist, cap on head, even though it was officer's country, brought some
papers for Rowan to initial. Higgins frowned severely at the machinist and fingered his new silver bars. The machinist smiled

agreeably. He had long ago stopped removing his cap before deck officers.

"I never get fat," said Rowan. He began eating, with steady, rhythmical jaw movements, a platter of cold scrambled eggs.

"Not even a scrap," said Higgins. He wrinkled his nose at the thought of so many names, so suddenly and completely blotted from the book of life. He turned to you — "This ship," he said, "I'm beginning to remember things I know never even happened to me."

All ships carried ammunition, and you had not thought much about it when informed that the last part of your journey to Iwo would necessarily be made on the ammunition ship *Achilles Victory*. But by the second day you had begun, like everyone else aboard, to think about it a good deal. In four days you had built up a handsome reserve of thoughts about this subject, while most of the officers and crew, aboard for two years, had now accumulated a lifetime supply of thoughts about ammunition ships.

All around you bombs, torpedoes, shells, explosives, mines, powder, were stuffed in an ingenious variety of containers, and these assorted engines could be advised to pursue you under water, in the air, over hills, underground, they could explode you on impact or after a seemly delay, they could obligingly wait till you had sailed or walked over them six times before going off on the magical seventh, they could follow out your warmth, your noise, your slightest pressure — and given a suitable occasion, they were more than willing to explode, not one by one, but simultaneously and everywhere.

"I'm leaving tomorrow," you said to Higgins. In your mind the old shanty persisted, *The white man loved the Indian maiden, Away, you rolling river* —

A desultory steward wandered in, surveyed you without interest, and slid in front of you a cold omelet which you had ordered half an hour earlier. By its side were two strips of bacon whose grease had long ago, perhaps early yesterday, congealed.

Engineer Rowan examined your breakfast closely. "With us the impossible takes a little longer," he said. You offered the cold omelet to him and he took it. "I never get fat," he said. "Where's the A1 sauce?" he asked the steward.

"Sauce?" said the steward without interest. He sloped off, promising nothing, not even the water you asked for.

Sure that the steward would not reappear for another fifteen minutes, Rowan leaned toward you and said, confidentially, "White slavery."

His bushy eyebrows went up and down like mechanical butterflies at the thought of man's inhumanity, here not to woman but to man. The good ammo ship *Achilles Victory* had been stationed (since ending her sustaining role in the Visaya campaign) in the Aleutians, at the recaptured island of Zhutchka — your old friend, Darling Beetle. (With notions his canoe was laden, you thought.)

"Left us anchored there for three months," said Rowan. "What did they expect our crew to do in their spare time? Embroider the powder bags? Why, there wasn't even a goat."

You started to ask about the goat, and then you stopped, not really wanting to hear about the erotic possibilities of an Aleutian goat.

Rowan told how a small group of nautical entrepreneurs, with the aid of some soldiers ashore, had established a homosexual white slave ring. Navy justice, still way to the right of Freud and Havelock Ellis in these matters, had at last caught up with the ring. Already the *Achilles Victory* had lost some of her crew, and would soon lose more, in her most vital parts, too, since the investigation had moved sluggishly from fo'c'sle to galley.

"We're shorthanded enough as it is," said Engineer Rowan. "Damn it all, don't they realize we have to eat?" He seized your arm in a hard, metallic grip. "Now about that souvenir stamp," he reminded you. His jaws worked smoothly through your cold omelet. You searched your pockets for the rubber stamp. The few crumpled pages of Leilani's diary fell to the deck. You picked them up and smoothed them flat.

Not a diary in the usual sense, it was rather a series of phrases, of words, all dated, written during the month you had lived together, at Abuyog, on Visaya. Once early in the month she had written, "A thousand things, all existing, all at the same time." And the next day, the ideograph, the same in Japanese and Korean, for "joy." The name of a medical officer in the Station Hospital, and after his name a Korean proverb, "Sit on a stone wall for three years — you'll warm it." Later the words "wrath, grief, the wounded." Your name once, and the Korean for "tall." Phrases that seemed specially hers, the hardwon Korean wisdom of the borderland — "With the food of others, let the pleasure of New Year's Day begin." The Korean word for mother — *omoni* — with a line penciled through it. A description of yourself, which you tore up. The longest entry was near the end. She feared childbirth, not for herself, but that without her the child might not be loved by a foster mother. At the end, undated, "Flowers from a lofty height."

Your Grandmother Brady, you remembered, had sung "Shenandoah" to you when you were a child, in her soft old voice that quavered a little when she sang "I love your daughter." In your Grandmother Brady's house, under the long Pennsylvania rifle of your ancestor, the revolutionary fighter Sam Brady, had hung a brownish picture of Ally, your mother's sister, at the age of eight. Ally was the last of your Grandmother Brady's six children. She was the favorite, said your mother. Ally, with the happy, petted expression of the favorite child, so much beloved, who had died at the age of eight.

A few last rhythmic, powerful bites of toast, and Engineer Rowan stood up, exuding force like a dynamo. His strong fingers renewed their pincer grip on your arm. "Let's get those souvenirs," he said.

Lieutenant j.g. Higgins looked up from his game of dice solitaire to advise you sternly, "If we blow — *nothing*."

"Dignity —" you wanted to say, but your voice never even started on the word, and Higgins continued, "Not even a scrap."

You nodded, to assure him that you understood clearly there was no future for an undertaker on this ship. The dice rattled on the green baize and rested, cocked, against each other. "The Captain wants you to lay up to the bridge and report to him that you're aboard," said Higgins. "He's funny that way."

Engineer Rowan snorted. "Never mind the Captain," he said, pulling you along with him. Like all engineers Rowan thought of himself, rather than the Captain, as really running the ship. To be sure, the Captain, assisted by lamentable deck officers such as Higgins, occasionally gave orders and mucked up the ship. But the Captain and his bumbling helpers merely put into words what the engine-room telegraph was already thinking. Down in the engine room was the working level of the ship.

Enthused by this notion, Rowan insisted that before you could go to his cabin and stamp as souvenirs his mementos of Zhutchka, you must see the real ship, the ship below.

Your route led down through a central hold, delightfully air-conditioned. A bulletin board announced movies: *Son of Dracula, Love Comes to Dinosaurland, The Fighting Sheriff of Labonza County* — in the dim red light you saw a technician start to test a few feet of film that you vaguely recognized — Ghostly Granpap, and Chicken Hero flickered by, and Gassy the Wunderhund — "The damned dog won't bark," said the technician in disgust. And in fact something had gone wrong with the sound strip — silently Lulukins highkicked her way through college, while Chicken Hero beat out a soundproof rhythm on his classbooks.

Your fingers curled on the stiffwire caging that walled off the sides of the hold, and you touched one of the red-eyed flashlights that hung every few feet along the caging. Then you understood the airconditioning. It was for the 16-inch gunpowder bags. Twice a day, in the movie and main ammunition hold, you could slip into your movie dream sack, watching first and second-run showings of *Sensual Longing, Ignorance, Desire for a Separate Existence,* while conveniently to hand were materials for achieving permanent Nirvana. *Whosoever loses his Irony shall save it, and whosoever saves it shall lose it again.*

In the reddish light you saw black paint cans that took up a whole corner of the caged area. FJB was stenciled on the cans. "We leave them at Guam on our way back," said Rowan. "I hear some idiot on the staff is planning to have them dropped on a Japanese mountain. Stripe it like a zebra. A few more ideas like that, and the war may go on forever."

While you marveled at the continuing vitality of Operation FUJIBLACK, wonderdog Gassy squealed in terror and began a long wavering bark, that suddenly disappeared in the whirl of tangled film loops through the projector. "Wham bam," said Rowan. "Thank you ma'am," said the technician. He switched on a cone of light that glinted off the silk powder bags.

Engineer Rowan's steelhard grip tugged you below to the engine room. Diesel cylinders throbbed and sucked the fanblown air. Proudly Rowan showed you how he held cracked cylinders together by metal tie rods and bolts. He led you to the next room. "What's this 'wham bam thank you ma'am'?" you asked him.

"Oh, there was this female rabbit made of iron —" his voice trailed off, he was lost in admiration of the great propeller shaft, of the huge metal rod slipping round, metal within metal. You smelled hot steel and oil. Here was the source of the trembling you always felt aboard a moving ship.

After you had seen the Holy Place, you were allowed to go back up to Engineer Rowan's cabin.

He fumbled in his safe, drawing out moldy logbooks from the sunken freighter you had once boarded, long ago, with Sanky, at the mouth of Zhutchka harbor. You remembered looking down a flooded hold at an unexploded bomb. One of the notebooks held in its pages the sharp smell you had first learned to know at Q — the smell of the dead. Quickly you stamped it SOUVENIR PASSED BY JOCPOA and tossed it back in the safe, but the smell, once established, lingered stubbornly on.

From Rowan's head a toneless voice chanted:

> I never been
> Satisfied
> Went down in
> Satisfied
> New farm field
> Satisfied
> Rattlesnake bit me
> Satisfied
> On my heel

Water from a shower gurglingly closed over the voice.

"Too early for some mountain dew?" asked Rowan, offering you a nip of Scotch from the back of his safe. You rainchecked him, and began stamping the remaining logbooks SOUVENIR SOUVENIR SOUVENIR.

Water gargled and guggled down the drainpipe, Rowan's shower turned off and a last explosive hawk coughed its way through the ship's plumbing. The voice bellowed on:

> Satisfied
> That didn't make me satisfied
> Satisfied
> That didn't make me satisfied
> I never been
> Satisfied —

With pleasure you called out, "Bulflash." He stuck his head out. "Taste it," he said, flipping the water your way. Sure enough, the shower, labeled SALT WATER, ran fresh. Engineer Rowan radiated modest pride. It had been no mean plumbism to hook his shower pipes into the ship's drinking-water tanks, and not only that, heat the water besides.

Rowan poured out two shot glasses of Scotch. He and Bulflash held their glasses high. "Remember the *Maine*," cried Bulflash. "Remember the Alamo," cried Rowan. They drank and held their glasses so that each could inspect the bottom.

"You're writing up the landing on Iwojima?" you asked. Bulflash tossed a peanut up near the ceiling and caught it expertly in his mouth. You had underrated him, the extravagant toss suggested. No longer were you talking to Bulflash the Boy Amphibious Correspondent, creator of *Joe Blow, Let's Go.* Grossman's magazine *Penetration* had discovered the real Bulflash, the *symbolic* Bulflash. His dispatches from Adak, Zhutchka, Rarawa, Visaya, so *Penetration* informed its readers, had an outer and an inner meaning. Sometimes two or three inner meanings.

Lost in wonder at his own miracle of metaphor, Bulflash helped himself to more mountain dew. "Did you realize everything I wrote stood for something else?"

You saw that Bulflash, like the readers of *Penetration*, had crossed the thin barrier that separates the successful symbol seeker from more ordinary human beings. Already *Penetration* had collected his richest dispatches, along with a powerful preface by Grossman, into a volume titled *Basilisk or Buttercup*, an Other Directions Book Club Dividend.

You began to understand. "You're on this ship at the suggestion of *Pentration?*"

"That's us — *The Ship of Fools*," said Rowan, beamingly giving away the title of the new project. "Toads and gardens," he went on, misquoting the subtitle. "Nobody can bang those symbols like Bulflash."

"You pistonhead," said Bulflash, "I've told you a million times —"

Hurriedly you interrupted. "Your newspaper will buy an allegory about an ammunition ship?"

Bulflash winced. "Not allegory. *Symbol*." Bulflash was no longer

383

supported by a newspaper, but by a Foundation Grant. Audiences were irrelevant when you were a Foundation Writer. He stumbled over a set speech that needed just a bit more polish — "I write about imaginary toads with real gardens inside them."

"That's us," said Engineer Rowan amiably. "Imaginary toads."

Bulflash tossed his peanut even higher in the air, but this time missed it. Once in a while, to be sure, he did little sketches of the old *Joe Blow* type, as honored guest in various national columns — "Like an abstract painter cutting out silhouettes on Sundays," he explained. And his greatest project was already in galley proof. Like nine out of ten American newspapermen Bulflash kept in his luggage a half-finished novel, and like nine out of ten American newspapermen he had named this unfinished Great American Novel *Black Narcissus*. Thanks to a suggestion from Grossman, he had changed its plot slightly, to the story of a reporter who is unable to finish a novel titled *Black Narcissus*. It had proved ridiculously easy to finish a novel about not finishing a novel. "Why this kind of book writes itself," said Bulflash, awed at his newfound powers. "Like Queen Victoria said, we heal our sicknesses in books."

"And the sequel?"

"A natural," said Bulflash. "That will tell how *Black Narcissus* was made into a musical."

"That's when the hero really loses his pants," said Rowan.

"His soul," corrected Bulflash sternly.

Dry though your throat was, you waved off a gratulatory potion of mountain dew. You clung to the bunk of the corkscrewing *Achilles Victory*, while Bulflash and Rowan turned to the real business of the day.

"You may fire when ready or not, Gridley," said Bulflash. He lovingly unwrapped a stock of 8- by 10-inch photographs.

Rowan brought out a similar stack. "Damn the torpedoes, full steam astern," he cried. They drank off their Scotch, and held out the glasses to each other for bottomry inspection.

For Rowan's scrutiny, Bulflash offered a photograph, a simple study in *déhanchement*, for its nude model had posed her right leg and hip in an enticing, forththrusting curve. Her right hand was brought across her softly rounded body below her breasts, and, smiling face tipped towards you, she leaned against a twisted column.

"Like your tail, nightingale," conceded Rowan. "But try this for rabbit habit."

His nude photograph was of a girl and some drapery. A great deal of drapery, in fact. But somehow it had not been possible to wind the drapery around her torso any higher than one delightful knee. This nude model also held one hand as if to cover herself, but by a bit of misjudgment she held it too far in front of the area in need of coverage. With her other hand, presumably, she waved to a distant friend.

"Strapped it to her kneecap purty," muttered Bulflash, pretending an indifference he was very far from feeling. "Made her boyfriend's fingers hurtie."

Rowan lectured proudly: "The same distance between breasts as from breastline to navel, and from navel to leg division."

Here was connoisseurship indeed. You had come a long way from captured pictures of geisha. Bulflash yielded a point. "All right, so she wins the procelain hairnet." But he rose sturdily to the challenge. "Just match this for largeness of charge."

After much searching he found a color photo, of a nude model powdered in gold, standing on a large blue globe. Her sole costume consisted of a strip of pink gauze, that she stretched tightly, perhaps for exercise, across small applehard breasts.

"Does she give you the deep undying hots? Or does she?"

"The leg division is a shade low," said connoisseur Rowan. "But I'll be generous. Mechanically I can't fault her."

"'Generous,'" repeated Bulflash, breathing heavily. He clenched his fists. "Mechanically you can't fault her!" For a moment you thought the photographic battle would be replaced by a less spiritual combat.

Rowan overhauled his own stack, and found his color masterpiece. His choice was a deep-breasted model — you could almost feel her texture, so perfectly had she been photographed. And she seemed to stand, or rather float against a blue background of space, all studded with golden stars.

"That's pretty cheeky chickie," granted Bulflash. "But study this — does she turn you off or does she turn you on?"

You tiptoed out to the corridor. The motion of the ship made the passageway seem to twist around you, and your room was no better. The nude photographs had done their work, you found yourself thinking of Leilani, you were maddened by the vision of her tiptilted figure in the room you had shared — never had she seemed so real, for a moment you were sure you had felt her shoulders against yours.

The ship gyred round you, groaning, and when you went outside to scan the waves, your eyes dazzled from the strange light, bright graygreen in color, sifting through clouds from the invisible sun above. The surface of the sea lifted and fell in large square sheets half a mile across and you were struck all the more by the forces that wrenched and shook at the ship from beneath these calm-seeming flats.

Without destination you clutched your way along the tilting superstructure deck. Just below the bridge deck you heard what seemed a familiar voice: "In the Behring sea . . . love those seals . . ." A long spyglass seemed to poke itself around a corner and aim down at you, and — not wishing to find out if it was, as you feared, your old drill master Martivet — you fled up the ladder to the boat deck, to a recess between the stacks.

A shaft of hot yellow light flashed from the strangely hidden sun, flickered over the two blowers, two deck engines, and two boats that bounded your symmetrical rectangle, lingered over an empty gun tub with a Negro telephone talker who wore an outsize helmet over earphones. The sunlight vanished into the oppressive green overcast.

The ship seemed calmer in your soothing rectangle; you felt guarded by the gun tub and the hooded pompon gun. You swallowed down your thirst and took out Arkansaw's letter. Since Visaya he had begun to write more systematically, to a wide group in Q, as though, once out of the Navy, he wished to try to preserve some sense of community he had once found in it.

You learned that Gordian was studying prisoner subgroups in the Japanese prisoner of war camps. Napoleon had just opened a *karate* parlor for the headquarters yeomen. Fresh from the vastness of Australia, Commodore Fantasy was an advocate of what he called Bigthink, and was talking of upgrading Feverton's old rubber sub into a rubber dreadnaught. Begel was flying to New York from Pearl to speak at Yale on "The Coming End of the War." The date, allowing for the international dateline, was today.

Arkansaw had heard recently from Grossman, and at length. In the Saipan experiment with the *Section 8 cases*, Grossman had played a considerable part. At the first meeting of the schizzos, the army psychiatrist had suddenly fired a gun in the air, and had recorded with much satisfaction that all his experimental subjects jumped. At the next meeting, Grossman had seen to it that a Japanese grenade went off, rather close to the psychiatrist, while he and the schizzos played it straight. It took the Army a while to find a new psychiatrist (psychiatrist #1 retired to Walter Reed with a temporary grenade complex); when #2 appeared he substituted for the gunshot sessions a close reading and explication of inkblots, with elementary and advanced classes. Few could equal Grossman when it came to fantasies erected around inkblots; often his contributions could be placed without further editing in *Penetration*. Readers spoke of new strength and maturity in his work, and a New York agent, sensing under Grossman's abstractions the healthy American he-man who needed only a little encouragement, advised Grossman to consider different — and paying markets. Soon Grossman was selling to such magazines for men as *Atlas, Muscle, Biceps, True Biceps*, and even *Hairy*.

Arkansaw's letter ended with some suggested Book Sequels — *Sinbad at Yale, The Return of the Screw, Ben Hur's Other Chariot*.

On the margin of his letter you scribbled: *The Sun Also Sets, An UnAmerican Tragedy, What Maisie Didn't Know*. The ship lurched and tumbled about in the strangely flat sea. You decided to open your father's letter some other time. But as if in a dream, you saw a boy about fifteen, his face hidden, reading under thick yellow lamplight. Under another cone of light, the boy's mother was sewing. Suddenly she stood up and screamed, walked toward the boy, fell across him, slid down to the floor, froth clung to his hands. *O holy and most merciful saviour deliver us not into the pains of eternal —*

She took a long while to die, the doctor said to the boy. A very brave woman, said the nurse to the boy. He wanted to ask why she screamed, doctor, and as if sensing his question the doctor said, she was unconscious. Here is your book, boy, said the nurse kindly. *Of whom may we ask for succour but of* — A voice, like the voice of Chaplain Simon, but not his voice, you had not known Chaplain Simon then. In a rage the boy flung the lamp to the ground and smashed it, he ran from the house and fired a rifle in the sky —

In the gun tub the telephone talker spoke into his gray mouthpiece, and without your noticing it, the Negro gun crew, muscular, alert, well trained, jumped into the tub, took the canvas hood off the pompon, prepared shell cases.

Your senses heightened, you felt a keen desire to live, to survive, and it was impossible to forget that you were on a ship where the slightest scuff of metal heel on metal deck, the smallest bullet or bomb, could be fatal, you watched for a great hail out of the heavens.

Nonchalantly the gun trainer was humming, "Life would be the BUNK, I'd become a MONK."

"Now this irony animal," said the captain of the gun crew, "this animal had the shape of a rabbit, but it ate iron, anything made out of IRON. Bullets, FRYING pans, red-HOT iron, anyTHING made out of IRON."

You had a sharp, agonizing vision of Leilani beckoning toward you, and vanishing. The gun trainer sat back in his seat, facing the sky, and said softly:

Little black train is a comin

The gun crew answered:

Get all yo busness right —

He led again:

Go set yo house in ordah

And they replied:

For the train may be here tonight.

From the stern of the destroyer ahead, a string of colored balloons shot into the air. You relaxed. It was, after all, merely a target practice.

The captain of the gun crew spoke sharply and the men were silent. They were very proud of their ability to shoot and they concentrated on the balloons.

Yellow, red, blue, one striped, the balloons fluttered overhead.

But the order to fire did not come, nor were they told to secure from the drill. You recalled a greenclad Filipino madman shouting "Why did you poison my food, why did you take my brain out?"

In the gun tub, much thumbed and worn, was your pamphlet on suicide attacks — *Recommended Attack Doctrine, Divine Wind Decisive Forces* — "just before attack descend to 500 meters, when beginning attack —"

Thinking you wanted something to read, the gun trainer tossed you the latest copy of *Scientifiction.* On the cover a Venus fly trap, half naked woman, half plant, reached out for brilliant biologist Jack Anderson, while in the background, red white and blue horses galloped away, one of them bearing his fiancée Mary Cristal. You threw it back. Sandwiches and coffee came up, and the Negroes, smiling, offered you some of theirs. "What's your name?" you asked the gun trainer. They all laughed. "He name Sin Killer," one of them said. The ship twisted on through water that heaved in flat sheets several acres across. The gun crew explained the workings of the pompon to you. Continually the greenish light flickered down from the clouds overhead, where the sun lay hidden.

A spyglass seemed to sidle round the corner of the bridge, it started to lift itself in your direction, you caught sight of a face muffled in a rain hood, and you sat down quickly behind the gun tub. When you looked, a few moments later, the spyglass was gone.

Men drowsed, played cards, sat, slept, talked. Still the alert continued. You saw Leilani, lying back on the bed in your room at Abuyog. Korean girls are sorcerers, she said. Sanky, you cried, in a burst of anger, and she turned toward you eyes full of tears, questioning — your own eyes tingled, you started to stretch out your hand to wipe away her tears (the irrelevant, cheerful voice of Prince Mokuaweoweo broke in — Has she a friend who bites?) —

"Those white girls all look black after a while," said one of the gun crew. In the gun tub Negroes laughed. "Now everybody talk," said the gun captain. The telephone talker, forced to be silent, stamped his feet. The gun trainer, called Sin Killer, began chanting, softly at first, "It's turtle singing time." "Now everybody talk," said the gun captain. Sin Killer chanted, "Now the king has brought me to his pad, I am black but good-looking."

"Hear it, hear it," they said in chorus. "Hear it, hear it."

You had tried to read Begel's "Brief Preliminary Account of the Last and Greatest Naval Battle," but now that you knew he was speaking at Yale, you were stimulated to finish his preliminary masterpiece. Was he at this moment in New Haven tying a string to an eraser and pushing it back and forth, so as to give his audience a feeling for the pendulum of history? You thought it likely. And as you read, the words spoke themselves in his voice, you saw his head, so large and firmly set on his short body, and you were startled to find that he always referred to himself, now, in the third person, he told how "he had been part of the stream of history which he described."

Documents for him were only one third of the historian's life, and so, when war came, "he knew that he must sail and fight in those waters where Magellan had sailed and fought before him; like Herodotus, this historian knew he must take part in life's historical pageant." Like Herodotus, a footnote advised, he had learned to use annexes and postscripts.

("My dear friends," said Sin Killer, "we seen my little sister, she has no breasts, what shall we do for our sister?"

"Hear it, hear it," they chanted softly, "hear it, hear it.")

Wearing his new historical purple, Begel pontified: "He urges his readers not to get lost in contemplation of the Battle for Visaya Gulf, great though it is in naval annals, for as a prophetic historian, he must warn that it is only a part of the greater world-wide struggle, between the heartland — EastEuroAsia, and the sealand — WestEuroAmerica."

(Sin Killer rocked happily back and forth — "If my gal a wall, we will build her a palace. If my gal a door, we will build her boards of cedar."

"Heya heya," said the gun crew, shuffling their feet softly on the metal deck, "Heya heya.")

You skipped eagerly to the climax, the two days at height of the battle. It was vintage Begel, in his richest shade of purple — when after the war, this chapter became a book, it would surely be among his best. With what fervor he described "that grand tactical motion," the mystic crossing of the T!

("Choose your seat and sit down," chanted Sin Killer.

"In the two chap two," answered the gun crew.)

With what heroic compassion Begel told how the Japanese guns blazed in their dying fury all along South Strait, with what a spirit of Calvinist New England predestination he told of being aboard one of the instruments of justice, an old battleship raised from the mud of Pearl Harbor to slay her enemies.

And though he had been asleep when the T was actually crossed, he had described it — so you thought — far better than dozens of encounters during which he was awake.

(Sin Killer's voice sank to a whisper: "Flowers on the earth, in the turtle singing time."

Softly the men replied: "Hear it, hear it.")

You turned the pamphlet to the second day, you read how the historian waited deep within the gulf for the Japanese fleet to enter — it was hard at times to remember there had been anything more in the gulf than Begel and a rowboat.

(More loudly Sin Killer said: "I am in the garden lover, how beautiful with shoes."

The men echoed his rhythm, "Pull im along, pull im along.")

Here Begel's prose reached even more commanding heights, when he told how the Japanese Admiral, victory in view, turned away to the north — to the oriental make-up of this Japanese flag officer Begel had been unable to keep from adding just a tiny touch of Greek hubris. But how Begel made the pendulum of history swing on this climactic day!

("Return, O black gal, return return return."

"Pull im along, pull im along.")

And there was an annex explaining that an age of catastrophes was a golden age for histories — so it had been for Procopius, Josephus, Rashīd-ad-din, so it had been for Herodotus and Thucydides, and so it was now for Begel.

("Lover, your breasts feed among the lilies, hurry, lover, hurry, along the mounting of myrrh —"

"Hear it, godamighty, hear it.")

And a postscript told how a monument had been designed, with an inscription reading, They gave their souls to God, Their bodies to the soil of Visaya, Their hearts to America.

("Among the rose, my love, among the thorns, my love, tomorrow never come."

"Tomorrow never come, tomorrow's in the barn.")

But sternly, in the tone of Pericles to the war-battered Athenians, Begel declared that a naval battle leaves no trenches or trace, the waves roll over it and on, rising — forever, cresting — forever, and forever — indifferent — falling.

("Lover, your breasts like grapes."

"Godamighty, hear it.")

From a dark corner of the bridge a spyglass seemed to raise itself and aim at the crew in the gun tub, and a voice muffled by a rain hood shouted, "Pipe down." The spyglass shifted to you and stayed on you, too late you ducked behind the gun.

The men fell silent, the squawk box gurgled and barked, deep in its electrical larynx, "Now hear this, secure —" There were sounds of static, a woman's blaring voice — "the fundamental things apply —" a long screech like a fingernail on glass, the sound of feet slowly and heavily stepping down the bridge ladder, a new voice speaking angrily through the squawk box, "Secure from general quarters, set the steaming watches —"

At the far end of the boat deck a spyglass swung lazily round the corner as if by itself, and you fled down the nearest ladder, and down again.

Looking for water to quench your thirst, you stopped at Engineer Rowan's cabin. He and Bulflash had resumed their contest and you heard Bulflash saying, with satisfaction, "The Greeks had a word for it."

Bulflash had chosen a photograph of a short, plump little charmer, sprawling her nudity on yellow satin, and scrutinized from a corner by a stone Cupid of dubious moral caliber. You considered her lovely bottom. The Greeks indeed had a word for it. From long forgotten days the word came to mind. *Periprochtian.* A coquettish jumping of the rump.

"Surrender be damned, I have not yet begun to retreat," said Rowan. He got out the mountain dew and the ceremonial of bottoms up was solemnly honored.

Rowan found a photo of a nude woman clasping a necklace round her throat, while lying on her side on a lion skin.

"Boing boing," yielded Bulflash. "But as the rabbit said to the iron rabbit, if it's subtlety you want —"

He presented a photo of a nude girl sitting in a park beside two fully clothed men, beside them an open picnic hamper.

"Fight her till she floats, and don't give up the ship," grumbled Rowan, a bit desperately. "Where's my Cooky Nookie?" he asked himself. He turned to the safe again, and found the envelope he wanted. In his hurry he knocked the Zhutchka logbooks to the deck, but he paid them no attention. From the envelope he extracted a picture of a nude wearing a wool scarf round her neck, a fur coat over one arm, and leaning against an ancient wooden wagon wheel. "The four textures," he said in triumph. "Classical."

"Classical schmassical," said Bulflash. He offered a photo of a nude reclining, asleep, one hand covering herself, a sheep peering wistfully at her.

You heard the uneven sound of motors, of low-flying Japanese planes. The strident call of General Quarters, doors clanging shut, feet running down passageways, hands swinging down ladders.

There was a crash, you fell to the deck, picked yourself up, you began running, you were driven upward by some sort of instinct, once your clothing singed and you seemed to wade through a tiny puddle of fire, but you went ever upward till you reached the boat-deck gun tub.

Overhead the old planes came, the old Zeroes, so terrifying, so magnificent, so agile at Pearl Harbor, now flying antiques, good only for suicide attack — *gyokusai*, for *gyoku* the king, and *sai*, to kill, as with a rock, in the imperial way.

You held your ears against chatter of the pompons, of the five-inch gun astern, of the heavy machine guns. Someone had told you once — was it Gordian — that in their last moments both Japanese and Americans called out Okaasan, Mommy.

The Negro gunners worked in fury at their pompon, your pamphlet on suicide attack blew about the tub under their feet, they trampled on it. Still the planes came on, three of them, four, with their pilotfish escorts scudding low across the greenish sunless sky. From above and abeam, two suicide planes, one haloed with smoke, slowly nosed over and dived at the ammunition ship, diving slowly down, not to eat, not for love — you watched the two swerve as they fell, among blossoms the cherry among men the warrior — they swerved again, spiraling, nudged by tracers from your pompon, and collided with each other, dissolving into a huge ball of fire, sunspotted with fragments, that hurled headlong down flaming into the sea.

As if pushed up by a giant hand, the cover of the central hold blew open, the movie projector started up, by itself, proclaiming to all ignorant hearts that Gassy the wonderdog was doing her tricks, tap tap tap te tap tap te tappy tap went the metalsoled chorus, smoke boiled out of the main ammunition hold, in the thick and greasy smoke Gassy barked and barked.

The heaving sea turned intermittently golden, mist began to blow away in the upper air, shafts of sunlight burst here and there through the clouds, far off stood a gray island with fire dots winking over it. Iwojima.

The ship turned abruptly west southwest, it gained speed and the lurching, corkscrew motion smoothed out a little. The Japanese escort planes dove down quickly on their strafing runs, and from the other side, one of the two remaining suicide planes pushed over into a flat, final dive, through the curtain fire of the escort destroyer, through your ship's pompon and machine gun barrage. Part of one wingtip disintegrated in the air, the plane skidded up, righted itself. Once again the *Victory* slowly turned, and the suicide plane sluggishly followed. You wheeled with the curving ship, you saw yourself and Leilani walking together, how real she seemed! But it was no use, she would forget, the child would never have known — what after all was Ally to you, once the family favorite, so petted, so much beloved?

You lowered your head, flung up your arms, men dived from the gun tub, the suicide plane, guns still firing, its pilot dead, hung one wing tip on the bridge, pinwheeled over, plunged into the water. Tiny, growing explosions from below decks stung your feet.

Your lips cracked with thirst, you turned to the gun tub. The men slumped in it, around it, the pompon, still loaded, swung free. With surprise you saw how close the boat deck now seemed to the water.

The sky steadily lightened, and the sea stopped heaving in its great patches, the ship no longer tossed and turned, but soddenly held to its course, ever more slowly. And then at last you realized that below you the lifegiving vibration of engines and propeller shaft had ended.

From far astern the last Japanese suicide plane began its run, at a height of 500 meters, flying completely by the book of doctrine that you knew so well. You climbed into the gun tub and fixed the elevation of the pompon, you had a terrible feeling of the mystery of your life and that of the suicide pilot, each life moving toward the other. You got ready to fire — for every suicide attack there was a suicide defence — and from the bridge a spyglass dawdled round the corner, fixed on you, not to be shaken off, a voice muffled by a rain hood called your name. The ship rocked from side to side, shaken by a small explosion from within, and startled, a school of flying fish lifted themselves from the water, caught the brightening sunlight in their rainbow scales, soared high and far on a sharp gust of wind that left one to flutter birdlike on the deck beside you — was it true, you asked, was Irony what you had instead of God, was it true, you asked, did you hate God and adore his creatures? Irrelevant, indifferent, the fish flew to meet your grasping hand — it was wonderfully light, you felt its scratchy scales with joy — in its wings, in its cunning body, as much as in your own, were all the secrets of nirvana and parinirvana, of void stacked on saddleshaped infinite void, all secrets of all motion and all flight. And you had a vision of life as something that lived itself everywhere, at once joyful, indifferent, and true, both within and beyond your power —

You flung the fish out to the wind in a great, seaspraying arc, the fish turned golden and rose-colored in the broken sunlight, you forgot the onrushing suicide plane, you forgot the swinging gun, you forgot the drillmaster's voice screaming at you from the bridge, you turned your head to follow its arching miraculous flight, its slow cresting dive beneath the plunging waves and down into the deepest, darkest blue.

There was a roaring sound, a noise that seemed all the stored up noise of the world cracked against your eardrums — did they think to drive you from your world by dreadful sounds? Your eyes stung with broken lights, iron beams crumpled like wood around you, the bridge slumped down, a steel column pinned you to the deck.

The ship, still blazing from small scattered fires, still smoking ominously from its open hold, suddenly trembled again. Rowan had got his beloved engines turning, a propeller thrashed at the water.

With a sharp pop, like that of a cork from a giant popgun, Bulflash blew out of a deck hatch, clutching the precious nude photographs;

there followed a fountain of black paint, from Operation FUJI-BLACK. He bent over his precious photos to protect them, and slipped on the paint, while the wind caught the nudes from his hands. Dotted with black, scorched from occasional fires, they flew high over the ship — they settled down — a girl with one breast exposed, and one thigh, another completely undraped, women in a bath toweling themselves, thirty-six Japanese views of Mount Venus, a nude stepping into her bath and testing the hotness of the water, a nude Negro girl looking down at a nude white girl on a sofa, a nude just starting to disrobe, a masked figure seen in a mirror, staring at a nude, a woman stepping nude from a plastic streamlined disc to the shore. They swirled in the air, they clung wetly to the ship, they seemed everywhere.

The trembling motors faltered and stopped again. Sounds of swearing, of pumps forcing water over the sides. Courage, you said, dignity, you said, and with a great heave you rolled the steel column slightly to the side. The engines started again, the ship nosed forward, still settling, just barely underway. Leilani, you called, your hands cut on the steel, how quickly the time passed, you boasted to Leilani that you could jump an 18,000-mile somersault, no she said, tears in her eyes, half laughing, you cannot jump from my hand, but you rushed off beyond space and stars to the edge of the universe, and there, on the pillars that hold up the edge of the universe you wrote Monty was here — back you rushed to Leilani who opened her hand, on her finger was the writing, and smiling, with her tears that were not tears at all she brushed your dry lips —

You woke still thirsting, you knew the ship was moving faster, and from the open hold came the discordant sounds of a movie, all this time Chicken Hero and Lulukins had continued their story, they were now dancing their way through boot camp, you laughed, you knew from your thirst you were still alive, you were stronger than war, than death, than wrath, in the shape of Leilani you were alive, in the child within her you were alive, you pushed at steel and made it move, you were life itself, you were — *you were —*

on the coverlet her sleeping fingers traced a phrase *windblown, a thing called life,* then she awoke at the squealing clash of metal against metal. Clumsily a truck shifted down in gear, and tugged the long, flatbed trailer uphill, to the fort that was hidden inside the volcano above her house. On the flatbed trailer, tied by wire cables, was a long battleship gun barrel stenciled *Wyorada*, and behind that truck still another with a trailer, and a gun barrel, and another, and another. In a languid ambiguity of mind she thought dutifully, as the Lotus Sutra taught, that there was no sharp, no significant distinction to be made, between her house, the land she had just bought, the truck, the trailer, the guns, her thoughts described an encompassing circle that included these things, and herself as well.

On the mantel before a picture there was a bowl of rice, an empty soup bowl, a tiny blue saucer, brass chopsticks, a porcelain spoon. She began, still almost asleep, a half bow with both hands on her right knee, and then a full bow, so that her hands touched the floor — she caught herself, with a start, and looked, afraid, at the picture. But a comforting trick of light sent her own strong reflection back from the glass, and not really fully awake, now drifting back to sleep again, she sank back in her bed, her hand stretched under her pillow as if to grasp not just the paper deed but its land as well, but first she touched, and felt deep within her, the stirring, growing child.

When she reached deepest sleep again, her unknowing cheeks were wet with tears; these dried quickly in the tradewind.

The sun rose first on Palisades, Connecticut, then it rose on Coaltown in Pennsylvania, it rose on a Missouri gas station with two pumps, it rose on the Golden Gate, it found its way across the Pacific to a knot of men at the stern of a fleet tug, and let its dawn reach them through a blinding, bluegray spray.

"Goddamn fucking ship," said the captain of the tug. He stared at the hulk of the *Wyorada*, stripped of her gun turrets and their long-barreled guns, stripped of her railings and fittings, trailing behind her a towing cable that hissed in and out of the roiling water like a serpent of the sea.

The men clustered round their captain, whom they liked, and they watched the *Wyorada*. The tow had failed, but they had been ordered by The Admiral to stand by her until she finally sank.

"She won't go down," said the engineer. But he did not mind

waiting in the fresh air and having a cigarette. He could smell breakfast back in the galley. Eggs, bacon, coffee, cornbread.

The leatherfaced mate spat with the wind, and said, thinking hard, frowning, "I was on her at the Sesquicentennial."

"What the hell was that," asked a young sailor, wanting to sound tough. "The Sesquicentennial?"

They blinked their eyes. With unbelievable speed the *Wyorada* upended, slid stern first high in the air, then faster and faster down, at last, without dignity, sucking her way below the surface.

They all thought of her spiraling slowly down, past green light, into the dark blue light, into the deepest blackest blue of the great marine deep, where phosphorescent eyes would wink open at the sight, where gentian blue turns at last to black.

The saffron fingers of the morning sky began to brighten on the waters. Over the sunken *Wyorada* the waves whirled round in a circle, not very violently.

The tug heeled round, obedient to her helm.

"The Sesqui," said the mate, contemptuous and friendly, "man, that was before you were born."